"Does my betrothal to Lord Campbell anger you?" she asked.

"D'ye wish it to?"

"I wish it to anger you," she whispered, watching his mouth.

"It does anger me," he replied and lowered his lips to her neck. His breath whispered against the fine hairs, making them stand on end, dissolving her French resolve.

Niall rested his forehead against hers. "I despise Campbell more than I did when I awoke this morn. He has so much. With ye as his wife he will have wealth beyond mortal measure."

"He will not." The words barely escaped her lips. "He won't have this moment."

Niall smiled. "True."

He drew her nearer, as if that were possible. Her lips tingled with anticipation. Her breath quickened.

His lips met hers, tentatively, before he pulled away, eyes searching her face. Was he looking for her approval? Not Niall MacGregor, Highland king! This man could never want for any woman's approval.

Here in this hidden place, this moment was theirs. They were the only two people in the world. Surely, Niall knew that as well as she.

Then he clasped her to him. His scent, one of the land, captured her as his breath caressed her face in soft waves.

"This time is ours," he whispered.

She heard herself speak from so far away, "*Oui . . .* ours. . . ."

She fell into his kiss with a frighteningly deep and aching desire. There was no escape . . .

Heaven
and the
Heather

Elizabeth Holcombe

JOVE BOOKS, NEW YORK

If you purchased this book without a cover, you should be aware that this book is stolen property. It was reported as "unsold and destroyed" to the publisher, and neither the author nor the publisher has received any payment for this "stripped book."

This is a work of fiction. Names, characters, places, and incidents either are the product of the author's imagination or are used fictitiously, and any resemblance to actual persons, living or dead, business establishments, events, or locales is entirely coincidental.

HEAVEN AND THE HEATHER

A Jove Book / published by arrangement with
the author

PRINTING HISTORY
Jove edition / November 2002

Copyright © 2002 by Elizabeth Holcombe Fedorko
Cover art by Dave Stimson
Cover design by Marc Cohen

All rights reserved.
This book, or parts thereof, may not be reproduced in any form
without permission.
For information address: The Berkley Publishing Group,
a division of Penguin Putnam Inc.,
375 Hudson Street, New York, New York 10014.

Visit our website at
www.penguinputnam.com

ISBN: 0-515-13402-3

A JOVE BOOK®
Jove Books are published by The Berkley Publishing Group,
a division of Penguin Putnam Inc.,
375 Hudson Street, New York, New York 10014.
JOVE and the "J" design
are trademarks belonging to Penguin Putnam Inc.

PRINTED IN THE UNITED STATES OF AMERICA

10 9 8 7 6 5 4 3 2 1

For Dan and Owen, always.

Acknowledgments

This endeavor was not, gratefully, a wholly isolated pursuit. For that very reason, I wish to offer my unwavering and deepest appreciation to those who have indulged me with their support, expert and enlightening opinions, and a few symbolic whacks with a big stick when panic set in.

To my awe-inspiring and enormously talented friends and critique partners, Karen Smith, aka Karen Lee, Courtney Henke, and Catherine Abbott-Anderson. Especially to Laurin Wittig, fellow Jove author and maven of techno and moral support; Julie Moffett, who drenched me in her positive attitude; and Mary Burton, lifelong friend and the most levelheaded person I know. And a huge thanks to my extended family of authors in Washington Romance Writers where there are no shortages of support or valuable resources.

I am enormously fortunate to be working with a stellar group of publishing professionals. Thank you to Kelly Sinanis, assistant editor at Berkley, who certainly knows how to make my year, and for her expert editing, kind words, and enthusiasm. And thanks to Gail Fortune, senior editor at Berkley, for her kind encouragement, and for requesting this tome. I am enormously grateful to my agent, Jennifer Jackson, of the Donald Maass Literary Agency, for handling all of the details with her experience, intelligence, and wry wit.

Thank you to the ever inspirational Barbara Shugrue

and her mother, Grace Gorrie, two of the finest Scots I know. And thank you to Wayne Clark for many years of teaching me the Scots Gaelic. *Alba gu bràth!* Thank you to Kevin and Suzy Spence for enduring support and friendship. And a big thanks to Shari Mahoney, my "biggest fan."

To my family, I offer my deepest gratitude for a myriad of reasons too numerous to mention here. I have received an unending supply of love and support from my parents, Calvin and Carolyn, since I decided to be a writer after reading *Harriet the Spy*, by the late, great Louise Fitzhugh. I love you deeply. I also give huge thanks to my brother, David, and to my delightful parents-in-law, Joseph and Patricia. And never last or least, to my husband, Dan, and son, Owen. You are my life and true inspiration . . . always.

Prologue

In 1561 the world was a dismal place for anyone named MacGregor. On August 19, hope arrived on a royal galleon from France bearing Scotland's new sovereign, Queen Mary Stuart. For one of the MacGregor clan, hope did not wear a crown. It bore a crippled hand and a bleak heart.

chapter 1

Le Pays des Sauvages

19 August 1561, Leith Harbor, Scotland

M *on pere est mort."*

"My father is dead. And I can never go home."

Sabine de Sainte Montagne stared at the paper in her twisted right hand. She had done so many times since she had sailed from Calais on the royal galleon bearing Mary, Scotland's new queen. No matter how many times her eyes swept over the paper, it did not change the harsh truth. She was condemned to be a prisoner in this land.

She had received the letter, which bore a crimson wax seal and a ribbon as dark as the inside of a wine cask, just before stepping upon the gangway at the French port. She did not have opportunity to read it until the galleon was in full sail across the English Channel.

Her father had died of the king's evil. She knew well of the elegant whores who languished in the halls of Château de Montmerency as frequent as winter snow came to the Alps. Her Alps. They shadowed her beautiful home. For that she mourned, not for her father. According to the letter from her father's *avocat,* the château and all within it had been left to a woman Sabine had never met, another of her father's river of lovers, the last lover.

Sabine could not bear to read the letter any longer or to have it in her possession. She crushed it in her mangled fist, ignoring the pain that suddenly tore up her arm with the subtle purchase of a lightning strike.

"Adieu, mon papa," she said, tossing the paper over the salt-encrusted gunwale. "May you find solace where the heat touches upon your flesh."

Her father had been so in name only. His cruelty, his banishing her five years ago to royal servitude, had been his parting endearment. Sabine's curse into the mist that surrounded the galleon was the only endearment she could summon, the kindest words she could say.

He was gone, leaving her nothing but a crippled right hand.

"And a promise to my queen that I shall marry a good man."

She peered over the wood railing down to the slate-black water below her. It was all she saw of this Scotland. The good man was there, beyond the mist, waiting for her, by the queen's command and her promise to Sabine's father.

Her intended was a man she had only met briefly when he had come to France to express his deepest sorrow to Mary after the death of her mother, Marie de Guise. He was a Scottish noble, not a savage. His appearances gave her reason to believe that, to hope that, but her heart would not soften to this man, this Lord John Campbell, self-proclaimed master of the mysterious Highland Kingdom. He was a tamer of the people who lived there, so he said.

"Le pays des sauvages," she murmured. "The country of the savages . . . *l'Écosse.* Scotland. The Highlands."

She had heard the whispered rumors of Mary's attendants. She felt she knew well of this Scotland and of its Highland wilds. Men were said to wear clothes which bared their legs. Women were said not to wear shoes. These savage people lived as they wished, sweeping down from their remote hills and mountains with long, terrible swords, ready to fight and die for the meager life they lived in the wild. These were things she had heard ever since Mary had proclaimed that she and the whole of her court would go to Scotland.

Sabine strained to catch a glimpse, but the weather was against her. She gripped the gunwale. One hand held fast to the crusty wood better than the other. The mist was as thick as an Alpine blizzard. An impenetrable curtain to her curiosity.

Hope rose in her, because she had a way to escape royal servitude—this land of savages, and the man who by the queen's command would marry her.

She would make her life her own, even with the mark of her father's anger upon her crippled right hand. That, one day, too, would not exist. Hope was a gift she had given herself. Hope was her companion since the day she was forced from home five years ago.

Sabine reached down under her sapphire velvet cloak, which hung heavy and damp from her shoulders. She forced two gnarled fingers around the string of a soft leather *sac* pinned at her hip. She could not hear the crinkle or clink under the leather, but the small vibrations against her fingertips echoed the only bit of security and familiarity she had known.

Scraps of paper rested inside. Worthless to anyone except her. Sabine clenched her eyes shut, her right hand cramped a little. She fingered a small, fist-sized woolen ball. Each day, with its help, ignoring the pain in her hand became a little easier.

She extended her fingers as far as she was able. The tips of her two middle fingers brushed the cool, familiar feel of four gold pieces. Four? She stretched her fingers again, ignoring the pain, held her breath, and made a quick mental count.

Un . . . deux . . . trois . . . quatre. . . .

"*Cinq.*" She breathed. "Good."

These five pieces of gold, a gift from her mother countless years ago before she died, would save Sabine's life. These five pieces would give her freedom from all that lay before her like a borderless dark path, dismal and foreboding. She would never marry a man she barely had made acquaintance, much less loved, and for the keeping of a royal promise to her father. The queen would never see the folly of that promise, 'twould be treason to inform her.

With the gold she could travel far away from the savage

land that remained veiled behind a stubborn mist. The queen would not miss her. She had ten other attendants and five ladies-in-waiting. Sabine could return to France, sort things out, then continue with the course of her life, by her will.

"Hope," she breathed, *"mon amie."*

Above her on the masts, the great sails lowered, shouts from the galley's crew shattered the muted, misty silence.

"Le port! L'Écosse!"

She opened her eyes and stared forward. But where? As much as she strained, she could not see a thing! Her fears of coming to this land would be easier to face if they indeed had a face. Mist was all she had seen after they had rounded the east coast of England, ruled by Mary's cousin, the flame-haired Queen Elizabeth, and protected by her fleet of over-bearing ships.

Her heart tightened at the pictures that remained in her mind. Her beloved Alps and the way the seasons made them magical. She puzzled why home, which held so much cruelty, still called to her heart. Scotland was a fearful unknown, the devil she did not know. France, her home for better and worse, was the devil she had known all her score of years.

"L'île des sauvages," Sabine whispered. "Why would Mary wish to return here?"

"That question is not yours to ask, impudent fool."

She whirled around to face one of the queen's five ladies-in-waiting, all Marys. This was the uppity one, Lady Mary Fleming. Her earth-colored hair was concealed beneath a dark velvet cowl. Her face, prunish at best, held perpetual disapproval.

Offering a brief curtsy, Sabine eyed the proud Scots-woman, the only one of the royal court, other than the queen, whose blood ran from this land hidden by the misty pall. Sabine prayed the loathing in her eyes was similarly shrouded.

"Madame," Sabine said with a nod. A sudden puff of wind stirred about her, teasing several thick, corkscrew strands of black hair about her face. She lifted her chin higher. 'Twas not just the Scots who held the repute for fierce pride.

Lady Fleming narrowed her pale eyes. Her gaze dropped to Sabine's right hand and paused. "Get ye to the others," she said, forcing her gaze up. "A common *femme de chambre* with spirit is as worthless to Her Majesty as a blind footman."

"I emulate Her Majesty's independence of spirit, to glorify her," Sabine said proudly. She meant this with all of her heart. Mary was indeed independent, going against her French councilors and returning home as sovereign. Home. Were royals the only ones destined to find home?

"Insolence will be your undoing, *la petite chienne*!" Lady Fleming grabbed Sabine by the arm. "To the bowels of this ship with the others of your station. Now!"

"Sauvage," she whispered, shrugging away her grasp. "You've come home."

Lady Fleming raised a hand to strike her. It would not be the first time. "What did you say?"

"I said, 'you're fortunate to have come home,' m'lady." Sabine stared hard at her. The breeze heightened. It buffeted the hood from her head and sent the tumble of black curls spiraling about her face.

The Scot slowly lowered her hand.

"Ever since your father sent you to Her Majesty's gracious service, you've been but a bane to my very existence."

"I did not ask for her charity."

"Five years have not tempered your selfish yearnings. Your concern should be for the needs of your queen. Now, to your position."

Lady Fleming stole one more glance at Sabine's hand before padding across the deck toward a huddled grouping of the femmes de chambre, ten in all, clucking at them, waving her arms. The queen was on her way. Sabine took a deep breath and walked carefully across the deck slick with sea spray. She stopped and curtsied low. She loved her queen, but she loved France more. To leave royal service would be treason, yet she could not perish the thought. Not as long as a loveless marriage and a life in Scotland were her only choices. Perchance, her queen would understand. Perchance. The coin weighed against Sabine's thigh. Hope. Royals were not the only ones who possessed it.

Mary Stuart, the queen of the Scots, passed before her entourage. Sabine caught a glimpse of golden brocade, strands of pearls and jewels, and hair that rivaled the fiery foliage of autumn in the French Alps.

The galleon lurched. A sudden stinging oily scent mingling with the mist made Sabine's eyes water. Distant shouts rang up over the gunwale.

Sabine stood upright.

"*L'Écosse,*" she whispered in frightened awe.

She turned around and looked over the gunwale. Through the mist the gray wharf teemed with gray, dour people. The stench of tar and garbage rose up to greet her. Sabine cupped her left hand over her nose and mouth. The crowd on the dock stared up at the royal galleon. Their pale faces shone out from beneath moldy hoods and mist-dampened cowls.

Sabine swallowed hard.

This place was just as dismal as she had feared.

She clutched her hood and drew it up over her head. She willed one foot forward toward the gangplank, into the mist.

Scotland. *Mon Dieu!* She walked slowly, her gaze searching the wharf for any of these savages that came down from their mountains with swords in their hands and death on their lips.

Her *sac* banged against her thigh. Soon she would seek a way out of this wilderness.

I will get justice for my clan. I will seek revenge for the murder of my father and brother."

Niall MacGregor, chief of his besieged clan, saw the shadow of a large ship looming over the wharf. The vessel was magnificent, worthy of royalty. Hope surged in him for the first time in forever. This was the queen returning to Scotland. With her, there was hope for his clan.

He fervently wished his father, the great chief of his clan, could be here instead of dead beside Niall's older brother, Colin. Yet they lay in graves a fortnight old on the side of Beinn Tulaichean, which guarded Niall's home and his clan in the Highlands. He had left his home for one purpose, revenge against an auld and persistent enemy.

His father and brother had come to the Canon Gait, neutral ground just north of Edinburgh, eleven miles from Leith, and had died there.

"Peace," Niall silently hissed. "Our enemy gave them peace eternal."

Niall looked away from the ship as another wave of mist roiled in between his hiding place in a shadowy, narrow close and the great galleon. His eye caught sight of a post and a notice on it.

He read quietly to himself: "By order of the Privy Council of Scotland and the Isles . . ."

His throat tightened. Privy Council. Lord John Campbell was the bloody Privy Council in the Highlands, so he declared with his castle, men, and vast wealth and influence. Campbell would shoulder with this newly arrived royalty. Rumor was that he had already gone to France to express grief to the new queen over the death of her mother. It was rumored that he alone influenced Mary to return to Scotland, that as tithe for his kindness, she had gifted him with one of her attendants, personally arranged the betrothal. Some French maiden was the queen's political pawn who would bring Campbell and the Highlands closer to court.

Niall knew Campbell's true character, which Mary was so blinded to. No viler, nastier heart beat in Scotland. No man hated Clan Gregor more than Campbell. The proof was printed on a wrinkled and torn notice before Niall's eyes.

He stared at the paper. The words, printed in the darkest ink, the boldest letters, slammed him in the face.

Be it known to all good subjects of Her Majesty, Marie Reigne, Queen of Scotland and the Isles, that conscription has been imposed against all who embody allegiance to Clan Gregor, all claiming themselves as MacGregor, and the like. All nobles and good and loyal subjects of Her Majesty are ordered to forthwith pursue Clan Gregor with fire and sword. It is forbidden for all lieges to help Clan Gregor in any way with food, drink, weapons, shelter, care for the sick, or transport.

Campbell had not put his name to this piece of rubbish, but the timbre of the words bore his stench. So did the deaths of Niall's father and brother. Of this he needed undeniable proof. He also needed the help of his new queen. The penetrating question was how he, a hunted outlaw by virtue of this paper, would get an audience with the queen to warn her of the vermin in Scotland, to tell her the truth of his clan.

He stepped out from the close, hood over his head, concealing his flame-colored hair, as much a mark of Clan Gregor as was his plaid, dyed from an azure heather that grew in profusion in the glen.

Mind reeling, Niall stood alone amid the bustling crowd. No one paid him any notice, his face shrouded in shadow and mist, his stature that of an average man. His will that of a hundred.

"I will not die by fire and sword," he whispered. "Neither will my clan."

He narrowed his gaze at the galleon through a thinning patch of mist.

"By God we will not."

Niall took one step forward.

The mist from the Firth of Forth obliterated just about all in front of him. Oddly grateful for the concealing Scottish weather, he wove through the gathering crowd. The mist was as much a part of Niall as his damned flame-colored hair and condemned name. He made his way to the bottom of the gangplank to seek an audience with the newly arrived queen, to make his clan and their loyalty to her known.

He would sacrifice his freedom, risk imprisonment or death, to tell her that the edict set forth by the Privy Council, by Campbell no doubt, was a lie. All she had to do was hear him out.

"In a bloody dream, perchance," he told himself. There was no way the queen, fresh from her journey, would deem to listen to him. But he damn well had to try.

"Misneach is sith," he whispered in the comforting Gaelic over gnashed teeth. Then in the tongue the queen was certain to understand, "Fortitude is peace." He paused. She was coming from France. *"Le courage est la paix."*

A sharp breeze thinned the mist for a moment and pushed the hood from Niall's head. He grabbed for it just as he saw her. The woman cautiously stepped off the gangplank, clutching her velvet cloak to her throat, a hood concealing her hair. Niall stopped in the center of the wharf, the crowd flowing around him. Was this stunning beauty the queen? He wished she did not have the hood over her hair. He would know immediately if this breathtaking woman was the queen or not if he saw her hair. It was reputed to have the same fiery hue as his own.

He stood, rapt, a few dozen steps away from her. She turned and caught his stare with the most beautiful eyes on a face straight from his wildest . . .

". . . dreams, " he gasped.

A dark shadow suddenly raced past him in a fury of hoofbeats, almost knocking him off of his feet into a stall laden with fragile-looking baskets of chickens and various other poultry. He caught himself from faltering into the pile of clucking madness and droppings. He stared ahead, a dozen paces away, as darkness settled close to the beauty, halting its mount so near her.

"Campbell," Niall hissed.

The crowd quickly closed in around him. They, too, knew the queen had arrived in Leith that day. Only Niall seemed to know the devil himself had come to greet her on a black steed.

He glanced at the stall of chickens. An audience with the queen. He would have to distract those about her, and, in the same instant, come to her rescue.

The man Sabine was ordered to marry by the queen's command had come to greet her. She reached down and tapped her *sac* to comfort her turbulent mind.

She told herself not to be foolish. Lord Campbell had come to see his queen. Seeing Sabine had to be secondary. This thought brought her little succor.

Sabine followed Mary off the gangplank onto the muddy wharf. Fifteen people preceded her, the ladies-in-waiting and ten femmes de chambre. She was last in the procession. The instinct to turn and flee to the galleon and hide deep within its salty hold surged many times in her. She had to will her leaden feet forward, each step taken with determination.

Urgent whispers rippled through the line of velvet-cloaked ladies and attendants.

"Has no one but Lord Campbell and this gaggle of commonfolk come to greet Her Majesty?" Sabine heard Mary Fleming whisper.

At the foot of the gangplank she allowed the others to walk away from her. She strained to see along the wharf through the gathered crowd and the mist. The savages were out there waiting. She could feel them as well as she felt the tremor of her own fear of the many unknowns before her.

Sabine stepped forward from the plank into ankle-deep mud. She grabbed her cloak and gown and lifted them up as best she could while retaining courtly dignity. The others had walked far ahead of her, so her embarrassment was her own. She pulled her feet out of the filthy quagmire with a rude sucking sound. Her slippers were a complete loss.

"Merde," she said under her breath.

"I have but a cursory understanding of the French, lassie, but I'll wager you're not at all happy with my country so far."

Sabine froze. She stared up the long, bony body of a man immaculately clad in dark stockings, pantaloons, and doublet. Equally as dark were his neatly trimmed beard and peppery curls of hair under a jaunty velvet cap topped with an ostrich plume. His face was flushed as if he had been on a recent and hard ride.

"Oui," she uttered, "I understand you, *monsieur.*"

"Good," Lord Campbell said.

He stared up and down at her.

Sabine, in turn, stared at his pointy face, at the wide eyes, the raised brow, the sneer of surprised disgust on thin lips. His reaction was more common than she cared count.

She hastily glanced away from this man to the queen. The ladies and the femmes de chambre, too distant to conceal her, hovered protectively about their sovereign.

"Pardon, monsieur," she said, stepping away from the man in dark velvet and brocade.

"Her Majesty arrived a wee bit early," he said. "We were expecting her in a fortnight."

Sabine tipped her chin up, craving the huddle about the queen. A crowd of spectators had gathered around them—a ring of pink faces and gray wool clothing. The queen appeared not vexed by the situation. She looked radiant with the hushed adoration of the crowd about her.

As if sensing her worries, he said, "We have met, you know, on several brief occasions in the French court. Yet, allow me to introduce myself again, as I fear you may have forgotten me. I'm Lord John Campbell, at your service"—he paused and tossed a glance at the crowd—"and Her Majesty's, of course." He looked long at her. "I have ridden from Edinburgh on another errand only to find that Scotland has been made more lovely . . ." He stole a glance at her right hand, paused, then said, ". . . now that you have arrived."

"Your thoughts should only be for your queen," she snapped. Were all Scottish men as rude as he?

"And for my betrothed," he said, taking her right hand and raising it to his lips. He looked at it, paused, and gave the back of her hand a quick, dry kiss, much like the peck of a hen in dust.

Sabine could only glance away with a bitter swallow as she took possession of her right hand and tucked it beneath her cloak.

"Ah," he said, looking up the cobbled street, a ghost of relief on his face, "the carriage has arrived. I shall assist Her Majesty. Never fear, I shall return to assist you in good time."

Sabine watched him walk away. Good. She would never fear as long as that *fripon* was a good distance from her. Escape from him and this nasty country would come none too soon for her.

A cry rose up in the crowd.

Sabine whirled around and was suddenly filled with more fear than the day she sailed from Calais.

"Mon Dieu!" she cried.

A chicken flailed toward her, parting the crowd, then terrifyingly sought sudden refuge under her skirts. She flapped the many layers of velvet and brocade at the excited bird as it raced about her legs. Tiny claws ripped into her silken stockings, scratching her tender flesh.

She dropped her skirts. Birds calmed in the dark. She prayed this was true. Then she looked up.

A horrible man, *non* a monster, rushed toward her. His dark cloak flapped open. A crosshatched-patterned wool skirt beat against powerful reddened knees above calves wrapped in strips of frayed wool. Piecemeal leather shoes pounded the mud. Hair the color of a fiery sunset after a storm blew back from his face. Then he threw his body at her feet and disappeared halfway under her gown.

Sabine tried to leap away from the creatures beneath her gown, but the crowd had pressed around her, staring. She could not help but act a consummate fool and shriek when savage hands grabbed her legs, taking advantage.

Her body turned rigid as the monster rose before her.

All she could do was gasp.

Penetrating, bright, fierce eyes, the blue of an Alpine river, stole her breath. Damp, wavy, auburn locks framed a heart-stopping face of perfect furrows and ridges. His lips turned upward into a grin. Sabine forced herself to breathe. This was a true savage of Scotland.

"Got ye," he said, sounding more Scots than Lady Fleming herself.

Sabine heard herself breathe from far away, *"Oui."*

She feared her struggle with the *sauvage* before her had just begun.

N*iall dropped the chicken. It weaved away into the crowd.* His plan had worked. He had not saved the queen, but he was nearer to her, very near to this intended of Campbell's, this royal pawn.

While staring deep into the dark eyes that studied his own with as much intensity, he silently celebrated this wee victory. This woman, a beauty among beauties, was Campbell's prize from the queen. That much he had heard and seen, 'twas no longer rumor. Yet, from the conversation Niall had overheard, from the way this French lass had looked and stood apart from Campbell, she was none too fond of the impending nuptials. He had found a kindred spirit, tenuous at best, but they seemed to share the same sentiments toward Campbell, if his eyes and ears did not deceive him. He feared, though, he would only have a moment to state his demands to her, so a moment would have to suffice.

The woman tipped her chin up a little, revealing the long line of her neck to the stiff collar of silk and lace concealing her throat. Her dark gaze, as sparkling as the spring waters of Loch Katrine, captured him and disarmed him.

She had the presence of a queen. She was of noble, regal bearing, as she condescended to him with one gaze.

Niall swallowed again. He was so close to her. His left hand rested inside her cloak, his fingers brushing a soft leather purse. He clenched his fist about it without thinking, a reflex. Dear God, how lovely she was standing there taking small, nervous breaths over perfect lips. She stared hard into his eyes as if she was afraid of him, as if she expected him to do something.

"Scotland *sauvage*," she said with a toss of her head. Her hood slipped down. Hair darker than pitch spilled out. It glistened in the mist. The tendrils dangled against the porcelain skin of as lovely a face as he had ever seen. 'Twas a shame she was a French snot.

Niall's mind turned over rapidly. He must seek an audience with Her Majesty through this woman. He did have a repute for charming the lassies of his glen. This comely lass should be no problem. If she would only lower her chin a wee bit.

The beauty reached up with a twisted hand to replace the hood over her hair. He gave her hand no more than a passing glance. Her eyes were far more interesting.

"Aye, well," Niall said, finding his grin, "the true *sauvage* is—"

"A MacGregor!" A horrid and familiar voice rang out behind him.

Niall jerked around, taking something, the soft leather purse, with him. He stabbed his free hand under his cloak for his dirk.

But it was as futile a gesture as deeming to soften one of the royal court to him. Several pairs of hands grabbed him, jerking him roughly away from her, jerking his hands from his knife.

"Ye're ruining a lovely moment, lads," Niall said. Jest was all he could find for the moment. He struggled against his many captors.

He was whirled about. His head was yanked back by a fistful of his hair, forcing his chin up. His gaze met that of Satan himself.

"Campbell," he rasped.

"The *mademoiselle* knows you better than you know yourself, MacGregor," Campbell said.

"Then she must also realize that ye arc but shite beneath her feet," Niall hissed.

Campbell slapped him. The leather gauntlet stung the side of Niall's face, but he remained steady, giving his enemy not so much as a wince.

"Ye hit like a lassie," he said. "Weak, like yer claim to Gregor land!"

"Take this scum to the tolbooth," Campbell snarled.

"On whose authority do you do this, Lord John?"

Campbell bowed low to the queen, a stately woman with hair more fiery than Niall's. Her clothes rivaled the sun with their brilliance.

"Release this man," she commanded.

The guards obeyed her. Niall stumbled toward the queen.

He bowed before Scotland's new sovereign. Hope for his clan burned deep inside his soul. He prayed the queen had not heard the lies against his people, had no knowledge of the edict posted against all MacGregors.

"Lord John, what say you to this disruption?" the queen asked.

"Your Majesty, I heartily apologize—" Campbell began.

"I did not ask for apology," she said, voice firm. She waved a hand forward. Still bowing, Niall looked up through his hair. The French lass stepped forward. She was more lovely than her sovereign. Surely, that must be treason in itself.

"Our Sabine, what say you to this disruption? You appear to be the source of it."

Niall's grin escaped. He now knew her name.

Sabine curtsied. "I regret, Your Majesty, that I cried out. I was affronted."

"Affronted? By whom?"

Campbell stepped forward. "That MacGregor, Your Majesty. An outlaw from an outlaw clan. Your Privy Council decreed it, in your name."

"We did not solicit a response from you, Lord John. We are most affronted that policy is made by our Privy Council without our knowledge. We have yet to determine the truth of any accusation you bring to one of our subjects."

Niall held his head higher and threw a wink at his queen. She was a lass after all. The merest hint of a smile played at the corners of her mouth.

"But, Your Majesty, MacGregors are—"

"Enough!" The queen stifled a yawn with bejeweled fingers before her lips. "We are weary from our journey. This matter can certainly wait." She turned away to the carriage and the huddle of nobles that had seemingly appeared from nowhere. Sabine continued to curtsy but took a furtive glance at Niall.

He mouthed her name. *Sabine.*

She blinked, gasping. Good. He deserved something from her, even if it was a startled reaction. If she had not disarmed him with such beauty, he would not be in this predicament.

"Take him away," Campbell said to the guards.

Niall suddenly dropped to the mud. Like a newt, he slipped through the muck, evading the grappling hands. With one hand he reached for his dirk, neatly sheathed, hidden in a fold of his kilt. Brandishing the weapon, he parted the crowd in a hail of gasps and startled breaths. He ran through Leith with the speed and fury of a spring storm, to the outskirts, to a forest where his horse was tethered and hidden.

He vowed to see Sabine again, for the sake of his clan. She would get him inside the palace, but how?

He looked down at his left fist. He had not unclenched it since he had been torn away from Sabine. He opened his fingers one by one, revealing a small, leather purse in his palm.

An idea leapt to mind. He sat down in cover of the forest and opened the purse.

S abine stared into the mist as a light rain began to fall. "He has escaped, no?" she asked Lord Campbell.

She knew the answer to her question. One as bold as that MacGregor could leave her life as quickly as he had entered it. She could still feel his firm touch upon her legs, see his fierce yet heavenly gaze in her mind.

"Curse all MacGregors," Lord Campbell replied to the mist.

Sabine allowed him to escort her to her queen. This vile and savage place was her new home and not for long.

She reached inside her cloak, down to her *sac,* with her right hand, stretching the fingers, strengthening them, reaching to the symbol of her freedom—

Her heart froze, and her spirit plummeted to harsh reality. She rustled her hand frantically under her cloak until all about her gave her hard stares. She stopped, forced her hand into view, and stood quiet and demure as a good attendant should. Inside the depth of her mind and soul she was screaming.

Mon Dieu! Her *sac* and the hope it bore were gone!

Lord Campbell stared at her, face frozen in confusion, unsure what to think of her. Then he offered her a thin smile and his hand.

Sabine had no choice but to place her hand in his. She offered him her left hand this time. He gladly took it and escorted her to the waiting carriage.

N iall *sat against a stout oak. He allowed his breathing to* calm. His mount chewed lazily on the undergrowth of fern, the chomping a distant sound.

He opened the gut strings wide and reached into the purse. He pulled out what at first glance looked like brittle autumn leaves, but upon closer inspection he realized they were scraps of paper with images from another place drawn in charcoal.

"She drew these," he guessed out loud.

He picked up one of the papers. Set before his wide eyes were jagged snow-topped mountains. The sun shone on these bold outcroppings from the knife's edge of a fir forest. Niall did not have to see the winter sunlight to know its power and rarity in these select charcoal markings. He also knew this place was not Scotland.

He looked at another paper. A man with a small mustache

and pointy chin whiskers stared back at him. One thin brow was cocked jauntily above a glinting eye. The realism was startling. The fact that this man was naked was more startling.

"A lover, no doubt," he mused wickedly. This man was not Campbell. "I wonder if the bastard knows about this."

Amused, he thumbed through the other papers. More beautiful scenery met his eyes, but no more revealing portraits. He looked to his lap. There, resting in the center, nested in the dark plaid like an egg—it was a ball made of strips of wool wound round and round.

He picked the ball up. He lifted it to his nose, savored her delicate flowery fragrance. He drew her scent in deep and captured her. A curious possession, aye, but no more curious than this woolen ball.

Niall recalled her right hand. A minor flaw on an otherwise perfect beauty. Perchance, it was not a flaw at all. He gave the ball a squeeze. The muscles in his fingers tightened against the slightly resilient orb. He squeezed as hard as he could until the veins on his forearm stood out against the pale, mud-streaked skin. He relaxed his hand, his fingers felt a wee bit stronger.

The purse still weighed heavy in his palm. He upended it. Five gold pieces fell into his lap.

"A bloody ransom!" was his first reaction.

He then clapped a hand over his mouth. He glanced through the wood, and up and down the road. He remained alone.

Five gold pieces! 'Twas wealth as he had never held before, yet alone seen.

"She'll want this back, oh aye," he said with a grin.

He shoved the papers and the wool ball back into the purse. He dropped the coin one by one into the opening and cinched the gut strings tight.

He was no thief. He was chief of a clan that would be slaughtered if he did not seek out the queen. The MacGregors could remain hidden in their remote glen, fend off an attack, but for how long? As much as he hated to admit it, he needed help.

He could not help but grin to himself. He knew several of

the French lass's secrets. Perchance he would know more,
after he forced her to do his bidding. If she wanted it returned
she would take him to the queen. This leather purse was his
key.

Sudden hoofbeats seized his attention. He reached under
his cloak for his dirk and held it at the ready while he waited
in the tree shadows.

The rider wore a cloak that blew back from his shoulders.
It ill concealed his dark plaid and the chaotic black curls of his
hair.

His best mate, Rory Buchanan, a hapless but loyal soul
fostered a score ago into Clan Gregor, slowed his mount to a
stop before the stand of oak. He puckered his lips and let loose
with a poor imitation of a woodcock trill. Niall relaxed and
placed his dirk back into its sheath at his hip.

"Aye, aye," Niall said stepping from the wood. "I hear ye,
ye daft bastard." He glanced down the road. "What news of
the Canon Gait? Any witnesses against Campbell?"

Rory slumped a wee bit in the saddle. He sighed and raked
a hand through the rat's nest on his head.

"What is it?" Niall asked, taking the reins of Rory's mount
as his friend thumped to the ground. Rory would not leave his
father alone. The Buchanan, a giant, but with as much brains
as a midge fly, was the chief's champion, his protector.

Rory looked askance to nowhere in particular on the
horizon.

"What news?" Niall demanded.

Finally, after heaving another sigh, Rory looked Niall in
the eye and said, "Nowt."

"Nowt?" Niall stood firm. There were no witnesses? Not a
bloody one?

"None." Rory's voice trailed off on a meandering, unintel-
ligible path.

Niall held tight to Sabine's purse. Rain began to fall
around him. He looked to the south. One word crossed
through his mind and his lips. He shoved the purse into his
sporran, a humble satchel that hung from the belt that cinched
his plaid to his waist.

He turned and walked determinedly to his mount. He
climbed into the saddle over the horse's rain-slicked back and

faced the beast north to the palace at Holyrood, eleven miles away.

Sabine's purse weighed heavy inside his sporran. She would help him. She had to.

chapter 2

Hope, Lost and Found

Hope had abandoned Sabine, and she had been in Scotland but a day.

She raced from the queen's chambers, where she had pretended to unpack Mary's extensive wardrobe while searching desperately for her *sac*. No one saw her leave. No one noticed the frantic look upon her face when she made her most horrible discovery.

Sabine blindly wound her way through the polished wood corridors of this Scottish palace, humble in comparison to the great Palais Royal they had occupied in France. She ran as fast as her legs could carry her, heart pumping with the steady flurry of a moth around a flame.

She took it on faith that her destination was ahead of her, around the next corner. All palaces had one. This palace of Holyrood had an abbey, or part of one, if the rumors Sabine had heard were correct.

Only Saint Giles, France's famed hermit and patron saint of cripples and hopeless causes, could help her now.

She passed a surprised guard who had no time to lower his pike and bar her way out of the corridor. She stumbled through a pointed stone arch and skidded to a halt. All around her were ruins only to rival that of the remains of Pompeii, from what she had seen in sketches in a book . . . once.

She looked about her at the blackened timbers, the soot-stained stone walls. A score of years ago, Henry, the father of the English queen, had ordered his soldiers to sack the abbey.

Saint Giles had guided her here, and perchance he would listen to her. Sabine prostrated herself before the wreckage of the altar under the glowering faces of the burnt icons, praying.

In the rainbow-colored reflection of the broken stained-glass windows on the sooty stone floor Sabine prayed for strength from her beloved patron saint. The damaged traceries held the jeweled fragments of glass. Perchance, Saint Giles did not come to such a desecrated church. He brought no answers to Sabine's prayers. Only truth. Her *sac* was gone. She no longer had a choice to her life. She would have to marry Lord Campbell and live the rest of her life in his Highland Kingdom. She saw nothing but dread ahead of her.

Sabine gripped a stick of charred timber with her right hand, strengthening her twisted fingers. She had to think some more. There had to be other choices.

She rose to her feet and raced from the abbey, from the stink of burned wood, from decay, into the vast palace garden where the heady air of early evening was resplendent with the fragrance of hundreds of flowers and herbs.

Despite the beauty that surrounded her in the rising moonlight, desperate thoughts rattled in her head as she walked in the cloistered gardens. Beyond the manicured rosebushes, the fruit orchard, and the fragrant knot gardens lay a wild and untamed country. She knew this to be true, though she had to take it on faith and from the stare of that untamed MacGregor.

Sabine closed her eyes and inhaled the sweet scent of the sprays of lavender blossoms about her. The color blue loomed on her mind's horizon, the blue of this waning Scottish summer, and the blue of the eyes that had captured her soul for one unforgettable moment. Her heart missed a beat, startling her.

She placed her right hand over her left breast, over the black and crimson velvet and silk of her gown. She had sewn it herself, the stitches uneven, yet sturdy enough. Many times during her sewing she had to stop and relieve the cramp in her twisted fingers, and listen to common sense implore her to use her left hand to do the work. *Non*. That would not do for Sabine, ever.

She opened her eyes to the soft slope of the green hills swelling above the garden walls. Such a lovely green. Hills wore many cloaks depending on the season. This rich green mantle was Sabine's favorite color next to the blue of late-summer sky. The thought was comforting, but she needed to think of harder things. To ease her mind. Then she might remember where she could have lost her *sac*.

She wandered past the knot garden to a small orchard of fruit trees, plum and fig. Under the soft boughs, in the dappled light, she found private sanctuary. There she turned the paper over.

Slowly she reached into the top of her gown, between her breasts, and withdrew a scrap of paper no bigger than her palm. The ragged edges were decorated with fragments of Her Majesty's elaborate script. The paper was something the queen had crumpled and dropped on the floor, rubbish to anyone but Sabine. She did not notice the words, could have cared less. She knelt on the dew-damp ground and smoothed the paper over one thigh.

Sabine gripped the charcoal tighter in her gnarled right hand. She took a deep breath and soon her hand glided across the rough surface of the paper. She easily became unaware of anything other than the motion of the stick over the paper. Her right hand cramped and protested. When she could ignore the pain no longer she dropped the charcoal and stared down at her sketch.

Sabine gasped.

The MacGregor looked up at her. The soft and strong lines, contours she had sketched, were enmeshed into one vivid, captivating image. She had sketched his hair in a wild mass of lines jutting from his head and flowing around his strong, corded neck. She had drawn his grin, a razor's-edge smile that pierced her heart and haunted her dreams, and framed it with furrowed dashes on the corners of his lips. The bold cleft in the center of his chin was there as well. Sabine surprised herself for remembering so many details about him.

Her art did not suffer from the damage in her drawing

hand. It flourished fresh and new. The lines more expressive. Was this because of her daily prayers to Saint Giles? Or was this because of her new subject?

"*Le MacGregor . . . ,*" she breathed. Her heart trembled, or was it the wilds of her imagination?

Her once beloved, always remembered, *le maître,* her instructor before she had to look to Saint Giles for strength, would have been so pleased. He would have adored this sketch of the wild Scottish creature. Sabine lifted it high over her head. Maybe he could look down from Heaven and see her coveted creation. But he would not be completely satisfied, as she had not taken that next step, the step he could not have taught her because he had left her forever. She had not used color, had not gathered the pigments. Yet, in her memory, this Scottish MacGregor savage was replete with color.

Sabine closed her eyes and summoned the MacGregor's colors, locked them in her memory. The colors found in Heaven and placed on one who surely was one of hell's minions.

"And a thief!" she shouted to the stars.

Oui! Of course! She had been a fool not to guess he had stolen her *sac.* And why had she not guessed it from the start? She looked to the sky as if the stars and the silver moon would give her answers when all she had to do was look to her foolish heart. It had blinded her to the very real possibility that the MacGregor had stolen her hope. His azure eyes had pierced her soul and her good sense.

She shunted her eyes to the west, to the high stone garden wall, and beyond to the moon-shadowed hills. Far beyond those hills savages dwelled.

She clasped her arms about her body, suppressing a cold shudder that rose up from her toes. The cold quickly yielded to the building anger that originated in the pit of her soul.

The MacGregor had, in all likelihood, taken her *sac* to his lair, burnt her sketches to keep warm for a moment, and spent all of her gold on drink and whores. That was what men did. Especially savages.

Her *sac* and all in it were lost forever. She would not see this MacGregor again except in her memory, and in the sketch she held in her hand.

Her first instinct was to tear it to as many bits as there were stars in Heaven. She acted on her second instinct, folded the paper and tucked it between her breasts. She might need it. That hope remained with her like a burr on wool.

"Where are you, silly girl!" Lady Fleming screeched from the direction of the palace.

The Scotswoman shoved aside the low boughs, ducking her veiled head, before stopping abruptly before her charge.

"Why did you leave Her Majesty's chambers without a by-your-leave?" she asked, one thin brow raised, arms folded across her bosom.

"To pray," she replied.

"Do you still mourn the loss of your father?"

"Mourning is never over, m'lady," Sabine replied, throat tightening. "Not while the heart is alive."

Lady Fleming narrowed her gaze. "Why do I suspect that it is not your father you mourn for?"

"Because you knew him, m'lady. He gave me to you."

She nodded. "What a willful child you were then. What a willful child you are now. You should be grateful, with . . ." She paused and glanced at Sabine's hand. After a swallow, she said, "Your father is not cold in his grave, and you show not the slightest remorse."

Sabine displayed her hand to the woman. She forced her twisted fingers to straighten. Lady Fleming's eyes widened. "'Tis a miracle or witchery," she breathed.

"*Non,* m'lady," Sabine said. "'Tis sweet Saint Giles who gives me strength. Remorse, as you say, would only further cripple me. Perchance, that is what you wish?"

Lady Fleming straightened and cleared her throat. "The queen requests your presence in her outer chamber. *Now.*"

Numbly, obediently, Sabine followed Lady Fleming out of the orchard, past the lavender and germander knot gardens, past the rose hedge, and through a dreary gray stone archway into the palace.

Their footsteps on the waxed wood floor echoed around the great length of corridor, up to the ceiling with its painted and gilded floral carvings. They stopped before an ornately carved door of flowers and fruits, the same one Sabine had rushed from a lifetime ago.

Lady Fleming rapped briskly on the wood.

"You may enter," Her Majesty said.

Lady Fleming opened the door.

Mary sat in a chair that made the rich carving on the door leading into her outer chamber humble by comparison. Embroidery rested on her lap. To one side of her chair the hearth blazed with great snapping and hissing logs. Even the damp of this country found its way into the queen's chambers. Sabine stepped onto the woven rush carpet and into a low curtsy.

"You may rise," the queen commanded.

Sabine jumped upright. *"Ma Reine."*

"Your period of mourning has come to an end." Mary tipped her chin up a bit. Gold and black pearl earrings swayed lightly from her earlobes. Then she smiled. "We feel quite strongly that our attendants have abiding happiness."

"Yes, Your Majesty," Sabine said, trying to conceal the suspicion in her voice.

"Come forward."

She did as she was commanded. How was Mary going to grant her happiness?

"You shall marry Lord John in a fortnight."

Sabine halted. What?

"The wedding must take place soon, as a promise we made to your father. We promised him that you will marry a good man. Lord John is such a man."

"A fortnight, *madame*?" Sabine asked. Because of a promise to a man who was now quite dead!

Sabine wished to speak further, to thank Her Majesty for her generous concern, and to tell her that she was in no way endeared to Lord Campbell, to tell her the truth of her father.

The door burst open.

She turned about, into Lord Campbell's path.

He threw himself into a deep bow, sweeping his hat from his head. The stiff skirt of his dark doublet pointed to the ceiling.

"Rise, Lord John," Mary said. "We have taken the liberty

of expressing to our Sabine your wish to marry her in a fortnight. We give you leave to speak to her in privacy."

"Yes, yes, Your Most Gracious Majesty, we shall take our leave."

Lord Campbell backed toward the door past Sabine, trailing a scent one would have to find in a *parfumerie*. She stared at him, mouth open, her eyes wide. Love did not exist in her heart for this man, but love was not a reason to marry, was it?

"Come, *mademoiselle*," he whispered, a hint of urgency in his tone.

"Our Sabine, we have given you permission to see Lord John in private. We suggest you take the opportunity before you attend to your other duties."

"Your Majesty," Sabine began, "I beg your forgiveness and appreciate your generosity. I . . . I do not. . . ."

"You do not . . . ?" Mary asked, one thin red brow raised.

Sabine let out a long breath. "I do not know how to aptly express my appreciation for Your Majesty's concern for my happiness . . . and for the memory of my father." After that lie, she offered Mary a low curtsy, bowing her head.

"Take your leave . . . and you as well, Lord John."

"Yes, Your Majesty," he said bowing in front of Sabine, giving her a good view of his better side, concealed by velvet pantaloons. For the briefest moment, she mused as to what the MacGregor looked like beneath that woolen skirt he wore, then as quickly crushed the image from her mind.

"*Oui, madame.*" Sabine backed toward the door. Suddenly she wanted to run as far away from the palace as she could, until her heart burst from her flight.

Lord Campbell was waiting for her. There was no escape. The once familiar weight of her *sac* inside her gown was a ghostly feeling now. One brought to her by that MacGregor. He had gifted her with hopelessness.

She forced in a deep and nourishing breath and slipped around the door.

Lord Campbell immediately grasped her left wrist and pulled her toward him.

"I can see in your eyes, *mademoiselle*, that you're much surprised by my proposal," he said, lips glistening.

Sabine tried to pull from his hold. "You have proposed nothing to me, *monsieur*."

He towered above her, pressing her into a niche along the corridor. She grasped his arms, trying to free herself from his presence. There was nowhere for her to escape from the cramped space.

"I love a fiery spirit. You French are reputed to have such passion in everything you do. One thing in particular intrigues me above all else. That I wish to discover on our wedding night."

"Wishes, Lord Campbell, are for the very young. Are they not?"

" 'Tis not a dream, *mademoiselle*, 'tis an edict from your queen." He released her. "That you cannot deny." He stared her up and down.

Sabine thought of the MacGregor. Entrapped by Campbell, her will betrayed her and softened to another truth about the Highland thief. He had looked into her eyes that misty morn and, for a moment, had freed her soul with his fierce gaze. He had not rudely sized her up like meat in a butcher's like this supposed "noble" was doing to her now. Despite his untamed exterior, he had not been as rude as Lord Campbell was being at the very moment. The MacGregor probably never had to force his will on any woman. Or get a royal command to have a wife.

She blinked and tossed those foolish musings aside.

"You should be grateful, *mademoiselle*," Lord Campbell said, "that I have made allowances and can overlook your, uh, affliction."

Fire burned to her very core. "There can be no allowances made for your rudeness," she snapped. "You're the one who is 'afflicted'!"

Campbell's eyes grew dead. Sabine felt the same in his stare.

"I'll take my leave, *mademoiselle*, to prepare for Her Majesty's welcoming masque on the morrow. At which time I will formally announce our engagement to all present. Do me the honor of displaying your pleasure at that time."

He slid away from her, a man of influence and wealth, a

man twice her score of years. That was all she knew about him. It was all she cared to know.

"Sweet Saint Giles," she whispered, "I need your help. I need your strength."

On another breath, she said, "Send that MacGregor to me."

The night of the queen's masque, Sabine walked through the moonlit gardens grateful to be alone again, aware that her solitude would be short-lived once Lord Campbell discovered her absent. She savored this time in the garden, inhaling the lavender scent thick in the night air. Tonight the queen's court and all of her guests would know that Sabine was to wed Lord John Campbell. Banns would be posted. And in one day less than a fortnight, she would be wed.

Lord Campbell would have to find her first.

She wound her way through the plum and apricot grove into the dappled moon shadows. She walked pensively among the spindly trees, laden with aromatic, sweet fruit. She stopped a dozen steps from the wall, a stone affair twice her height. Getting out was impossible. And where would she go if she did succeed? And with what means?

Sudden rustling, a thud, followed by a grunt, then again, the same noises repeated. Sabine froze under a plum tree, her gaze fixed at the base of the wall.

Someone wanted to get in when all she could think of was getting out. Who was this fool? She ducked behind the gnarled trunk of the tree, digging into the bark with bloodless fingers. Who would be so bold to try to break into the royal garden?

Sabine stared through the bluish patches of moonlight. She gasped. Not one bold person, but two had penetrated this royal sanctuary. She held her breath and gripped the tree harder, fascinated.

The figures, cloaked by the darkness and the garments they wore, moved steadily, hugging the wall. The first intruder stopped and the other one ran into the back of him. The leader of this duo lowered the hood of his cloak.

Robbers! Savages!

Sabine could not breathe. Silhouetted in the moonlight, she

saw the sharp profile, arrogant slope of nose, determined curl of lips, and waves of hair. She knew this intruder. She could not hold in her gasp.

He turned at the sound. Hoping he could not see her, Sabine sunk into the darkness as his penetrating blue eyes took in all corners of the shadowy grove. Savage creatures always surveyed their surroundings before attacking. She remained very still and deathly silent.

The Highlander swept off his cloak, revealing a broad expanse of linen back. A swath of the crosshatched fabric draped across it and wrapped over his lean hips. Another item adorned the Highlander's back. It was the longest sword Sabine had ever seen.

The other figure removed his cloak also, exposing a confused mass of black curls and a grim mouth. This creature seemed not as bold as his leader, as he removed the sword. A hint of moonlight touched the blade, glinted silver, and then was gone. The man swiftly stashed it against the base of the wall.

Sabine held her breath and tried to become one with the tree shadows. The savages were now walking toward her. She had two choices: fight or flee.

Gathering her skirts and her wits, she took the latter choice and raced toward the ruined abbey. It was so far away, across the expanse of grove and garden, where beyond its broken pillars and burned timbers a pair of guards stood vigilantly by one of several entrances to the palace. With each pounding step, sanctuary seemed to grow further away from her.

She tore through the grove, hoping to reach the lavender knot garden where the guards might hear her shouts from beyond the cover of the trees, when her feet suddenly left the ground. She landed fast and hard on the grassy path. Her breath left her in an undignified whoosh! The heavenly scent of the fruit and herbs was quickly masked by a heady, male smell, of soil and sweat. Sabine fought to get up, twisting her body around to face the Highland savage. He lay half on top of her, holding her captive in his arms and in his piercing gaze.

"Le MacGregor!" she whispered.

"Ye honor me to remember my name," he said, pressing her closer.

"'Tis not my intention," she said, renewing her struggle. He held her tighter.

Their lips were so dangerously close, she could taste his spirit-tinged breath.

"Release me," she said. "Or I shall scream for the guards."

"To it, *Sabine*," he said. "The guards are on the other side of the abbey and willnae hear ye. I checked that they were far from here before we bothered to come over the wall."

"Do not call me familiar. And how is it that you know my name?" she said, then demanded, *"Let me go."*

"I cannae do that, *mademoiselle*," he said. "Ye might run away."

"You aren't as much of an *imbecile* as you look, savage."

"The name's MacGregor. *Niall* MacGregor," he snarled, breath hot against her face.

"Well, MacGregor, Niall MacGregor, you're crushing me."

Still holding her wrist, he slipped off her. He helped her to her feet, and they faced each other.

"Would you be so kind and release the rest of me?"

Surprisingly, he complied with her demand.

"How regal ye sound," he said. "Tell me, did ye learn such ways of speech from Her Majesty, or do all of ye French lasses raise their chins so high?"

Sabine blinked. "As much as all Highlanders are savages . . . and *les voleurs*."

He certainly would not know she had just called him a thief to his face.

"Does one who lives such a charmed life commonly disparage those she doesnae know? 'Tis a popular game of the royal court, aye, Sabine?"

"You pretend to know me in the moment we have been together, Niall MacGregor, do you not?"

"Perchance. Would ye like to get to know me? I can make it worth yer while." He reached up and took a plum from the bough above his head.

Sabine blinked. This man spoke crazy gibberish. She abruptly turned right into the other Highlander, the one with the rat's nest of black curls. She whirled angrily back to Niall MacGregor.

"I want an audience with the queen," he said, taking a bite of the plum. Juice exploded onto his chin, trickled into the cleft.

Sabine, taken aback by his bold demand, replied, "You're an amusing man. Are you actually that stupid?"

He took another bite and spoke, his mouth full of fruit. "Ye wish me to break ye in two now, or shall I wait a bit?" he asked.

"Don't try to impress me with your strength. Unless, of course, it is your way of making amends for your puny brain."

His companion snorted in what sounded suspiciously like laughter.

Niall yanked her against the unyielding firmness of his broad chest. The juice on his lips and the hard contours of his body beneath the rough linen tunic tempted her to allow her lips a tiny taste. *Non!*

She swallowed, withdrew her hand into a fold of her gown, and denied what stirred deep inside her. It was an ignorant beast and one best kept hidden. She tried to pull away. He held her so tightly. Damn him. He had stolen her hope, would he steal her body as well?

"'Tis a fight ye willnae win," he said. "I see it in your eyes that ye agree not to leave my embrace."

"My eyes and every part of me agree that you're a cretin."

He held up the half-eaten plum. "Want a bite? Or are ye full from chewing my bloody head off?"

She reached up with her right hand, grasped at the fruit, then took it. She squeezed it. Juice trickled down her cramped fingers to her palm. She gave the MacGregor a challenging stare as she tossed the fruit over her shoulder before the juice made its way to her silk sleeve. No more games. Instinct told her that hope was alive, but for how long?

"Oww! Bloody hell!" came the harsh whisper.

She glanced briefly over her shoulder at the MacGregor's friend, who wiped one eye with a grimy sleeve of his tunic.

Niall grabbed her wrist. He pulled her right hand to his lips and licked the juice from the back of it. Sabine froze, not breathing. His blue eyes stared steadily into her as he wrapped his tongue around each finger, sending thousands of tiny bolts of sensation through her entire body. If he was not holding her tight with his other strong arm, she would surely have fainted right to the damp grass.

"I know your secret, *mademoiselle*."

He could not possibly. "Beast," she breathed. *"Animal."*

"Insults will get ye nowhere," he whispered. "I have a key to the palace, thanks to ye."

Sabine blinked. He was insane as well. "You have nothing."

But my only hope for leaving the prospect of a life as horrid as the one I left.

He moved his free hand down, never taking his stare from her, and reached into his own skirtlike garment. In a blink, he dangled her *sac* before her eyes. She did not know whether to scream in joy for seeing it again or to scratch his eyes out for stealing it from her.

He nodded, eyes flashing in the moonlight. "I thought that would wake ye up."

She snatched at the bag with her good hand and only grasped air. "'Tis mine!" Her tone was far too desperate.

He held it over his head, taunting her. Heat flared behind Sabine's eyes. She saw her father standing over her, his fist full of her drawings, crumpling them, before he tossed them like dead leaves. The heat built behind her eyes. It rivaled that of the fire in her father's enormous hearth, the fire that had turned her work to ashes. She stared hard into this Highlander's eyes as he tormented her with her own property, with her hope, and with his mere presence. How dare he!

With one mighty kick, she sent her slippered foot into the softness between his thighs, making contact like she did to many a French noble who came too close in the royal court. Like she planned to do to Lord Campbell on their wedding night.

Niall MacGregor slumped to the ground. He landed on one knee, the purse clenched in his fist. His mouth pushed out a surprised *whompf* of air. Sabine reached down as swift as a cat and grasped one of the braided gut strings that cinched the top of the *sac*. She tugged, but the MacGregor would not relent.

He looked up at her and flashed that grin. "Good thing me

mum waulked my plaid extra thick, or I would have to forgo having any weans."

"Let go, mongrel," Sabine said. "It is mine."

"Enough," he whispered from the ground. His eyes searched the far end of the garden, in the direction of the palace. "Enough."

Arms grabbed Sabine around her waist. She did not have to turn around to know his friend had her in his noxious embrace. He would do well to visit one of dozens of *parfumeries* in Paris.

Niall MacGregor rose before her. Once again he held her *sac* aloft before her pleading eyes.

"I looked inside," he said. "There's much value within as well as yer secrets." He gave her a wink. Sabine knew to what secret he referred. The heat built behind her eyes again. He had invaded her person by stealing her purse, and he had invaded her soul by looking at her sketches.

Her father had said the same thing—well, almost. He had called the drawings an "atrocity." Niall had smiled and called them "secrets."

"Only a crude person like yourself would dare say such a thing. You have looked at my private works."

"Aye," he replied, "I have taken more than a keek at them."

Sabine narrowed her gaze.

He grinned anew. "They're quite lovely. Captivating in fact. I've not seen anything like them."

No insults shuttled down from her brain to her tongue. No one had described her art in such nice words, no one except *le maître,* her beloved teacher.

"We will make a trade," he said. "Your purse, and *all* its contents, for—"

"I do not bargain for what's rightfully mine with a thief," she hissed. She squirmed out of the other Highlander's arms. She squared her shoulders at Niall MacGregor, her stance as stiff and defiant as the marble water bearers on the Fontaine des Innocents in the courtyard of the Palais Royal.

"Ye will take me to the queen," he said.

"You are but a fool," she replied. "I love my queen and would not see her harmed by the likes of you."

Brows knitted, eyes flashing, he jerked her closer to his body, as if that were possible. His masculine scent enveloped her. "Ye're no different from Campbell by thinking ye know me and mine."

"You know Lord Campbell?" she asked, surprised.

"I know he's an unholy bastard who would do anything to have more power and more land. He has lied against my clan because he wants our land. He has murdered twice that I know of to get closer to it. These things I will tell the queen. She must know who she has allowed into her court, she must take away the edict against my clan."

His gaze grew more fierce with his every word.

Sabine stared hard into his eyes. He knew much of her intended, or convincingly pretended to.

"How do I know you are not telling me lies?" she asked.

He held her so tight, the weight of her *sac* dangled from his hand and rested against the small of her back.

"Marry Campbell," he said, his tone a dare. "I know 'tis ye he has as his intended, dinnae deny it. Marry him and find the true mettle of the man for yourself. Decide for yourself whether I lie or not."

"I . . . I will not marry Campbell," she blurted out.

Of course she would unless . . .

Niall held up her *sac*. "'Tis your choice," he said, voice soft.

She stood in the moonlight, captivated by this Highland ruffian, one of the wild creatures of this vast wild land. His words could not have touched her bruised heart more. Choice. He was offering her hope in exchange for a simple request.

"*Oui,*" she whispered. "I will try to get you into the palace, but you must make me a promise."

"Aye?"

"That you will not harm or disparage Her Majesty. She is my queen."

"She is mine as well," he said.

The moonlight captured the fire in his hair and the sapphire glint in his eyes. She had to remember to breathe.

"I shall help you" was all she could say.

His grin widened as if he knew she would give in all along.

He made a low bow to her and tucked her *sac* into a crude pouch he wore on his waist belt. *"Merci beaucoup."*

Sabine would ask him later how he knew French. She would have time to ask him a great number of things when he sat in the royal prison. He would never make his way into the royal court, into the masque—

She paused. Masque!

Perchance Niall MacGregor would greet the queen after all. And she would get her *sac* back. She silently thanked Saint Giles for returning hope even if the bearer was a Highland savage with eyes the hue of Heaven.

chapter 3

The Duck and the Vixen

This French nymph's wiles surprised and intrigued Niall. She was doing his bidding in a most fascinating manner. His life was actually perfect for one bloody moment.

" 'Tis about time," he whispered from a burned-out recess of the once grand and glorious Royal Abbey.

"What?" Rory asked into his ear.

"Wheesht!" Niall hissed. His friend was the master of shattering one's concentration.

After one hard blink, he resumed his vigilance on the French lovely and the guard she appeared to be charming, seducing, or both. He took a few silent steps forward and stopped in the shadow of a charred timber. He felt the weight of his dirk, cold and heavy, inside the wool and fur wrapped about his calf. The temptation to unsheathe the knife gnawed at him.

"I apologize, *mademoiselle* de Sainte Montagne," the lanky guard said. "I thought you asked me to evacuate my post. That I canna do, even for *you*."

So the guard was not a eunuch to the beauty before him. He was falling to the feminine subterfuge, the bloody Lowlander.

"Non, monsieur le garde," she replied sweetly and, Niall hoped, without sincerity. "I was most concerned with something I saw in . . . *le jardin.* . . ."

Sabine's coyness appeared to be working. Niall could not help but grin. Clever lass.

"I saw something *disturbing,*" she said with false drama.

"I dinna—" the guard began.

She stepped back from the doorway into a yellow circle of torchlight. The guard followed, pike in hand, like a dog on the scent.

"Oy!" Rory whispered urgently. "Is she leading the guard toward us?" The unmistakable swish of him unsheathing his dirk brushed Niall's ears.

"Stand down, lad. Stand down," he whispered.

Sabine turned and glanced in Niall's direction.

He stiffened in the shadows, instinctively reaching down for the handle of his dirk. He, like Rory, was Highlander to the core. Always prepared for the worst, always watching one's back.

"What is it, *mademoiselle?*" The guard stepped from the archway. "What is in Her Majesty's garden?"

"A creature," she replied. "Perhaps two."

The guard stared into the darkness beyond the ruined abbey, squinting, craning his long neck forward, then shaking his head. "Sorry, *mademoiselle,*" he said in his nauseating Lowland voice. "I dinna see anything."

"Look," she said gesturing urgently toward the night. "By the wall."

Niall released the dirk. The lass knew exactly what she was doing. She did not appear to need his help.

The guard shrugged, gripped his pike with both fists, and took one long, reluctant step away from his post. "I'll have a look. "

"Oui, we would not want the queen to be in danger."

Sabine took one step back, out of the torchlight, deeper into the archway.

The guard puffed out his hollow chest and aimed his pike at the dark. Niall watched him disappear into the garden, on a mission to save the queen from a bloody phantom.

He switched his gaze to Sabine. She stood beneath the

torch twenty-odd paces away, not looking at him. Even from this distance he could see the details of her face. Flickers of torchlight defined her profile. Her rounded forehead met the determined slope of her nose, slightly upturned at the end. Niall traced his gaze over the soft swell of her lips, perfectly even, top and bottom, so very soft and pink. His journey ended at her jaw, a hard angle. He suspected that hard edge was cast closer to her true spirit than her other features.

Or perchance her eyes told her story? Taut wee jewels stared at him now. He had surely gone away in the head with such musings.

She beckoned him with a frustrated shift of her eyes. He slipped his glance to her twisted hand. It must tell another story, one he was not sure he cared to know . . . at the moment anyway.

Staying close to the burned and ruined wall, Niall moved quickly toward her. His heart matched the rhythm of his footsteps. He was so close to the palace, nearer the queen, nearer Sabine . . . nearer the guard. Niall could smell the Lowlander's approach in the damp night air.

Avoiding the fringes of torchlight, Niall slipped past Sabine and stepped into a deep archway. Rory loped in behind him. They stood in the deep recess of an inner doorway, at one with the velvety shadows of this, the queen's house. Niall held his breath once more. The guard returned to his post, several steps away.

"I'm quite sorry, *mademoiselle,*" the guard said. "There's nothing in the garden. I should escort you back to the great hall . . . to ease your fears."

"My fears would be eased all the more if you would kindly do your duty, *monsieur le garde.* I am not the one to be protected. Search until you find the intruder or find evidence that he has left the garden."

Such boldness! Niall could not help but grin.

After a long pause, the guard sighed, "At your service, *mademoiselle.*"

Niall cocked an ear toward the archway and listened to the sad shuffle of the lowly guard's footsteps. As that forlorn sound faded completely into the garden, the determined whisper of slippers on the stone landing grew.

"Give me my *sac*," Sabine whispered flatly.

Niall looked into the hard eyes reflecting snatches of torchlight. He was not overly tall, unlike Rory, who could rival the height of a Scotch pine, but this lassie should have been intimidated by him, no matter his height. Her fierce gaze told him otherwise.

"I havenae seen Her Majesty yet," he whispered.

"Sweet Saint Giles! You said my *sac* was the key to getting you and this other barbarian into the palace."

"When we're in, ye'll get your purse."

Sabine huffed and grabbed at the latch with her damaged hand. After three unsuccessful tries Niall reached for the latch to help her.

She shot him a fiery stare. Niall immediately withdrew his hand. He had insulted her.

She turned away from him and, on the next try, opened the door. Niall pretended not to notice her rubbing her right hand with her good one.

He walked into the palace, into the longest corridor in Scotland.

Sabine walked beside him. Niall kept her in his periphery, realizing that she was leading him. She stopped abruptly before a large door set into the wall. Niall walked to it. He took the iron latch in his fist but it did not move. Rory stepped in to help, bracing his shoulder against the door. Niall just shook his head, giving his friend a withering look. He turned and placed his back to the closed door.

He sniffed. What was that? Flowers? Very strong flowers.

"I still have the key," he told Sabine. "Where is the queen?"

Sabine gave him a vacant stare. "Soon Highlander." She reached around him and rapped on the door.

"What?—" Niall began, reaching up to grab her arm before she knocked again.

The door behind him opened. He stumbled backward, Rory fell with him, into something large and unyielding.

"Vite! Vite!" A voice with the timbre of thunder wrapped around him.

Before he could turn around, Niall was jerked back by the neck of his tunic, cutting off his wind. Helpless, he was pulled through the open doorway. Sabine followed him, a queer smile on her face.

There was no time to struggle, no time to escape. Niall cursed himself a hundred times over for being caught blind, for putting his vigilance down, for not being prepared. He reached for his dirk, held tight beneath the belt that cinched the plaid to his waist.

Before him stood a mammoth dressed in a crimson field of stocking, pantaloon, and doublet.

"Ah! Mademoiselle de Sainte Montagne! Vous êtes très belle cette nuit! Très belle!" the mammoth said.

"Merci, monsieur Le Canard," Sabine said with a smile. She curtsied briefly then closed the door behind her, sealing all of them, including herself, in this giant's lair.

The stinging pall of the man's perfume pinned Niall flat on his arse. The giant engulfed Sabine in crimson silk and kissed her on each cheek.

Niall scrambled away from the colossus.

"Och, bloody hell. . . ." he breathed.

The giant turned his scouring gaze on Niall, grimaced, and shook his head. The waddles under his chin flapped to and fro. *"Non, non, non."* And in English, probably for Niall's benefit, he said, "This costume is too, how do you say, *ordinaire*? Common? It will not do."

The giant regarded Rory briefly before turning back to Niall, snatching a great fistful of the plaid. Niall bashed the giant's hand away, sending sparks of pain up his own arm. He thrust his dirk up, inches from the man's face.

The giant just smiled. *"Bon, bon.* So much like the Highland beast, you are. *Perfect!"*

"Out of my bloody way," Niall snarled.

"Imbécile!" Sabine shouted. "This man can help you!"

She insinuated herself between Niall and the Goliath, standing so close to him that their noses almost touched.

"Dinnae ever call me an imbecile," he spat.

"I doubt you know what it means," she replied, shaking her head in frustration. *"Monsieur* Le Canard is the finest *costumier* in all of Paris," she said proudly. "He has fashioned the most glorious costumes for all of the royal *comédies*. He was a favorite of the queen's mother, Marie de Guise. Allow him to practice his art, and you will see Her Majesty." Then under her breath, "Unless you have not the conviction."

Niall narrowed his eyes. "*Mademoiselle,* I think ye've gone soft in the heid." He cut his eyes to Le Canard, who stood over Rory. There was an odd shine in the giant's piggy eyes. Niall looked back at Sabine. "That big *co-sheòrsach* would much rather have a go at what's under my kilt than help me see the queen."

"Your tongue is as guttural as your prejudices are unfounded," she retorted. "*Monsieur* Le Canard can get you into Her Majesty's masque and can give you the opportunity to let the queen know the *MacGregor.*"

This woman standing before him was more vixen than courtesan. And he was her hare. She had brought him into her den. How far could he trust her?

"Is this how ye honor our agreement?" he asked. "Putting me into some sort of drama, orchestrated by Goliath over there?"

"*Non.* It is not," she said. Her eyes held a triumphant twinkle. "You said you have a key. I gave you the door. That's what you wanted."

Niall stared at her. MacGregors never had favorable coincidence nod their way. Nothing was easy.

"In *monsieur* Le Canard's capable hands you will see the queen; would you still trust me?"

"Aye, but at what cost?"

"Do you care?"

Niall shook his head. "I dinnae."

"Well, good, Niall MacGregor. You will have your wish."

With that she took her leave. She only had to try once to open the latch with her deformed right hand.

"Vixen," Niall whispered. He turned to Le Canard, the Duck, and suppressed a hard swallow.

He still had Sabine's purse. She wanted it, and he had come this far.

For now, he had to trust her.

• • •

Sabine paused just inside the grand entrance to the great hall. Moments before she had been with that Highlander, and now she stood on the cusp of the most civilized gathering in Scotland. Before her a glittering, colorful crowd danced and engaged in animated conversation. The feathers on some of their masks bounced lightly with restrained nods of their heads. Sabine stared in wonder at the lavish costumes. If Heaven required adornment for its occupants, this is surely what they would wear. Gold, pearls, and shining gemstones matched the elaborate array of colorful silks and velvets on the fine gowns and doublets. Sabine was practically dizzied by the colors.

Or was it because her life was more contorted than the plum boughs in Her Majesty's orchard?

She stole a glance over her shoulder. The MacGregor had not followed her. Good. He had listened to her. At least he was not a fool.

But why did a tiny bit of her wish that he had insisted on escorting her? She imagined the astonished faces of the lords and ladies when she entered the great hall escorted by what certainly must be as fine a Highland man as the royal court had ever seen. Lord Campbell's look of shock alone would have made such an endeavor worthwhile.

Suppressing a giggle behind her right hand, Sabine took one step forward into the masque and tucked her right hand into a fold of her gown.

She adjusted her mask over her face. It was a papier-mâché falcon decorated with a multitude of black, sepia, and white feathers. At her nose was a pointed beak, a perfect representation of the royal bird of prey made especially for her by monsieur Le Canard. Falcons were willful things, kept prisoner for the service of the monarch, *this* Sabine understood with all of her heart.

The aroma of cooked meats, piles of fruits and nuts, pastries, and the finest French wines wrapped invisible tendrils about Sabine's nose, reminding her that it had been quite some time since she had eaten. She wove her way toward the groaning board through the groupings of lords and ladies, the Scottish and French elite, with a few Italians sprinkled in.

She spied one of the Italians at a long trestle table, staring expectantly in her direction. He was Davide Rizzio, a dwarfish, well-muscled man, and Mary's closest advisor. He wore a mask that, like her own, covered the upper half of his face. His was that of a rat. It sparkled with silver dust on the fur. He patted his pudgy little hand on the velvet cushion of the dark, carved chair beside him before he stood and offered her a bow.

"*Signorina* Sabine. You look to be searching for a chair. I have one just for you."

"How did you know it was me?" she asked.

"Your hair. It is the color of obsidian. I'd know you anywhere, *signorina*." Rizzio, unlike others, would never be so rude to tell her the truth, that her right hand betrayed her identity to him.

He slid the chair out from the table.

Sabine sank into it, grateful to be off her feet, grateful to have the chance to put some food in her hollow belly. The Italian raised one dark brow as he poured her a generous glass of wine from a cobalt glass carafe. She glanced beyond the table to the area before the queen's empty throne, where servants hastily set up the props for this evening's entertainment.

She mused at what could be grand and strange entertainment if that Niall MacGregor and his tousle-haired *ami* joined the *comédie* under monsieur Le Canard's direction. She doubted those Highlanders could follow much direction. Such would be their mistake. Niall and his friend surely would spend this night in the gaol.

"Tell me what you know of this Scotland, *signorina*."

Sabine lifted the goblet and took a sip. She set it down thoughtfully.

"*Signore* Rizzio, I know nothing of Scotland beyond the boundary of this palace. 'Tis not in my capacity to wonder on such things." That was as much of a lie as she could concoct. She was wont to wonder and wonder since she had met Niall.

Rizzio smiled, his tiny, dark mustache spreading across his upper lip like a woolly caterpillar. "Certainly Her Majesty has organized travels of her kingdom."

"I'm not privy to such, *signore*." Sabine took another sip of wine and glanced about the great hall expecting turmoil to arrive at any minute. Niall MacGregor would step onto the stage before the queen and her lavish court and hang himself. Even a master of *l'art de la comédie* as was monsieur Le Canard could not transform a Highland beast. Was that what she had truly wanted? The Highlander's imprisonment or death?

The wine tumbled her thoughts. Where was the food?

"You look pale, my darling. I am most worried," Lord Campbell said, startling her.

Sabine wrenched her gaze upward. The goblet almost slipped from her fingers.

"M'lord," she managed, shakily placing the goblet on the table. *"Bonsoir."*

He wore a black mask, feathered to look like a raven. His cruel mouth and pointed chin were clearly visible beneath it. Sabine had no trouble recognizing him.

"Bonsoir to you, my darling."

Her belly roiled at the endearment.

She offered him her hand. Let the farce continue. Her mind had been so occupied with Niall MacGregor that she had forgotten the reason for her being in the garden in the first place. Was there no escape from this man who was now pressing his dry lips against the back of her hand? She pulled her hand away. Lord Campbell sat down and took up her goblet.

"Signore," Rizzio said, "I would be most happy to pour you a fresh glass of wine, as I'm certain *signorina* Sabine has not finished what I have poured her."

Campbell slammed his fist on the table. The plates rattled and the goblets toppled, spilling the wine onto the dark wood, puddles spreading out like blood.

He leaned forward. The pointed feathers of his mask thrust toward the ceiling, glistening in the candlelight. His eyes, ringed by glossy black feathers, narrowed at the Italian.

"That mask suits you very well, *Rat-zzio.* 'Tis so very odd that Her Majesty would allow you in her court, joining those of us who have legitimate influence. You are an anomaly here, a freakish royal pet. So, presume not to tell me how to behave with my intended."

Mortified by his behavior, Sabine tried to rise from her place to leave. Campbell rose as well.

"A delightful idea, my darling," he said. "Her Majesty requested that you and I join her for the evening's entertainment. Afterwards, I will publicly announce our betrothal."

"You would dare marry one who is not as perfect as yourself?" she asked, raising her right hand from her lap. Lord Campbell could not help but stare.

He reached out and wrapped his long fingers about her arm. In one painful squeeze he pulled her from the sympathetic gaze of Davide Rizzio, her only ally in court. Campbell seemed to know this very well.

"Some things are best kept hidden, *mademoiselle*," he growled.

She struggled to free herself from the grip of this demented fool Her Majesty had seen fit to pair her with. No one should be allowed to order the path of another's heart, not even a monarch. Yet, the queen had, and there was nothing, beyond outright treason, Sabine could do about it.

Campbell escorted her roughly through the masked revelers, some dancing, some drinking, some eating. A low rumble at the base of her belly reminded Sabine that, other than a large goblet of wine, she had not had the chance to sample the array of delectable royal-worthy delights. Before she could utter a word of protest, Campbell released her, bowing so deeply that the feathers of his mask brushed the polished wood floor.

Mary had entered the great hall. The crowd hushed and bent to her like wildflowers in a summer breeze. Sabine curtsied low; the drink in her head threatened to topple her balance. Where was the Highlander? Had he taken control of his senses and left? She prayed he had changed his mind and run all the way to his Highland den, but he still had her *sac*!

The rustle of rich silk and velvet signaled the queen taking her place on the throne. The swish of her royal gown against the floor, the scent of the finest French perfume, and the contented sigh were clues Sabine knew very well.

"Arise," Mary commanded.

Sabine joined the others and carefully stood upright. She blinked away the dizziness into the dazzle of the queen's mask, a lavish affair of gold and silver decorated with dozens of little arrows pointing toward the ceiling, each topped with a precious stone. She was Diana, goddess of the hunt.

Sabine shifted her gaze to Her Majesty's escort, a thin, bored-looking young man with wispy, dark hair. He was dressed in deep purple velvet pantaloons, a shining black leather doublet, black hosiery, and finely cobbled leather shoes. His eye mask was made to look like an eagle, the feathers bright and sprinkled with gold dust. He took his place to the right of the throne, into the path of Her Majesty's adoring stare.

"Our Sabine," the queen said with a lilt to her voice, "how delighted we are to see you with Lord John." Sabine nodded. She could not have been less delighted.

"Lord John, I believe you know my guest, Lord Darnley," the queen said.

Campbell regarded the wiry man briefly. "No, Your Majesty, I'm afraid I haven't had the pleasure." And from his tone he did not want the pleasure either. Sabine glanced at Lord Darnley. He looked to be no more than ten and seven. Mary certainly had him in her favor. The queen was allowed to follow the path of her heart, no matter who or how young, no matter—

When Mary had said "we" she had not just been referring to herself at that moment, she had been referring to her five Marys and the ten attendants clustered behind her throne.

Sabine caught Lady Fleming's hard stare.

"Merci beaucoup." Sabine gave the queen a small, slightly faltering curtsy.

"Set you down, Sabine, and Lord Campbell." Mary gestured to two vacant chairs to the far left of the throne. The Marys and attendants took their places in two semicircles of chairs near the throne, in Sabine's periphery.

Light, bright applause broke her thoughts. She looked toward the props set before the throne. Monsieur Le Canard stood there and winked at her. Then he bowed low before the queen.

"Your Royal Highness and honored guests!" he boomed. He stood upright and thrust out his great chest. Spittle leapt from his lips as he roared, "I indulge your entertainments this evening by presenting for Her Majesty's pleasure *L'Histoire de l'Écosse!*"

He waved his arms toward the props: painted trees and

dark, brooding hills. With as much flourish as a big man could muster, he leapt clumsily out of the way.

Sabine sat rapt. The wine made her vision a little misty. She fought to concentrate on the players who moved out from behind the painted scenery.

"Norse marauders!" Canard shouted. "Viking invaders from Denmark! Men in furs and longboats! A terrible sight to behold!"

Sabine searched the players, dressed in rainbow shades of satin trimmed with white fur, wearing gilded pointed hats with gilded horns, and could not find Niall in any of them. Perchance he had taken flight, found some sense.

She relaxed a fraction in her chair, keeping her back perfectly straight. She let her breath out and tried to ignore her hollow stomach. The "Vikings" rode their longboats through waves of blue velvet. The players chanted poetry about pillaging and defeating Scotland. Then they disappeared behind the scenery.

Lord Campbell yawned while everyone else applauded.

"Delightful!" the queen exclaimed. She leaned in toward Lord Darnley, who forced a wan smile in her direction.

Sabine clapped as monsieur Le Canard stepped out from behind one of the false trees. "*Alors!*" he exclaimed, a hand to his ear. "Savages remain in Scotland. Men with wool on their backs and little else! Men who hide like the fox and the bear in dark, unhappy hills. *Alors!* They come . . . beware!"

He slipped back behind the "trees" with a flourish.

Sabine leaned forward, her hands gripping the arms of her chair, steadying herself. A hush fell over the spectators, collective breaths held in anticipation of the next act.

The servants waved long green cloths. Two figures stepped tentatively out from behind the scenery. One was taller than the other and wore a bear mask that covered his entire face. The other, a head shorter than the bear, wore a half mask of a ginger-haired fox. This figure stepped forward into one of the wavering cloths.

Sabine leaned to the edge of her seat.

The "fox" aimed its pointed snout to the floor, throwing his profile Sabine's way.

She gasped at the sight of the thick waves of auburn hair

flowing from under the mask touching the top of . . . what was he wearing?

She recognized the length of wool—it looked cleaner, brushed. His common linen tunic, the one he wore when he invaded the palace grounds, was gone, switched with a doublet of saffron and green. The garment was open to the center of his chest, revealing muscle forested with dark auburn hair. His crosshatched wool was wrapped about his hips in the same familiar fashion. She dropped her gaze to his legs, well-muscled, powerful, partially concealed in strips of red brocade over the calves down to his own pieced leather shoes, covering his rather large feet.

The fox continued to regard the undulating green wool barricading him from the throne before he grabbed it with one fist and yanked it from the hands of the astonished servants. He dropped it unceremoniously on the floor, leaving no barrier between him and his royal audience.

Monsieur Le Canard nervously cleared his throat. "Unh, the fox . . . unh . . . the prince of the forest commands the wood, allowing nothing to deter him."

The Highland bear lumbered behind the fox.

Sabine sat up very straight, her spine as rigid as a pike. She stared into the eyes of the Highland fox. The fox grinned slyly back at her, displaying perfect pearls of white teeth. In her periphery she saw Lord Campbell staring at the fox, then at her.

Niall took another step forward and bowed low before the queen. She nodded.

He stood upright and spread his arms wide.

"Round and round!" he cried out. "This ginger fox roams!"

His blue eyes gleamed through the holes in his mask. The grin wavered a bit, then disappeared. He looked ceilingward. "Uh. . . ."

Then monsieur Le Canard's anxious whisper from the side: "An errant Highland—"

"Oh," Niall said, lowering his gaze back to his audience. "Aye . . . aye." He aimed one hand at the ceiling. "An errant Hieland beast without a home. Away from sight of those that prey, to run by night, rest by . . . uh . . . day. . . ."

He allowed his words to fade away, his gaze becoming fiercer, like the beast he portrayed.

He took one step forward, closer to the queen. Sabine held her breath and dug her nails into the arms of the chair.

Monsieur Le Canard whispered urgently, "And, so, I travel from—"

"Wheesht!" Niall whispered back. He closed his eyes for the span of a gnat's age, before opening them and centering his stare on Sabine.

"Oh, to find peace," he said, his words slow, determined. He stepped forward, arms open. "Oh, to find peace, where death haunts me not! 'Tis best my blade—" He reached down, the movement so quick Sabine barely noticed, and pulled his knife into view.

The entire assemblage gasped in horror.

Niall held the blade aloft. Sabine wondered how anyone could be so blatantly stupid.

"'Tis best my blade stills my heart," he said.

Someone's blade will still this fool's heart. Sabine glanced at the agog faces surrounding her.

"What beguiles my spirit to live, to soar?" Niall asked the air. Then he thrust his free hand inside his doublet and pulled out Sabine's *sac.* He cut a direct path to her with his steady blue gaze. "What beguiles my spirit to live? . . . to soar? But this key I return . . . uh . . . as I've found the door."

She could barely find the strength to move, then stared into the eyes of the Highland fox. He smiled at her and bowed low before his queen. Before *her.*

Applause drowned out Sabine's confusion and dizziness.

"Enchanting! Delightful!" the queen proclaimed.

Sabine was not relieved. She took a deep breath but could not steady herself. The wine. No food. Not good.

Niall continued to bow.

"We are most amused," Mary said. "Rise."

Niall stood upright. Sabine tried to watch his every move. He concealed his knife back in the brocade wrapped about his calf.

The queen regarded Niall curiously. Then she smiled. "We are not familiar with your work, good player. 'Twould please us to know you." She waved a hand toward Niall's mask. "Would you be so kind . . . ?"

"Non," Sabine whispered. Inside, her head took a nasty spin. She grabbed the arms of her chair.

He bowed slightly and reached up and grasped the bottom of his mask with his strong thumb and forefinger.

"Aye, Your Majesty. 'Twould be an honor," he said.

No one is that bold or foolhardy. No one but this savage Highlander.

"Sweet Sainte Giles," Sabine breathed, closing her eyes. "Help *us.*"

And the goodly saint shoved her backward into darkness.

chapter 4

Deep in the Royal Lair

Niall stared down at Sabine. His purpose for being in Holy-rood Palace was suddenly replaced with concern for her.

He stood with the others: ladies-in-waiting, attendants, men in fancy doublets, women in gowns worth as much as a half-dozen cattle. They stared down at Sabine, crumpled on the floor beside her chair. Her mask still covered the top of her face, and she looked like a conquered bird.

She had imbibed too much spirit. He could smell it on her. The prospect of marrying Campbell was too much for her to bear sober.

He swore he caught a glimpse of fear in her eyes before she was so quickly introduced to this finely waxed Scots pine floor.

The queen remained calmly seated, her gaze on Sabine, and the bored fop beside her yawned and waved his goblet for more wine. The many elite who had come to this party stood behind Niall, wrapped in hushed whispers, no doubt perturbed that their masque had been disrupted by one fainting lass. Perchance they were used to two or three fainters in one evening.

Niall knelt beside her and gently removed her mask. She

had never looked lovelier than this moment of unwonted sleep and of not insulting him to his face.

"What is this disruption?" a familiar voice shouted. A shadow soon fell over Niall. He looked up, over Sabine, through the holes in his mask.

Campbell stood over them like a dark menace. His eyes narrowed behind the raven's mask he wore. Mask or no mask, Niall knew that bloody scourge anywhere. Campbells always sat shoulder to shoulder with the Scottish monarchy no matter what the royal bloodlines. He took in a deep breath. If he had not hidden his claymore in the garden by the wall he could silence this bastard right now. And as a consequence lose all chance of a word or two with Her Majesty. It was a chance he was willing to take. The good of his clan came first.

He rose to his feet. It was time for a MacGregor to find favor with the Crown. First he had to pretend he was someone else.

Sabine stirred. Lord Campbell insinuated himself over her, lifted her arm, and dropped it to the floor.

"You, servants!" he ordered. "Repair *Mademoiselle* de Sainte Montagne to her chamber." He centered his dead-eyed gaze on one of the attendants, a fair-haired wilting flower of a lass. "You! See that the *mademoiselle* is revived and returns to this masque soon and in good spirits. I desire to wait no more than an hour or I shall attend to her condition *myself*." He paused, then bowed to the queen. "If it pleases you, Your Royal Highness, of course."

The queen nodded. "It pleases us that you have concern for our Sabine."

Niall gripped Sabine's mask hard with one fist. His first instinct was to stuff it down Campbell's wretched throat. He dug his fingernails into the feathers and papîer-mâché. He had to be someone else, for his sake, and, quite possibly for Sabine's

He stepped back into the crowd, keeping Sabine in his sight. Two servant lads lifted her from the floor. The onlookers dispersed to their food, drink, and dancing. Niall turned to follow Sabine and stood eye to throat with Campbell.

"I believe that is *Mademoiselle* de Sainte Montagne's

mask," the bastard said, the feathers of his mask stiff and steady.

"Aye . . . *oui*." Niall kept his tone even. He held the mask harder, the papier-mâché within crunched in his fist.

Campbell held out one hand. "Give it to me."

The queen suddenly rose, placing her hand in Lord Darnley's. Niall bowed, as did Campbell. The glorious couple whisked by them without so much as a glance to the center of the great hall. The musicians struck up a lively tune, and Her Majesty danced with her man-child in dark velvet.

Niall stood upright, this time into the cloud of Campbell's growing annoyance.

"Give the mask to me."

"'Tis only a prop for the farce, m'lord," Niall said, almost gagging on the politeness of his words. "I must return it to *Monsieur* Le Canard."

"A farce," Campbell repeated. "'Twas a most interesting farce, and one unfamiliar."

"'Tis the latest farce from Paris," Niall said. "This is the first time it has been presented outside of Fraunce."

Campbell cocked an ear toward him. "*Fraunce*, did you say?"

"Aye—I mean *oui, Fraunce.*"

He tried to erase the Highland Scots in his voice, but was doing as poor a job of it as when he had recited Canard's verse. Niall had composed the second part of the verse himself as he stood before the queen. Sabine's doubtful and terrified look had been his inspiration. He had proved her thoughts about him wrong. He was no *sauvage*. Well, perchance in bed, but there was little chance she would find that out about him. Being in her presence was temptation enough for him to reveal it, though.

"You, sir, are a most odd French player," Campbell said. He raked his gaze over Niall. "Your height dictates that, aye, you could be French, but your brawny figure indicates a man who has spent much time afield, perchance, too much time for one in your profession."

Niall rolled his eyes. How did Canard behave when he dressed him in this odd mixture of plaid and silk? He was a man who certainly enjoyed his work. That was the most kind thing Niall could think of for that sort of man. If he did his best imitation of such a man Campbell was surely to leave him alone. Of course, with MacGregor luck, Campbell may be the type of man who sharpens both sides of his sword and would take Niall up on his false offer. He had to try anyway.

Choking down the bile rising in his throat, Niall stepped forward and flared his eyes at Campbell.

"My figure, as ye so kindly put it, m'lord, is betrayed by this costume? Would it be that ye would wish to see more of it, to satisfy yer keen eyes?" Niall stepped back a little. Bloody hell! Had the course of his life come down to this? This was a new low for Clan Gregor, one the bards would never sing about, much less know about.

Niall was besieged with the sudden urge to take up his dirk, end his flamboyant guise, and dispatch this bastard to his reward in hell. It ebbed when Campbell suddenly blinked and walked away, quite quickly, to a table burdened with enough food to feed a Highland family for a year.

"Another day, ye bastard," Niall whispered. "I'll see ye sent to the Danes for what ye've done. Ye'll wish ye were in hell then." He sighed. "I could do with an ale myself. Oh, aye, I could. . . ."

"There's no ale to be had in this fancy place," Rory said, the stupid bear mask still on his face. Niall had been aware, but had not acknowledged, his champion's absence until now. The food, no doubt, had been too tempting for his friend.

Niall looked past Rory to the small doorway where the servants had taken Sabine.

"Ye need a shave, lad," he said, pushing around him. "Enjoying the repast?"

"Oy, that's grand funny, that is," Rory said, wiping his lips with back of his hand. "I was watching ye from the table, waiting far ye to give Clan Gregor's auld enemy a kiss."

Niall swung around, seized Rory by the throat, and slammed him back into the shadows from which he came. "Say it again, Buchanan, and I'll show ye my dirk," he growled.

"Like ye were gonnae do to Campbell a moment ago?" he asked, managing a sly smile. "Show him yer *dirk*?"

Niall released him. "If that was the case, a dirk would pale in comparison to my *claymore*." With a wink he turned and walked away to the door where Sabine had been carried.

Rory fell into step beside him. "So, where are we going now, oh, great leader?"

"Through yon door." A guard was posted there. Niall told himself there should be no problem. He was a royal player after all, allowed access to the depths of this privileged lair.

"Och, why would ye leave this grand festival? I've no' had a sample of the drink."

"Stay, if ye will. I'm going—" Niall began before he felt trouble approach.

"Get into another costume! *Vite! Vite!*" Canard shouted, stepping in their paths.

"Sorry, big lad," he said. "But I've done enough playacting to last my bloody life."

"And what will *mademoiselle* Sabine say when Her Majesty's guards chop you into little pieces?"

"Being glib doesnae fit a man of yer stature, Canard."

"Monsieur Le Canard," he corrected.

"Aye, aye, whatever," Niall said, "If ye let us pass, I'll promise ye a dance."

The French giant raised one thick brow while his eyes swept over Niall. *"Oui,* I would like that very much, but not here, out in the garden, under the moonlight."

He tossed Niall a wink and lumbered away.

Rory leaned over and whispered, "Ye're gonnae dance with that pansy?"

"No." Niall headed to the doorway.

"Then that giant's gonnae thump ye hard, ye know that?" Rory asked, keeping pace with him. "If ye dinnae honor yer agreement with him."

Niall watched as Canard whispered something to the guard, who looked scandalized and stepped to one side of the door.

"Ye're a good man to know, Canard," Niall said walking up to him. He paused and pointed into the great hall. "See that man with the raven's mask?"

"Oui, the tall, thin one? Oh, *oui,* I do."

"He would love a dance. Escort him to the garden. He may struggle, but that means he likes ye."

"This dance, it is not with you, *monsieur* Le Highlander?" Le Canard asked.

"I cannot dance," Niall said, feigning disappointment. He patted his leg. "Wounded in battle."

Canard glanced down dejectedly.

"Oy, big lad," he said. "Ye'll find that Lord Campbell is more yer type."

The sun brightened on the giant's face. "I shall go, then, while the queen's occupied with her escort."

Niall slapped him on the meat of his arm. "Hurry before he gets away."

Canard turned with no semblance of grace at all and left in great haste.

Spared from a fate he dared not muse on a second longer, Niall sighed relief and stole into the corridor.

"The queen is in the great hall," Rory said as he followed him along the corridor, well lit by stout candles on iron sconces. "Should ye no' be trying to speak with her?"

"In good time. First I'm gonnae prove to one of her court that a MacGregor honors an agreement." Niall glanced back at Her Majesty, dancing and smiling at her escort, her gaze tied only to him. "I will see Her Majesty in due time . . . after her dance."

"Oh, aye . . ." Rory said, confused.

Niall walked deeper into the palace than good sense told him to travel. But he had left his good sense at the garden wall with his claymore.

After endless steps and endless minutes of wrestling with himself that being here was pure folly and he should leave, Niall stopped before one of the many doors. It was ajar. A female's voice, French, not Sabine's, wafted into the corridor. He peered inside.

Niall took a deep breath and a step deeper into a world he never thought he would see. 'Twas a bloody dream he saw asleep on the bed in the dim chamber. Now, if only she would welcome him. . . .

Lord Campbell stood before Sabine, a nasty grin spread across his face. Slowly he displayed his hands to her. His *palms were coated in blood. The red was more vivid than the brightest realgar, a pigment so poisonous le maître used to tell her to avoid it at any cost.*

"Come forward, my darling."

Lord Campbell's voice clamped long icy fingers about her soul. Sabine floated to him, unable to control herself.

He thrust his hand at her. Methodically, with great care, Sabine lifted her damaged hand. It clenched a brush. She dipped it into the crimson in Lord Campbell's palm.

"Show me your art, my darling," he said.

Sabine turned and placed the brush, heavy with pigment, against a piece of parchment. The paint ran in rivulets, building upon each other, thickening. The metallic odor assaulted her. Sabine reeled backward, dropping the brush.

Her mouth opened in a silent scream. The parchment was finished. The blue eyes of the dead Highland fox she had painted stared back at her. She could not help him. . . .

S abine sat up with a start.

She gasped, unaware of where she was, terrified that she was still trapped in that nightmare. Her head throbbed, so she must be.

"Chérie, chérie. Your dream, was it bad?"

Sabine fell into the embrace of one of the attendants. "Oh, what has happened? Did Lord Campbell slaughter the Highland fox?"

"Comment? I do not understand this, Sabine."

The attendant pulled away and took a plate from the small table beside the large bed. She offered Sabine a scrap of bread dipped in honey.

"Eat this. You need your strength. Lord Campbell wishes you to return to the masque in an hour."

Sabine ate the bread, not because of Lord Campbell, never because of him, but because her belly was empty. The honey dripped down her tongue, nourishing her, reminding her of the sweet plum juice Niall had licked from her fingers. What had become of him?

She glanced about the chamber, her thoughts too much on Niall and his fate and her deep secret hope that she would see him again. Instead she saw a well-lit, strangely cheerful hearth, tapestries of dancing nymphs covering the walls, and heavy, dark furniture against the walls like brooding centurions. But a gaol was a gaol no matter how decorated. Niall was certain to be in the bowels of the royal gaol by now, he and that friend of his, awaiting some dire fate. Sabine quickly prayed to Saint Giles it was not true.

She swallowed the lump of bread, lifted another piece to her lips, then paused. Her gaze fell upon the shadows by the chamber door. What was there? A Highland fox?

She turned back to her food, shaking away her imagination. Another thought occurred to her, one that made the bread go down smoother. Niall could be well away from this place after his ridiculous performance. Surely, he would not have shown his true face to Her Majesty. A Highland fox would not be that foolish, would he?

"Highland fox," she whispered. "Absurd."

"Aye, absurd, my thoughts exactly."

Her falcon mask landed in her lap.

Sabine dropped the uneaten bit of bread to her lap as she sat up on the bed. She was face-to-face with the blue-eyed Highland fox. "How dare you invade this chamber! No man is allowed within!" Her harsh tone concealed her relief that he was not imprisoned or dead.

"Not even a Highland fox?"

Niall walked boldly and arrogantly over to her bedside. His companion, wearing the bear mask, followed.

"Begone!" the attendant cried. "Or I shall call the guards!"

"Take care of her, Rory. See that she doesnae leave," Niall ordered.

Sabine watched in horror as the bear stalked over to the hapless attendant and pressed her into the tapestry-covered wall with his body.

"Do not harm her!" she shouted.

"Wheesht!" Niall said. "Rory'll not hurt her, unless she tries to rally all the queen's men against us."

Sabine sat higher on the bed, tipped her chin up. "Leave."

"I only came to honor our agreement." He reached inside his doublet and produced her *sac*. "Ye fainted before I could give it to ye, before I could speak to the queen."

"I never faint." Sabine grabbed for her property. Niall held it beyond her reach. "I had drink on an empty belly. You delayed me from returning to the masque, so I had not the opportunity to dine before the *comédie*. I got you into the masque. I honored my word."

"As I recall, *mademoiselle,* ye were wandering about in the garden, unescorted. You could have dined. Yet, ye were escaping from the masque, or was it something else?"

"Nothing else, Highlander. Give me my *sac!*"

"You are a *breugadair,*" he said moving closer still, retaining her property.

"Comment?" she asked.

"A liar," he replied. "Ye dinnae wish to marry Campbell." He shook her *sac.* The coins jingled. "Ye want to escape farther than the royal gardens, oh aye." He shook the *sac* again. "*Very* far."

Sabine stole a furtive glance at the other Highlander and the attendant. The burly Highlander held the attendant's complete attention and both of her hands. Those two were oblivious to her conversation with Niall. What beasts these Highlanders were with their animal brutality and lack of decorum, taking advantage of hapless girls. She turned to look at Niall, who stared and grinned at her. She shuddered under his gaze. He knew the mettle of his woolly friend. Yet, would he press his advantage upon her as well? She should not ponder such matters because . . .

"By the order of my queen I must marry him," she said, and glanced down at her hands. "I am a loyal servant."

"Ye mean a loyal pawn, d'ye not?"

She stiffened. "I am no pawn."

"Ye will marry Campbell and bridge Her Majesty's power to the Highlands, or will it that by marrying Campbell ye'll bridge him to the royal court."

"How do you know these things?" she asked, glancing at her *sac* dangling from his fist.

"I've lived in Scotland for all of my score and three years," he replied. "Ye've lived here for what . . . three days?"

She looked away. Of course he was right. She would never let him know, of course!

She deemed to return her gaze to him, heat grew behind her eyes. "You must go now after you return what is mine."

Embarrassingly, her stomach rumbled.

Niall grinned and took up the bit of bread that she had dropped to her lap and raised it to her lips. "Ye're a muckle peckish. Eat."

For once he spoke with sense, at least she thought he did. Those Scottish words were so confusing.

She opened her mouth and allowed him to slide the bread onto her tongue. Let him serve her. The honey left a trail on her bottom lip and on Niall's finger. She closed her lips softly around it. Her tongue flickered over the honey on his finger until it was clean of it. How liberating to do something so absurd! It must be the wine gone to her head.

"Lovely," Niall said, sliding his finger over her lips. He swiped it through the honey on the plate. This sweetness he did not give to her, but kept for himself. "So, very lovely," he said. Did he speak of her?

Sabine straightened and blinked. "Remove that mask. You look absurd."

"Oh, aye? I thought I look quite dashing. Yer lover didnae even recognize me."

"Lover? You speak a lie, Niall MacGregor. I do not love Campbell. I hardly know the man."

He reached to the bedside table and took up a knob of beef from the trencher. He took a large bite of the meat. "Campbell seems to enjoy having you for a pet. But that is the way of the wealthy, marry someone ye dinnae know and suffer the rest of yer life in gilded glory." She tried to snatch her *sac* from him. He immediately held it beyond her reach.

She huffed. "You are so very rude. And that is my supper that you seem to be so very much enjoying."

Niall stopped chewing. "Was this yers?" He held the beef out to her.

"You know very well that it is mine." She looked away, catching a glimpse of the attendant and the Highland bear, now unmasked, sharing what appeared to be intimate conversation before the tapestry of dancing nymphs a dozen steps across the chamber. The woman twirled a lock of her golden hair about her forefinger and looked at the Highlander through her dark lashes, a coy smile on her lips. If the attendant heard her and Niall, they seemed unconcerned, oblivious. Sabine looked away, disgusted. "How dare you call me Campbell's pet."

"You deny that he doesnae enjoy having ye beside him."

"Campbell relishes his proximity to Her Majesty more."

She could not help but look into the blue eyes of this Highland man, sitting so close to her.

Free me.

Sabine gasped. Had she said that aloud? Niall's face showed no reaction. He took another bite of meat before setting it back on the plate.

"Why are you really here, away from your wild home?" she asked.

He swallowed. The sinew of his strong neck tightened. "'Wild home.' Ye speak of the Highlands with a soft music in yer voice, as if they were far more agreeable to ye than this place. Do they entice ye a wee bit?"

"I have never been to these Highlands. How can they possibly agree with me, much less entice me?"

Niall leaned forward on the bed, the warmth of his breath touched her face. The scent of the meat on his breath drew her nearer to him than she would dare. Her belly rumbled again.

He reached around her, his knuckles brushing the side of her breast. She thought, or did she hope, he was going to hold her, but the next thing she knew, he held the knob of beef before her astonished eyes.

"Eat, and I'll tell ye why I'm here."

"Perchance I do not wish to know."

"If that were true," he said, "ye would have screamed for the guards."

Sabine harumphed and took the meat from him. She was not going to let him feed her again. She bit into it. The juices exploded on her tongue, filling her mouth. She chewed and swallowed, then took another bite before realizing Niall was staring at her.

"And ye called *me* savage," he said. "Ye eat with all of the delicacy of a wolf on fresh prey."

"I eat because I'm hungry. I eat with ferocity because I'm angry," she snapped.

"Why?"

"I want my *sac*. You waste time with me here, when you could go to the queen."

"Aye, I will go to her, and I havenae been wasting my time with ye. I will honor our agreement. I wish ye to know this and more."

Niall reached into the pouch at his belt and produced a folded piece of paper. He snapped it open and displayed it before her eyes.

She read the harsh edict set forth by the queen's councilors before Her Majesty had set foot in Scotland.

"By fire and sword!" she gasped.

"Savage words, aye?" he said, taking the paper away and tucking it into his pouch.

"Oui," she breathed. "They are quite savage."

"The name MacGregor is a blight upon the land through no fault of our own. More powerful clans have courted the monarchy against us. When Mary arrived I saw hope that, aye, she might agree that MacGregors have a right to live in peace without fear our land will be taken and our people killed as her Privy Council has decreed, as Campbell has enacted by murdering my father and brother. I have no doubt that I will be next, then the rest of my clan, one by one or more."

"This is how you Highlanders live, in fear?" Sabine tried to understand.

"Not all of us. Some have the monarchy to protect them, like Campbell. He despises my clan because our lands share the same boundaries."

"Is that the only reason?"

Niall stared at her, his eyes narrowed. "Does there need to be any other reason?"

"In civilized places, *oui,* there does."

"Will my returning yer precious purse mean anything to ye?"

Sabine paused, the meat juices dripping from her fist. "It means you can keep a promise. That you're a man of honor, in one regard."

"Aye, that was my hope."

Niall reached up and took the meat from her. He placed it

back on the trencher. With the hem of his woolen garment he wiped the juices from her hands. She found her gaze lowering to his exposed and powerful thighs, for a moment curious as to what lay in shadow beneath the wool.

"Are ye trying to learn more about me?" he asked, never missing a thing when it came to her. How irritatingly perceptive.

Sabine jerked her gaze up to meet his. "Certainly not! . . . I mean, *oui,* what is that odd wool you wear?"

Niall dropped it back to his thighs.

"'Tis my plaid, fashioned into a kilt. 'Tis a goodly garment. Keeps me concealed afield, keeps me warm, keeps the rain from my head, perfect for my 'wild home.'"

"Wild home," she breathed. "Kilt . . . plaid." The strange words felt comfortable on her tongue.

Slowly, Niall cupped both of her hands and raised them to his lips.

She tried not to close her eyes and give in to the moment. Yet, from his touch a flurry of sensation overtook her. He kissed her wrists, at the place where her blood pulsed so fast and so hot. She forced herself to resist his bold manner, but he took her farther away from this chamber, deeper into his free spirit. She shivered as he pushed her sleeve up her right arm, kissed the sensitive flesh there, all the while cradling her damaged hand in his large strong one. She could not help but close her eyes. Hardly aware of what she was doing, she flexed her twisted fingers around his thumb and squeezed. A low moan escaped her lips. She had to return to the bedchamber, to the masque, or they both could face the gaol.

"You must take your leave from this chamber," she whispered. Then she cleared her throat delicately and said more forcefully, "You have to go."

She released his thumb and took her hand back. She sat there, eyes closed, trying to catch her breath.

"D'ye want that?" he asked from far away.

She opened her eyes. Niall stood at the side of her bed. He had abided her wishes, damn him!

"Oui," she replied mournfully. "'Tis true." She tucked both her hands deep into her lap. "You must leave. Go back to your home." Her face was suddenly warm. Sweet Saint Giles!

Were those tears misting her eyes? "I beg you, leave my *sac* and . . . go."

"Aye, I'll go," he whispered. "Ye'll get yer purse after I see the queen."

He gave her one sapphire wink and a hint of unforgettable grin before turning his broad back to her.

He took a deliberate, direct path to the door. Was leaving just as difficult for him as it was for her? She had to erase such thoughts. Sabine glanced at her right hand. She grasped a fistful of bedclothes and squeezed tightly. Strength. Sweet Saint Giles give me . . . strength.

"Rory, get yer hands out of the lassie's skirts," Niall ordered his friend. "Let's away to the queen."

Strength. Sabine squeezed harder. The pain wrapped around her hand and seared up her arm. She willed herself to remember something pleasant, anything. All she saw was Niall's back as he stepped to her chamber door.

Then he paused and said, "Oh, to find peace where death haunts me not, 'tis best my blade stills my heart." He slowly turned to face her from across the chamber.

"You spoke those words during the *comédie*," she said, releasing the bedclothes. The pain remained. "They were your own, were they not?"

"Aye," he said, "they were."

The pain ebbed away as Sabine considered the words, so poignant, so beautiful, so much from the Highlander's heart. "Do you believe you will die if you cannot find peace?" she asked. "Why do you want me to know this?"

"Because it is why I must see the queen."

"She will be angered that you have broken into her masque. You could be imprisoned or die."

"Would she have given me an invitation?" he asked, stance so stiff and firm on the rush carpet.

Sabine shook her head. "Of course not."

"Yet, you gave me an invitation," he said.

"You have my *sac,* I had no choice."

He paused, hand on the latch. "I will give it back to ye." He opened the door and slipped out, his friend behind him. "Yer hope lies within."

Sabine gasped. Damn him for knowing her mind! And bless him.

Niall, a contradiction in plaid, a cretin with culture, had left her more confused than in her entire life. He walked a strange and crooked path, one that was so intriguing it made her ache with longing to know where it would lead.

As much as she hated to admit it, Niall MacGregor was far more a noble than a savage. Perchance that was what he wanted her to believe all along.

But would Her Majesty believe the same? Sabine trembled. She slipped off the bed to prepare to return to the masque. Soon, she feared, she would have her answer.

chapter 5

Audience for an Outlaw

Niall and Rory hunkered in a niche in the great hall. *They* wore their masks and shared the dark, cramped space with a massive iron candleholder, the candles long gutted. There were many other candles lit, too many, illuminating the vast space. They had found the only safe place in which to observe the revelers. And for Niall to gather his wits. He would have one chance with the queen this night, best he make it a good one.

"So, now what do we do?" Rory asked. He glanced quickly at the door they had just come through.

"I ken yer mind," Niall whispered. "Ye wish to return to that French lass."

"She seemed willing enough. But I'm no' the only one who was captured by the French."

"One sympathetic member of the queen's court could bode well for our clan."

"Is she? Sympathetic to our clan, I mean?"

Niall stared at the door, more than a dozen paces away.

Sabine entered, mask on her face. "I don't know," he replied.

* * *

Sabine glanced about the great hall. Niall was not in sight. Had he found common sense and abandoned his futile plan? She glanced anxiously toward the throne, where Mary sat with her escort. Niall was not there stating his case. She knew he would try to do so, and soon. The summer sky in his fierce, determined stare had told her so. It had stolen her breath, and she would never forget it. Soon, she hoped to sketch it from her memory.

Sabine walked stiffly toward the queen. She wanted to be near her when Niall returned.

Lord Campbell suddenly stepped in front of her. He was breathing hard and smelled of the garden. Were those flower petals and bits of grass decorating his doublet?

"I'm relieved to see you're well and good, *mademoiselle*," he said, swiping at his clothes.

Sabine curtsied. "Yes, m'lord. I am better." She stood and eyed him, fighting laughter. "But I fear you must tell a far different story."

Lord Campbell glanced swiftly over his shoulder. "I have spent the last hour evading the French oaf who produces those ridiculous plays. Someone told him I was . . . I was . . . never mind. When I find who told him such a thing, I'll hang him from the highest rampart of this palace."

Niall was the first name that came to Sabine's mind.

"It could've been true love, m'lord," she said, concealing a smile behind her misshapen hand. "You are fortunate. 'Tis an impossible prospect for most of us." Niall had to have been behind that wry bit of trickery, otherwise he could not have made it to her chamber without attracting Campbell's notice.

Lord Campbell grabbed her right hand and gave it a painful squeeze. "Join me in the dance. We have much to discuss."

"We have noth—" she began, despite the agony swelling in her hand, stiffening her fingers even more.

"Precisely. Come," Lord Campbell interrupted.

He practically dragged her to the center of the dancers, then stopped, released her, and bowed as if suddenly remembering his social graces. Sabine followed protocol and curtsied. They began a French *danse basse,* a favorite of Her Majesty's. Fingers interlocked, her left, his left, they stepped lightly across the floor. Sabine looked everywhere but at Lord Campbell and still did not spot Niall.

"I will propose to you after this dance," he said, his tone more of a threat than promise. "Then all will know you're mine."

"Is that what I am to you, a possession?" she asked.

"What else is a woman to a man but a possession, a thing to be treasured? You're a fine thing to be kept, much like the queen's falcons. Your mask is quite appropriate, my darling."

"How ironic of you, Lord Campbell. I didn't think a man of your importance would appreciate poetry."

He paused, then quickly regained himself. "The falcon is the most beautiful and cherished of all of the royal menagerie. 'Tis a great compliment that you are selected to wear that mask."

"I fail to see where the compliment is on me, m'lord, for a falcon is but a kept beast, brought out for royal pleasure."

"And it pleases Her Majesty to see you wed to me."

"Whatever pleases Her Majesty," Sabine sighed, "'twill please me." No words were more difficult to speak than those.

"Does it not please you?"

"I do not love you, m'lord," she boldly confessed, as if that would be enough to dissuade him from marriage.

"Love? Instead of wishing for such trifles as love, you should be grateful." He glanced at her right hand at her side. Sabine tucked it in a fold of her gown. She realized she had not done that in front of Niall.

Lord Campbell looked toward the throne. "See how Her Majesty revels in her childish attraction to that Darnley. 'Twill not be the first fateful decision she has made this night, I'll wager."

"What do you mean?" Sabine demanded.

Ignoring her question, he looked off through the crowd.

"M'lord, I ask you again, what fateful decision has Her Majesty made?"

Campbell's eyes suddenly narrowed as they caught sight of something across the great hall. His lips tightened into a grim line. "MacGregor . . . damn him."

"What—" Sabine wrenched her gaze in the direction of Lord Campbell's, in the direction of the throne.

Niall knelt on one knee before the queen, fox mask in hand. His friend knelt beside him, the bear mask still on his face.

"Non," she breathed.

Lord Campbell suddenly shoved her aside, breaking through the dancers, on his way to the throne.

She took a quick path along the periphery of the crowd, to her place beside the Marys and the other attendants. All of the women of court stood silent with eyes very wide at the sight of this Highlander kneeling before the queen. None of them were more rigid and attentive than Sabine.

"Most Gracious Majesty, I am Niall MacGregor, chief of Clan Gregor. I beg a word with ye." He bowed his head.

The luxuriant locks of his cinnamon-colored hair tipped his shoulders. In the doublet monsieur Le Canard had given him, Niall looked like a prince, yet he called himself chief. Highland nobility! Sabine's mind reeled at the possibility of a kingdom of people like Niall.

Mary stared down at him, her face, save for one raised ginger brow, betraying no emotion. She beckoned a servant to hand her a goblet of wine. After a sip and a visibly long, hard swallow, she spoke.

"While we are most intrigued by your presence, we are most disheartened by your intrusion."

"Regrettable, Yer Majesty, but necessary." Niall held her in a steady blue gaze, one Sabine knew so well. Perchance, that was why the queen had not yet deemed to send him to the gaol.

"Necessary?" Mary asked.

"Yer Majesty, there are more than stone walls and guards keeping me from speaking with ye. I am, and will be to the day I die, in loyal service to the sovereign of Scotland, yet there are those who would lay a false face to the name MacGregor."

"Not false at all, Your Majesty," Lord Campbell interjected. He stepped into a brief bow. "But well deserved. This man is part of a clan of thieves and raiders." He pointed at Niall, who remained strangely calm. The Highlander in the bear mask trembled.

Niall continued to kneel before the queen, his gaze set on

her from under the fervent arch of his eyebrows. "I *ask* Yer Majesty not to heed the ravings of this man who represents the generations of Campbells who have stolen land from and murdered my people."

Sabine studied Niall's steady form, kneeling there before the throne. A man like this would only *ask* of his queen. He would never beg.

"Such charges are not to be brought to this court at this time," Mary said. "Or any time. You, MacGregor, have invaded the royal palace. That action is worthy of the gaol."

"I shall summon the guards," Campbell offered eagerly.

"See that the MacGregor and his companion are repaired to the tolbooth. They must pay for their transgression against us," Mary decreed.

Niall stood, never once regarding Lord Campbell, keeping the queen firmly in his sight. "Yer Majesty, I must concur. For how could I be in yer presence unless I had used less than favorable means?"

Sabine unconsciously tipped her chin up. Niall bore more pride than a thousand men. She could not see that it would save him.

"Less than favorable, you say?" the queen asked. She leaned forward the slightest bit. "Tell us, MacGregor, who allowed you to have these 'less than favorable means'? One of my guards? Tell me, and perchance this court will deem to hear your plea, in our own good time, after you've been properly punished in the gaol."

The floor nearly slid out from under Sabine. The entire great hall was silent as Charlemagne's tomb, awaiting Niall's reply to Her Majesty's question. Sabine died a thousand times waiting to hear if Niall would betray her to the queen.

He took in a long breath. "Yer Most Gracious Majesty, I entered yer presence on my own."

Sabine breathed again, her relief brief as a blink. It turned to concern for Niall. He stood before the queen, supplicating himself, asking for her mercy.

Her heart died when Mary said, "MacGregor, you came to us on your own, and you will leave in Lord John's custody."

Lord Campbell stepped up to Niall, gesturing to the guards who had made their way to throne.

Niall stared hard at the queen, devouring her words with the blue fire of his gaze.

"The tolbooth is too good for you, scum," Lord Campbell said. "Since you refuse to tell her who let you into the palace, you will pay for your insolence . . . *dearly*. I'll see you sent to the Danes."

"Campbells always speak the shite," Niall said more calmly than his situation would dictate. As quick as the fox he portrayed in the *comédie*, he produced a large knife from under his plaid and placed the tip at the center of Lord Campbell's throat.

"Rory," he said, "we know when we're not wanted."

The other Highlander removed his bear mask reluctantly and took out his knife. He aimed it randomly at the stunned spectators.

Niall gave the queen a biting stare. "I wish we could've spoken on more civil terms, Yer Majesty, but yer reaction keeps with a great majority in this land."

He cocked his head toward Lord Campbell. "This vermin murdered my father and brother with the muscle of yer Privy Council behind him. The question ye should ask yerself, Yer Majesty, is why. Why d'ye allow loyal subjects to be slaughtered, hunted down? We have done nothing to affront the law of this land. All we have done is fiercely cling to our land that another wants. That person is this bastard here. 'Tis his hand that influences yer councilors, for his own ends. He did this while ye were at sea on yer way here. He took advantage of yer absence."

Niall jabbed his knife a little deeper into the skin of Campbell's neck. A trickle of blood and a strangled moan escaped his open lips.

"Our Privy Council acts in our best interests when we are not in our kingdom."

"Aye, keep telling yerself that lie," Niall said.

Sabine gasped. He was as good as executed for saying such things to the queen.

"Guards," Mary said. "Take this *sauvage* away."

Sabine lowered her chin. She had called Niall the same, but now as she looked into his azure stare, which stabbed her queen, she saw pain deep within. He was no savage. He had not given her away, told the queen she had let him into the palace, all for the price of her *sac*.

"Let yer guards take one step nearer," Niall hissed. "And I'll give this bastard what he deserves before yer own royal eyes."

Mary raised a hand. The guards stopped.

"You have no proof against Lord John," she said. "Release him, and we'll see your execution is merciful."

"A skilled axman and a well-honed blade are tempting enticement," Niall said with a grin. "But I'll have to decline, so I must bid you *adieu*."

He broke his stare from the queen only to give Sabine a quick wink. She gasped, scandalized. Lady Fleming glared at her.

Blade still biting slightly into Campbell's neck, Niall managed a slight bow to his sovereign. He forced Lord Campbell backward through the crowd, Rory flanking him, knife keeping the crowd at bay.

Sabine held her breath. Niall would never escape the palace alive.

He shoved Campbell from the great hall. His companion, Rory, slammed the doors behind them.

Immediately the crowd began excited murmurings. They had a taste of the inhabitants of Scotland's wild, remote places and seemed to think it was an entertainment.

"A most reckless soul," Mary observed. She took a sip of wine.

"Yes, I agree," Lord Darnley said.

A sudden crash echoed from beyond the door. Then shouts.

"Ah," Mary said, "they've got the intruders."

The door burst inward. Lord Campbell stumbled into the great hall, his clothing askew, a hand clamped on his neck. He stumbled through the crowd to the throne, not bothering to bow before his queen.

"The MacGregor and his man have escaped . . . crashed through one of the windows . . . through the glass! We should hunt them down!"

Sabine's heart danced. Niall escaped! The Highland fox would surely return to his lair. She slumped at the prospect that he would never return to the palace, unless he was insane, and her life would be far less exciting for it.

"Calm yourself, Lord John," Mary said. She glanced at Lord Darnley. "Would you like to join us on a hunt?"

"For that Highlander?" Darnley asked, stifling a yawn.

"And other Highland wildlife," she replied with a smile. "'Tis time we visited these Highlands. A good sovereign should see more of her country. On the morrow we will depart."

Sabine's knees weakened.

At one time, only hours ago, she wished to see beyond the palace walls. Now her heart told her these walls were far safer for her than the world of a wild Highland fox with sapphire eyes. Eyes that could bring her down with one piercing look.

chapter 6

❦

Betrothed to a Nightmare

If there ever was a place that could make Sabine wistful and fearful at the same time, it was the Highlands, at Castle Campbell Dubh. She had been in this gloomy place for three days, her mind occupied with settling in Her Majesty's many accoutrements.

After three day's travel in the queen's entourage, she was still exhausted from riding in the carriage behind Her Majesty's. The pain from endless bumps and jarring to her entire body was practically gone, save for the dull throb that remained in her backside, and the occasional stab of pain in her spine. She swore she was a good inch shorter after all of that.

During the journey she had abated her misery by snatching glances out at the vast and changing landscape from behind the velvet curtains Lady Fleming preferred to keep closed. Mirrored lakes shaped like fingers appeared at every turn. Deer drank freely from them, startling when the royal procession disturbed their idyllic silence. Birds soared above the emerald hills that grew higher and higher with each league they traveled. And Sabine, wrapped in the stolen glances at this grandeur of Scotland, remembered that she would be abandoned at their destination, abandoned by the queen into the hands of Lord Campbell.

Sabine opened one of the queen's cavernous *portemanteaux*. Her body groaned with the effort. Her attention to duty was fractured with thoughts of her impending marriage. Soon banns would be posted in the royal chapel, and her fate would be sealed. She had to keep her mind on duty to save her sanity.

She removed a heavy cloak and carried it to a dark table. Her mind tickled with the realization that Niall MacGregor was somewhere in that vast landscape. Did he know she was at the verge of his wilderness? Something told her that he did. The same something told her the Highlander would seek her out and make good on his vow. She had to believe Niall would return her *sac*. It was a scrap of hope, and her wedding day would be here soon enough. A small bit of hope was the only thing that kept her from screaming to the rafters.

Sabine smoothed the cloak on a table with a sigh. She looked about the expansive chamber given to the queen for her time here in Campbell's Highland castle—the dark furniture, a long table, two thronelike chairs, and a bed the size of southern France, which gave her a start. She eyed the dark, almost black stain of the wood. Only one thing could have deepened the color of the wood beneath so well, ox blood. Her father had owned much dark furniture in the château. It suited his nature.

She quickly decided that if she did not rein in these errant thoughts she would throw herself from the highest gloomy rampart. Lord Campbell would find her, no doubt, with more unwanted attention. Was it so terrible to be called the most beautiful woman in Scotland over and over again, to be coveted so much . . . to have a man who "made allowances" for her imperfection? *Oui*. It was.

To assuage her restless mind Sabine turned back to attending to Her Majesty's extensive, rich wardrobe.

She took a boar's-bristle brush and ran it carefully through the ermine collar of the lush cloak. She barely heard herself humming a nervous and disjointed tune, trying hard to ignore the reality that she was indeed in the Scottish Highlands. She was in the land of Niall MacGregor.

"Mon Dieu," she whispered and focused on the ermine, but Niall's image quickly intruded again. How annoying! She set the brush and the gown aside and walked to the window.

The summer breeze stirred loose tendrils of her hair. She imagined Niall living out there among those silent sentinels and the brooding forest that swelled through the valley like a dark green river before it disappeared over the horizon. She closed her eyes and prayed to Saint Giles she would never see him again. And she prayed to the depths of her hope she would.

Sabine opened her eyes and backed away from the window, ceasing her torture if only for a moment. Unrelenting shivers swept through her. She turned away from the window into an attendant's curious stare.

"Are you well?" the woman asked.

"Oui." She took the brush and began methodically grooming the ermine collar.

"You are most worried about that Highlander, are you not? I see it on your face." Her memory of that night in Holyrood when Niall invaded Sabine's bedside was too clear.

"You see nothing except my annoyance at your silly words." Sabine folded the gown more roughly than she should and practically threw it into an ornately carved oak press.

"On the journey to this isolated place I saw you peering from the carriage curtains," the attendant continued. "Then you were standing before the window locked in a dream. If you were not looking for that Highlander, then for what were you searching?"

"Peace," Sabine whispered.

She held her breath. Had she actually said that word aloud? It was Niall's dream, he had told her. But it was her dream, also! She could not share it with that Highlander, she should not share anything with him. Ever since she could remember, peace had eluded her. It was not the peace that comes after battle, surely what that Highlander had known, but the peace that came deep from within one's soul. She tried to flex the twisted fingers in her right hand. The pain became easier to ignore when she thought of Niall—

"Merde!" she hissed. It should not be that way! He was a barbarian and she was . . . wellborn, French.

"And a mere servant to the Scottish queen," she said.

Sabine knelt before the portmanteau.

"I can never understand you," the woman sighed.

She knelt beside Sabine and took out a riding skirt of the finest Florentine serge, a violet color rivaling a winter's sunset. "Her Majesty will need this on the morrow?"

"Oui," Sabine replied.

She took the skirt from her unwanted companion and rose to her feet and smoothed the serge with her right hand. On the morrow the queen would hunt deer.

"I am commanded to go," she said mournfully.

The attendant glanced at her twisted hand.

Sabine caught her stare. "Not for the archery, to discuss the posting of banns," Sabine interjected. "The next step to my nuptials to Lord Campbell." Saying it to another made it far too real. A steady cry of despair suddenly rose within her, one so deep her lips could not release it. There had to be something good within this predicament. Her scrap of hope slipped away. Niall could never invade this castle and return her *sac.*

"I . . . I must go," she stammered. "Get some air."

She stole through the warren of corridors and snaking stairways barely lit by sconces with burning, musty bricks of something these Scots called peat. The corridors that housed the queen, Lord Darnley, and her ladies were illuminated by candles. Lord Campbell had insisted on the best for his queen. He was always preening before Mary, vying for her to notice that he was the most loyal of her subjects in Scotland. It was a quality that Sabine had never desired in a husband. Would Lord Campbell be as loyal to her, after they wed, as he was loyal to his queen?

She walked silently, her slippers barely making a whisper on the stone steps and plank floors. She was lost in this horrid dank place, *non,* it was just a series of corridors. Nothing to frighten her as long as she remained calm. She took a deep breath and continued. After a few dozen steps she saw a twisting stair just beyond a stone archway and an ajar door. She paused before the arch, carved with heads of deer. Sabine stopped and peered around the door.

With care she opened the door wider to get a better look. She gasped.

Scattered about a dark wood table and ornate, thronelike chair were dozens of scraps of paper. Some were crumpled, some torn. They looked like autumn leaves scattered across the floor.

Sabine stepped inside. The vast chamber was vacant. To one side of the table a large hearth smoldered and hissed with a dusky peat fire. On the opposite wall an enormous posted bed with dark velvet drapery sat like some foreboding sentinel. Sabine shivered. This had to be Lord Campbell's chamber.

The need for her art overrode the fear that should have made her leave this place. Fear stung her enough to make her rush across the scabby rush mat that covered the floor. She skidded to a stop at the table, the papers blowing up and settling at her feet.

Sabine looked down at the papers and scowled. In France one did not toss paper on the floor unless it was worthless garbage, and even then one did not.

She knelt down into the papers, as good as gold to her, and began greedily scooping up the scraps. She stuffed them down the front of her gown, filling her cleavage.

In mid scoop she paused, her eye on one large piece that was more than a scrap. The words on the paper made no sense at all. Gibberish, some language of this land. There was a cracked red wax seal. Sabine turned the paper over and made a squeak of delight. The reverse was blank! Unheard of except in some official document. What she could draw with such a luxury of virgin space! Maybe there was some worth to Lord Campbell after all. His wastefulness was a blessing to her.

She knew exactly what she would draw on that field before her . . . Niall MacGregor. She tingled at the thought. His image would come from her mind. She would capture every detail on paper. She halted those thoughts. Was she that much of a hypocrite? One moment she thought Niall a wild savage, and the next she trapped his image on paper without so much as taking a charcoal stick to it.

"He's so free, and, yet, he holds my thoughts captive. The memory of his grin, of his eyes, of his very being . . ." Sabine shook him from her mind. "'Tis best I forget we ever met," she breathed, the truth hurting her like a blade drawn slowly through her heart.

Voices and heavy footsteps coming up the stair arrested her thoughts. She searched wildly about the chamber and spied the bed. A childish, yet lifesaving notion grabbed her. She scrambled into the dark, dusty space under the bed. The footsteps and voices invaded the chamber. Sabine gripped the large paper in her right hand, balling it tight. She peeked out at Lord Campbell and another man, who stood in the papers scattered about the desk.

Sabine held her breath and waited. This was a rare treat, to observe the man who would be her husband with his character stripped bare to her when he did not know she was in the room. She prayed he would give her a pleasant surprise about himself. He could not be the demon Niall had said he was. Lord Campbell was a noble, and Niall was nothing but a . . .

A man, she mouthed.

The man who joined Lord Campbell stood in shadow with his profile to Sabine. He was overly tall. His hair was curly, the end of his nose rounded like a knob. He wore a dark cloak wrapped about his body, his hood down about his neck.

This man spoke an odd language. It sounded like guttural nonsense. And Lord Campbell must have shared her opinion, because he chose to respond to the man in English. Perhaps he thought that other language was beneath him.

"What proof have you of your skill? Must be better than the royal archers, who prefer to play that absurd game of golf on the palace green than practice their skill. I daresay your treachery is unmatched by your presence here, but I've no knowledge of your hand with the arrow. Am I to take your word alone in exchange for my coin?"

The shadowy man took in a long breath before declaring, *"Tu tha bi fo fiachaibh do!"*

He slammed his fist on the table. The candle, in an iron holder, jumped, wax sprayed onto the wood, the flame flickered madly.

"How dare you call me worthless! We have struck a bargain. If it is done to my satisfaction, you will get payment." Lord Campbell lifted an object from the papers littering the table. "And do not speak the Gaelic to me. If any of Her Majesty's court would hear it they would be most . . . confused."

Sabine stared hard, her curiosity growing. He held an arrow. The point reflected the hearthlight. The shaft was painted a smooth white, ending in the most beautiful green and blue feathers. They must have come from a drake, the color was so brilliant, so distinctive.

He regarded the arrow briefly before handing it to the man, who took it and tucked it away into his cloak.

Lord Campbell looked down at the desk, strewn with every manner of paper. "Where is that agreement? Did you return it to me?"

"Tha," the man said. Sabine assumed that meant "yes," as he nodded also.

Lord Campbell swept the papers to the floor with one arm. They fluttered down like leaves. "I'll never find anything in this rubbish! The servants have been so lax to my needs, now that Her Majesty is within," he raged. "I'll compose another. I'll see that you receive it in due time. I must now prepare for Her Majesty's return." He paused, smiling. "I should be falconing with her. Engaged in frivolous royal pursuits, making my loyalty known."

"Cretin," Sabine whispered.

Lord Campbell paused and suddenly looked toward the bed. Sabine pulled back into the dark, praying he had not seen her.

She did not breathe as she listened harder.

"I have no doubt that you agree with me when I tell you that, in my observations at court, Her Majesty has made foolish choices, one being falling in with that Lord Darnley," Campbell said. "What an unabashed fop he is! The queen's duty is clouded by this childish attraction. She barely listens to my council on the Highlands. No one knows what's best for Scotland better than me."

Sabine heard the big man shift his weight on the plank floor. "Is yer loyalty to Her Majesty heightened because of that fine piece of French quim she's given to ye? I saw her round the great hall seeing to the queen's person."

She did not know what *quim* was, but by the way the man

said it, she knew it was far from a compliment. Lord Campbell was certain to reprimand him for such indiscretion.

"There is more than one piece of French quim in this castle. How would you know which is my betrothed?" Lord Campbell asked.

"The lassie has a fine figure, warm looking hips and arse, and tits generous enough to fill yer hands. And her black hair is a goodly length for taking into yer fists, and having yer way, for holding her face beneath yer kilt."

Cochon! Highland dog! Sabine dug her fingertips painfully into the wood, trapping small bits of wood and grit under her fingernails.

"I do not wear a kilt," was all Lord Campbell said.

"Ye're reputed to be a man who favors only the best and the grandest of everything. Ye pick yer lassies as well as ye pick yer horses," the Highlander said. "Have ye given her the three fingers up the tirlie-whirlie that ye give any filly ye're gonnae buy?"

"She's intact," Lord Campbell said. "She'd best be."

Sabine covered her mouth.

"Ye have doubts," the man asked with a short laugh, humored by his question. Sabine could not have been less amused.

"She is French," Lord Campbell said.

"Aye," the Highlander said, "I believe that she is true to her kind, as much a whoredaughter as the one she serves."

Head spinning, Sabine pressed farther back into the shadows. *Whoredaughter.* The very same name her father had given to her. She knew there had been no love lost between him and her long dead mother, the woman he called a whore until the day the fever consumed her. And that day, before she was shunted off to Her Majesty's service, he had called her *whoredaughter.*

"Marriage will no doubt put me in the best position to do my work without suspicion," Campbell said firmly.

What work? Sabine's mind screamed.

"And the whoredaughter?"

"I will saddle that bitch, and make her mine." Campbell sighed. "I grow weary of her displays of spirit, of having to suffer through her petty bouts of disdain, of bowing to her

every whim, pretending that what I do is only in her best
interests."

"Teach her what she should know."

"I will, and soon," Campbell said. "She will learn that she
should serve and obey me, not try to rule and command me.
Beauty, despite her flaws, and the willingness to shed her
shank to the first lad who lifts her skirts, will not protect her."

Sweet Saint Giles! Sabine could not breathe. Her heart
pounded, threatening to burst. She prayed it would and end
her agony. Campbell knew about Niall. That day she arrived
in this terrible country he had to have seen Niall chase a
chicken up under her gown!

"She will not be protected by any palace or castle, for she
has chosen her fate by leaving France. And she will die by it,"
Campbell declared. "I'll see you out, but not by way of the
great hall. You're presence here is known but to me. Her
Majesty's court would not understand."

The man met this statement with a grunt.

The sound of waning footsteps and the diminishing echo
of agreement from the Highlander told her she was once again
alone.

She waited, clutching her belly before she slipped out from
under the bed and out the door. Bile rose in a fiery trail onto
her tongue. She clasped a hand over her mouth to keep from
retching.

She needed fresh air. And a great deal more.

Sabine ran away from the narrow stair, the one she was
sure Campbell and the Highlander had used. She ran until she
came to another stair, one wide and familiar. She forced her
legs to propel her down the steps. Grateful, relieved, she
stumbled into the great hall, a cavernous and cold space,
sparsely decorated with a few tapestries and rusting swords.
The only signs that the queen was a guest were the fresh rush
mats on the floor and candles in the sconces.

Sabine ran faster than she had in her entire life, the large
paper balled inside her right fist. She knew she had to get outside, past these suffocating stone walls, if only for a moment,
to think, to clear her mind.

She raced through the great hall, past stunned servant boys
into the courtyard, past a lowly line of farmers bringing tithe,

and onward to the massive portcullis, which was kept raised
for the farmers to pay their lord. Two leering guards stepped
in her way.

"Suffer Her Majesty's wrath for not allowing me egress!"
Sabine threatened.

The royal guards immediately stepped back to the shadows
of the thick wall.

Taking in great gulps of air, she raced over the drawbridge,
spanning a dingy, weed-choked moat. She did not look back
as she filled her lungs with the cool air, with the essence of
this wild place that even Campbell could not corrupt.

Not far from the castle, a less-used path branched off from
the wider road. Sabine chose it. The path was more of a trough
through the meadow, leading down toward a winding stream
partially hidden by birch and bracken. A narrow wooden
bridge made of roughly hewn planks, just wide enough for a
horse and rider, spanned the stream. Sabine halted her flight
on that bridge. Beyond, on the other side of the stream, was a
darkened forest and an infinite horizon of misty mountains.

She looked back at Castle Campbell Dubh, Black Campbell. Such a fitting name for so dreadful a place. It was now
diminished, small and unthreatening on the horizon. At this
distance the frightening, hard edges of the jagged crenellation
on the two towers that framed the large gate were softened in
the heavy air. She could barely make out the small windows,
nothing more than afterthoughts on an endless facade.

"I fear that castle will be my gallows," she whispered.

Campbell's words were like the arrow he gave to that man,
well sharpened. There was no mistake that he wore more than
one face when he was with her. No mistake at all. It chilled
her blood. Her father had called her *whoredaughter* once. A
vulgarity she would never forget.

"But there is nothing I can do . . . unless I run away. But
that is impossible. I do not know this land. I would be hunted
down like a hare."

She could tell the queen what she had heard. Sabine
quickly shook her head. "I am but a lowly, crippled servant to
Her Majesty, an oddity like Rizzio, and Campbell is a respected Scottish noble . . ." She paused, the trickle of the
stream below her suddenly sounded like her words and

thoughts: mournful, lost, confused, not strong. "Why would he wish to have me murdered? Is it because he thinks I'm in league with Niall MacGregor?"

She looked up, toward the mountains. Was Niall there, hiding, waiting for a reason to come out from the den where he dwelled?

"Niall," she whispered so quietly, "where are you?" He, after all, still held fast to her *sac*, as much as she held fast to her fading hope that she would not marry Campbell and could return to France, anywhere, as long as it was not here.

"Save me, . . . Niall," she breathed.

As if she had called forth the demon of want that dwelled within her and the one that dwelled in these Highlands, cold, wet talons grasped her ankles, digging into her flesh.

"Ohhh!"

Sabine soared backward, the ball of paper burst from her hand. She landed with a loud splash into the stream, which was far deeper than it had looked from the bridge. She sank beneath the water, her skirts weighing her down, her hair loosening from its pins, floating about her face like dark sea grass. Bubbles rushed over her body as she thrashed beneath the surface. What terrible creatures lived in these Highland streams that fed on people?

Something strong wrapped around her waist. A tentacle! It pulled her roughly to the surface of the pool, bitter comfort, as she was certain to be devoured by this creature.

Breaking the surface of the water, she gasped in huge swallows of air trying to find a spark of strength. The creature dragged her out of the pool into the shallows of the stream. She struggled, her slippered feet skidded on the mossy rocks. Then she was dropped to her belly on the bank.

She rolled around ready to face her attacker, to fight, to die in this terrible place. She whipped aside her dripping locks with a defiant toss of her head and stood up.

Niall grinned at her. Shocked, she fell to the bank, hard on her rump.

"Cretin!" she cried. "Bastard!"

Niall bowed, sweeping his hand down over the surface of the water. He stood knee-deep in the stream.

"At yer service, *mademoiselle*." He straightened up. "Ye

did say, and I quote: 'Save me, Niall.' Or was it a voice on the wind?"

"I did no such thing!" she protested.

Niall nodded. "Ye did."

His auburn hair was slicked back from his face, save for a few wavy strands that tickled his forehead. The plaid he wore hung in a great soggy mass from his lean hips. His tunic clung to his broad shoulders and gaped open down the front, revealing damp lines of hair strewn across the muscled chest. Sabine scooted backward up the bank. Temptation was the most dangerous creature here, and the most alluring.

The handle of a great sword thrust up from behind Niall's right shoulder. Sabine narrowed her gaze at so large a weapon.

"Do you intend to use your sword on me now? Or do you always pull unaware wayfarers into cold streams?"

"A dousing in the burn does most anyone a wee bit of good . . . clears the head," he replied, leaning forward, his warm breath caressing her face.

Sabine moved away on her soggy bottom until a thorn in the bracken pricked her neck.

She did not cry out, certain Niall would like her to do so.

"*Mademoiselle,* you are a stranger here. I had to save you from imminent danger."

"By nearly drowning me? Tell me, Niall MacGregor, where is this terrible danger?"

"On yon hill coming this way. I'll wager Campbell thinks ye have run away. And from the way ye rushed from his castle, I'd say ye fled from something quite terrible."

"*Oui . . .*" she began, then shook her head. "*Non.* I mean . . . mind your own affairs!" She was not about to let him know he was right about Campbell, yet.

Sabine sat up, craning her neck to see through the bracken. It was far too dense for that. She began to stand to get a better look. Niall lunged forward, shoving her roughly back to the ground.

"What did you do that for?" she demanded.

"Bide yer time, and Campbell will soon be here. I'd wait if I were ye, with yer gob shut and yer body hid."

Sabine leaned forward on the bank, looking through the

branches to downstream. The bridge was only a dozen paces away if one chose to wade through the water to get to it, which she did not. She was as chilled to the bone as a person could be. She considered climbing up the bank, but it was too overgrown with a confusion of vivid colors. Saffron flower petals, emerald leaves, ivory-pale birch trunks, and ruby berries nestled among the bracken thorns. She began to reach into her gown, knowing that she now held a wealth of paper to—

"A wealth of soggy, useless paper," she whispered. Sabine stared hard at Niall, who stood protectively beside her. "'Tis all your fault. My papers are now worthless."

She stabbed her hand down the front of her gown and produced a fistful of soggy paper. She stared at Niall, narrowing her gaze. He stared back, amused, then reached forward and lifted a soggy scrap that clung to the top of her breasts.

She gasped and slapped his hand away. "Cretin!"

"Campbell is going to have yer lovely head if you dinnae hide it and haud yer wheesht," he said, dropping the paper.

The rumble of hoofbeats grew like thunder in the small river valley. Instinctively Sabine shrank back from the noise against Niall, who pulled her deeper into the undergrowth, using the swag of his plaid to shield her from the thorny bracken. From there, Sabine spied the ball of paper, high and dry, near the edge of the bridge. The last of the wealth from Campbell's chamber. She wanted it, wanted one good thing to come from this day.

"I'll get it," Niall whispered into her ear, reading her thoughts. "After . . ."

He kept her close to his body and trembled against her back.

Campbell suddenly rode into view and halted his mount on the bridge. "Where did that wench go? I'll thrash her for taking her leave without my permission."

"I did not know that I required his permission to take my leave," Sabine whispered.

Niall squeezed his arm about her. She quieted.

Campbell looked upstream in their direction. Niall pulled Sabine closer against him, wrapping both of his arms and his plaid around her, drawing them both deeper into the bracken. They were one with the vegetation, a Highland disguise.

"Sorry, m'lord," one of the guards said. "I thought she was allowed to leave with Her Majesty still being out on the hunt."

"No one goes in or out of the castle without my permission!" Campbell snapped. He waved a dark, gauntleted hand at one of the guards. "Ride ahead, see if you can find her. I'm back to the castle to await Her Majesty's return, play the happy host."

Campbell jerked the reins, rearing his horse about on the bridge. The boards creaked and rattled. The ball of paper bounced, threatened to fall into the water. He rode at a fierce gallop back to the castle, spraying clods of earth in his wake. The guard rode off in the opposite direction.

Sabine did not move. She remained sheltered in Niall's arms. Her heartbeat thundered in her ears as a light rain began to fall. Real thunder cracked in the distant mountains, a mirror of her pounding heart. She started forward, toward the bridge, reaching her hand out. Her paper sat perched near the edge of one board, despite Campbell's rough departure.

"I'll get it," Niall said, pushing past her.

He waded through the stream to the pool under the bridge. With agility common to any wild creature, he dove into the pool with hardly a splash. Niall surfaced almost as soon as he entered the water. With one arm, he grasped the edge of the bridge. He pulled himself out of the water far enough to grab the paper.

"Catch," he said matter-of-factly, and threw the ball of paper over his shoulder at her.

She faltered on the slippery stones, but managed to catch it before landing in the stream on her already bruised backside. She held the paper aloft over her head and looked up at Niall as he climbed out of the pool.

He looked down at her, grinning that grin that made her knees weak. Good thing she was sitting down.

"Why have you come here?" she asked. "Is it to speak to Her Majesty against me? To tell her the truth, that I was the one who let you inside the palace?"

Niall furrowed his brow. "Is that what ye think of me? That I would scorn yer name to elevate my own?" He smiled. "No, *mademoiselle*, that I would not do and I have proved it, have I not?"

"I do not have my *sac*," she said.

"Ye will, in due time," he said. "Trust me. 'Tis possible, because I've come to trust ye, little by little anyway."

He offered her his hand. Sabine paused, then took it. He pulled her from the stream and led her to the bank. The rain fell harder now.

"Come," he said, "unless ye wish yer precious paper to meet a soggy fate, I'll take ye to a dry place."

"Non," she protested, folding the paper several times, tucking it into her hand, trying to keep it dry. "I will not go with you until you tell me why you came if 'twas not to return my *sac*."

"Ye'll get yer purse," he repeated. "I dinnae break a vow."

Niall looked into her eyes. His blue eyes reflected the glowering sky.

"Storms can bring more than rain, Sabine. They can clear the air and bring sun and calm," he said. "Let me give ye a wee bit of shelter. Ye need it, or did ye speak a lie on the bridge?"

"I did not lie," she said, tipping her chin up. Niall was as condemned as herself. He came here to face his enemy. But he had not when he had the opportunity. He had chosen to save her. She offered him her right hand. He swallowed it in the warmth of his hand. She would go with him, to save her life, and because she saw a glimmer of hope wink at her. Or was it Niall?

chapter 7

Something in Common

Niall could not tell Sabine why he had really come, because he was not certain himself. He had to form a plan, and from the look in her frightened eyes he was certain Sabine would help him. The queen was within Campbell's castle, this he and many knew. He had seen the cortege, had heard the hoofbeats a league or more away. All Her Majesty had needed to further announce her arrival on Campbell's lands were Gideon's bloody trumpets.

Aye, he and Rory had stayed close by, waiting, planning . . . for what, they did not know . . . yet. From the look on a Sabine's face, he might know soon enough. And from the news Rory might bring him. He had sent his friend a day ago to reconnoiter the castle, learn what he could. Yet, his concern did not yield to Rory as much as it now did for Sabine.

He looked at her expectant gaze. He should tell her he had hidden her purse in a very safe place. It was more secure in his hiding place than on her person in Campbell's lair. However, Sabine did not look prepared to know where he had placed it. He needed her trust and her will to help him when he needed it. First he needed more information from her.

She was trembling as they walked. What in God's name happened to her in that castle?

She stopped and looked at him, eyes wide, face too pale.

"Why are you here?" she whispered.

"I'll tell ye," he said, "after ye come with me to a drier place." In that time he might come up with a reason to tell her why he was here, and a reason to save her, something she so obviously needed now, more so than her purse.

Hesitantly she offered him her left, undamaged hand. Niall took it. He wrapped his calloused fingers about her fine-boned hand, over the soft flesh, swallowing it whole with his hand. She looked up at him, plaintively so, then immediately glanced away when he caught her eye.

Niall led her away from the bridge, his mind trapped in a whirlwind.

What was wrong with him? Did he really need this complication in his life? Ever since he and Rory had taken flight from Holyrood, he had beat himself inwardly. He had been a fool to think he could appear before Her Majesty without royal appointment and prove his clan were not the savages a murderer like Campbell claimed. He had fled with the knowledge that the queen subscribed to Campbell's ideas. Of course she would.

The urge to barge into Castle Campbell Dubh and slay his enemy clawed at his good sense. Such folly would bring his swift death—and what good would he be to his clan then? Or to this lovely French woman? A MacGregor had to watch his back, his front, and either side. Campbell knew he was alive, knew he had taken on the mantle of chief of Clan Gregor. Reason enough for Campbell to want him dead.

He led her along the bank of the burn, further away from the distant den of his auld enemy.

Rain pattered down through the birch leaves, obscuring his vision. He swiped his eyes with the soggy sleeve of his tunic and plodded forward. Proof. What an elusive dream that was.

"Where are you taking me?" Sabine asked suddenly.

"My lair," he said, teasingly.

She huffed and jerked in his grasp. He squeezed her hand and pulled her along.

"You're an . . . how do you say . . . *outlaw* here," she said as he led her further up the burn. "The queen will have you put in chains," she added.

"That would be a relief. I thought she meant to execute traitors."

"What do you mean by that?"

Niall pushed aside a birch branch, letting it whip behind him. He took a quick glance back at Sabine who, gasping in surprise, ducked the branch.

"Beast!" she hissed.

He suppressed a laugh. What else could he expect from her but French indignation?

Rain fell harder about them as they plodded forward. The banks of the burn were steeper here, and taller. Niall found what he was searching for, a small cave in the stony, moss-dripping face of the bank. He and Rory had slept here the night before, planning and arguing about their next move, before he had sent Rory to see what he could see at the castle.

"I'll not go in there," Sabine protested.

"Fair enough," Niall said. He released her hand and stepped over some large rocks into the stony shelter.

"Are you just going to leave me here in the rain?"

"No," he replied, turning, one brow cocked, "I'm just gonnae stand here and savor some fine French 'whine.'"

He offered Sabine his hand.

She huffed and stared at the rocks separating them. "Those, I cannot climb."

Niall grinned. "Very well then. . . ." He turned away and paused.

"Well!" she cried. "What am I to do? . . . What are you going to do?"

Shaking his head, he turned and stepped back over the rocks. Without a word he hooked one arm around the small of her back. He scooped her into both of his arms.

"What are you doing?" she demanded indignantly. "This is—"

"This is me doing your bidding. Now shut yer gob for once."

He carried her over the rocks.

"If you drop me, I'll . . . I'll . . . ," she began.

"Ye'll break yer backside, that's what," he said, ducking

into the cave. It was barely tall enough for a man to stand upright. In fact, barely wide enough for two men to sleep with a fire between them.

"You are a scoundrel and a *beast*," she hissed, wriggling in his grasp.

Niall blinked. "Ye may be the most beautiful woman I have ever seen, but yer mouth is pure vinegar."

He suddenly pictured dropping her to her well-bred arse, but thought better of it. He would only hear more complaints.

He eased her gently to her feet.

Sabine smoothed her skirts and ran her fingers through the long length of her damp black hair. Niall propped himself against the stone wall, arms folded across his chest, observing her. She looked nervously out of the shelter at the rain, then she shifted her gaze to him.

"It's not much drier in this place," she said. "I'd be better off outside in the middle of the river."

"Do as ye wish."

He knelt to the charred branches that had given him and Rory warmth last night. He held his hand over the sticks. Heat touched his palm. He hoped there was enough life left in this pile to make a proper fire. And he knew Sabine would stay right where she was, with him instead of out there in the rain.

Surprisingly, though, she knelt beside him instead of standing there with her arms crossed and a scowl on her lovely face.

"What type of wood is this?" she asked, shifting the wadded paper from her right hand to her left. A precious drawing, no doubt, one she wished to keep private. He wondered for a moment if it was of Campbell, then quickly banished the thought as his gut roiled.

"The sticks?" she persisted.

Niall had to think for a moment. He and Rory had just gathered fallen bits and branches, not paying attention to what they were, just that they were dry. Did he have any more? "Birch or willow. Why?" He searched the ground for any twigs or bits of dry grass to ignite these coals into flames.

"I have my reasons," she said.

Niall picked up a handful of dried grass and tossed it on the coals just as Sabine stuck her gnarled hand to the base of the charred sticks. The grass burst into flames that licked the back of her hand.

She yelped and snatched it back, dropping a charred twig.

"What'd ye bloody well do that for?" Niall asked. "Let me see yer hand."

"There is no need. I am fine," she replied, wincing.

"More stubborn than fine, I'd say. Give me yer hand."

Sabine raised her hand under Niall's nose. The twisted fingers twitched. She was trying to straighten them. He concentrated on the back of her hand, on the red burn there.

"See?" she said wincing. "I'm very well."

"Oh, aye," Niall said, studying the red marring the delicate skin on the back of her hand. "I've got the cure for your wound but not for that bigsie way about ye." He reached into his sporran and wrapped his fingers about a small vial. He wondered for a moment why he was attracted to Sabine, when she had only shown her appreciation by being a bloody pain in the arse.

"Bigsie?" she asked.

"Conceited," he replied, cradling her hand in his. "Now, dinnae move."

"What are you doing?" Sabine asked.

"Making amends for yer stupidity with a wee bit of Agnes's cure," he replied with a grin. The aghast look on her face was worth the teasing he gave her. 'Twas a shame he could not give her more of himself. There was a wall about her, one she had built at Campbell's castle. He saw it in her frightened eyes. He had not seen it at Holyrood.

"Who's Agnes?" she asked.

"A lass," was all he would divulge. Was all he would ever tell her.

He pulled the cloth stopper out with his teeth and spit it to his lap. Carefully he daubed a small amount of the mysterious, but effective, concoction of herbs and fats onto Sabine's burn.

"So, tell me," he said, releasing her hand. He reached down to the bottom of his kilt and tore off a thin strip. "Why would ye stick yer hand in the fire?"

"I am certain I'm not the first to do so."

Niall grinned. "Good point, but that's not what I meant.

What would make ye wound yerself like that?" He would chisel away her wall stone by stone if he had to.

"'Twasn't with intention," she said. "But someone like you would not understand." She continued to hold her hand out.

Niall covered her wound with the strip of his plaid. He wrapped it carefully around her hand, under one finger that seemed perpetually bent to her palm.

"Aye, I understand," he said. "Ye need the stick for yer art."

"You know about art?" she asked, brows raised.

"Dinnae look so bloody surprised. I'm not without culture, although such learning was not my choice, I assure ye."

"Why is that?"

Niall tied off the plaid wrapping. "Another time . . . maybe . . . I'll tell ye. . . ." He had his own wall, too.

"I do not wish to know your Highland secret," she said, tipping her chin up.

Niall returned to the fire. "Then we've something in common, because I dinnae wish to tell ye them."

He piled the remains of twigs, grass, and larger sticks on the flames, pleased that Sabine did not rummage about for another twig. He bent down on hands and knees and blew gently on the coal. After a few puffs the weak flames grew into a healthy, crackling fire. Niall sat back on his heels, smiling at his accomplishment.

"Congratulations," Sabine said. "Now, what do we do?"

"Hide," he replied, looking at her shiver slightly.

He reached behind him and took his relatively dry cloak from the ground.

She stiffened.

"Dinnae be frightened," he said. "I see that ye're cold."

"Is that supposed to be a joke?" she asked, eyes flashing.

"*Cold* is the last thing I'd call ye." Niall dropped the cloak to her shoulders and scooted back a little.

"I don't bite," she said, eyeing him over the low flames. She clutched the cloak tight about her.

"Ye look as if ye think I will."

She sniffed. "Are you now ready to tell me why you came here?"

"The queen is within yon castle, and her repute for a good hunt has made it far into these bens and glens," he said. "'Tis sure that she will hunt for deer during her stay."

His reply to Sabine was more his own scheming than it was an answer for her. Why was it when he was with her his thoughts could be so muddied and so bloody clear?

"How would you know that? Were you spying?" she asked.

"Not spying, just remembering. Every Highlander knows, especially my own kith and kin, when the royalty come here to hunt, there's profit to be made. Takes the monotony out of earning coin from sheep and cattle." Saying this made his belly turn. Highland farmers, rarely warriors like himself, often joined in what Niall thought was a task far beneath them. Royals would pay them to drive deer and roebuck from the forested bens. It was a dreadful, demeaning affair, but money was a loud hue and cry.

Sabine stared at him.

How could one like her understand the problems that had plagued these hills longer than the auld ones could recount?

"Her Majesty will hunt on the morrow at first light. All in her court will join in the *grand amusement*." Sabine furrowed her delicate brow. Niall stared at her until she caught him. He blinked and looked into the fire.

"I take it that ye arenae too fond of the hunt," he said.

"I certainly am not fond of it! I have no hand for the arrow. Her Majesty will only see me as a foolish cripple, but then why should she be any different?" She looked to the flames while winding and unwinding a lock of hair about a twisted finger.

"Different from whom?" Niall asked.

Sabine looked to the fire. Wisps of her hair, dried by the sparse heat, drifted across her face. She pushed them out of the way. "Lord Campbell," she said deliberately, dropping her gaze. "He is one who thinks I am foolish and a cripple to be pitied."

Then she looked back at him. Her eyes reflected the fire, and reflected something else. Fear.

"Campbell knows ye not," he said.

What in bloody hell had Campbell said or done to her?

Niall swallowed, deciding not to ask her right now, decided to get to know her a wee bit more.

"Are you king of your clan?" she asked suddenly, hopefully.

Niall straightened. Did the mere thought that he could have that kind of power excite her? He smiled inwardly, relaxed. She was intrigued by him. But he could only offer her truth. In that he hoped she would see honor.

He looked at her. Eyes wide, taking furtive glances outside, jaw set, and her body as rigid as a pike.

"I'm not their king," he said. "I'm an equal with them. I offer my clan protection and my vow to take the name of MacGregor to glory and respect, which my clan is sorely lacking."

"That is why you wished to see the queen?"

"Aye, but that was fraught with trouble from the moment I entered her court, from the moment I saw Campbell at her side . . ." He looked at Sabine over the flames, the heat building on his face not from the fire but from deep within him. ". . . and from the moment I saw Campbell with ye." Niall wanted to bite back that last confession. It would cause him more trouble than it could possibly be worth. Yet, he could not help notice she had not asked in a long while about her purse.

*S*abine stared across the fire at Niall. The heat warmed her face. Niall's wool cloak warmed her body, the musky scent wrapped around her, the scent of male. Enough to keep her warm. Or was it his penetrating stare under fiercely arched brows? Her words certainly were not warmth to her. They were nothing more than icy truth. "Campbell's a man with power, land, and eventually me. He has everything." Except the paper tucked in her left hand. She moved it to the top of her gown, drier now, and slipped it inside between her breasts.

"Aye, but that's where ye're wrong," Niall said. "Campbell is typical of all the chiefs with power beyond measure. All he wants is more land, more wealth, more power." He let out a bitter laugh. "I daresay he has entertained the notion of usurping the throne. The queen is a fresh monarch. I've no doubt that Campbell sees her as an easy mark. He's just biding his time, like a wolf, waiting to strike when his quarry is unaware."

Sabine stared at him. Niall was speaking about herself. She was Campbell's quarry.

"Sabine?" he asked.

Under Niall's thick cloak she trembled.

"Nothing," she stammered, rushing to her feet. The cloak slipped from her shoulders and puddled about her feet.

A sudden wind whistled into their hiding place and swirled the flames almost to extinction. Niall leapt up and grabbed Sabine by the arm, whirling her about to face him. She was comforted, almost, in the thought that perhaps Niall was the one person who could save her from Campbell.

"What vexes ye so? Tell me."

"A demand from you? I have faced a lifetime of demands, and you give me one more when all I want for you is—" She bit off her words. She could not speak of those terrible things Campbell and the shadowy Highlander had said about her.

"Is what?" he asked, his gaze searching her face. He did not demand. She could see it on his face that he wanted to know.

He paused and heaved in a great breath. His gaze sharp as a knife's edge.

"Tell me what has Campbell done?"

The world splintered before her eyes. She sagged against him with no choice but to tell him, to save herself.

Niall held her tight. He said he was a protector, not a king. Would he protect her? Sabine took a deep breath toward the first step into finding the answer.

"Campbell has threatened me," she said, trying to calm her voice. "After we marry, after he's had his way with me, he will kill me." Sabine broke down into tears. Just speaking of what she had overheard made it so much more real.

"How d'ye know this, Sabine?" Niall asked, his lips brushing her ear. "What proof have ye?"

"Only what I heard him tell another man in his chamber."

"What did Campbell say, exactly?" he asked, his breath warm on the side of her face.

Sabine swallowed. The words would not leave her mouth. She swallowed again.

"Take yer time," Niall whispered. "I want to know every-thing." His tone was firm, not demanding.

"Campbell described me in the most vile and unspeakable ways," she said. "He doubted my *virginité*."

Niall raised an eyebrow.

Sabine stiffened. "Do not look at me so, or I shall not tell you more."

"Ye will, because I see it in those lovely eyes that ye want me to know. So, continue. Why d'ye think Campbell wants to kill ye?"

"He said that he grew weary of my displays of spirit . . . my flaw. That he suffers through my bouts of disdain while bowing to my every whim."

"Not a fair description of ye, I must say." Niall held her closer.

"Are you daring to make jest again?"

He shook his head. "Go on, tell me more."

She searched her mind, and did not go far to find the essence of her fear. "He said that beauty, and the willingness to . . . um . . . 'shed my shank,' I think that was the vulgarism he used, to the first lad who lifts my skirts, will not protect me."

She froze, Niall captured in her stare. "'Tis your fault that Campbell wants me dead. He saw you under my gown on that wharf, when you were chasing after that silly chicken. He thinks I have affection for you, that you are a threat to him."

He burst out laughing. Sabine jumped a little.

"Me a bloody threat to him?" he said. "I wish that was the truth."

"But of course it is true. Campbell said it, did he not?" What was the matter with this Highlander? Why did he not believe her? "He called me the most vile name as well."

"What did he call you?"

She did not reply right away. The word was far too hideous to pass her lips. Having it pass more than once through her mind was bad enough. But she wanted to prove to Niall what she heard from Campbell was true. She had to tell him.

Sabine stared into his eyes and managed to say, "He called me a 'whoredaughter.'"

Niall blinked and released his hold of her just a fraction. "He called ye a . . . a what?"

"I will not repeat it. You heard what I said."

"Whoredaughter," he repeated.

She raised her chin. "*Oui,* that is what Campbell called me."

Niall took a step backward, a faltering step. He shook his head. "He did not call ye that."

"He most certainly did," she said. How could he deny her? *"I heard him."*

"It wasnae about ye, Sabine."

She placed her hands on her hips. Niall was certainly out of his Highland mind. She drew a thin breath over her lips and prepared to unleash her anger upon him, slightly grateful she was no longer so afraid . . . for herself, but now for whom?

Through one fallen lock of auburn hair, Niall leveled a steady gaze on her. "Campbell was speaking about the queen."

Her first instinct was to call him a fool. But she had learned it was not best to act on her first impulse toward Niall. He held as many surprises, she suspected, as did these Highlands. "How do you know this?"

"'Tis common knowledge that the queen's late mother, a Frenchwoman named Marie de Guise, wasnae held in high regard with many of the Scottish nobles or many Scotsmen, especially those in Edinburgh. My brother and I spent more than our fair share of time in the taverns of that fair city, escaping our tutors and hearing opinions about the late queen regent. The favored phrase to describe her was none too respectful—*whore.*"

Sabine winced and crossed her arms over her breasts to keep from shaking. The poor Queen Mother, what a horrid thing to say about her. She had been French, one of Sabine's "kind." Campbell had said so, just before he called Queen Mary, *her* Queen Mary, a . . .

". . . Whoredaughter," she whispered.

"Aye," Niall said, taking a step forward. "That's what I heard said by men who considered themselves noble . . ." He said the last word as if it was poison on his tongue. ". . . After the queen regent's death, those same men cheered and toasted to the arrival of the 'whoredaughter.'"

"Terrible," Sabine breathed. But Campbell was so generous to Her Majesty. He provided her with a relatively stately refuge in these Highlands. Provided her entertainments and gave her the opportunity to . . . *Mon Dieu!*

". . . To hunt!" Sabine cried.

Niall cocked an ear toward her. "What?"

Mind reeling, she tried to grip on to her thoughts and steady her wavering legs. She toppled backward. Niall was there to catch her. His strong arms bound her to his body—and protected her. But she was not the one who needed his protection.

"The queen," she breathed, "I must save her from Campbell."

"Ye must . . . do what, Sabine?" he asked.

She snapped her gaze to his. "*Oui,* that is what I said. The queen must know. I must tell her."

Niall turned her about. He held her at arm's length and stared directly into her eyes. "This ye cannae do, Sabine. T'would place yerself in harm's path."

She shook her head furiously enough to make her hair flail about her face. When she stopped, she breathed so heavy she thought she might faint. She stared at Niall through the hair that had fallen in front of her face. He brushed the long locks away from her eyes. "Sabine," he said, "ye dinnae know Campbell as I do."

They stood apart, but only for the span of their breaths in the damp air.

"I know what I heard," she said. Her face warmed, throat tightened. She felt like she had swallowed broken glass. What kind of world was this where a monarch could not rule until she breathed her last, after living to the ripe old age of two score and ten, maybe more? Where a queen's most trusted advisor wanted her dead to satisfy his own drive for power?

"I know what Campbell wants," Niall said.

"Power," she said, "is that it?"

He blinked, surprise in his eyes. "Aye, and more land."

"The two go hand in hand, do you not think so?" she asked.

He nodded again. She was not too pleased at his sudden look of astonishment that she would know such things about men. But Niall did not know about her life in France, where she had experienced the evil depths to which a man would drop to press his will over anyone who so much as disgruntled him.

Niall glanced away. He stared over her shoulder, grinding his jaw. She started to ask him what had entered his mind, if anything, when he suddenly looked at her and said, "We need proof, Sabine."

"What? . . . *We?*" she asked, taken aback.

"Aye, *we*. Campbell has Her Majesty's confidence. He's her Highland liason. D'ye think if ye just walked up to her while she sat on her grand throne and announced that ye've come to save her from a murderer that she would believe ye? Especially when ye tell her that her accused murderer happens to be the golden lad of the Highland nobles, none other than Lord John-bloody-stinking-bastard-Campbell?"

"I am a member of her court, her attendant," Sabine said.

Somehow that title did not seem so significant at the moment. What was she to Her Majesty but an obedient maid who cleaned her wardrobe and stood silently by in wait for the next petty order? But Mary was good to her, never cruel.

"I love my queen," she said. "I made a vow to be vigilant to her needs. And the need to protect her, to *warn* her has arisen. I must leave this place, and go to her."

"And put this pretty neck in Campbell's noose for yer trouble," he said, gliding a finger over the nape of her neck, sending an explosion of shivers down her back.

"But I cannot sit idle with what I know," she protested. "I must protect my queen."

"Protect?" he asked, amusement in his tone. "'Tis a difficult thing to do . . . *protect*." His gaze suddenly disarmed her, comforted her somehow. This was what Niall did for his *clan*. He *protected* them.

"Protect," she whispered. "'Tis a good word, is it not?"

Niall nodded. "Aye. 'Tis."

He reached out and took her by the waist. He pressed his fingers into the back of her gown and drew her near him. Niall wrapped his arms about her, and pulled her closer until their breaths mingled.

Sabine stiffened a little in his hold. He trapped her arms to her sides. She did not struggle. Anticipation aroused curiosity in her. She had been through so much this day. Niall's embrace calmed her in the wake of his promise to help her. Surely, his offer came with a price.

chapter 8

L'essence d'Amour

Who watches over ye, Sabine?" he asked, his breath brushing her cheek. His Scots burr softened each syllable, lingered over them. "Who protects ye?"

He was so dangerously close to her. A fine, pale scar cut through the coppery brow over his left eye. Her gaze glided effortlessly down to a small, dark mole that rode the edge of a furrow at the corner of his generous mouth. Niall's details were so wondrous!

"Sabine?" he asked again. "Who protects ye?"

Sabine tipped her chin up. "No one, but myself," she replied quickly.

"Stop being so bloody French for one moment. Answer me truthfully," he said gruffly.

"I protect myself," she said. "I survive."

"Survive," he repeated with a scowl, a swift downward glance at her damaged hand. "Have ye *lived*, Sabine?"

"I do not know what you mean. Tell me." Her tone challenged, although she did not mean to make it so.

Niall drew in a deep breath. He looked to search for just the right response, probably something to shock her. "*D'ac-*

cord, mademoiselle, avez-vous le sens d'amour? D'ye know the meaning of love?"

"You know French?" Sabine gasped. "How do you know my French?"

Niall held her tighter. "Answer my question first, *chérie*," he replied. "And I might answer yours later."

"No one knows the meaning of love, especially me."

"Poor Sabine, has no one loved ye?"

"I do not like sarcasm."

"'Twas not sarcasm," Niall said. "'Twas concern."

Sabine freed her right hand from her side and tried to slap him. Swifter than she could have imagined, Niall grabbed her hand. His gaze captured hers as he slowly raised her gnarled fingers to his lips and kissed each one.

Her knees weakened. He tightened one arm about her waist. She had to remind herself to breathe.

He released her hand and offered her a wide smile. "Is that why love hasnae found ye, Sabine? Because ye act on your first impulse?"

"What do you expect me to do, now that you have me captive? *Kiss you?*" She gasped, wishing she could take back her words.

Niall drew her closer, sifting his fingers through her hair, entwining them in her curls. "Is that your second impulse?"

She was so near him, unable to stand on her own if he released her. She drew in a deep breath and took in his scent, one so fervent, so male. It made her dizzy.

"Kissing you," she lied, "is the absolute last thing on my mind."

"Lying doesnae wear well on ye," Niall said. He cupped her chin between his thumb and forefinger.

"And being a brute does not wear well on you," she said.

His face, his lips, were very close to hers. His voice was soft, his words deliberate. "When Campbell has ye to his marriage bed, will love find ye or will ye look to these hills for it?"

"Does my betrothal to Lord Campbell anger you?" she asked.

"D'ye wish it to?"

"I wish it to anger you," she whispered, watching his mouth.

"It does anger me," he replied and lowered his lips to her neck. His breath whispered against the fine hairs, making them stand on end, dissolving her French resolve.

Niall rested his forehead against hers. "I despise Campbell more than I did when I awoke this morn. He has so much. With ye as his wife he will have wealth beyond mortal measure."

"He will not." The words barely escaped her lips. "He won't have this moment."

Niall smiled. "True."

He drew her nearer, as if that were possible. Her lips tingled with anticipation. Her breath quickened.

His lips met hers, tentatively, before he pulled away, eyes searching her face. Was he looking for her approval? Not Niall MacGregor, Highland king! This man could never want for any woman's approval.

Here in this hidden place, this moment was theirs. They were the only two people in the world. Surely, Niall knew that as well as she.

Then he clasped her to him. His scent, one of the land, captured her as his breath caressed her face in soft waves.

"This time is ours," he whispered.

She heard herself speak from so far away, "*Oui* . . . ours. . . ."

She fell into his kiss with a frighteningly deep and aching desire. There was no escape from this man she had scorned only moments before. She believed that somehow his life and hers were linked because of this dreadful thing they knew about Campbell and the queen.

Thunder sounded in the distance. It echoed the wild beating of her heart. She tasted him, and wrapped her fingers through his hair. She pulled him closer and kissed him deeper. This kiss was without compare. It was her first and, she vowed, would remain her secret.

A small moan escaped her throat. Niall moaned as well, a guttural, wild sound. He kissed her with far more passion than he had at first. He ran his hands confidently up her confining bodice. His fingers dug eagerly into the stiff fabric covering her back. Niall's exquisite touch sent shivers up and down her spine. Maddened sensation rang through her. She craved more of him, wanted to hoard these new feelings.

She pulled away. Was it to draw breath or to study the lively blue of his eyes, the sharp corners of his mouth, the furrows on either side of it, and the cleft in his chin? More details for her memory.

"What?" he asked.

She shook her head, beat the demon of denial back into the dark recess of her mind, and kissed Niall anew. The thunder grew louder. The frantic beating of her heart threatened to give her away to him forever. It drummed louder and louder—

Non!

Niall held her, his lips brushing hers, his breath hot and moist, fueling her need again when he must not.

"What is it . . . ?" His question trailed away. He must have known as well as she that the distant thunder was the queen and her entourage returning to the castle.

This moment had to end. "I must go," she said.

"Ye said the queen is going on a hunt on the morrow?" he asked.

Sabine searched her memory. Had she mentioned a hunt before? She could not remember.

"Oui," she stammered. "I will be there as well."

"The hunt could be the place Campbell would choose to murder the queen," he said.

"I don't know," she said, suppressing a shudder. "I have to warn my queen. I have to get her alone, which is near impossible, and tell her." She looked at Niall. He grinned at her.

"Why are you smiling?" she demanded. "Sweet Saint Giles, you are insane!"

"Ye're not gonnae be on the hunt alone, Sabine," he said. "I will be there. I will protect Her Majesty from Campbell. She will send him to the Danes when I'm through."

"Is that bad?" she asked.

"The worst sort of bad," he replied. "The Danes know how to do things to a man far worse than Satan himself. Campbell will pray for death, but they will show him no mercy. Rest easy, Sabine, I will protect the queen."

She could not find the words right away, then she looked into his eyes. "You are placing yourself in danger for a queen who has sent her guards after you, had run you from the palace."

"Mary's *our* queen. I hope she will see my protecting her as a sign of fealty. It would be to the benefit of my clan anyway." He grinned.

A smile tugged at the corners of Sabine's mouth. Niall's grin was infectious. For one moment she thought things were not so bleak as they seemed.

Sabine glanced down at his strong fingers, at the lines of sinew on his hands under skin roughened by hard work. She looked up at his face and memorized every feature. This night, while the castle slept, she would put his image on one of the papers she had found. Then she would tuck it away, and no one would ever see it. And every time she dared look at the sketch, for a brief instant, her life would be free. Niall would be with her always, a free man of the Scottish Highlands!

"We havenae proof, beyond what ye heard, that Campbell means to threaten the queen's life."

"Proof?"

"A paper, an order to another party," Niall said. "Campbell would not be the one to do the deed, but he surely would be the one to plan it."

"Proof," Sabine said. "'Twould be difficult for me to get. But I will try."

"Who said anything about ye finding it?" he asked. He seized her. "Dinnae do anything daft."

"I will do what I must."

"Then I willnae let ye go to do this foolish thing."

She wrenched away from him and crawled quickly up the bank. He snatched at her hem, tugged her back a little, but she was too fast and escaped his hold. On top of the bank she turned and glanced down at him. Niall glared at her.

"I'll let ye go," he said. "But I trust ye'll not do anything to bring harm to yerself."

When she did not reply right away, he scrambled up the bank and grabbed her hand. "Sabine, promise me ye'll not do anything foolish."

After a pause she said, "I promise." She meant every word.

She breathed deep, pulled from his hold, and turned toward the castle. She ran up the path, away from the bridge, and the afternoon, that suddenly seemed so long ago, and the Highland MacGregor was nothing more than a dream.

She raced past the crossroad, breathing hard, gown flapping about her legs, breaths exploding within her. She did not pause until she reached the drawbridge into Campbell's castle. Her Majesty needed her more than ever. Sabine had to prove it with more than words repeated from eavesdropping on Lord Campbell. It was a dream as absurd as the one she had just lived in the arms and kisses of Niall MacGregor, Highland king.

W*ith Rory at his side, Niall looked through the thin stand* of trees up the slope to Castle Campbell Dubh. The last rays of the setting sun stained the western face crimson. From this distance the castle looked no larger than his hand. He held it in front of his face and made Campbell's lair disappear. Soon, darkness would do the job for him.

"Why are ye doing this mad thing?" Rory asked. "'Tis just putting yerself into the lion's mouth."

With a sigh Niall slipped down from his horse and handed Rory the reins. "If Campbell is spoiling for the throne by means of laying threats to the queen . . . this I must know."

"Why should ye?" his friend asked over a sigh. "What proof could ye get? And why in hell are ye the one to go get this thing that doesnae exist?"

"D'ye wish to go?" he asked.

Rory raised his hands. "Unh uhh, no' me! Ye're the one with a promise to keep . . . ye're the bloody chief of this clan—"

"Now ye're getting it," Niall said. He unhooked a coil of rope from the back of his horse's saddle and spread it on the ground.

"Och, and ye'll just take these things ye may hear to Her Majesty and tell her ye've come to save her from Campbell, the head of a clan who has remained shoulder to shoulder with the Stuart monarchy since for-bloody-ever?" Rory continued.

"If it'll result in restoring the good name of Clan Gregor it will be well worth my trouble," Niall said. He began picking up sticks of dead wood and dropping them on the center of the rope, his back to his friend.

"Well, good luck to ye then. Especially with *her*."

"Daft bastard."

Images of Sabine suddenly flashed across his mind. He hoped with all his heart that she was safe. He would make it part of his mission to see to it that she was.

He dropped more sticks into the growing pile until it was large enough for his purposes. He knelt on the ground and wrapped the rope around the bundle several times, then tied a knot, cinching the sticks tightly together. Niall lifted the bundle with one hand and stood upright.

"I'm away."

"Aye," Rory replied with a sloppy nod. "See ye return."

"I'll see ye back in the glen before last light on the morrow."

Niall used his free hand to slide his claymore from the sheath beneath his cloak. He slipped the weapon cleanly into the bundle of sticks, concealing it quite well.

"I've got to ask, finally," Rory said. "What's with the fardel?"

Niall hefted the bundle to his back and hooked his arm through one of the loops in the rope. " 'Tis my key to the castle."

"Oh, aye," his friend mused. "That's as bloody clear as muck."

Niall sighed. "Did ye not learn a damn thing from our experience at Holyrood? This is a disguise, ye tosser. See?" He dropped his hood onto his head and hunched over just a bit. "What do I look like?"

"Some git with a fardel on his back," Rory smirked. "Aye, aye, I get it. Ye're a farmer bringing his crops of dead wood to yer lord, am I right?"

"As right as ye're able. D'ye remember what they were burning in the sconces at Holyrood?" Niall did not wait for a reply. "Wood! Not peat. Heaven help us if the queen had to breathe in peat smoke. I'm just making a delivery."

Rory nodded. "Aye. . . ."

"All I need do is bluff my way into the castle . . ." He adjusted the bundle on his back and grinned. "Who'd have believed it?"

"Believed what?" Rory asked.

"That I'd learn a few things from that Frenchman, Le Canard."

He would have to tell Sabine that very thing when he saw her in the castle.

She may find it amusing. Perhaps as much as his presence. She would be the only one in that castle to think so.

Sitting up in her bed, Sabine stared down at the strip of plaid wrapped around her right hand. She remembered how Niall had carefully wound the wool from his Highland garment around her hand, under her twisted fingers, keeping them free. A more careless person would have just bound them together, not taken the time to slip the wool between fingertips and palm. Nothing about Niall was careless.

Sabine stared down at the colors that practically sang out from the wool about her hand, hues as bold as the Highland landscape leapt out at her: the deepest crimson, found in the last gasp of the setting sun; the blackest pitch of a moonless midnight sky; and a thin strip of saffron as rich as gold honored the humble woolen warp and weft. This piece of fabric was as much a part of this wilderness as was Niall. The colors were subtle yet so strong! So much like these Highlands.

A chilling night wind blew in through the open window, banging the glass against the deep stone sash. But there was another sound, one subtle, menacing. The door to her chamber opened inward. The hinges squealed in protest. Sabine looked up. She instinctively thrust her hand under the covers, slipped the plaid from her hand and hid it there just as Lord Campbell stepped inside. His stride did not falter as he cut a direct path to her bed.

Sabine sat up, trying desperately not to cower from her intended. The way he stared at her gave her a nasty chill. Now, and all during supper, it was as if he knew her thoughts. Did he know what she had heard that day?

The curtains shuddered with the promise of more rain as

thunder rumbled near enough to rattle the water carafe on the table beside her bed.

Campbell gave her a small bow.

"I looked for you this afternoon, before the evening meal. The guards said you left in a hurry."

Sabine sat up a little higher. "I wanted to see more of this beautiful country . . . I needed fresh air."

"You should not leave the castle without escort," Campbell said. The hearth light cast stark shadows against the hollows of his face.

"I did not want to disturb you, m'lord," she managed to lie.

"You should've waited until I was available to show you the grounds."

"And if I had waited, m'lord, for your guest to leave, you would've shown me the grounds in the rain."

Campbell blinked. "Guest? My only guest is the queen, and she was falconing for the afternoon."

Sabine forced herself to contain the contempt for this man growing inside her.

"I assumed a man of such a magnificent castle and land would have many guests. 'Twas a guess, 'tis all, m'lord." She swallowed. "Of course, I would've preferred you to escort me. But I cannot have everything I want, can I?"

Campbell stood beside her bed, his question still thick in the dank air. "Well," he said, "be that as it may, I made report of your absence to Her Majesty moments ago."

Sabine silently tipped her chin higher and stared hard at Campbell, defiant.

He moved closer. The light from the chamber's hearth slashed across his face. "You are an arrogant girl who needs discipline. After we are wed—"

"Non," Sabine whispered, bile rising in her throat, "t'will never be."

"Your queen commands it to be so. Her Royal Highness commands you to remain under my watch as long as you're in my castle. She says you wish to get to know me better."

"She must be mistaken." Sabine bit her bottom lip. She should never have spoken against Mary aloud.

"I only follow Her Majesty's wishes," he said, taking a few steps back from the bed. "You should rejoice in doing the same. She wishes you to remain in the castle unless escorted beyond. I gave her my word that I would see to it that your wings are clipped."

"How can you do that, exactly, . . . m'lord?" Sabine dared ask.

Without a word, Campbell turned, walked away from the bed, and out of the chamber. He took the massive door latch in his fist and slammed the great wooden door with a heavy blow. The noise rang in Sabine's ears, almost deafening her from the clank of the key in the lock. She sat stunned by Campbell, who had made very good on his word. The devil.

"I knew this place would be my gaol," Sabine said with a heavy sigh.

The curtains blew inward. Rain leapt in through a break in the dark wool, dampening the foot of the large posted bed and the moldering crimson-velvet bed drapery.

She gazed up at the rafters, at the shadows that leapt amongst the rough-hewn timbers. This was the highest garret of this castle. The farthest chamber away from Her Majesty.

"My queen must know about Campbell," she whispered. "But without proof, I might as well be speaking into the rain. However, I must do something to warn her."

Sabine thought for only an instant, the answer too obvious. On the morrow's hunt she would warn Her Majesty that Campbell is a villain, not to be trusted. She prayed Mary would consider her accusation as truth. She prayed such news to Mary's ears would also stop her betrothal as well as save Her Majesty's life.

Wind pushed the curtains deeper into the chamber. Sabine looked to the window. She was locked in without hope. Niall, who was free out there in the darkness, could never come to her. This castle was as impenetrable as Campbell's heart. Why would anyone want to try to get inside?

"There's enough freshened air in this chamber to last a lifetime," she mumbled bitterly. "Time to close out the night. Then, perchance, I may sleep."

Barefoot and clad only in an ankle-length linen tunic, she padded over the plank floor, which was covered in a frayed rush mat. The wind rippled the garment against her legs. She clutched it to her body against the chill. Once she closed the windows, she might sleep in silence and warmth. Sleep was what she needed to clear her mind, to prepare her for a full tomorrow.

She released her tunic and reached for the curtains. She managed to grasp the edges and step into the billowing, musty wool. The wind made the curtains dance, as if they held life. She shook her head. This chamber was full of too many shadows.

She grabbed the latch on the window and drew it in, the rain pelting her face. With a bit of effort, she closed the window, then paused gazing far down through the glass and rain, to the edge of the moat, at a small parade of torches. The flames flickered wildly in the wind and the rain, shining weak, broken light on those who carried them. Guards, out in the rain, doing Campbell's bidding on some stupid errand, no doubt.

"Imbéciles," she said, stepping back out of the curtains, backing into something very hard and unyielding.

She whirled around, biting off a surprised shriek.

Niall stood before her, dripping on the rushes, a grin frozen on his lips, his sapphire eyes sparkling as did the raindrops that clung to his hair, his plaid, and his face. The shadows and candlelight played off the strong furrows and ridges of his face. His hair, darkened by the damp, hung in shimmering strands framing his face. One lock adhered to his forehead in a dampened curl. Temptation rose in Sabine to glide her fingertips over his dampened brow, wrap the lock about her finger as Niall stared down at her, as his breath left his lips in brief bursts. What exertion had he performed to find his way here? She was as tempted to touch him tenderly as she was tempted to strike him for foolishly placing himself in danger. Yet, she stood captured by his stare and was paralyzed by the mere sight of him in her chamber, her gaol.

"Better those guards get an eyeful of yer fine figure in yon window than mine," he said.

Then she blinked, allowing frustration, anger, and relief to cause her to react on her first impulse. She slapped him hard. His grin did not disappear.

Then, on the next breath, she flung herself into his strong embrace.

"You must leave," she said into his sodden wool, her heart breaking to speak so.

Niall held her firmly.

"That, *mademoiselle*," he replied, "I cannae do."

Damn her traitorous heart, she was very happy to hear him say that very thing.

chapter 9

❧

Artist's Eyes

You frightened me!" she exclaimed.
A wave of emotions crashed down on her, almost
knocking her out of his arms. She wanted Niall gone, back
into the rainy night. And she wanted him to stay, here, with
her. Why was it that he brought confusion to her with just one
glance? One grin?

She managed to pull from his embrace and take a few steps
back.

"I had not meant to scare ye." Niall paused and looked
about the chamber. "So, Campbell does keep France's fairest
flower in the highest garret of his castle. Lucky for me."

"How did you get to the window from the outside?" she
asked, clasping her arms across her breasts, convincing herself it was to fight the chill. "Did you climb up the wall like a
lizard or did you come down from the roof like a bat?"

"The second one," he replied.

She winced. "How did you get that far?"

He would not tell her the truth. "A trick I learned from
your friend, Le Canard. Only this time I didnae have to recite
some daft poem."

"*Monsieur* Le Canard? How? A disguise?" she asked.

"Aye." Niall removed his cloak, the great sodden mass of it, and surveyed her, all of her. She shuddered. "Nice tunic, keep ye warm?"

"You are not here to inquire to my comfort . . ." She narrowed her eyes. He should leave quickly for both of their sakes. That was what common sense told her. Her heart on the other hand made her ask, "Are you?"

Niall continued to hold his cloak. The leather-wrapped handle of his great sword thrust over his left shoulder. The part of the blade Sabine could see glistened in the firelight, the steel as brilliantly polished as the queen's jewels. "Perchance aye, perchance no," he replied.

"A well-used sword would not shine so," Sabine said into his curt response.

"Aye," Niall sighed, turning his back to her, as if purposely affording her a full view of the long weapon in the leather sheath strapped to his back. She was impressed, but for all the wrong reasons.

He laid his cloak before the fire, spreading the swath of dark wool inches from the coals.

Shivering slightly from the rain-damp on her tunic, Sabine took a step to the bed and gathered up a blanket. She paused, then offered it to Niall.

He raked his dripping hair away from his eyes and took the blanket with his other hand. He swiped a corner of it across his face. His blue eyes bore into her, to the depths of her soul.

"Is there a way out of this chamber, or are guards just beyond that door?"

"There's only the way you arrived, unless you wish to use that sword to break the lock on the door."

He regarded the lock. "Cannae do it with any blade. The keyhole is too wee. A battering ram may get us out, but I've not got one of those under my kilt."

He looked at Sabine, one brow raised. She held her breath and braced herself for another bawdy remark. "Did Campbell lock ye in because ye ran away today?" he asked.

"I did not run away," she said, chin up. "But since you've come here, we're both prisoners."

"I can leave anytime I wish," he said, tossing a glance to the curtained window. *"Can ye?"*

"With Campbell's guards circling, you must remain as well. 'Tis certain they know something is amiss if they search in the rain, do you not think so? 'Tis best you stay until the guards stop circling." What was she asking of him? Of her heart?

"Is that a wee bit of concern for me I hear?"

Sabine straightened. "Perchance."

"Aye, well . . . good," he said with a quick nod and the trace of a smile.

Niall strolled to the hearth, removing the sheath that had held his sword on his back. He slipped the blade into the leather with such utter care that to Sabine the act looked like some sacred, Highland ritual. Carefully Niall placed the sword on the folds of his cloak.

He stood upright. His achingly blue eyes took her in again. "That tunic is a bit flimsy for a Highland night. Couldnae keep a weevil warm in midsummer." He thrust the blanket out to her. "Perchance ye are the one who needs this."

"*Oui,* my garment keeps me warm enough," she replied. "What other garment would one wear to slumber?"

"If a person needed one. . . ."

The sly smile that crossed Niall's lips sent a thin shiver up her back and a vivid image to her mind. What did he look like without all of those Highland trappings?

She shook her head furiously. She did not need to know the answer to that question, not now anyway, here, locked in Campbell's garret. Stiffly she pointed to the blanket in his fist. "Dry yourself off, then you can tell me why you're here."

"Aye, well," he said, removing the silver brooch holding the plaid over his left shoulder. The soggy wool immediately slipped down to his waist. He placed the brooch in a pouch at his hip. "I've come here . . ." He reached for the buckle to the belt that cinched the plaid around his waist. Sabine drew in a sharp breath. ". . . because of ye, Sabine, and because of what ye claim to know."

He unbuckled his belt and let it drop to his feet. Sabine gasped and spun away from him.

Niall laughed. "I didnae think that ye French were oh, so, innocent. I've heard that there's a lust about your kind that's unmatched in all the world."

"Does rampant stupidity compel you to believe such things?" she asked.

She could hear Niall behind her, wrestling off his wet clothing. She stood tense and shivering, with only her tunic and thoughts of what Niall must look like without his clothes to keep her warm.

"Does rampant curiosity compel ye to turn round?" he teased.

"You said you came because of me, did you not?"

"I came to see if I could find proof behind yer words against Campbell. That would be a sweet discovery."

Sabine turned slowly around.

He stared at her. She stepped closer to him. The sinew on his neck tightened up to the hard angle of his jaw. The furrows around his mouth deepened.

"What we know is worthless. Lord Campbell is a saint in Her Majesty's eyes," Sabine said.

"Campbell is as much a saint as is Satan himself," Niall growled.

"You would do whatever is necessary to protect your clan?" she asked.

His expression softened. "Aye, I would. 'Tis why I'm here, locked in this room with ye, waiting for the guards to retire, waiting for my clothes to dry." He drew in a deep breath.

"Are wet clothes all that deter you from pursuing Campbell now?" she asked.

"I'm better at wielding my sword when my clothes are dry, besides we are locked within and there are guards without. I have to stay . . . for a wee while."

"I thought you came to rescue me," she stammered. What had she just said? She covered her mouth with her gnarled hand. Niall glanced at it.

"Sabine," he said, gaze sympathetic, fixed on her hand.

She dropped her hand and hid it in a fold of her tunic. "Sympathy I have, a king's ransom of it. I do not need more."

"Ye willnae get it from me," he said. "Ye're the strongest woman I have met. 'Twould be a waste to give ye sympathy."

Niall, half naked, walked toward her, his body bathed in dampness, more of a distraction than she could stand. And as if that were not enough to make her heart beat wildly, the memory of the kiss they shared burned so bright in her memory that it nearly blinded her.

He stopped before her, the hearth light warming half of his face, the other half deep in shadow. "I didnae come to save ye, but I do confess that your well-being is rapidly becoming a concern of mine. Ye're my greatest ally here."

"I do not need . . ." Sabine began. She placed her profile to him, but she could still see his shadow on the wall before her, a worthy enticement. She clenched her eyes shut. If it did not look stupid, she would gladly slap herself a few times to rid herself of these musings, to stop this war raging inside her.

She opened her eyes. Niall stood in front of her, a breath between them. Sabine stiffened. He placed a finger to her lips.

"Shh," he said softly, "there's no need to deny the truth. Ye need me. I felt it when ye were in my arms, when we kissed."

Sabine stepped back from him. Warmth flowed through every part of her body. Even the chill brought through the thread-bare tapestries covering the stone walls of this chamber did not bother her.

Niall was too near. Heat radiated off his lean, well-muscled chest. Here was a man who worked hard with his hands all his life. He used his brawn to make a place for himself and those he cared for. He cared for his clan so much that he willingly placed himself in the path of harm for them. Oh, 'twould be bliss eternal to be in the path of such unconditional caring.

She raised her right hand and drew tentative, twisted fingertips over his shoulder, over the lean muscles under pale skin that the stingy Highland sun had not touched. With both hands she traced his arms. The bold contours enticed her, slowly melted her resolve. She should be exploring him with her eyes, not her hands.

He reached out and enveloped her in his arms. Was he caring for her now? Unconditionally? Did he know she had begun caring for him when he came through that window, perhaps before? Did he know she was gradually sorting out her confused feelings about him? Would he care?

He touched her chin, then he bent his head down and kissed her.

She fell into the kiss, remembering the wondrous rush of heart-stopping sensation shooting through her the first time their lips had met. Her body relaxed in his arms. She placed her hands on his bare back.

She dug her fingers into the hard ridges of muscle. She ran her fingertips down, down to the top of the blanket about his waist. She shuddered and quickly stepped away from him to the fire. He had to go! He had to stay!

She touched the plaid spread on the floor with her bare foot. The garment was still damp. She bent down and lifted it from the floor. Feeling his gaze upon her, she gathered yard after yard of the fabric into her arms. The weight of it caused a small grunt to rise from her throat. A scent of the earth wafted up from the wool as she rubbed a corner of the fabric between thumb and forefinger. It was surprisingly soft. Slowly she draped the plaid as best she could over the back of an ornately carved chair next to her gown.

"If we're not going to take the kiss further"—Niall came to her side—"what d'ye suggest we do? Play chess?"

Sabine spied the large paper she had taken from Campbell's chamber on the chair's seat, nestled in the folds of her gown. A few pieces of charcoal she had scavenged rested on the small table beside the bed. *"Non.* I have another idea."

She whirled around, her tunic swirling about her legs. "I know something better than chess—" The words she was about to say evacuated her mouth on a whoosh of breath. She had made the mistake of looking at Niall just then.

"So do I." He was resting on the floor, back to her. He faced the hearth, head propped on one arm in casual aplomb. The blanket was spread out beneath him, a corner of it barely covered his lean hips.

Gathering her breath, Sabine blindly groped behind her for the paper. She grabbed it up and clasped it against her belly. Then she reached to the table and took a charcoal stick in her right hand.

"I can tell ye're looking at me," he said. "Come round before the fire, so I can see ye."

Containing her eagerness to rush over to him, she strolled the few steps to the hearth. Slowly she eased down to the warm hearthstones and tucked her legs beneath her tunic. A sliver of her garment touched the edge of Niall's blanket. Finally she raised her eyes and met his gaze.

"Why are ye looking at me like that?" he asked. "Like ye're forgetting to breathe."

She let out a sigh. She did not speak. Instead she chose to study him in silence, just for a moment. She traced her eyes down through the soft whorls of paprika-colored hair on his muscled chest, to the powerful length of his thighs, to the solid knees and calves. He crossed his ankles as if he did not have a care in the world. From the tense lines in his neck Sabine knew that was far from true.

"Show me your truth," she whispered to herself, unfolding the paper and smoothing it on a dry corner of the plaid.

"What?" he asked.

"Please, do not move or speak," she said. "I want to look at you as you are now."

She rose to her feet and padded across the floor. She took the candle in a spiral iron holder from the table beside the bed. She cupped her hand before the flame and eased back down to her place at the hearth. The fire warmed her back. The sight of Niall warmed every other part of her. Carefully she placed the candle beside her.

Brows knitted, Niall eyed her. She took up the charcoal stick and paper.

"What're ye doing?" he asked.

"I want to sketch you. Indulge me, please." She smoothed the paper over her lap. The candle flame illuminated it.

Niall raised one brow. "Oh, aye? Instead of chess? I do know some interesting and challenging moves." He patted the blanket.

She rolled her eyes. "I've no doubt your Highland repertoire is as varied as it is shocking."

She looked down at the blank side of the paper. With the charcoal poised firmly in her twisted fingers, she looked at him.

"May I?"

"Och, be my guest," he said with a shrug. "If this is the only way I can bide my time, then, aye, do yer art if it makes ye happy."

"It does make me happy." And free.

Sabine put the charcoal to paper, not concealing the smile growing on her face. The stick fit well in her gnarled fingers.

Niall had not noticed that she used her twisted hand to sketch. Or was he just ignoring it?

"Aye, now that's what I want to see, a lovely smile," he said. "That makes me happy. There's not much that makes me happy in this world."

"What?" Sabine asked absently. Her gaze shifted constantly up and down, from Niall to the paper. She could not stop sketching for any reason—

"Ye've quite a lovely smile. I havenae seen ye smile much, but when ye do . . ."

Sabine sighed and looked up from the paper.

Niall continued, ". . . When ye remember to smile, 'tis a—"

She laid a finger on his lips. "Shh. I should have told you that the subject should remain still and silent. That's what makes me smile the most." She gave Niall a large smile, just to make them both happy.

She had never sketched in front of anyone, or from anyone since *le maître*. But she had to tuck that memory away or she could not continue. Sabine glanced at Niall. She said a silent prayer to Saint Giles to help her complete this glorious task. Yet, this time, she did not need him. Her heart was enough.

N*iall took her smile and held it close. He would play this* odd French game for a little while. Only a very little while, then he would have to leave this glorious respite and tend to the matters of his clan.

There were some advantages to being in this unfamiliar state, posing for Sabine and her art. Niall could think of two. The first was he could spend a few moments in quiet company with the most beautiful and spirited woman he had ever met. The second was he could plot what he had to do after these precious moments ended.

Campbell was somewhere beyond that locked door, safe in his bed at so late an hour, unaware that a MacGregor was so near. Surprise would be Niall's greatest weapon. It had worked with Sabine. She had not tossed him back out the way he had come.

He stared at her, savored her. Her eyes dragged over his

body, aye, and her hand moved in swift strokes across her paper, but she was not here.

She was herself this night. The rich gown she usually wore lay draped over a chair. His plaid and tunic rested beside her silk brocade. Her lean, lithe body was modestly clad in a long white tunic of fine linen. The firelight turned the soft edges of the pale linen transparent. Soft, perfect curves of her body silhouetted before him, his own private view. She did not know of his advantage. He allowed his gaze to linger a second longer before he looked up at her hair loosened about her shoulders. It framed her face in soft waves of black, like the night waters of Loch Katrine.

Her eyes, cast down on her paper, cast up, looked him over, then cast down again. The damaged hand that held the charcoal was in constant motion. How odd she used that hand, in particular, to make her drawing. He suddenly wanted, more than anything else at that moment, to know her.

"Tell me, Sabine," he whispered, "why are ye here?"

"Hmmm?" She looked up from her paper, her hand stilled.

"Why did ye leave France to come to a country ye so obviously despise?"

"I had no choice in the matter," she said curtly.

"We all have a choice, Sabine. Ye chose to attend Her Majesty. Why?"

She put the paper on the floor and began to rise to her feet. Niall grabbed her wrist and pulled her down beside him.

"And I asked ye, 'why?' "

Sabine sighed. "I did not choose royal servitude." Her warm breath washed over his face. "My father made me leave Chamonix. It is a small village in the shadow of Mont Blanc. My father had built the largest *château* in all of the Alpines. That was where I spent most of my life."

She laid much weight on her words, as if a memory she did not wish to meet again had arisen in her mind.

"Why are ye in service to the queen?"

Sabine's eyes flashed. Aye, he had exposed a nerve, but bloody hell if he was going to let it ruin this time they had together.

"Truth is difficult to face, Sabine." He was so close. His lips brushed hers. Their breaths mingled to one.

"'Tis difficult," she echoed.

He swallowed and wove his fingers through her hair. Her evocative scent, a fragrance that was entirely her own, curled around him. He sighed, eyes closed. When he opened them Sabine was once again looking at his body.

"Through an artist's eyes?" he asked. "Is that how ye see me?"

She averted her eyes from his. *"Oui."*

His smile widened. Dear God, he did enjoy being with her. If only the moment would last.

"Well, if ye must draw me, go ahead. I'm your servant."

He tore off the blanket. Let her see all of his charms.

*S*abine, startled at what Niall had done, allowed curiosity to tear at her. She kept her gaze firm on his azure stare. He dared her with his eyes, dared her to look at what he had just revealed. She wanted to very much, without her artist's eyes, but she would not reveal that to him.

"Crétin," she breathed, a smile on her lips.

"Certainement," he replied.

This would not be the first time she had seen a man undressed. She flexed her twisted fingers, ignored the pain.

It would be her second. And so deliriously different from the first time.

She took a deep breath and continued her sketch, haltingly so.

A distraction was in order. She could not bear to have him staring at her, so very smugly, waiting for her to weaken, to forsake her sketch. She would have to contain the curiosity that beat at her to look at this man with anything other than the eyes of an artist. She would just have to suffer his stare and his dare for the sake of her art.

"Tell me, Niall MacGregor, how do you know French?" she asked, hoping it would distract him from trying to shock her.

His smirk suddenly faded.

"My brother and I learned French in Edinburgh from tutors. Are ye listening to me?"

She shunted her gaze from her sketch back to Niall's eyes. "*Oui,* I am listening."

"Our father sold quite a few cattle to pay for our education . . ." Niall stopped. "Sabine?" Her gaze and sketching scurried back to his navel, and over to the angle of bone and sinew of his hip, the hard line angling down to a thick nest of dark auburn hair. . . .

He suddenly took her right hand in his. She dropped the charcoal stick.

"Am I boring ye?" he asked.

"*N-non,*" she stammered.

"'Tis alright, Sabine, I was boring myself as well," he whispered.

He held her hand close to his lips, his breath warming her fingertips like dozens of butterfly wings brushing her flesh. "I didnae mind learning the French," he said. "It smoothed my burr a bit."

She smiled.

"I like your burr."

Gently he kissed each of her fingertips. His lips barely touched her skin, but it was enough to send a thousand sparks crackling through her. She closed her eyes and waited until the last spark vanished.

"I am glad that you learned the French," she breathed.

"Why?" he asked. He teased her with one final kiss on the back of her hand.

She could barely speak. "It has brought us together, has it not?"

He grinned, sending another flurry of sensation through her. "As I remember, it was a chicken that brought us together."

He cupped the back of her neck and drew her closer. His other hand fell gently to her breast. Sabine let out a small breath, one of yearning. Niall obeyed her and pressed the linen of her tunic to the heated flesh beneath.

Sabine allowed her hand to wander down Niall's chest, over the ridges of muscle, through the soft chest hair. His warmth radiated against her palm.

He kissed her neck, caressing it with his lips, sending bolt upon bolt of lightning sensation through her. Her breath beat the same time as her runaway heart until she thought she would burst. He moved his kisses down to the lacings on her tunic and pulled them open with his teeth.

Sabine told herself that Niall was here because her common sense had taken a respite and let him stay. She would treasure that moment until reality knocked again.

Yet, reality was a dream away. There was nothing between them but the building heat as Niall freed her breasts from behind the linen and took a nipple in his mouth. Sabine fell further away from the reasons why she should tell him to leave. He tugged gently at the bud of engorged flesh with his teeth. Sabine arched her back. He caught her in one strong arm and eased her to the hearth. She never had felt so emboldened and so wicked at the same time. To find such raw temptation in this wild Highlander was a heavenly gift, one she knew was worth cherishing.

Her desire heightened upon itself, building, compelling her to seek that hardened part of him pressing into her thigh. He would not disappoint her. He must have wanted her to venture there as badly as she wanted to go. The tips of her fingers tingled as her hand traveled down to grasp him. Only inches, and she would be there. So tempting, so wicked, so desirous—

The door latch rattled, and broke the spell.

As if buried under a sudden avalanche, Sabine could not catch her breath.

But Niall was far more accustomed to such a swift change of situation. Perchance it was the Highlander way of things, to live one's life always ready for trouble. He leapt to his feet. In one movement, he swept his garments from the chair and tossed them over one shoulder as he took his great blade in hand.

"To the bed," he ordered her in a harsh whisper. "Now."

Stunned, trying to assess what he meant to achieve by such a statement, Sabine rose on shaky legs. By the time she stood upright, he was at the door wielding his sword and . . . a chair?

He dared steal a swift glance over his shoulder.

"Bed," he mouthed, "now!"

He turned about. His plaid and cloak dangled down over his body.

Sabine jumped up into bed. She knelt on top of the blankets and peered through a gap in the bed curtains. Niall shoved the chair under the iron plate that held the latch. It rattled again, then stopped abruptly. The door pushed inward only a fraction. The chair skidded an inch on the planks and stopped.

Sabine looked at Niall, a flush of pride warmed her cheeks for his cleverness at giving them a moment before the inevitable. Moments of joy were all she had these days. He ran toward her, toward the bed.

"I will find ye," he whispered. "On the morrow."

He delivered to her a grin that made her swoon. She gripped the bedpost. Her fingernails dug into the myriad carved fruits and flowers. She would remember that grin as long as she lived—be it a moment or a lifetime.

He disappeared behind the window curtains just as the door burst inward. The chair skittered across the floor.

Sabine gasped, cinching the strings across her breasts. She boldly slipped out of the bed. A guard stepped inside, glancing about, his pike firm in his fist. He caught sight of Sabine, made a rapid bow, then backed out of the chamber. She waited for Lord Campbell to enter.

But unexpected intrusions were quite normal this evening, so she should not have been so shocked when Lady Fleming walked into the chamber.

"'Tis a sorry state this chamber is, girl," she scolded. "But not as sorry as the state in which you have placed yourself before Her Majesty's favor."

"Lady Fleming, I am most disturbed that the queen would think me anything less than her loyal servant," Sabine said.

"You are most disturbed? You? Well, my girl, I wish you had considered the consequences of abandoning the castle without a by-your-leave. Lord Campbell was kind enough to give Her Majesty's court accommodation and use of his household for her entertainments of sport, and you show your gratitude by running off on the first childish whim that strikes your fancy."

Sabine winced. Niall was far from a whim to her, especially after this night when he had stolen a large piece of her heart. She dared not glance toward the curtain.

"M'lady, I assure you that I have not—"

"—Been acting the grateful guest of the lord of this house who is also your intended?" Lady Fleming snorted. "Her Majesty's generosity knows no limits with you, girl, for she has commanded your presence on the morrow's hunt, at Lord Campbell's insistence, I might add."

Lady Fleming bent to pick up the blanket strewn by the hearth, the same blanket Niall had warmed with his body. She lifted it between thumb and forefinger as if it carried the plague. "Why is this bedcovering on the floor?" She held it higher, as if by doing so Sabine would reply more urgently. Instead, the sketch she had made of Niall fluttered out, wafting to the floor, promising disaster should Lady Fleming dare look down. Which, of course, she did. A hawk's sight would have been no less sharp.

Sabine dove down to retrieve it, but Lady Fleming was closer by a few steps and took the advantage. She crumpled the edge of the paper in her fingers as she stared at it, her eyes perilously wide, her lips colorless with rage.

"'Tis nothing, m'lady," Sabine managed, reaching forward for the paper.

"'Tis everything, girl," Lady Fleming hissed. Her stare seethed. The coals in a thousand hearths did not have as much heat.

"Just a sketch, a mere . . . whim, m'lady." Sabine wanted to slip through the cracks in the floor. This was Chamonix all over again. Except Lady Fleming was in the place of her father.

"An abomination! Is this what passes through your thoughts as of late? Such distraction will mean your end, my girl. Remember your father's reason for sending you to the queen's court? Or has there not been enough bloodshed because of your foolishness?"

Sabine shook her head furiously, fighting back hot tears.

"*Non,* m'lady! Do not say such things! My heart guides my hand, always. There is no blood upon it."

"Such pathetic excuses have brought down one man. Shall you bring down another? Lord Campbell is your intended. He has offered the best possible future for you, with the blessings of the queen. He forgave your infirmity. You will wed him."

Sabine thrust her right hand under Lady Fleming's narrowed gaze. "I will not!"

The old Scot took the paper in both fists and tore it into several pieces.

"Non!" Sabine cried. "You cannot!"

"For you, I do this. Accept my pity."

She dropped the pieces to her feet.

"The hunt begins at first light." Lady Fleming pointed to the torn paper on the floor. "And dispose of that French trash!"

With an abrupt turn on her heel and a turn of the outer latch, Lady Fleming left Sabine alone in the chamber.

She fell to the hearth and gathered up the dozen bits of paper the embittered Scot had so ruthlessly torn. Clasping them to her breast, she raced across the floor to the curtains, knowing that Niall was well gone the way in which he came.

She stared out of the open window. All that greeted her was the open blackness of night. Chill wind blew in, circling about her body, threatening to tear the papers from her hand and cast them out over the stone sash.

Sabine held tight to the torn sketch, a most indelible memory of this night. She also held Niall's hasty Highland vow that he would find her. She wanted to believe him, to know that she was not alone in the world.

She closed the window and the curtains. She took her gown from the chair beside the bed. She would mend the sketch with a little flour-and-water paste, or hide glue from the scullery. She tore open a seam at the top of her gown and secreted the papers and a charcoal stick between the layers of silk and velvet. They would hide over her heart.

Like an obedient royal servant, she took to her bed for a good night's sleep.

"If I were truly obedient to my queen, if I were my father's daughter," she whispered to her pillow in lieu of prayer, "I would burn the sketch in the hearth myself. Yet, I shall show my loyalty to Mary in another way. I shall save her life . . . together with Niall."

Her throat tightened at the thought, and her right hand

ached. She clenched her fingers and shut her eyes. Tomorrow, she feared, would bring a storm down upon her and Niall. Tonight she would dream of him and nothing more. Dreams and the torn sketch were all she knew she could keep of him, no matter what tomorrow brought.

chapter 10

At What Cost Valor?

The morning sun broke through the forest and warmed Niall's face. He squinted at the rays that illuminated the edges of the departing storm clouds. Streaks of light, like God's veil, escaped from the puffy, violet clouds and spread across the heather that surrounded him. The raw, powerful beauty of the Highlands after a storm strengthened his soul. It always had. But today he felt as if he looked at the land with new eyes. Sabine had awakened a new confidence in him. He took a deep breath and called it forth.

"I have more than my clan to protect," he said, to believe it himself. "I have my queen to protect and, God help me, I want to protect Sabine."

That exceptional moment when he first met her on Leith wharf seemed so long ago instead of little more than a fortnight and five. So much had happened since then. He felt as if he lived on the edge of forever with Sabine at his side. He allowed himself a foolish dream now and then.

He climbed onto his horse. His cloak weighed heavy on his shoulders, the hem dew dampened.

Niall gripped the reins and waited. He stared at the forest, at the thick stand of pine and ash, at the tangle of undergrowth that grew about the slender trunks. He spied a deer trail, a thin cut through the foliage, and nodded to himself. Beyond the forest, several miles away, lay Castle Campbell Dubh. Sabine was the one guest in that vile place who he felt was on his side. And he hoped Rory would return soon and tell him she was just beyond that forest, down the hill, and waiting with the other royals in Glen Fuil—Glen of Blood.

The sound of distant hoofbeats caused him to look north, to Rory on his horse, rounding the trees as fast as Beelzebub's messenger.

Niall straightened his shoulders and waited. Thoughts buzzed about his head. His need to find proof against Campbell last night had failed albeit gloriously with Sabine in his arms. He would not give up until he got the proof he needed to expose Campbell for what he was: offal, shat out into the Highlands by generations of those just like him. The question was when? And how? The *how* vexed him the most.

Rory thundered up to him, then halted his mount, sending up a spray of soil and bits of heather.

"A bonny morn to ye," he gasped. "Glad to see ye arenae Campbell's prisoner."

"Where are they?" Niall asked immediately.

Rory pointed to the forest. "The royal hunting party, dozens of them, dressed well enough to shame the rising sun, are coming to Glen Fuil from the east. They left their horses, carriages, and I don't know what all, on top of the eastern rise. In minutes they should have made their way into the glen. Ye know what bothers me, though?"

"What?" Niall asked. He did not have to ask though. He knew.

"Glen Fuil is a wee glen. There's an abandoned croft on one end and a stone circle on the other, and not much heath in between. Any farmer Campbell hired to chase deer down into that glen might get slaughtered with their quarry."

"Aye," Niall sighed. "I knew Campbell would choose that glen, to insure the queen's success in the hunt." He looked at Rory expectantly.

His friend nodded. "Aye, she's there. All of the queen's attendants are there. She's not with them though. She's with Campbell."

The world dropped out from under Niall. He swallowed and asked, "In the glen?"

"Aye. She was beside him . . . *is* beside him."

"Beside the Devil himself," Niall whispered. "Foolish, foolish lass."

"Why do I think that jealousy isnae the reason for that look in yer eyes?"

"She's in danger," Niall said.

"Campbell is the enemy of yer clan," Rory said. "His influence couldnae go as far as France, to Sabine's clan, could it?"

Niall managed a smirk. "There are no clans in France."

"Then why is the lass in danger?"

"She's beside Campbell, bound to marry him," he replied. "'Tis much danger, aye?"

"Aye."

"I've got to go," Niall said.

"To Glen Fuil?"

He looked at his friend. "And ye as well."

"In Glen Fuil?"

"Aye."

Rory glanced to the forest, to the sun, to the heather, then back to Niall. He looked as if pondering that question ached his mind. Finally he asked, "What d'ye want me to do?"

"Go to the south of the glen. Keep hidden. Watch Campbell. Watch the queen. I need your eyes."

"Watch for what?"

"Anything unusual."

"Oh, aye . . . unusual. That's helpful," Rory's words faded. Then he snapped to life. "D'ye want me to go to the south of the glen, in the direction of the stone circle, thereabouts?"

"Go there, watch. I'll go to the north end."

"And if something happens, something *unusual*?"

Niall stared at the forest. "Then just follow my lead."

"Will ye watch that fine lassie as well?" Rory asked.

He did not reply. Niall had wanted to believe that this morning Sabine would not, by some miracle, be in that glen. He knew, as a loyal subject, he would step in harm's way for his queen. His heart told him to do no less for Sabine.

• • •

*S*abine bowed her head toward the dewy ground. The heather with its tiny, delicate, bell-shaped flowers, met her gaze. The color was the exact blue of Niall's eyes.

"Risc," Mary said.

Sabine rose from her curtsy and stood with the many others, including Lord Campbell, who was by her side. But not in her thoughts, she reminded herself. She stole a furtive glance at his profile, at the patrician nose and dark, neatly trimmed beard. There was nothing inspiring about him. His uninteresting face did not compel her to flex her gnarled fingers and reach for a charcoal stick and paper. She knew what lay beneath his facade. He was wholly predictable to her now . . . too predictable. Such knowledge crumpled her soul. There was no art here, only an absorbing darkness named Lord John Campbell. And she was to marry him.

Slowly she reached down and touched her gown over her heart, over her mended sketch of Niall. She had arisen before the rest of the castle and repaired her precious drawing with a small amount of hide glue she found in the scullery.

"Bona sera, signorina."

Sabine looked down at Rizzio, the little Italian, at the jaunty way he wore his velvet cap, at his saffron satin cape tied over one shoulder with a gold cord. His garments matched his jovial face.

"Bona sera, signore Rizzio," she replied.

Campbell moved closer to Sabine, his arm brushing hers.

"Leave us, Rat-zzio," he said under his breath.

The little Italian hung his head and joined the gallery of onlookers.

"Pest!" Campbell hissed. "Freak."

Sabine looked at him aghast. No truer bastard lived in Scotland, 'twas obvious to her, yet, she feared, to no one else, especially her queen.

"We wish the hunt to begin," Mary announced. "The morning will not wait."

"But the sun would wait to rise and set for you, Royal Highness," Campbell said. "If you commanded it."

Mary smiled demurely from beneath the brim of a green velvet hat lavished with pearls and peacock feathers. Lord

Darnley stood beside her. Sabine wondered if his face could hold any expression other than boredom.

"Explain to us again this Highland way of the hunt," Mary said. Then added, "For Lord Darnley's benefit."

Lord Darnley straightened, glanced at Campbell, then gave Sabine a small smile from the shadow of his wide-brimmed hat. She hastily looked away to a large pile of rubble a dozen or more paces away, to the west. Anything to distract her, anything . . . was Niall out there as he had promised? She stared hard at the rubble, at the forest beyond, her heart beating a little faster.

"Well, Your Majesty, it's quite simple . . . ," Campbell began.

Sabine narrowed her gaze at the rubble, which was not a haphazard pile of stones. Timbers, half rotted, thrust out from the moss and vine-covered remains of a stone wall. This was the remains of a cottage, a humble Highland dwelling.

". . . My tenants are in the west wood as I speak," Campbell continued. "Up the hill . . ." He pointed toward the ruined cottage and up to the forested hill that bordered the small valley.

Sabine glanced at the forest, which loomed up the impossibly steep hill. They had entered the valley from the east, on a heathered slope, gentle in comparison to the wall of tree and earth to the west. Nothing short of an Alpine goat could traverse such a landscape.

". . . They will chase the deer, and if Your Majesty is fortunate, the great roebuck from the forest," Campbell said with a swell of pride in his voice. "Your arrow should bring one down quite easily, as your repute of the hunt is far and wide."

Sabine's stomach rolled at the idea.

"What fun, " Lord Darnley sneered.

"When will this happen?" Mary asked. "How soon?"

"I will signal your archer," Campbell replied. "He will send an arrow with a red silk aloft. The hunt will commence."

Mary smiled. "Lord John," she said, "have you something for our Sabine?"

"Perhaps my gift will make the *mademoiselle* more agreeable to the hunt," Campbell said. "I sense her hesitation."

Sabine shunted her gaze to her intended.

You should sense nothing but my contempt, she thought. Nothing short of a miracle could make her agreeable to anything this hopeless day.

He placed a hand under his cape as a sly smile played upon his lips. He looked directly into Sabine's eyes.

She dared not look at his face for more than a moment, lest she run screaming into the forest on the other side of this small valley. She steeled herself for the gift and glanced at her queen, so regal, so very unaware of the serpent in her court. She glanced nervously at the dozens of courtiers, at the pages distributing archery equipment. Then she looked to the forested hill. Was Niall there, hiding in the pine shadows, concealing himself behind the bracken?

And he should stay well hid, she thought quickly. What good could he do if he showed himself? He would be taken prisoner, or he would die. That would not do for the queen or for herself.

"Mademoiselle!" Campbell snapped.

Sabine jumped. *"Oui?* M'lord."

"It seems the landscape has enchanted our Sabine, as much as it has us," Mary commented with a refined laugh. "These Highlands are most captivating."

Sabine nodded to her queen.

"Yes . . . yes, well, if I may, Your Most Gracious Highness. I'd like to present the *mademoiselle* with my gift," Campbell continued.

"Oh, yes, Lord John, please . . . do carry on," Mary said with a flip of one bejeweled hand.

With a flourish Campbell produced a slender bundle from beneath his cape. He unwrapped the wool and dropped it to the ground. In his hand he held a bow and three arrows.

Sabine did not know what to say or how to react. This man and her queen, no doubt, actually meant for her to hunt! She had just assumed that she was to join the royal hunt as a spectator.

She forced a thin smile of gratitude to her lips, nodded to Campbell, but could not utter a word of thanks. He flourished the bow and three arrows under her nose, then up in the air for everyone to see. There were polite nods of approval all around.

Sabine suppressed a shudder and stole a glance at the forest.

"You've rendered her speechless," the queen said. "No more delays. To the hunt." She regarded Campbell. "Where shall we be at best advantage?"

Sabine stood firm. Her best advantage was beside Mary.

"Ah, yes, Your Majesty," Campbell replied. "You will be most able to bring down one roe, perhaps two, from this very spot. They will most likely run into the center of the glen. Here the sun will be at your back. However, I most respectfully suggest that your entourage stand further down the meadow so as not to impede your success."

"Do you, Lord John?" Mary asked, one ginger brow raised. She glanced at Lord Darnley, who stood picking at his doublet. "Lord Darnley and myself shall remain at this spot and await our quarry. *Signore* Rizzio may take my ladies to a place they feel is suitable." She paused and glanced at Sabine, who was inching closer to her. "Lord John, escort our Sabine across the valley. You will not only have vantage of the quarry, but will have opportunity to speak with her. We fear that marriage holds as much appeal for her as does the hunt."

Sabine stared at Mary. Her queen knew her all too well.

"We expect that, for her own good, she will find marriage and the hunt quite appealing soon," the queen concluded with a snap to the last word. And with a flip of her hand, she waved all her court away.

Sabine did not move at first. How could she protect Mary from the opposite side of this small valley? She would be a good quarter mile away.

She turned and finally looked at Lord Campbell, who offered his arm and a vapid smile. At least he would not be near the queen either. Small comfort, but comfort nonetheless.

She walked in silence toward the other side of the valley. Now and then she glanced over her shoulder at Mary and Lord Darnley, who stood, heads close together, in hushed conversation.

Campbell took her arm and roughly urged her through the heather. "Show your pleasure at Her Majesty's graciousness."

"I will not be happy as long as I have you beside me," Sabine said on a wave of anger surging inside her. "Marrying me will only bring you one step nearer the queen, and further from my heart."

"I do not need you to place me nearer the queen," Campbell laughed. "Foolish, girl. Don't you realize that the queen offered me your hand because she wants to be one step nearer her Highland people and one step further from France? 'Twas not a promise to your father, I assure you."

"Impossible," Sabine snorted. But she knew it was true. Niall was right. She was a pawn for Mary.

"Keep that tongue back in France, my dear. It has no place in my castle."

Sabine struggled in his hold. "Why do *you* wish to marry me?"

"'Tis quite simple, my dear," he said, face close to hers. His hideous breath swept across her on a puff of breeze. He gnashed his teeth in the most uncivilized manner. "A man would be a fool not to want you in his bed, not to want you to bear his heirs . . ."

She shuddered. Campbell's heirs? She would rather die than be responsible for bringing his spawn into the world.

Campbell's words were distant. His harsh tone was a wall between his voice and his sincerity. Sabine doubted if anything about this man was sincere other than his sincere effort to be a *bâtard*.

He practically dragged her the remaining steps to the other side of the valley. Sabine glanced over her shoulder. The queen and Lord Darnley were no more than the size of dolls on the heathered landscape. She turned her gaze back and stopped. What was this before her?

Stones. A circle of them, standing at attention in a wide ring. The stones were twice as tall as a man and three times as wide. They were gray monoliths with weathered edges and a soft patina of moss and lichen. Curious, Sabine took a few steps toward them. They rested on top of a small rise, a dozen and a half strides from her.

"Go sit among them," Campbell sneered. "Revel in Highland spiritual legend and lore, if you must. They've only brought great tragedy, or so I've been told."

"How could stones cause tragedy?" she asked, mesmerized by them, if only for a moment, taken from her worries.

"A long time ago, in the time of the Bruce, two clans met inside the stone circle and perished," he replied.

Sabine shifted her gaze up at him. "They disappeared?"

"Aye, by blood and sword, all because of one thing they could not have."

"What?"

"Love." He said the word as if it bittered his tongue.

She winced. "Love, m'lord?" she stammered. "Impossible."

"'Tis an old legend. Love is for naught. The legend of two clans proves it. Clans Lamont and Lachlan aren't the powers they once were because of love. Now, their ancestors are scattered to the wind because two of their kind thought love would unite them. A hapless union, all because of trifles like love. Certain factions of society should never mix. Don't you agree?"

Sabine blinked. What did Campbell suspect? If he knew anything he did not let on. That was what frightened her.

"Love has brought down many leaders. It steals their common sense and fills them with feelings." Campbell tossed a glance at the queen and Lord Darnley.

Sabine turned from the stones and glanced across the heather at her queen. The breeze stirred a few strands of hair from her braid. "Will love bring you down, m'lord?"

"It will not," he snapped. "Because I don't believe in such foolish things. My father never—" He bit off his words and took her roughly by the arm.

Sabine stared at him, surprised. She and her intended had one thing in common. Only one thing. Her father never loved her either.

Campbell cleared his throat. "This hunt is long overdue. Time we began."

He looked toward the queen. "Time we began," he whispered through his teeth and released Sabine.

A chill sliced up her spine.

Aye, ye bastard, time ye show all these good royal folk yer true character," Niall whispered. "And by the way, if ye touch Sabine like that again, ye bastard . . ."

He bit his bottom lip and hunkered down over his horse's neck. The rubbled, mossy remains of a cottage provided ample cover for him to see the proceedings of the morning. Fortunately for him, the proceedings could not see him. Sabine had looked his way, and he was certain she had not seen him either.

Two of Scotland's elite strolled in his direction and stopped a few paces from his hiding place. Niall grimaced at the sweet endearments spoken between the queen and the young fop with her. He jerked his gaze across the small glen at Campbell, who raised one hand high in the air. He slashed it down like an ax to the block. One of the royal archers raised his bow and shot an arrow festooned with a ribbon of red silk high into the air. It soared toward the forest.

"Let the hunt commence!" Campbell shouted.

Niall wondered if the deer and roe had also heard the command as he saw Campbell force a bow into Sabine's hands. She managed to hold the bowstring in her twisted right hand and held the yoke firmly in her other hand. Campbell wrapped his thin arms around her and placed an odd white arrow to the string. He stepped back and folded his arms across his chest. Sabine stood frozen to the spot where he had left her. She looked to be posing for a painting, a goddess, Diana of the hunt.

Niall squinted across the glen. Sabine was about three dozen paces from him, but he could see her expression. Fear.

He gripped the reins of his mount with one fist and silently slid his claymore from the sheath on his back. Thunder rose in the forest behind him, a cacophony of shouting men and frightened beasts pounding the earth.

He did not take Sabine from his sight. She looked to the forest. The thunder grew, interspersed with the lightning crack of breaking branches.

Niall gripped the claymore tighter. His mount shifted beneath him.

Campbell was shouting something to Sabine, but Niall could not hear over the din of man and beast. He stared at her. She was struggling to thread the bowstring. Her twisted hand failed her for several attempts before success. She held her weapon at the ready. Campbell stood right beside her. He was yelling in her ear. Niall saw his thin lips form one word.

"Shoot!"

An arrow whizzed past his hiding place. It speared the center of a great roe's chest. He clearly heard the queen squeal in triumph as the beast went down into the heather with an earth-shaking thud.

He looked back at Sabine. She was doing Campbell's bidding. She shot her arrow . . . Niall grinned . . . into the bastard's foot.

"Well done," he mouthed.

He suddenly broke his stare. An arrow, white and gleaming like hers, soared up from the standing stones behind her, its archer unseen. Niall looked up as the arrow sailed high into the gray sky. His practiced eye followed its intended path, downward, toward the queen.

"Rach air muin," he cursed under his breath.

He jerked the reins and raised his claymore high above his head.

There was only one thing for him to do. But at what cost?

chapter 11

Flight

"Non!" *Sabine breathed, throwing aside her bow and racing forward, Campbell's howls behind her.*

Niall and his mount soared over the moss-covered wall, waving his great Highland sword over his head. He raced directly toward the queen.

"Non!"

Niall, the Highland *sauvage,* was going to murder Mary. Why had Sabine trusted him? Why was she such a fool!

She ran faster, gown bunched in her hands, her throat burning, tears swelling in her eyes. He had lied to her!

Niall slammed his horse to a stop before the queen, sword raised. Lord Darnley screamed and crumpled to the ground.

Sabine raised her left arm. *"Non!"* she gasped.

She stumbled to the heather, bashing her knee against a rock. Despite the pain, she scrambled to her feet, limped a few steps more and fell just short of Niall's mount. The Highlander looked down at her, winked one blue eye, then looked to the sky just as an arrow, gleaming white like the one Campbell had gifted her, stabbed through his stained tunic into the meaty part of his right shoulder. The hard "thunk" sound reverberated sickly in Sabine's ears. Instantly she knew her eyes had betrayed her. Niall had ridden to save her queen. He had made good on his vow. And now he was going to die.

Or not.

Niall reared his horse, scattering the queen and all about her out of the way. All except Lord Darnley, who remained in the heather. Sabine stood just as Campbell's angry words rang behind her, just as Niall, arrow in his shoulder, rode back in the direction he came, to the forest.

"Get him!" Campbell bellowed to the guards who ran across the valley, pikes in their hands.

They were no match for Niall and his warhorse, well gone. Sabine never felt so alone as she watched him flee.

"Arrest the MacGregor!" Campbell screamed, as if that would make the royal guards run any faster into the wood. He limped to a stop beside Sabine and grabbed her roughly by the arm. He looked at Mary, who silently observed the melee about her, and Lord Darnley at her feet. Campbell pointed at Sabine, then to a guard who had taken his place just behind the queen. "Arrest the *mademoiselle*, too! She tried to shoot the queen with her arrow!"

"*Comment?* What?!" Sabine cried. "This, I did not do—"

"Fortunately, the *mademoiselle*'s arrow struck that Mac-Gregor before it could dispatch Your Majesty to an untimely end," Campbell declared.

Mary stared at Sabine. "If one did not know better," she said. "One would think that Highlander had taken the arrow for us."

"He did, Your Majesty!" Sabine cried. "I know this to be true!"

"How do you know this?" Mary asked. "How know you this *Highlander*?" She had stepped too near Sabine's heart and made her mute. There was nothing she could say at the moment to escape this horrid predicament.

Lady Fleming and the other Marys quickly joined their queen, voices steeped in hushed concern. The old Scot, who had seen the sketch of Niall, gave Sabine the nastiest stare. She glanced away. Her world was splitting apart again. This was a disaster to match the one she had lived through years ago in Chamonix. Only this one, she feared would mean her end.

"I know not the Highlander, Your Majesty," Sabine protested. She meant she knew him not in the biblical sense. She would never lie to her queen. "I saw what he did. He saved your life."

Campbell tightened his grip on her arm. "And you tried to take it! 'Twas your arrow!"

"'Tis a falsehood, m'lord!" Sabine shouted wrenching from his grasp. "'Tis a truth you should be pointing at yourself!"

"*Mademoiselle* Sabine!" Mary cried. "Kindly remember your place!"

"But Your Majesty, I . . . I . . ." Sabine could not find the words to defend herself. With all of these disbelieving eyes staring down at her, she may as well have tried to climb Mont Blanc in the middle of winter.

"The arrow is yours, is it not? And do you confess to know this Highland outlaw named MacGregor?" Mary asked.

"Your Majesty, I do not understand—" Sabine began.

"We had hoped for so much more from you. Your late father had hoped the same. You are such a disappointment to us all." Mary stole a glance at Sabine's right hand. "You will have to be confined until your innocence or your . . . guilt is proven."

Sabine clasped her hands together as best as she could. Would that she held real, undeniable proof against Campbell, her world would not be so bleak!

"Most Gracious Majesty, I would never—" She suddenly unclasped her hands and held her right hand out to her queen. "I could never—"

"How do you explain the wound to my foot?" Campbell shouted. "Your hand with the arrow is fine despite your malady."

Sabine glanced down. The side of his leather boot was slashed open, exposing the arch of his foot and a thin line of blood. She had simply grazed him. He needed a cobbler more than a healer.

"Take the *mademoiselle* to my castle," Campbell ordered the guard. "Place her deep within the gaol."

The guard, pike in hand, stepped briskly over to Sabine.

The thunder of hooves suddenly reverberated in her ears.

"Blowing hot wind across the glen, ye Campbell bastard?" Niall shouted from behind her.

Sabine whirled around, her heart flooding with relief, her mind seeing disaster.

Niall rode toward them, at full gallop.

She stood very still, in his path. He was putting his own head on the block by returning to the valley. Niall was indeed foolish . . . or incredibly brave.

"Niall," she breathed. "*My* protector."

The guard who approached her leapt back, out of the way of Niall's horse. Sabine did not move. She closed her eyes.

In seconds she was soaring, her body clasped in one very strong arm. She imagined herself flying from this nasty scene. The man who had saved her queen's life was saving her from the gaol and certain horrible fate. No one would believe her innocence. She was a cripple, suspect with one glance. As Campbell had said about Rizzio, she was a *freak*. No one believed a freak, no one but a Highland outlaw.

Sabine landed soundly behind Niall. She clasped her arms around his taut waist so she would not bounce off. She glanced at the stunned and angry faces below her.

"Listen to *mademoiselle* Sabine, Yer Royal Highness!" Niall shouted. "She knows who the pestilence is in yer court!"

He reared his horse back around, toward the forest on the impossibly steep hill. She could not go there, to his wilderness. Where else would he take her? To France? That was the only place she belonged. And Niall still held her gold, hidden in his Highland home, no doubt.

"Bloody bastard!" Campbell hissed. "Guards! Kill him!"

"This is such a nice day," Niall said. "Why ruin it by dying?"

He reared his horse. Sabine held him tighter, suddenly aware that she was making a horrible mistake. The suppressed anger on her queen's face told her so. There was no proving her innocence now, no proving that she heard Campbell's plot to murder the queen.

"Watch your back, Your Majesty!" Niall shouted. "Choose your minions with care!"

"Get him!" Campbell bellowed at the guards. But the order

was nothing short of delusion. Niall would not be his prisoner this day. Neither would Sabine.

Was that what she really wanted? To be a hunted outlaw like Niall?

He gave her no time to ponder that dilemma when he spirited her away from the heathered valley into the dark pine forest, past a group of confused guards. Any defense of her innocence evaporated behind her. And that, she decided, was a very, very bad thing.

Sabine pounded Niall's back as they climbed the forested hill. *"Arrête!"* she shouted. *"Arrête!* . . . Stop!"

Ignoring her plea, Niall hunched over the bobbing horse neck. Sabine had no choice but to mirror him. She peered around his linen and plaid at the arrow that protruded from his shoulder. She glanced at his face, in profile, at the expression that betrayed no pain, just stubborn determination to get wherever he was going. Sabine clasped her arms tighter about his waist.

They rode deeper into the forest and higher up the hill. She closed her eyes and felt the horse ride down and up and down again. She prayed her belly would not betray her and wished desperately to wipe away this horrid, topsy turvy day.

Sabine had no idea how long or far they had ridden when Niall stopped the horse in a thick glade of pine and bracken.

"This is a good place," he said.

Sabine glanced at the trees, undergrowth, more trees, and more undergrowth. The clouds and thick boughs overhead blotted out the sun, giving the forest a gloomy, foreboding air.

"Non," she said. "We cannot stop here. You must take me back to my queen."

"Ye can walk back," he said under his breath.

"Comment? What did you say?"

Niall reached up and took the arrow protruding from his shoulder in his fist.

"What are you—?" Sabine began.

"Wheesht!" he hissed, then snapped the end of the arrow off.

She gasped. Slowly Niall shifted to the right and fell from the horse carrying Sabine with him. They thumped to a carpet of moss and pine needles. She immediately rose to her knees beside him. He lay faceup on the ground, staring, his eyes a dull gray-blue. His breaths came out in hard gasps. She touched his forehead. The flesh beneath her fingertips was cool and clammy. She looked down at his tunic, at the stump of the arrow protruding from a ragged bloody hole in the cloth.

"Sabine," he whispered, startling her.

"*Oui,* Niall?" she said. She smoothed back his hair, when all she wanted to do was shout at him for being so stupid for placing himself in the arrow's path, for being so blindly brave to protect her queen. And she wished to kiss him for that as well.

"I need your help," he said, as if it pained him to admit it.

He propped himself up on his elbows. Sabine reached out to help him, them withdrew her hands.

"You should lie down," she said.

He shook his head and scooted back a little until he rested his back against the trunk of a pine tree. "No time for that," he said. "I'll rest after. . . ."

"After what?" she asked, fearing his reply.

"After ye push the arrow the rest of the way."

She shuddered. "Rest of the way?"

"Through my shoulder. Letting the arrow continue its journey is the only way to get it out. I cannae do it on my own." He tipped his head back against the tree. His chest rose and fell with his heavy breathing. He relaxed his arms at his sides, his legs were splayed on the pine needle carpet.

"*Non!*" she exclaimed. "I cannot do that!"

"Get my dirk," he rasped.

"Your—?"

"Dirk. Knife. It's tucked in my leg wrapping . . . my right leg."

Sabine looked down at the powerful, muddy legs protruding from the woolen skirt he wore, his kilt. A ragged combination of leather, wool, and fur covered his calves. The leather-wrapped handle of a knife stuck out of the covering about his right calf, just like he said. Sabine reached down and took the handle in her left hand and slid it carefully out. Her knuckles brushed the auburn hair on his leg. What did he need this knife for? She was not going to do his bidding with it, *certainement*!

She held the knife out to him.

He stared at her and did not raise a hand to take it. Instead, he opened his mouth.

"Comment?" she asked.

"Put it in my mouth," he gasped.

Confused, she held the leather handle and placed the blade close to his lips.

"No," he said, looking at her as if she were completely mad. "The handle."

"Oh." She laid the handle between his teeth.

He clamped down, and shifted his eyes to the arrow stump.

Every part of Sabine's body, inside and out, froze in horror. *"Non.* I cannot."

He nodded furiously. That seemed to sap him of all his energy. He slumped a little, then strained to right himself, pushing air out of his nose.

Sabine took a deep breath. Niall needed her help. She had to put her squeamish fears aside, or else he could die and leave her alone in this Scottish wilderness. That was the very least she could do for the man who had taken her away from certain imprisonment, perhaps execution. She could help him, and then he could help her get back to France . . . or find proof that it was Campbell, and not her, who plotted to murder the queen.

She grasped a great wad of his plaid, cinched over his shoulder, and bunched it over the arrow stump. She held it there with her left hand.

Niall looked into her eyes. All she saw in those blue depths was pain on top of pain. He reached up with a trembling hand and took the knife from his mouth.

"Dinnae worry," he breathed.

"I am not worrying," she lied.

"They may come after me," he rasped. "But they'll never find me. They never have. And now, they willnae find ye. . . ." He lifted his arm and rested the back of his hand against her cheek. "Sometimes hiding is the best course. 'Tis what my clan has done for generations. 'Tis what we do best." He managed a weak grin.

"This is no time for levity," she said through the tightness in her throat.

"Oh, aye, 'tis all we have. Now, bear up, do this thing I ask ye. Wrap the wound when ye're done. I'll be alright. Ye'll be safe. 'Tis all that matters for now." He gasped in another breath. "Now, use both hands, quick and sharp about it."

"Or you may pass out."

"That, Sabine, is a forgone conclusion." He placed the knife handle back in his mouth and gave her a brief, weak nod.

Both hands. Sabine drew in a long breath and placed her right hand over her left, over the wad of wool over the arrow stump. She captured Niall's stare in her own. Bravery, fortitude, were in abundant supply in these Highlands if Niall was an example.

She gritted her teeth and pressed her hands down. He squeezed his eyes shut, leaving her to do this thing alone. She pushed. A low moan escaped through his teeth gnashed around the knife handle. *Quick and sharp,* he had said. She pushed hard, the end of the arrow pressing against the wad of wool, against her palm, painful but nothing compared to what Niall was facing right now. Sabine squeezed her eyes shut and placed all of her weight onto the arrow.

Her right hand suddenly seized on her, cramping so tightly that she saw stars in the darkness behind her eyelids. *Non!* her mind screamed. Sabine prayed to Saint Giles and forced her gnarled fingers to flex against the knotted muscles beneath her knuckles. She pushed until all she heard were Niall's muffled moans and the thunderous beating of her own heart.

She dared open her eyes to the sight of Niall slumped against the tree trunk. His eyes closed, coppery bristle-covered jaw slack, the knife resting in his lap. Sabine looked tentatively at the back of his shoulder, at the blood-covered arrow protruding forth. With trembling fingers, she pulled it the rest of the way out.

Tears rolled down her burning cheeks as she wrapped the wool tightly around Niall's bleeding shoulder. "Don't you dare die!" she cried.

She wrapped the wounds tightly, forcing the blood flow to slow.

"You're an idiot for riding in the path of that arrow! The queen showed not one ounce of appreciation! Why would she? You're an outlaw!"

She tied off the plaid as best she could, her twisted fingers crying out for her to stop using them. But she ignored the pain and smoothed back Niall's thick, cinnamon hair. The hue was so precious and rare, so like his spirit. He was fading from her, and there was little she could do.

"Niall," she whispered. "Speak to me. Tell me something to make me laugh. Tell me something *en français* or with your lovely burr."

"The circle of stones in Glen Fuil," he whispered so quietly that the pine boughs overhead in the breeze almost drowned him out.

"*Oui,* what about them?" she asked, lips brushing his whiskered cheek. All she could smell was blood, no longer Niall's scent of the earth, of his spirit.

"I'm sure Campbell filled ye with lies about them. Love did prevail," he rasped.

"You could not have heard us—" she began.

"I know the sense of what he told ye. I saw his face, saw yours. Enemies can and have united with success even with love, like Clans Lamont and Lachlan." He coughed. "Campbell has never chosen to believe it. My father went to him to seek peace . . . he got death. . . ."

"Do not speak of such things now. Save your strength."

Niall managed a small grin. "Aye, I willnae . . . yet, the proof we seek against Campbell is behind that stone circle . . . the wielder of the arrow I took for the queen . . . is the proof . . ."

He choked out a breath. "*Adieu, ma chérie.*" Niall slowly closed his eyes, blocking out the blue from her.

"*Non,* Niall, *non!* You must remain with me. I'll be lost, so terribly lost without you."

She rested her cheek against his. Tears rolled freely down her face. Her life had taken a sudden, unpredictable turn, and he was leaving her to deal with it alone.

"Niall MacGregor, you cannot go," she sobbed. "You cannot . . . *mon Dieu* . . . I need you."

His chest rose and fell with shallow breaths. Sabine tightened the wool further against his wound.

Then she felt a presence other than Niall's.

Her mind screamed, *Campbell*! She whirled around. Her hand still pressed to Niall's shoulder.

Rory sat on his horse. His face was pale, bathed in sweat. He looked down at her as if he were seeing her for the first time. His face did not show relief or concern. He glanced away from her, his dark brows were knotted together. His mouth was tight in concentration. He seemed trying to decide which path to take through the forest. As far as Sabine could tell, there were no paths in this forest, none that she could see.

chapter 12

In Niall's Wilderness

Rory took Niall and Sabine on an endless ride to a small valley surrounded by imposing, misty mountains. In the valley lay a huddle of cottages. To Sabine they looked nothing more than mossy piles of stone topped with thatch. The only evidence that these piles of stone and turf were dwellings was the thin curls of smoke rising from stone chimneys and collecting in the valley like a shroud.

Rory rode right up to the rickety door of one cottage, took Niall from the saddle of his horse, and carried him over his shoulder inside. He did not say a word to Sabine. She chewed her lip, deciding whether to go in or flee. Her need to be with Niall, to see him healed, was far greater than the fear of what could lay beyond that rickety door.

She quickly dismounted onto the loamy ground. She determinedly stepped inside and stood in a shadowy corner of the most humble dwelling she had ever seen. Several women gave her brief but scouring glances before they hunched over the rough-hewed bed where Rory had placed Niall. Sabine immediately realized she was as welcome here as a leper at a banquet. She tilted her chin up a little and remained in the shadows observing, listening to the strange guttural language these women spoke to each other, to Rory. She also could not help but take in the scent of smoke and cooking meat as well as the strange language.

The air inside the small abode was thick with musty peat smoke. Sabine strained to see Niall through it and around the gray wool and linen these women wore, all of them long in years. One of them might be Niall's mother, but Sabine could not tell which. Perhaps none of them were his mother. Niall had never mentioned that she could still be alive.

The sound of fabric ripping combined with stunned gasps made her jump and step forward a little, to get a better look. Rory stepped back, bumped into her, and gave her a harsh glare before he walked to the hearth with its large cauldron over a pile of orange, smouldering coals. He knelt before the coals, his back to Sabine. She returned her gaze to the women and Niall.

They had removed his clothes, or so she assumed from her limited vantage. The wool plaid and stained tunic lay in a heap at the foot of the bed. One of the women had retrieved a wooden bowl with water and a rag. It quickly disappeared into the huddle.

Their strange language rose in the smoky air, but Sabine could not tell if their tones were concern or anguish. She listened harder. They spoke in steady voices as if their task was one common to them. One of them placed the bowl and rag on the earthen floor. The water was now crimson, the rag the same color. Sabine took a step forward. Her own blood pumped through her body so hard she could hear it rushing with the fierceness of a spring river. Was Niall dead or alive? She had to know.

"Step back," Rory said suddenly from beside her, his voice gruff.

Sabine did as she was told. The Highlander held an iron poker, its tip brilliant orange.

"What are you going to do with that?" she asked, eyes wide, heart pounding. She feared she knew the answer. She had heard of cauterizing wounds with a hot poker, she just never expected to witness it.

Rory shouted to the women, all of whom bent to Niall and held him down. All Sabine could see of him was his pale profile, his coppery hair darkened by sweat. His eyes were closed, and a grimy rag was between his teeth.

Rory jabbed the poker down onto the hole in front of Niall's shoulder. Sabine clenched her eyes shut and heard the sizzle and the deep, wounded-animal moan that escaped Niall's mouth. She opened one eye. Every tendon on Niall's strong neck stood out, his ginger brows knitted together in anguish, his teeth clamped down hard on the rag. She flexed her fingers, and closed her eyes remembering a time when her own pain had been so hard. The most difficult part was the living after. . . .

Rory shouted to the women. Sabine opened both eyes. Was this over?

They sat Niall up. One of the women, with all the worries of the world etched across her sullen face, held him tight to her bosom. The side of his face, eyes closed, rested against her generous breasts. His arms dangled limply, like a poppet's. Rory pressed him firmly against this woman, whose eyes, a dusty shade of blue, held back stalwart tears. She hugged Niall's bared back, knobby fingers pressing into his well-muscled flesh. Sabine looked at the woman's cowl, at the wisps of cinnamon and silver hair escaping the grayed linen. This careworn woman, with tears in her dusty eyes, had to be Niall's mother.

Rory jabbed the orange end of the poker into the wound on the back of Niall's shoulder. Sabine jumped. The acrid smell of burned flesh dragged her into darkness. The last thing she remembered was the disapproving stare in those dusty blue eyes of the woman she knew was Niall's mother.

C*ó ris a bhuineas ise?" his mother asked from her place at* the hearth.

"She belongs to no clan," Niall replied, adjusting himself in the chair by the fire. "She's French, a *femme* of the queen's court."

He leaned back in his chair by the worktable. His wound pulled painfully at his shoulder. He fought to ignore it. What was done was done. He was on the way to mending, the pain was just an annoying part of it. He settled his mind on more comforting things. First, he looked at his mother.

For as long as Niall could remember, she was always at the hearth, stirring something in that great cauldron. The sight comforted him as much as the aroma of meat that came from the great iron vessel. And knowing Sabine was safe in this cottage, in his glen.

His mother stopped, stick in both knobby fists. She did not look at him. Her gaze was fixed on the supper. Niall knew she was puzzling over her new guest as night fell on the longest day he could remember.

He stole a glance over his shoulder, bandaged in layers of linen, at Sabine, who slept on his mother's bed, the only one in the cottage. His place was a shieling, up the side of the ben. It was one he shared with Rory, one they had built themselves, to be nearer the sheep they tended. They mattered nothing to Niall now. Sabine was the only thing worth his attention at the moment.

He lifted a horn cup to his lips and took a long sip of whisky. It helped dull the pain better than trying to ignore it. Sabine's fainting had done little to ingratiate her to his mother. Her sleeping now had done even less.

"Ar chreach-s' a thàinig," his mother mumbled from the hearth.

"Sabine hasnae brought ruin to our clan," Niall said, turning back to the hearth. The fire warmed his face and helped to dry his freshly clean tunic, which he comfortably wore unlaced to the center of his chest. The ragged hem rested across his knees. His mother had sent it and his plaid with one of the clanswomen to have the blood and other nasties boiled from it. The plaid now hung on several pegs near the hearth, all nine yards of it. It would not be near dry until morning. His tunic was enough covering this summer night.

His mother stood upright. Her stout little body was not much taller than a child's, but her eyes contained wisdom far beyond her age, which she kept a guarded secret.

"Since ye're intent on speaking the tongue of the Lowlander, m'lad," she snapped, "I will abide. However, I willnae abide that royal servant in my house. The queen's men will be looking for her, and if they find her, they'll find ye—her abductor."

"She came willingly," Niall said. He drained the cup of spirit, then reached across the plank table for the bottle. "We need her."

His mother snatched the bottle from his grasp. She unstoppered it and poured a dram or two into her own cup. "The wound has drained the blood from yer heid. Ye speak daft." She upended the cup and took a long drink.

Before Niall could tell her more of his mind, a futile prospect at best, the cottage door opened. The scent of heather and some strange concoction of herb blew in, curling inside Niall's nostrils.

He grabbed the bottle and poured himself another dram. There was not a man alive who could outdrink his mother. Not even himself. However, there was one woman who could match her dram for dram. And he did not have to turn around to know she had just walked into the cottage.

"Agnes," he said, lifting the cup to his lips. "I was wondering when ye'd come with yer witchery and potions. Keep them to yerself. I'm well into my healing." He took another drink of whisky.

A woman, with long hair the color of grain in autumn, stepped between Niall and the hearth. She bent down, affording him a full, close view of the attributes straining behind her moss-colored gown. The strange twinkle in her amber eyes told Niall one thing—trouble.

"Niall maiseach," she cooed. *"Ciamar a tha thu?"*

"Well and good," he replied stiffly. "Ye came for naught."

"I came to see the *Fràngaich.*" Agnes gave him a lingering stare before standing upright. Niall noticed a hide pouch at her hip, could hear the tinkle of glass when she moved.

He lunged from the chair and slammed the cup to the table. "Ye'll no' give her any of your poison, ye witch!" he shouted. The pain in his shoulder flared without mercy, causing a satisfied smile to cross Agnes's lips.

She stepped quickly closer to Sabine, who stirred under a wool blanket.

"Leave her be!" Niall ordered.

The witch reached down and took the blanket away.

"Fine brocade on a fine-boned figure. Hair as dark as a raven's wing. A chin she keeps tipped up even in sleep," Agnes said methodically, her assessment deliberate.

Niall grabbed the blanket and began to place it back on Sabine, when Agnes suddenly dropped to her knees. Eyes wide and dancing, she cradled Sabine's ruined hand in her own. Niall's mother stepped up beside him, and gasped.

"What is this?" Agnes breathed. "A wounding to such a fine lady?"

Sabine moaned lightly and tossed her head back and forth on the pillow. Agnes released her hand.

"This she cures herself. She doesnae need me," she said.

"Well, that's a blessing to us all," Niall scoffed.

Agnes laid her hand flat on Sabine's forehead.

"Her mind betrays her strength," she said. "It torments her in sleep." She looked at Niall. He froze in her stare. "Does it torment her in waking?"

"What know ye of this lass?" his mother asked suddenly, before he could reply to Agnes's biting question. "What have ye brought to us?"

"A lass who can help us," he answered immediately. He just wished he knew exactly how. She had been living in Campbell's castle, had heard him plot the queen's murder, had been blamed when Campbell's plot failed. Niall's shoulder flared. The arrow was shot by an unseen hand from behind the standing stones. Whose? The question was a plague on his mind.

Niall glanced down at Sabine's hand. Such deformities were common in Highland folk, those who lived like his kith and kin, fighting for their very existence, or hiding just to stay alive. Sabine was not of that life. She had been in royal service, in France. She had lived a privileged life in her father's château. He stared at her hand. How privileged?

"Look at yer son, mistress MacGregor," Agnes said. "From the look in his eyes, I fear your late husband's want for us to join."

Niall could only stare at her. What a muckle mess he was in if Sabine found out about Agnes and him.

Agnes had come to the glen by order of his father. She was to be Niall's bride. But so much had changed since that day, since Niall became chief, since Sabine had entered his life. He could not tell her, confuse her more by trying to sort out his troubles.

Sabine's lids fluttered open. At first her dark eyes mirrored confusion, then fright. Niall quickly knelt beside her bed.

"Niall," she whispered, voice husky with the remnants of sleep, *"tu vas bien?"*

"Aye, *je suis.*"

Niall did not glance at his mother or Agnes. He knew what was on their faces, in their minds. He bitterly agreed with them that Sabine could not stay in the glen. He stared into her dark eyes. His heart told him she would stay until it was safe for her to return to her life with the queen, one of refinement and security behind palace walls. Sabine would have to leave. This was not the place for one like her, and he could not possibly be the man for one like her.

chapter 13

The Waulking Party

A *gathering*.

That was what Niall had announced around his mother's table. Sabine looked at him, over her plate of tough meat and mushed root. He did not offer her an explanation, nor did she expect one. He continued to discuss the "gathering" with Rory, his mother, and a woman about Sabine's age, with straw-colored hair and penetrating eyes. Her name was Agnes.

Niall spoke of Highland things. Sabine did not wish to know of them. She wished she were anywhere but here, where she was clearly unwelcome.

Agnes continued to stare at her with those unsettling eyes. *Oui.* Sabine was most unwelcome.

"Rory," Niall said, "at first light ye will ride to all corners of our land and rally the clansmen for a gathering."

"A gathering," Rory repeated around a mouthful of meat, raising a thick black brow.

"Aye." Niall scooped up a large piece of meat and root with his Highland knife and dropped the food into his mouth. He chewed vigorously. No one could guess that earlier in the day he had been close to death.

"Can I ask ye what for?" Rory said.

"I was gonnae ask the very same," said mistress MacGregor.

"Campbell," Niall said.

Rory and mistress MacGregor quickly nodded. Agnes just stared vacantly ahead. Sabine could imagine what roiled through their minds. Campbell had affronted these folk longer than he had been a bane to her existence.

Mistress MacGregor was the first to break the stillness. She rose from the table and took Niall's empty plate and ladled a generous amount of meat on it and gave the plate back to him. He tossed her a wink and continued to eat. His mother paused and eyed Sabine. "The lassie has hardly touched her meal. 'Tis no' good enough for her well-born tastes?"

Sabine straightened and took up another piece of the tough beef on her knife, one of several Niall kept on his person and had lent her. Of course, his mother was not without her own weapon, her stares and curt comments were sharper than any blade.

"She doesnae belong here. The queen's guards will find her," mistress MacGregor said.

"No one has found us here," Niall said. "What makes ye think they'll find one lass?"

"She should leave!" mistress MacGregor shouted, her hands balled into fists on either side of her plate. "She doesnae belong here, I tell ye!"

Sabine knew she was not welcome. Her right hand cramped a little. Quietly, she rose from the table. The conversation ceased, faces turned toward her.

She opened her mouth to speak, but the words evaded her. She swallowed hard and found her voice. "I must go back to my queen and protect her." It was all she could think to say, all she wanted at that moment. Her own needs and hopes had evaporated on the needs of her queen.

She turned away from those pale Scottish faces and stepped toward the door. She was between lives with no path before her.

A heavy hand laid on her shoulder. She did not have to turn around to see it was Niall.

"Come back to the table. Eat yer supper."

She shook her head.

He leaned into her, lips brushing her ear. "No one will bite ye . . . except, perchance, me."

She could not keep her smile at bay. His breath warmed her ear. And . . . "Ouch!" . . . he did take a small nibble on her earlobe.

She looked into his eyes, at the path he offered her. One with him. For now, it was her only choice.

"Bring the lassie back to the table, m'lad," mistress Mac-Gregor ordered. "She needs a full belly before her journey."

"Her journey willnae be farther than this glen," Niall said. He took Sabine by her right hand and guided her back to the table.

"Eat. 'Tis a sure way to me mum's heart," he whispered in her ear.

Sabine took her seat. Niall released her hand. The warmth from his touch lingered a second, then was gone. She took up the knife in her right hand and brought a piece of the beef to her mouth.

Agnes smirked at her, gaze so deliberate, so rude, and oddly familiar. Campbell had looked at her with no less disdain.

Sabine squeezed the knife's handle as hard as her twisted fingers would allow.

"I am not a painting in the royal Salon," she said. "Why do you stare at me so?"

Agnes sat up a little straighter. "Ye tip yer chin up, *outeral,* and look down at us."

Sabine shifted her gaze to Niall, who looked at her expectantly, silently urging her to explain that which he knew. She looked back at Agnes and slowly raised her knife. Everyone around the table stared at her. Sabine tipped her chin high. She squeezed the handle then released it. The knife clattered to the center of the table.

"With every squeeze," she said, "my hand gets stronger. With every squeeze I can lift my chin a little higher."

Sabine slowly shifted her gaze to Niall. He was smiling, blue eyes shining. But it was his mother who spoke.

"Ye show a wee spark of the Highland spirit, lassie, and my lad for his own reasons wants ye here. I'll let ye bide a wee."

Sabine looked at her. "Bide a wee?"

Mistress MacGregor offered her best imitation of a smile. "Ye can stay."

Sabine's bed was a crude linen bag stuffed with straw, and was as comfortable as sleeping on a sack of pins. She rolled to her side for the hundredth time that night. Her gown bound about her legs. She did not bother to unbind the layers of silk and fine linen from her body. The extra warmth her garment provided was most welcome.

The scratchy wool blanket mistress MacGregor had given her scraped against her cheek, releasing a moldy scent. She wrinkled her nose. The scent was a part of this land as much as the lichen and moss that grew on everything.

Sabine glanced to the other side of the hearth at her begrudging hostess who slept under a heap of wool blankets before the hearth. A harsh melody of snores and grunts had earlier broken the chilling night, but now the Highland woman lay still and quiet as the gray light of morning began to seep in through the tiny window.

Sabine closed her eyes. She pulled the wool to her chin, trying to force her mind to want the rest her weary body craved.

She was an exile.

That very thought scratched against her consciousness all night. She burrowed under the wool. No matter how much she tried, she could not relax even to feign sleep. Nasty thoughts swirled in her mind, taunting her.

Campbell was out there beyond the mountains and the forests.

"Sweet Saint Giles," she whispered. "I must get proof of his treachery . . . somehow. . . ." The next voice she heard must have been in a dream. Maybe she had mercifully fallen asleep.

"We'll find proof . . . together. . . ." Warm breath brushed her face.

Sabine opened her eyes, meeting Niall's incredible blues. He was lying beside her, on his side. For an instant she could not breathe. Slowly she loosened her grip on the wool blanket. Niall pressed a finger to her lips.

"Shh," he whispered, "get dressed. I want to take ye somewhere before the glen awakens."

"I—" she began.

He shook his head, cutting his gaze to his mother, still asleep under her heap of blankets.

"I—" she said under his finger.

"Shh."

She pushed his hand away from her mouth.

"I'm already dressed. It is chill here."

Niall smiled, wide and long. He slipped off of the bed to his feet and offered his hand. She took it and sat up on her pallet. The wool blanket slipped from her body. She glanced down at her feet, clad in silken stockings. With a dramatic sweep of his other hand, Niall gathered the slippers that she had carefully placed beside the pallet and knelt before her.

He did not serve her, no, he was doing this because it pleased him. Sabine could tell this in the dawn light from the small smile on his lips. He wrapped warm fingers about her ankle and guided her foot into the slipper.

Before her, head bowed, he executed his task with far more care than was necessary. Compelled by his tenderness toward her, she touched his hair, tracing her fingertips across the contours of the thick locks. Niall took up her other ankle and placed the slipper on her foot. He released her and looked up through a roguish lock of hair that had fallen over one eye. Sabine did not mean to gasp at his gaze, but it startled her emotions. Niall smiled, reveling in this small victory over her, no doubt. She knew he had meant that.

Mistress MacGregor shifted and snorted under the covers. Sabine flinched and abruptly stood up.

"Let's go," Niall whispered. He, too, leapt to his feet.

"*Oui,*" Sabine breathed. She did not have the slightest notion what she was agreeing to, just as long as it got her out of that cottage. She willingly followed Niall outside.

As soon as she stepped into the morning air, Sabine halted and looked up at grandeur only Heaven must know.

"*Mon Dieu,*" she breathed.

"Aye," Niall said proudly. "God used the muscle of His talent when he made *Beinn Tulaichean.*"

"*Oui,*" Sabine quickly agreed.

The mountain, a *ben* as Niall called it, was skirted in an early morning, lacy mist that had settled into the rain-damp valley. Glints of morning sun touched the summit in streaks of orange and red across the lush green that seemed to touch the heavens. Clouds, dyed pink and yellow by the sun's light, glided lazily past the mountaintop, paying a brief visit and giving mere mortals a glimpse of the colors of paradise. Sabine covered her mouth to keep from shouting at the beauty before her, the beauty Niall had given her this morn.

"Och, Sabine," he said softly, "had I known ye would react so, I might have prepared ye before I showed ye *Beinn Tulaichean.*"

Swallowing, finding her voice, Sabine asked, "What does that mean?"

"Small green knoll."

"Knoll?"

"Aye, probably named by some Frenchman who lived in the shadows of the grand Alps," he replied with a grin. "That ben protects us well enough from intruders, it and the other bens that make up this wee glen." He paused, cocking a quizzical brow at her. "It might be best if ye didnae make this climb this morning. Ye look shaky." He began to walk away, toward the mountain.

"*Non!*" Sabine exclaimed, hurrying to walk beside him. "I wish to go!"

"If 'tis *mademoiselle*'s wish."

Niall took her hand. He led her forward, up and up.

"This is a good place to sort things out. I've climbed this ben as soon as I could walk. I know every bit of it, every tree, rock, and burn . . ." He turned and gave her a wink. "Ye could say I'm like a Highland fox in that respect . . . a *sauvage* fox."

Sabine blinked from the dart. "I never—"

He did not break stride, taking her with him, up and up, through the mist.

"Yer heart can be swayed, that I know," he finally said.

"How would you know my heart?"

"I know yer lips, can yer heart be far behind?"

"Prideful—" She huffed.

"So, I've been told," he laughed.

They walked in silence for a while, the mist roiling around them, until Niall finally spoke.

"If I can turn yer heart round, Sabine, there'll be one less person in Scotland who doesnae want 'savages' like me and mine in the gallows."

She was on the verge of telling him that the title *sauvage* she had given him so long ago was forgotten to her, but kept silent. Why could she not say those words? She tried to convince herself it was the beauty all around her, what she could see of it through the mist, that kept her speechless, and not the denial of her feelings for Niall.

He climbed up, over hillock and stone, cutting a path for her through the heather. The bottom of his kilt scraped the bell-shaped blossoms and sent them swaying in his wake. He was the king of this place, king of the "glens" and "bens" as he called them.

Not breaking stride, Niall walked up and up, one long stride after another. Sabine watched the way the plaid swung from the tight curve of his buttocks and brushed the taut hollows behind his knees. The joy she found in simple observation was not demanding. Little by little, she felt that when she was alone with Niall the world was theirs. So it seemed on this beautiful Scottish mountain. The higher they climbed the more the mist exchanged with sunlight. No one followed them, no one knew they had come here at the birth of a day Sabine imagined radiant with hope. Niall was here with her on an adventure away from the troubles that besieged the both of them. That she could not deny.

He stopped and released her hand and made a wide sweep with both his arms.

"Take a good look about ye. . . ." His words trailed off as he captured her with his gaze. ". . . Sabine?"

She had not taken him from her sight.

"Well? Take a look. I'd hoped ye'd be a wee bit impressed."

Sabine did not move.

A breeze tossed the thick, cinnamon locks of Niall's hair about the angles of his face. The ends brushed his strong chin, touching now and then the shallow cleft in the center. The early morning sun brought out an enchanting array of reds, oranges, and golds in his hair. If she ventured to count the many hues, she would be an old woman before she finished.

Niall creased his brow. "I thought ye'd like the view."

She did very much.

He turned away from her and plopped dejectedly down on an outcropping of stone, like a little boy.

Sabine smiled and kept sudden thoughts close to herself. She suspected that Niall had brought her here for more than the view. She allowed herself to muse of passion released while their bodies were cradled in the heather, their cries of rapture as she gave herself freely to a man as mysterious and free spirited as the mist that opened before her. The mist that opened to reveal a glimpse of Heaven. . . .

"Sweet Saint Giles!" Sabine stumbled backward. Niall was there to catch her in the strong embrace of his arms.

Beauty, that she had missed since she had left France, was defined for her.

R*apt she was, like a child with eyes anew on a magnificent* gift, the birthing of the spring lambs, the budding of the rowan trees, silvery salmon flipping through the burn, or the bonfire at a winter *ceilidh.* Sabine stared at the glen and the bens that made up this favored piece of MacGregor land. Niall had never dreamed that he would sit on the summit of *Beinn Tulaichean* with a woman like Sabine and the future of his clan in his hands.

She stood in profile to him, gaze fixed on the morning light that crept into the glen. Orange and red spears touched each cottage, spreading out and turning the mist into nothing.

"What d'ye find so appealing yonder?" Niall asked.

She closed her eyes for a moment, then opened them, her gaze on him.

"All of it is beautiful," she replied, adding, in a breathless whisper, *"Merci."*

Slowly, steadily they took a seat on a large, lichen-covered stone. Niall placed an arm around her waist. He did not allow hesitation to rule him, the same polite hesitation that bastards like Campbell thought was proper before they took what they wanted. He shuddered to think of that son of a whore touching Sabine. Hesitation was a trait that Niall could not afford to possess.

He had hoped that he could look down on this favored land, his home, and the way to protect it and all that dwelled here and yon would come to him. So far all he had done to save his clan was to send Rory to the corners of the land and rally them for a gathering on the evening of the morrow. What would he tell them? That they were to fight or flee Campbell? Those seemed the only options available. He stared down at the glen with Sabine so very close beside him. There had to be another way out of this incredible mess.

"Tell me of your people," Sabine said, "as I view the whole of your kingdom from here."

She was right in a way. From this summit one could see all of the bens and glens that made up MacGregor lands as long as the name had existed. Niall thought he could find solace here, by seeing the land from a hawk's view, knowing how bloody important it was to preserve it, seeing how fragile it all looked from such a great height.

Niall shifted on the rock. He reached into the swag of plaid across his chest and withdrew two apples. He dropped one in her lap. She looked at the fruit, then at him.

"Hungry?" he asked.

"*Oui*, but does this mean you do not want to tell me about your people?"

"Oh, aye, I do," Niall said, taking a bite of apple. "Eat and I will."

Sabine took the apple and bit into it. A trickle of juice glistened at the corner of her mouth as she chewed. He swiped it away with his thumb and made her smile. She quickly looked away, down the side of the ben. What was she denying herself? Or did she think of him as a common outlaw as the rest of Scotland did?

"MacGregors are the scourge of the Highlands," he said. "'Tis a reputation I did nothing to perpetuate, nor did any of my clan, or the clan before them. The hatred for the MacGregors travels so far back through the ages the bards dinnae ken how it got started. To my mind 'tis land, 'tis always land."

Sabine glanced about her. "Land."

"The head of Loch Katrine is considered a valuable waterway. It flows to the firth, to Leith and beyond. The clan who controls Loch Katrine can control trade from the Highlands to . . . anywhere."

"And your clan does this trading?"

"We protect those of us that do from time to time. There's not much trade from the Highlands . . . yet. I hope that one day we can trade wool from our lands, we have enough bloody sheep, a muckle wool, enough to trade."

" 'Tis your dream? To bring commerce to these wild lands? 'Tis a good dream."

"A daft dream," Niall scoffed. "As long as my clan are outlaws. Our name is tainted because others have wanted what we have, and because we have held fast to it, died because of it."

He looked to the south where the mist had begun to clear in the sunlight, to the dark mirror of Loch Katrine. The head of the loch broke into the glen like a jagged piece of mirror.

Sabine cradled her body into his.

He gently rubbed her back, gliding his fingertips along her spine. How he wished there were not the barrier of her fine brocade between them. How he wished. . . .

Her bottom lip trembled slightly.

"Tell me your mind," he said, stroking the side of her face with the back of his hand.

"Campbell planted a false face against me to my queen. I don't know why."

"I do," Niall said. "But ye willnae like the reason."

"Tell me," she quietly demanded.

He sighed. "Campbell has asked to marry one of her court that, to him and the queen, needs charity. Most important to Campbell, this person who is, say, *different,* could be suspect if harm were to fall on the queen's head. I know the character of this man, how he feels about anyone who is different, or who he feels isnae worthy of him. He wants them gone."

"Like Rizzio," she said with a shudder. "And me."

He looked at Sabine's profile, at the tilt of her strong chin.

He allowed his fingertips to glide over one soft cheek. "A fair *mademoiselle* shouldnae know such strife or such evil."

"I have known . . ." She took in a long sigh. "I do not wish to plague your thoughts . . . or mine anymore."

Sabine burrowed her face into the side of his neck. Moist warmth touched his flesh. She was crying. What she said next tore a lightning swath across his soul.

"Do not send me back to Campbell."

Niall held her tighter. Her body shivered in his hold.

"Why would ye think that I would send ye back to that bastard?"

"To save your clan," came the muffled reply. "So, he would not come here, after me."

"He doesnae know where we are. Nor would he dare come if he did."

Niall stared at her face. More lovely than the glen in spring, more lovely than anything he had ever seen in his entire life.

"I give ye my word that ye will never go back to Campbell."

"Your word?"

"A MacGregor's word is not to be taken lightly. Our strength is in our word. But if ye need proof . . ."

He kissed her. He took his time, and he kissed her, tasted her, wanted so much more. Sabine surrendered easily into his arms. She took his kiss and made it her own. Niall was only too happy to give her more to prove that his word and his will were hers. She should always feel secure with him. Whatever demons touched her past, whatever secret she could not reveal to him, did not matter now. He would vanquish those demons with one kiss, with many more if necessary, if that was what it took to bring her into his arms for an eternity.

He vowed to himself never to let her from his sight, as long as she deemed to stay.

Sabine broke the kiss. "I cannot stay here forever," she said, the tears welling in her eyes again. "I am not a part of this place. Your *mere* knows this all too well. I cannot cook. I can sew, a little. But this Highland life I do not know. I will not be welcome."

"Dinnae say such," Niall said. "Stay here. Remember I am chief . . . *king* . . . of the MacGregors." He grinned. "They will do as I command . . . even my mother." Of course what he said was pure tripe. His mother obeyed no one but the Almighty. But his words did bring a small smile out of Sabine. Oh, aye, that it did.

"I do believe you," she said, swiping the tears from her eyes with the back of her damaged hand.

"I know ye do," he said.

"How?" she asked.

"Because ye havenae once asked for your purse and the gold within, even when ye lost your good sense when ye thought I would send ye back to Campbell."

She blinked. *"Mon Dieu!* Niall! My *sac* . . . I . . . I—"

"Havenae cause to need it when ye're with me, aye?"

She paused, then smiled. *"Oui,* it is true, but where have you hidden it?"

"Nearby, 'tis safe."

"My *sac* isn't the only thing safe here," she said with a sigh.

He raised one brow. "Oh, aye?"

A light breeze wafted up the ben, rustling the long curls about her face. She looked to the sunny sky and breathed deep the scent that came up from the glen. The scent of *waulk*ing.

"What is that scent?" she asked.

"The women of the glen are *waulk*ing the wool. 'Tis the time to do it after the dying."

"Dying? Pigments from plants? You have that here in the Highlands?"

"Aye, I would think so, otherwise our colors would be quite boring. None at all actually, unless sheep is a color."

Sabine rose to her feet. The breeze grew stronger, rippling her gown about her legs. Niall stole a glance at the way the silk wrapped about her long slender legs. She turned toward him, her expression radiant, like it had been when she first surveyed "the whole of his kingdom."

He glanced down the slope. The faint sound of the women's *waulk*ing songs wafted up the ben on the morning breeze.

"What are they singing?" Sabine asked.

"'The Shepherd's Son'," Niall replied, a wee bit embarrassed. "'Tis a bawdy song. The women like it a lot."

"Translate, please," she said, a glint to her eyes.

He swallowed. "I dinnae—"

"Tell me," she whispered.

"Aye. . . ." He listened to the Gaelic words coming up the ben. Slowly he translated them for Sabine:

> *There was a shepherd's son*
> *Kept sheep upon a hill;*
> *He looked east, he looked west,*
> *Then gave an under-look,*
> *And there he spied a lady fair,*
> *Swimming in a burn.*
> *He raised his head frae his green bed,*
> *And approached the maid; . . .*

He stopped. "Are ye sure ye wish me to continue?"

"Oui." Sabine began walking down the ben as if caught in a dream. Niall walked beside her. He reached out and took her right hand in his and gave it a small kiss.

"Tell me more," she whispered.

> *. . . And then he approached the maid;*
> *"Put on yer claiths, my dear," he says.*
> *"And be ye not afraid.*
> *If ye'll not touch my mantle,*
> *And let my claiths alane,*
> *Then I'll give ye as much money*
> *As ye can carry hame. . . ."*

Niall stopped.

"The rest of the song is too bawdy to sing to a lass as well-born as ye."

"Tell me," she said firmly. "And if you call me wellborn again, I'll slap you."

"As best as I can remember, the lass in the song offers herself to the shepherd's son. The shepherd's son takes advantage of the lass right there on the bank of the burn while the flock concealed them from the lassie's husband."

"Delightful!" she exclaimed, startling him.

"Delightful?" he asked.

"Oui!" she cried. "Everything about this place. Delightful!"

She suddenly raced to the bottom of the ben. Niall was impressed with her speed and did not try to stop her. He was more impressed with the way her gown flapped up, revealing slender ankles and calves concealed in pale blue silk stockings. He was as much a bit o' a' lad as the shepherd's son.

His fetching quarry stopped at the base of the ben and walked quietly between two cottages into the center of the huddle to where the women, ten in all including his mother, sat round a worn trestle table.

Sabine kept an awed and respectful distance from the women. Niall stayed beside her. In a matter of a few blinks his and Sabine's presence was more than casually noticed by all of the circle. Their hands stopped moving across the long length of wool draped over the trestle table.

"Och, and look who's come down from the ben to join his kith and kin," his mother said. "My lad and his French lassie."

"Haud your tongue, Mum," Niall said, keeping his distance from the *waulk*ing table. Men were not welcome there. As much as women were not welcome at the gathering.

Agnes gave Sabine a hard stare from her place at the table. Despite this Sabine slowly broke stride with him and made her way across the mud and grass to the table.

He reached out to pull her back from the den of Highland lionesses, but all he got was a whisper of brocade from her sleeve between his fingertips.

The women stared at Sabine as she walked to their circle, as if she were a pestilence in silk and velvet come to join them. They quickly returned to their work as if that would make her leave. She held her chin even, steady gaze cast on the women and their quick-paced hands pounding the wool, tightening it, toughening it. Pausing at the head of the table next to his mother, Sabine knelt slowly to the ground. She placed one hand, her right one, upon the boiled wool, tracing over the plaid, over the greens, oranges, yellows, and black. Niall's mother, Agnes, and the rest of the women stared at her as if they expected something to happen but were not sure what exactly.

"Très belle," Sabine said, mesmerized. "From where did these colors come?"

Niall held his breath, waiting for his mother to lay through her with her blade of a tongue. Why had Sabine stepped into this exclusive circle?

"The horsetail," his mother replied steadily. "The heather, the onion—"

"Blackberry," Sabine added. "And the fuchsia. . . . *très belle.*"

"Aye, lass," his mother said, surprise in her tone. "'Tis. Have ye dyed the wool before?"

"Non. I have gathered the plants and soils to make pigment for the paintings . . . once . . . I do not do that anymore," Sabine replied.

Niall leaned against the cottage, eyes wide. What was happening here?

Sabine settled on the bench beside his mother. She glanced at him, at first with confusion in her dark eyes, then gave into the yearnings of her spirit. Her damaged hand glided over the wool. Her strength was in her hand. Dye water oozed from between her twisted fingers, and she tipped her chin up a little higher.

The women, one by one, tore their gaze from their guest and renewed their singing. Niall leaned against a cottage. For the first time in a long time, his worries were replaced by unencumbered joy. Sabine wore the very same on her face. But for how long?

chapter 14

❧

Freedom, mon Amour, Freedom

R*ight hand throbbing, chin tipped higher than ever, Sabine*
sat alone at what the women called a "*waulk*ing table."
They had finished their task and left her for their other mysterious duties. The table was mottled with purple and gray
puddles reflecting the increasingly cloudy sky. The color reminded her of rounds of slate from the roof of the Château de
Montmerency in the Loire Valley.

"So beautiful," she whispered, a smile tugging at the corners of her mouth.

Niall had departed on some task while the women had let
her sit with them. Although she did not know their Gaelic
songs, she had hummed as her hands skidded and pulled the
freshly dyed wool, the colors running out between her fingers
and toes, like rivulets from evening tide. Her right hand sang
with a glorious ache, one of her own making.

Sabine glanced at her hands, stained with the hues of the
Highlands. She closed her eyes and breathed deep.

"*De'n t-ainm a th'oirbh?*"

Sabine popped her eyes open. Wide-eyed children stared at
her.

"*Bonjour,*" she said.

The girls curtsied to her, and the boys made exaggerated bows, as if she were royalty.

Sabine smiled and bowed her head to them. "That is not necessary, *mes petits*. But I thank you very much."

The children were giving her curious stares, their heads tilted, grimy faces grinning at her.

"I wish I had something for you, but I confess I have come here with very little, however"—Sabine reached down to the top of her gown, between the layers of fabric—"I would very much like to draw your beautiful faces."

She took out the large scrap of paper, the pieces glued together. She unfolded it a little, hiding the sketch she had begun of Niall, and found a small blank space. She placed it on a dry place on the *waulk*ing table. Grateful the repair held and just grateful to be here, she removed a charcoal stick from her gown. The children gathered round her, curious faces cast down to the paper. One by one Sabine tipped up their chins. "Up, up, *mes enfants*. Let me see your pretty, pretty faces."

One of the girls swiped a smudge of soot from her face with a sleeve. She gave Sabine the sweetest smile she had ever seen.

"*Très jolie . . . mon Dieu. . . .*"

She sketched the unique qualities of each child. They continued to smile at her, not once regarding her right hand with more than a passing glance. Lost in her drawing, she added details, fleshed out the sketch, to make it complete.

"'Tis sure ye will steal the weans' souls with such marks upon yon paper . . . French demon."

The children shrieked and ran away, disappearing as quickly as they came. Sabine did not have to look to know Agnes had returned to the table.

"I was sketching those beautiful children. 'Twas no witchery except the way you made them disappear." Sabine slid the sketch and charcoal stick into her gown, feeling Agnes observe her every move. A chill, like the claws of something long dead, walked up her spine.

Wisps of straw-colored hair floated about the woman's face as she regarded Sabine.

"Ye wear such fine silk. It can keep one warm, but no' as warm as the body of a goodly Highland man."

Sabine rose from the table and stepped into a puddle of dye water.

"Her Majesty is no doubt missing you terribly, hmm?" Agnes brushed her fingertips against the sleeve of Sabine's gown. "Did Her Majesty gift this to ye?"

"She did not." Sabine remembered that Lord Campbell had given her the fabric shortly before she left France. She had made the gown herself, the stitches not perfect.

"'Tis a fine fabric," Agnes said. "No' a typical gift from a Highland warrior as is Niall. 'Tis typical of a Highland noble as is Lord Campbell."

Sabine wrenched her arm away from this woman. A flame ignited deep in her gut. What was wrong with this woman? Sabine had done nothing to her.

"Listen to my words outsider . . . , *outeral*," Agnes said. "There is enough trouble within this glen. For these Mac-Gregors, curses arrive unwanted on dragon's wings with nasty talons of fire. However, ye arrived in fine slippers with silk on yer person, a curse nonetheless."

Sabine stared hard at Agnes. *"Sorcière!"*

"My words are true, *outeral*. Best ye leave before Niall dies."

Sabine stopped. *"Comment?"*

"I said," Agnes replied, "if ye stay, Niall will die."

"Why say you this horrible thing?"

"He has ye here to protect ye. Campbell and all of Her Majesty's soldiers will surely pound his clan to dust to find ye."

Sabine blinked. "They will not," she said weakly, but Agnes spoke the truth. "Niall gave me his word." It sounded ridiculous the moment she said it. How could his word save her or anyone?

"He plied ye with 'his word,' did he?" Agnes laughed. "'Tis sure ye're no' getting the best part of him."

"Meaning?" she asked, hands on hips. Of course she knew the answer.

"Nothing that should vex ye, *outeral*," Agnes replied. "This clan is cursed, as cursed as yerself. I see the mark the Devil has placed upon yer hand."

"I see the Devil before me in dour dress," Sabine snapped. "Enough!"

"Then haste ye away, and save Niall and his from certain doom."

"You are the doom in his life," she said. But Agnes was so horribly right. Sabine would never tell her that.

She had to think, but where? Slowly her gaze stole up the mountain Niall cherished so much.

Leaving her stockings and the witch behind, she ran toward the base of that beautiful mountain Niall had showed her this morning. She dared not look behind her to see if Agnes made chase. Witches could fly. At that moment, Sabine wished she could too. Could fly away, back to France, away from Niall, possibly saving his life. She was a curse on him, a distraction from his duties to his clan. Yet, he wanted her here.

She ran as fast as her legs would allow her. The rush of air up her gown, across her flesh, only served to propel her further up the mountain, right into a downpour.

Her bare feet skidded across the wet earth between the heather plants. She regained her balance and ran.

Where else was there for her to go? Niall said this mountain with its view of the whole of his kingdom helped him to sort things out. There were two things Sabine had to sort out: to stay or to go.

And the decision was as hard as the rock she suddenly slid upon. First her knees, then her chest, then her head, struck the granite shelf. As she fell to the soggy ground, she wondered how anyone could survive in a place where it seemed all the four seasons could happen on the same day.

Niall had found Sabine, muddy, half drowned, with a bloody scrape on her forehead. He was never so happy in all his life.

And never so angry.

A sudden storm had swept down *Beinn Tulaichean* just as Agnes had found him, stolen a kiss, and announced "the curse is gone." Niall did not have to ask that witch what she meant by "curse." Agnes and her usual cachet of gloom and doom had run Sabine from the glen.

He smoothed back Sabine's thick hair from her muddied forehead.

She lay on as soft a pallet as Niall could fashion of straw and his plaid. He knelt beside her. His tunic dangling over his knees kept him warm enough in his and Rory's wee hovel on the side of the ben.

He glided his fingers over the damp curls of Sabine's midnight hair, silently grateful that Rory was off to get the rest of the clansmen for the gathering. His fingers tangled gently in the locks. The wound on her forehead was nothing more than a bump and a scrape. Niall had cleaned it with a handful of wet moss. Sabine would live. Eventually, she would awaken.

"I didnae tell ye the rest of the *waulk*ing song," he said over the steady beat of the rain outside. The sound was so much a part of the glen, he hardly noticed it.

He leaned down, lips a breath from her warm cheek.

> *O I'll not touch yer mantle,*
> *And I'll let yer claiths alane;*
> *But I'll tak ye out of the clear water,*
> *My dear, to be my ain. . . .*

Niall kissed her cheek.

"Non!" Sabine bolted upright, sending Niall hard onto his buttocks. His back struck an iron trough full of steaming water. Some splashed out and plastered the tunic to his shoulders.

Eyes wide, she looked about the small cottage before pausing on Niall. He scooted away from the trough back to her side.

"Where am I?" she demanded.

"My cottage, quite private."

"Private?" she asked, eyeing him warily. There was nothing private in this valley, as far as she was concerned.

"Aye, after your wee row with Agnes, I thought ye might like to sort things out," he replied.

Sabine stiffened. He knew her mind too well.

"I had gone to your mountain. 'Tis where you go to 'sort things out,'" she said, mocking his inflection on purpose.

"And ye're still on the ben, in a shieling. A grand one at that. We built it, me and Rory."

"Shieling?"

"A wee dwelling on the ben, so I can be near the sheep in summer." He winked at her. "And so I can collect any strays I may find. Makes the wee beasties feel safe."

"I am not a sheep."

"Not since I last checked."

Sabine shifted on the pallet, suddenly something more than usual seemed amiss.

Then she looked down at her waist. "My *sac*!"

"Where it is meant to be," he said. "'Tis yours."

She stared at him.

"Look inside," he said. "Make certain all is in order."

"I do not have to," she replied.

She lifted her hand to the top of her gown. Her paper was missing! Her eyes widened as she looked at him.

"'Tis drying by the fire," he said before she could gasp in alarm.

She glanced at the paper. "It seems to be well . . . as am I."

She glanced at the turf-and-wattle ceiling. "So very crude," she whispered. "More of a dwelling for beasts. The rain is leaking inside. . . ."

"I could've left ye on *Beinn Tulaichean* bleeding all over the heather if ye'd prefer." He grinned, moving closer, until his thigh touched hers. Sabine did not pull away, liking him near, feeling his warmth in the chilling damp air.

"I am grateful." She captured his gaze. "Most grateful."

"Why did ye go in such haste? Ye should've come to me. I would've told ye that Agnes's words are as empty as the queen's promises."

"I should not be here," she blurted out, remembering the nasty truths Agnes had told her.

"In this glen or in this cottage?" Niall glanced briefly at the sparse surroundings. "Of course, calling this place a cottage does it a great service. I know that it isnae a castle or a palace with a proper bed, but—"

Sabine bristled. "You talk too much, Niall MacGregor. I do

not need fine things to comfort my soul. I've been surrounded by them all of my life, and they've caused me no happiness. I do not miss them."

"We have the finer things," Niall said. "Ye just have to look a wee bit to find them—"

"You have to look more than a 'wee bit' to see anything fine about me. I must look like a beggar now covered in your fine Highland mud."

"Just a wee bit of good Highland soil on ye, 'tis all, I assure ye."

"No jest, Niall," she said. "I must look as horrible as I feel."

He smiled. "Did ye not just tell me that ye no longer have use for the finer things?"

She narrowed her eyes at him. "Do not tease."

"I ken ye enough to know that bathing in the burn is too . . . now, how should I say this? . . ." He loved teasing her, watching her cheeks flush, eyes flare. ". . . Common?"

Teasingly she raised a hand to him, but he jumped to his feet, narrowly missing striking the top of his head on a low beam. With a sweep of his arm, he pointed to the wooden trough and its steaming contents.

"Voilà!"

Sabine eyed the bath.

"I dragged the bloody thing across the ben. It was not as arduous as carrying water from the burn and heating it in yon wee cauldron to give ye the finest bath in the Highlands."

Sabine eyed the cauldron over the fire. Then she shifted her gaze to the trough, her bath, her gift from Niall. But one thing remained on her mind.

"What's amiss?" Niall asked.

"'Tis but a trough for the animals to drink," she blurted out.

Niall folded his arms across his chest. "'Tis a bloody trough, aye. I dragged it here and boiled four cauldrons of water to fill it. The least ye could do is show a wee bit of gratitude."

"You dragged water four times up the bank of that river in the valley?"

"From a wee fall of the burn right outside the door. I'm not daft."

A half smile played on her lips. "That is a matter for debate."

Niall snorted and grabbed the front of his tunic. "If ye're not gonnae put yer fair, sweet arse into yon water before it turns chill, I'm gonnae do it." He began to remove his tunic.

"Non! I will get in!" She tossed aside the plaid and jumped to her feet.

"Sabine! Mind the—!" Niall shouted.

Too late. Sabine struck the top of her head hard on a low timber.

"Merde! What is this? *Une maison pour les enfants?"* she asked angrily, rubbing the top of her head.

Niall stood by the bath, the steam floated up around him. Sabine walked carefully to the other side, loosening the top row of lacings on her gown. She stopped and looked at Niall. She would go no further until he said what she wanted to hear. She wanted him to decide right then, and quickly, to stay. If he delayed a moment longer, she knew she would tell him to go. He just stood there, staring at her, brow furrowed.

Sabine opened her lips to speak, but he beat her to the task. "I'll leave ye to your bath," was all he said.

He stepped away from the trough, scooped up his plaid and his claymore, and ducked out of the doorway into the rain. The door rattled on its wooden hinges after he slammed it closed.

Sabine remained in stunned silence. It was her fault he had left so abruptly. She had not given him an invitation, had banished him to the elements with one stare, because she was afraid. And, damn his Highland honor, he had complied.

She continued to unlace her gown.

The trough with its luxury of warm water looked most inviting. The last time she had sat in a *baignoire* was before the hearth in Campbell's castle, two days ago, the morning of her arrest before her queen. . . .

"Non," she whispered, letting her gown slip about her feet. "I will forget my troubles if only for a moment."

Dressed in a white linen shift, she took her gown and *sac* from the floor and placed them on a rough table near the hearth. She winced at the streaks of dried mud on the brocade. Why should that bother her so? Appearances, slovenly or otherwise, did not matter here in the Highlands, where living was done without pretense. The land was the true monarch.

"The Highlanders are free. Why not I?" she whispered.

The table was laden with quinces, pears, a joint of meat, and a loaf of *manchette*. She made a place for her possessions, took a pear, and stepped toward the bath. Inwardly she thanked Niall and wondered how far she had driven him away. She did not look out the door, guessing that he had not gone far. He could return if he wished, that was his choice. She would not open the door and call him inside in the wake of his Highland pride.

The bath beckoned her with steam and a heady fragrance. She looked down and saw small bunches of heather floating on the surface of the water. Niall thought of everything. Quite civilized of him. Sabine felt if she said so, he would violently deny it, as if it were a bad thing.

She removed her tunic and tossed it on top of her gown. The chilling air immediately puckered her flesh into thousands of tiny *chair de poule*. She stepped into the trough, gripping a cool side with her left hand while her right hand gripped the pear as she would her wool ball. She slipped down into the warm water, imagining all of the nasties on her skin dissolving to nothing.

She lay there, her hair dangled over the back of the trough. The popping in the hearth, the patter of the rain, and the gentle sound of her own breathing keeping her company, relaxed her.

She ate the pear and played with the sprigs of heather floating in the water. She squeezed them to release the sweet fragrance that was so much a part of this land. Sabine glanced about the dark rafters and corners of this very small cottage. This was a man's house, sparse and untidy. A man's house, and she was alone in it, naked, in a trough of water. . . .

Something moved in the shadows. It rustled, twitched, and . . . squeaked!

She flinched, splashing water everywhere. The something moved across the floor. She could see its eyes, small, round, and dark. It looked at her. Sabine could not make a sound, her breath was lost. She gripped the pear's core with her right hand, slowly raised it, and took aim.

With one smooth motion she threw the pear at the shadow with the beady eyes. It shrieked, mirrored Sabine's scream, and raced out of the cottage through an unseen door, just as Niall bashed in through his door. Sword drawn, he stopped over her bath.

"What is it?" he asked. "What made ye scream?"

"A rat, I think," Sabine replied. "*Oui,* a nasty rat with tiny eyes and long teeth."

"One of Rory's pets, no doubt," he said, lowering his sword and taking a long, impolite look at her.

Sabine instantly covered herself with her hands, a futile gesture at best. Futile and a lie. Slowly she slid her hands from her body, brushing aside her hair, gaze forged to his. She allowed her eyes to drop to his chest rising and falling steadily behind his mud-stained tunic and plaid. He was struck mute, and she smiled inwardly at her power over him, but on the outside her entire body trembled.

Niall finally found his grin. She loved his face when he smiled, the furrows on either side of his wide mouth, the way the dimple in his chin disappeared, the way his eyes twinkled and danced beneath arched auburn brows. It warmed her.

"Speechless?" he asked.

"You rarely are," she said breathlessly, "until this night."

Under Niall's admiring gaze she relaxed and trembled at the same time, the feeling strange to her and inviting.

"I have seen fine views and finer views," he whispered, "but this . . . well, there are no words. . . ."

There were thoughts, if not words, for this moment. She was here in Scotland before a man who took her heart and soul to places she had dared not go. She was free of her past, of her troubles, completely and utterly free.

She swallowed. Her throat as taut as an iron band.

"Where there are no words, Niall, there are actions," she said.

"Actions?" he asked, tilting his head just the slightest bit.

She smiled. She had disarmed him. *Très bien.*

Sabine sat up a little, her shoulders out of the water.

"Actions," she repeated.

Niall nodded, quick and brief as if he understood her. "Oh, aye. . . ."

Freedom swept over her like a spring avalanche. She held up her arms. Droplets plinked back to the water in the trough. She forced her body to stop shaking. The next thing that she said had to be done quickly, or else she would flee, or simply vanish.

"Join me?" she asked. *"S'il vous plaît?"*

"Oui!" he shouted, face exploding in a smile from ear to ear.

Niall leapt to the task. He tore off his plaid with his free hand, sent it sailing across the cottage where it landed on the pallet of straw. He then attacked his tunic, jerking it over his neck. He grunted and snarled at the fabric, which seemed intent on binding itself around his head.

Sabine gasped. Niall's full manhood was as exposed for her as his face was not. She felt naughty for staring at him while he struggled so. Perchance she should tell him to stop, to go away. But she could not speak as she stared at the one part of him that was at the ready, even if the rest of him was not.

"'Twould work better to remove your tunic if you laid down your sword," she managed over rapid breaths. What in God's name was she saying?

"Aye," came the muffled reply. The sword fell from one sleeve, tearing it on the way down.

"Niall—!"

The handle of the heavy piece of weaponry clanged down on his foot.

"Ow! Shite!" he exclaimed through the linen. He paused. "Sorry."

This would not work, she told herself. He had to leave her, now. She would wait until this *comèdie* was over, then tell him . . . perchance.

Two knives suddenly fell from his tunic and narrowly missed stabbing his feet. She wondered where he stashed those weapons, and just as quickly did not wish to know.

"Bloody hell!" Niall cried in frustration.

He tore the tunic from his body and tossed it over his head, where it caught on one of the rafters.

Standing there, over her, breathing heavily from his exertion with his clothes, Niall looked every bit the male animal. Sabine swallowed. The firelight to his right side raked shadows over the sculpted contours of his chest and abdomen in tempting chiaroscuro. The scar from his encounter with the arrow was a reddened star-shaped blotch on an otherwise perfect form, one the great Michelangelo would have coveted with hammer and chisel. The blood rushed from her face, the breath evacuated her body just to view such a magnificent sight.

"May I join ye?" Niall asked stepping over the knives.

"Formality from a Highland *sauvage*?" she teased. A nervous giggle escaped, betraying her confused emotions.

"Aye. . . ."

He leaned down and braced both hands on either side of the trough. "No invitation necessary, my love."

"My love?" Sabine smiled. *"Mon Dieu!"*

"Not quite—" Niall's hand slipped. He fell into the trough on top of her.

She laughed as he fought to regain any semblance of balance. Her tension evaporated as quickly as the water that leapt from the trough. Sprigs of heather flew out on tiny waves landing on the earthen floor. A splinter suddenly stabbed her buttocks.

She squirmed under him. "Ouch! Off of me!"

He scrambled off her, suppressing a laugh, and stood over the trough. Sabine stared angrily up at him. "Leave me," she demanded on a foolish whim. It was far from what she truly wanted, so she thought. She had no idea except what her body felt so strongly.

He laughed. "The time is ready for us, has been for a long time. I feel as if I have known ye for an eternity. To deny me with lies from your heart would be a crime."

All she could say was a breathless, *"Oui."*

He gathered her in his arms and carried her against his body to the pallet, where he laid her gently down.

He leaned forward until their lips met, wet and warm, with more passion than one kiss should have. Sabine yielded every piece of her body to him. Yet, she kept a small bit of her soul that allowed her to savor the moment in silent ecstacy. The moment when Niall would take her, when she would give herself to him. The moment she had anticipated, had dreamt of.

His hands roamed across her damp flesh, awakening her more and more, drawing her so close to him she could barely breathe. He glided a hand up her thigh and slipped it downward, fingers splayed and sweeping over the top of her leg. Her flesh danced under his touch as he gave her sweet torment with his fingertips.

Slowly, assuredly, he moved his hand up along the inside of her thigh. She ceased to breathe under the touch of such passion. His hand was fire upon her as it was so perilously near that place no man had ventured. She gasped and told herself to breathe so she would be a part of this moment and the moments she knew would follow.

Niall brushed his hand up to the top of her thigh and across the bottom of her belly, over the gentle swell there. She was suddenly awash in gooseflesh as he teased her so. Her desire to have him touch her more, to place the fullness of his hand upon her built to bursting. Never did she think a touch could do so much, could make her body crave so much.

He placed both of his hands upon her now, more enticement than she could bear. She could not help but willingly gave her body and mind to this enchanting, precious moment. He slid his hand down again to that place between her legs, that place consumed now with enough heat to melt iron. She slowly opened to him, and was quickly rewarded with his smile.

"A dèan gaol," he whispered to her. His burr lovely, comforting, becoming.

"What?" she asked breathlessly, feeling his manhood pressing down on her abdomen as he rested his body on top of hers. She trembled just a little. It was a good tremble.

"To make love, *amour,* Sabine," he replied. "'Tis what it means."

She reached up, burying her right hand in his thick hair. She took in his steady azure gaze, slowly found her voice and spoke the truth from her heart.

"I wish to make love . . . to you and no other."

He nodded slightly, a wry grin on his face. "'Tis what we are doing."

She smiled. *"Aye."*

He drew her nearer to him. He eased her, sensation by glorious sensation, into knowing that at this very moment nothing else existed but the two of them. His art of *amour* made nothing else matter to her, nothing but this very time.

He drew his kisses from her mouth and anointed them upon her waiting flesh. He kissed her breasts, circling his tongue about the dark rounds of taut flesh and heightening her desire more than she had dared dream.

Slowly he drew his lips between her breasts, down her abdomen to the top of the dark triangle between her thighs. Her flesh quivered and she released a tiny moan. Could such pleasure also be a torment?

Niall raised his gaze to meet her own. His eyes sparkled, rivaling the most precious sapphire, a gift he gave to her alone. She reached up and brushed the back of her hand across the strong angle of his jaw. *"Niall . . . mon amour . . . ,"* she whispered.

"Sabine," he said, brushing her desire with his Scottish burr.

Taking a deep breath, he slid a hand under the small of her back and brought her body up into a smooth arch.

She gasped, her pleasure too difficult to contain. Shivers ran through her like a raging Alpine river. She slowly parted her legs as he bridged over her on taut arms, swollen with muscle. He kissed her, stifling another gasp and the moan that rose in her throat as he slowly entered her. Nothing short of the world exploding would cause her to halt this moment.

He slid himself deeper into her, breaking the mantle of her maidenhood. A moan escaped from her throat at the sharp pain, which was rapidly followed by a wash of pleasure as she surrounded him, her blood pumping molten through her body.

"Mon amour. . . ." she breathed. "Again and again."

She soon joined him as they danced passion's *volte.* She matched his rhythm as they climbed the highest mountain in the Highlands. Breaths tore over their lips, lips that found purchase against each other's flesh. They held each other, kept time together, without knowing there was time to be kept. Wind tore up the mountainside, over their skin, raising row upon row of gooseflesh. The air rushed down over them, thundering in their ears, or was it the weather outside? What difference did that make when the summit was so near? They climbed up into air warmer than what they had left behind. The heat built upon itself. Their breaths charged out. Their heads dizzied. Bursting was inevitable.

And Sabine did burst from her very core, over and over, slipping down and climbing up again only to slide back down, over the top of a landslide that crashed down on her. Niall was there with her, every breath, every step, as her lover. She felt she would be warmed forever at the mere thought.

Awash in heat inside her Highlander's embrace, happiness had a new name for Sabine: *MacGregor.*

She fixed on his blue gaze. He had stolen a piece of her heat, yet she was not chilled, oddly enough she was warmed more. She did not mind that he had done so. Ever since she had seen him on that misty wharf, she had been revolted by him yet had wanted him. Now she lay coupled with him, a testament to the unpredictability of her heart.

He moved inside her. She closed about him when he kissed her, his tongue mingled with hers. He knew the French way of kissing very well. She had only experienced it once, and it did not compare to this. Nothing did. She hummed beneath him, lifted her legs, wrapped them about his thighs.

Niall looked down upon her. Damp locks of his hair hung from either side of his face.

"How d'ye feel?" he asked.

There were too many words to describe how she felt. All of them jumbled in her mind. She chose the first and not the most appropriate word.

"Hungry."

"Aye, me too," he said.

Niall climbed from the pallet. She did not let him from her sight.

"Mon Dieu," he whispered. Never had he experienced anything like that before. He had experiences, but nothing that matched what threatened to make his knees buckle. Trying to be steady on his feet, he walked the few paces to the table. He picked up a quince and tossed it over his shoulder. He quickly surveyed the rest of the food he had brought into the shieling. How could he think of his belly at a time like thi—?

He paused. A crunch and the scent of sweetness beckoned him to turn around.

Sabine sat up on the pallet, damp hair spilled down over one shoulder, breasts flushed with their recent lovemaking, nipples stiffened in the cool air, the fire laying shadows and light over the slender length of her body. A thin line of juice from the quince trickled down the hollow at the base of her neck down into the generous valley between her breasts and onward over her softly rounded belly to the luxuriant dark triangle between her smooth thighs. Niall's knees began to give way anew.

"A picture of insane delight," he whispered. "Even ye couldnae draw it."

Without warning, she shot him a seductive smile. "Can one find love here in your Highlands?"

"Aye, 'tis possible."

She smiled and took another bite of quince, her teeth penetrating the golden flesh of the fruit.

Niall grabbed her wrist and took a bite of the fruit. Sabine ate at the other side of the quince until it was gone, leaving them passionate kisses, sweet and sticky.

Niall broke the kiss and trailed his lips down her body to the dark triangle between her legs. He took freely of her own sweet juices, his tongue an instrument for her pleasure.

Weakened by rapture, Sabine slipped down on the pallet and opened herself further, as he made love to her in the French manner. She had only known of such ways in behind-the-hand whispers between Her Majesty's attendants. She had to bite her bottom lip to keep from shouting her ecstasy out to the shadowy rafters. Hands cupping her breasts, fingers digging into the flesh, thumbs toying the nipples into hardness, Niall took her to the brink, his methods unforgiving and expert. Then he kissed her and seized her with his powerful body for another climb through the wind and water, up the highest mountain in Scotland.

chapter 15

❦

Guarding a Secret

"*Stop eating,*" Sabine scolded. "*Or I shall sketch you as you truly are.*"

"Oh, aye?" Niall asked, lifting one brow. The firelight played seductively off his face. "And what am I . . . truly?"

She stopped sketching briefly and savored the recent moments as deeply as the current one. They had shared hours of abandon that would forever be upon her mind. A rare gift that no one could steal from her.

"You are an untamed *animal,*" she said. Praise sweet Saint Giles for that!

"Aye, well, I'm not the only beastie in this cottage. As I recall ye could have used a bit of tying down a wee while ago," he replied with a grin.

"That's why I'm sketching. Keeps urges at bay," she teased.

She continued drawing Niall, completing the sketch she had begun at the castle when her eyes were innocent of him. Recently acquired knowledge emboldened her right hand to render the lines and contours as confidently as the man reclining against a stack of peat bricks before her. The pain in her fingers did not exist, or had she learned to ignore it?

"My God, ye're beautiful," he whispered, swiping meat juices from his lips with the back of his hand. "I wish I could draw ye, but I'm not the artistic sort. Not much use for drawing and such in the Highlands."

"Implying what I am doing is futile?" she asked.

He shook his head, disturbing his pose. Sabine cleared her throat, reminding him to sit still. Niall settled back into his pose. "I wouldnae say what ye do is a waste, not as long as it brings ye happiness. I'm just saying that I've not an artistic bone in my body."

Sabine smiled a half smile. "From my vantage, Niall Mac-Gregor, there's much art about you. However, your true talents are best kept in private company."

He grinned, and Sabine quickly sketched the furrows on either side of his generous mouth.

"Ye enjoyed that, did ye? My 'talents' on the pallet, against the wall, and dangling from the rafters?"

"Dangling from the rafters?"

"Aye. Well, perchance, I've not shown ye the full extent of my abilities."

He slipped away from his place on the opposite side of the fire.

"*Mon Dieu,* Niall!" she protested. "How can I complete my sketch when you—"

He ended her words with a kiss that rivaled the heat of the flames snapping over the bricks of peat.

"Enough sketching," he said, taking the drawing from her lap. "'Tis time I showed ye my prowess on the rafters."

"But, Niall, " she said, "the paper . . . be careful. . . ."

"Dinnae fash," he scoffed, holding the sketch from her reach.

Sabine looked at him, at the paper between his fingers, at the tears she had repaired from Lady Fleming's cruel damage.

"Hold me," she said suddenly, throat tightening so hard she thought it would strangle her.

Niall placed the paper carefully before the fire and gathered her in his arms. He lifted her into the strong security of his lap. Sabine rested her cheek against his chest, the flesh warm under a cool sheen of perspiration that plastered the auburn hairs to his skin. She drew a finger up through the hair, up to his neck, to the bristles on his chin, pausing at the cleft.

"The beauty is in the details," she said, remembering a lesson of long ago in her past.

"Lovely sentiment," Niall remarked, combing his fingers through her hair and down the side of her face. The sensation of hundreds of butterfly wings danced up and down her flesh.

Sabine sighed. "'Twas not mine—the thought, I mean."

"Whose thought, then?"

He pressed his lips to the side of her neck.

She could not keep her memories to herself. Without intent, Niall had given her the desire to tell of her life, the need to purge her soul.

"'Twas from *mon maître*." The tears came much too easily. She gasped and covered her eyes with both hands. Niall gently took her hands away from her face. "Who is this person? *Mon maître.*"

"I cannot tell you." Of course she could, wanted to desperately. She had never trusted anyone as much as she trusted Niall. Yet, her truth was too terrible to speak.

"Aye, ye can," he whispered, calmly urging her to reveal the truth of her past.

"Non!" She tried to pull away from him. But he held her firm with one arm and reached for her *sac* with the other.

"'Tis mine!" she cried. She wanted him to have it, despite her protests, wanted him to know.

"Why d'ye guard these bits and pieces of paper as if they were the royal jewels?" he asked.

"Are you jealous?" she accused.

"I'm never jealous."

He thrust his hand into the *sac* and brandished the papers over her head before the fire. He dropped all but one to the ground. The sketches fluttered about her. He stared up at the sketch that remained in his hand. In a second, so did she.

"Please, don't," she whispered.

Please, do, she thought. Free me, Niall. I know of no one else who can.

"Answer one question," he said, did not demand.

"I hate it when you torment me." She gathered her

sketches and placed them back inside the *sac*. All but the one he held.

"I havenae asked ye the question yet."

Niall showed her the sketch in his hand. A ghost on paper stared back at her, one with a neat beard, a neck like a swan, and a body as stout as an Alpine ram. "Is this *mon maître*?"

"I tell you nothing," she said, folding her arms across her breasts. "You are jealous." Of course, he was not. He was concerned. She should be as much for herself. *Tell him,* her mind screamed.

Niall laughed. "Jealous? I've not been jealous in my life."

"Your tone tells me otherwise."

He rattled the paper before her nose and gave her a heartrending grin. "Please?" he begged.

Her heart melted. She could not deny him.

"Do not beg. Does not suit you."

He kissed her, and her wall crumbled.

"*Mon maître* was my, how do you say? My teacher?" she said.

"Teacher." Niall regarded the sketch. His lips formed into a smirk. "Is that what he told ye?"

She sat upright on his lap. "*Signore* Rinoletti was a fine teacher. He apprenticed under the great da Vinci."

"Da Vinci? Couldnae have been so great. I've not heard of him."

"Why would you? Living here in this wilder—" she stopped.

Niall sighed. "I'll admit that news takes a wee bit longer to make it to this glen."

"I did not mean—"

He placed a finger to her lips. "No apologies, no regrets . . . Come here."

He dropped the sketch and held her close.

"Niall. . . ."

"Aye?"

"Is the past so very difficult to forget?"

"Only if it blinds us to the future."

"So, you do not wish to know more about *Signore* Rinoletti?"

"It can wait, can it not? We are alone here, with a few hours before the glen stirs. 'Twould be a shame to waste it."

Sabine smiled. "Another time then, I will tell you." Or perhaps not at all.

She snuggled against him. "When you took me . . . when I took you before the fire and the times before . . . I never felt so free of the troubles that plague us, the past . . . everything."

"I'm always willing to oblige ye again with my Highland hospitality."

He laid her down on the pallet before the fire. Slowly he worked his body on top of hers. He cradled one hand under the back of her head and helped her to join him in another enchanting kiss.

"Sabine," he whispered, his Scots burr rolling over every letter of her name. "I lo— Oh, bollocks!"

"What?"

Niall rolled off her as quickly as if Her Majesty had just walked in.

"Shite!" he exclaimed.

"What is it?" Sabine asked. She watched him as he scrambled toward the hearth. "Oh, no!"

Niall slapped the flames into nothing on the earthen floor, the flames that had singed one corner of her mended sketch, the one of him.

"I should not have put it there. 'Tis my fault," he said.

Sabine slid the paper from beneath his hand. He was doing more damage by beating the flames into oblivion. She held the paper up and tried to wipe the soil from it.

"Wait!" he shouted.

Startled, Sabine dropped the paper. He caught it before it met the ground.

"What now?" she asked.

He held the paper before the flames. His azure eyes reflected the fire as he studied the sketch. No, he was not. The sketch faced her. Niall was reading the scrawl on the other side.

After a long moment, he looked up at her. "Sometimes the past has to come back to us, even at the most inopportune moment." He held the other side of the paper for her to see. The words were in that Scottish language she did not know. "Where did ye get this?" he asked.

Sabine pulled back from his predatory tone.

"I cannot remember," she lied.

I *dinnae believe ye,"* he snapped, but did not mean to. Sabine's expression was downcast. He hated himself for causing her any pain, for breaking this most beautiful night. But the paper . . . the bloody paper! It had changed everything.

"Sabine," he said, calming his voice and the storm inside his soul, "I'm not accusing ye of anything. This paper is written in the Gaelic. I know ye couldnae have written it, much less read it. Where did ye come by it?"

She wrapped herself in his plaid, tucking her legs up under herself. She looked at him as if she had lost trust in him.

"D'ye wish me to apologize, before ye'll answer my question?" he asked. He was met with silence. "Aye, well, I apologize, dear Sabine, from the depths of my heart. I would never, with intent, do anything to cause ye pain."

He knelt before her, taking her gnarled hand from the plaid and delivering a kiss upon it. "I give ye my word, and the word of a—"

"Oui," she said with a roll of her eyes, "and the word of a MacGregor is as true as the mountains that surround this valley."

"Ye learn well." He glanced at the paper crushed in his fist. "Sorry, again, I apologize." He smoothed out the paper on the spill of plaid coming down from Sabine's shoulders. He rubbed his hands over the drawing of himself, as naked as a bairn. "Ye have captured me well," he remarked. "*All* of me."

"'Tis as God made you."

"As God made me. . . ." A proper excuse for rendering one without a stitch on his body. She was a bold lass with her art. He could not help but love that about her, but there were other matters that must be addressed and quickly.

"Where did ye get the paper?" he asked again.

"Tell me what it says, translate, and I'll be better able to tell you," Sabine said, "because I really do not remember."

He took the paper up, gently this time, and read her the searing words.

"Call to action! The goodly sum of five Royal sovereigns is promised to the man who brings proof that the plaque set ashore of this country is no more."

Niall swallowed. He rubbed his thumb over the small red wax seal, the mark of his enemy: a stag's head inside a tower. Anger gripped him by the throat and squeezed hard.

"This is yet another threat against my clan—a warrant for my execution," he said, voice strained with anger.

"'Tis not a threat to Clan Gregor," Sabine said quickly.

Niall stared at her. "What say ye? How can this not be what I suspect, another affront to my clan?"

"How long has your clan been in these mountains and valleys?" she asked.

"Since the Danes, the bloody Norsemen, were driven out, and before that," he said. "Campbell should be sent to the bloody Danes."

"I've heard Campbell mention this in reference to you. What does it mean, exactly?"

"The worst possible punishment. Scotland sells wool to their merchants at a very fair price, and, in turn, we send them our worst prisoners, those devious, dire folk who would see simple execution as a blessing. The Danish prisons make them pray for death. Campbell deserves worse for what he has done to my—"

"Are you so blinded by the affront done to your people, that you have missed two very important words written there? The same words you translated for me?" she said, interrupting him. He had said similar words to her one time long ago.

"What say ye?" he repeated. "Make sense."

"I know where that paper came from."

"Campbell, but what of it?"

"Dare you say, Niall, chief, *non . . . king* of Clan Gregor, that paper affronts you and your people. Yet, in truth it affronts Her Majesty in the worst possible way, it calls for her murder. She is the one who had 'set ashore,' as the paper states, not your clan." She paused, took a long swallow. "Campbell has given us proof with his seal and . . . *mon Dieu . . .* I saw him."

"Saw who?"

"The man contracted to murder Her Majesty, a brute, who spoke in a guttural tongue. Campbell was searching for this paper to give him, but could not find it because it was in my possession. I did not know what I had until you translated it."

"Sabine, ye've got to remember, who was this person with Campbell?"

"His back was to me. He kept in shadow."

"Remember."

"Does it matter?" she asked. "Does it matter that Her Majesty may be dead by this person. I did not warn her, but was here, enjoying myself."

"Remember, Sabine. Remember the details of him. Ye're an artist. Tell me what ye know, and perchance I will know this hired assassin. *We* can save the queen."

Sabine paused. "Save Her Majesty, *us*?" she asked.

"Aye, we have evidence, proof on this paper, and much more should ye remember all of the details of this man in Campbell's chamber."

Sabine nodded. "I will think, place the details of the brute upon my mind. He was in shadow, his back to me, but I will think on it."

"Perchance this'll help clear your mind."

He took her in his arms and placed a kiss upon her lips. Sabine returned his kiss just as the door burst inward, slammed the wall in a shower of turf.

Niall held Sabine tight with one arm. He stared up at the hulking figure in the doorway, silhouetted against the blue-gray light of a new day. He grappled for his claymore, but it was woefully out of reach, laying beside the trough.

"What spine ye have disturbing this cottage!" he shouted.

Rory stepped into the light of the hearth.

"Och, ye've been putting our domicile to good use, aye? Well done, lad," his friend remarked.

"Bastard," Niall said, drawing his fingers frustratingly through his hair. Rory could test the patience of the sunrise if he had a mind. "Now, would ye bugger off?"

"Aye," Rory said, stepping backward, ducking under the lintel. He paused outside of the doorway. "Just in case ye were wondering, I rallied the men. They'll be here for the gathering this night."

Niall nodded. "Good work. Good man."

Rory closed the door as ordered.

Niall looked at Sabine. "Now, where did we leave off—?"

He stopped. Sabine's eyes were wider than his mother's best trenchers. She looked as if she had seen a terrible apparition, one that chilled her. She shook in his arms, and he held her tighter.

chapter 16

Sabine's Secret

A cool breeze brought afternoon mist into the glen. Gossamer fingers snaked up the face of *Beinn Tulaichean*, thickened and obliterated everything but the heather plants closest to Niall.

The paper in his fist fluttered damply, trying to loosen from his grasp. He held it tighter and read the nasty edict against the queen for the hundredth time that day, knowing he could never take this paper to Her Majesty. A MacGregor could never approach the queen and not suffer arrest. His one try at Her Majesty's masque had proven that.

But there was another whose name had fallen into recent ill repute by Campbell's word, one who could possibly vanquish the charges against herself and his clan with the evidence set forth in the paper Niall held.

"Sabine," he said, the name like honey on his tongue.

She was loyal to Her Majesty. The queen had just to look into her eyes to know the endless depths of her fealty. Sabine did not have the capacity to feign loyalty, or anything, if the night's past held the depth of her truth. There was no doubt in his mind that she would find a way to see her queen. And find a way for *him* to see Her Majesty as well. Sabine had done it before, only this time there was much at stake.

He had to make a decision and soon. As chief of Clan Gregor there was only one decision for him to make: to take Campbell's order of murder to his queen. It was undeniable proof, signed and sealed by Campbell. Sabine would have to help him, but it was far too dangerous for her to get near the queen with Campbell about. She would be tossed into the gaol once she showed her pretty head in court. Sabine would have to stay behind with his clan, whether she wanted to or not.

Something moved in the mist.

Seizing the handle of his claymore with both fists, Niall slid it soundlessly from the leather sheath and took steady aim.

"*Có thusa?*" he demanded.

No reply.

He raised his sword higher, ignored the tug of pain in his healing shoulder. The mist thickened about him. He stood in the damp heather, legs braced apart, feet firmly on the ground. His arms did not tremble, but his soul did. He had yet to kill a man with his claymore. That day, he feared, would come as certain as his own death.

"*Có thusa!*" he shouted to the mist.

A lock of hair fell over one eye. He dared not remove a hand from the claymore to brush it aside.

Something stepped up to him through the mist.

"*Có thusa!*"

"*Comment?*"

But the reply was too late. He had already stabbed his blade forward . . . into the basket Sabine carried.

Shrieking, she leapt backward. Niall reached out and grabbed her by the wrist, keeping her from falling.

"Dinnae tumble down the ben, *chérie,*" he said. "How did ye make it up here, alone, in the mist?"

Breasts straining against her brocade gown as she caught her breath, Sabine stared at Niall. He smiled at her, loving the way her dark eyes flashed.

"*Imbécile,*" she scolded. "I was born near mountains higher than this." She paused, then said, "You could have skewered my belly with that weapon. 'Twas *fortuit* that you skewered your *petit déjeuner* instead."

The basket hung ridiculously from the end of Niall's blade. He peered inside. A bannock was speared through, the meat was spared.

He grinned. "My blade is swift and sure when I wish to halve my bread. Care to join me in this fine repast?"

"'Twas my intention," she said with a small smile. "But, *s'il te plaît,* sheathe your sword."

Niall slid the blade from the basket and laced it neatly over his shoulder, into its leather sheath. "Does my blade frighten ye?" he asked, watching her bend down to take the basket from the heather, watching the way her gown hung smooth over her fine, firm bottom.

She stood up and stared him down. "'Tis not your blade that frightens me so, Highlander, but the sureness of your wielding."

He stepped forward, took her by the waist and pulled her close. She must have felt his growing passion. The small gasp that burst over her lips told him that she had.

"I'm glad ye're here," he said. "Ye're the most wonderful thing that has happened to me."

She looked into his eyes. "I shall say the same, Niall. For I have never been so light-headed with happiness as when I am with you."

"'Tis the Highlands that have lightened yer head, my love. Ye're up where the birds soar."

He kissed her, burying his fingers into her hair, which he noticed she had worn loose ever since she had come to the glen. She was herself here, free to roam the bens and glens without fear, protected by his kith and kin, free to let her hands slide up his kilt—

"Why, *mademoiselle*," he purred, "ye're a wee minx."

"I told you, Niall MacGregor, 'tis not your swift sword that frightens me. *Au contraire.* It intrigues me." She sealed his lips in a strong kiss. A moan escaped his throat as she unashamedly massaged him, bringing him to full fruition, until he thought his breath would leave him for good.

He took her down to the heather, on top of him. With both hands he slid her gown up her legs. She shoved his kilt up his thighs, bunching it to his waist, revealing him to the mist. Then she straddled him. He smiled in the knowing that he had played a part in embolding her, taught her what he knew in the ways of lovemaking. She was a very good student.

He reached up, cupped her breasts through the brocade. Sabine arched her back, sliding her body flawlessly over him. Niall grasped her rounded hips and pulled her harder against him. She wrapped her hands around the back of his neck and kissed him.

He closed his eyes. Bliss could exist inside him. There were more important things than his name. The first one was the completeness of his soul. Without that, how could he solve the problems that existed in the glen below them? He opened his eyes and wished he could draw, wished he could express in some material way the beauty of body and spirit before him.

He drew in the deepest of breaths and rode with Sabine through the mist.

"Ye make me complete," he breathed. "Ye give me strength."

"A gift that is mutual, *mon amour*," she whispered.

They remained coupled for an eternity that lasted at least until their stomachs rumbled for the food Sabine had brought.

"Y ou are wanted in the valley," Sabine told Niall around a dry bite of Scottish cake. "By your subjects."

"I'm not a king," he said, taking a large bite of meat. "I've told ye that many times. Is yer head full of *fromage*?"

She tilted her head, cocking one eyebrow at him. "Are you making fun of me, Highlander?"

"*Non.*" He grinned.

She would never slap such smugness from his face. It was too much of an endearing part of him that she had grown accustomed to. "We should not tarry."

Niall gave her shoulder a squeeze. "I like the way ye tarry, my love."

Sabine smiled. "Your mother told me to get you."

"*My mother?*" he asked, aiming a finger into the swag of plaid across his shoulder. "She told ye that?"

"'Tis not so crazy, Niall. I think she knows about us, has come to some agreement in her own mind. She helped me assemble this repast."

"My mother comes to no agreement. She decides when things are the way she wants them to be and gives her consent."

"She consents to me?"

"Ye impressed her by sitting at the *waulk*ing table, participating without pretense. If there's one thing my mum hates, that's pretense."

"We should go."

"The gathering is not until sunset. We have time."

A breeze blew a thick pall of mist between them. Something landed on Sabine's lap. She looked down. It was her drawing of Niall.

"Tell me, Sabine, why d'ye look so darkly when ye gaze upon this picture?"

"'Tis not the sketch, Niall."

"'Tis a bonny drawing. Looks just like me, too much like me. I pray Her Majesty willnae get a muckle eyeful when I show her the other side of this paper."

A bell as loud as the one in the belfry of Chamonix cathedral tolled in Sabine's head.

"Non!" she cried. "You cannot show it to my queen!"

She reached for the paper, but Niall grabbed it and held it beyond her reach.

"Give it to me," she said, refusing to plead for what was hers.

Niall lowered the paper. She took it from him, folded it several times, and tucked it into her bag. She did not raise her eyes to meet his.

"Why did ye act so?" he asked.

"No one can see this sketch" she said, the memory of long ago, of a woman-child who had witnessed the most shocking of horrors, rose in her mind. "Because you will die . . . Agnes was right—I have brought your death."

Niall took her in his arms and held her tight. She could feel his heart pounding against her own.

"Tell me why." He did not demand, he did not order her. His words and the way he said them were from his heart. She could not help but want to tell him everything, allowing the pain of memory out into the misty Highland air.

Sabine took a deep breath, and soon the words rolled icily over her lips. She had been on the cusp of telling him early this morning, but had joyfully been interrupted by their love-making. Would she be so fortunate a second time? Not likely after their most recent bout of bliss.

"Five years ago, I returned to my father's *château* from an outing near Mont Blanc. I had been sketching, had waited in vain for *mon maître* to join me afield, but he did not arrive to teach me more."

She swallowed down the lump forming in her throat.

"Inside the *château*'s *grand foyer* hung a massive iron chandelier. It was old and looked like a giant spiderweb that hung from the vaulted ceiling by four thick lengths of chain. Some of the candles were lit, some were guttered into nothing more than reedy drippings, frozen on the black iron and . . . stained with the blood. I looked up and droplets of blood fell like rain on my arms, the palms of my perfect hands, and my face."

"Who was it, Sabine? Whose blood fell on ye?" she heard Niall ask from so far away, from his place in another life that she wished could be hers forever.

"*Signore* Rinoletti," she whispered. "*Mon maître.* His neck was severed, almost all the way through."

"Oh, dear God," Niall breathed into her neck, his forehead pressed to the side of her face.

Sabine continued, her words rolling from her mouth.

"My father's servants must have put him there. He could not have lifted *Signore* Rinoletti or raised the chandelier . . ."

Niall held her closer.

". . . But 'twas my father who murdered *mon maître.* His hand could wield the knife, that I know. He left the body for me to find. *Signore* Rinoletti was a respected guest in our house, until Father found my portfolio. I killed—"

"No, Sabine," Niall said quickly. "Ye dinnae kill anyone."

The truth attacked her with the ferocity of a midwinter blizzard.

"Everyone I have ever loved has died. *Ma mère,* she died when I was eleven, of the consumption. My brother, Yves, died in the war with the English a year later. Father became so protective of me. He suffocated me. Kept me prisoner. 'Twas no wonder that he thought *Signore* Rinoletti a threat when he found those sketches."

She looked up into his face. Her hair blew in errant strands across her face. "*Oui,* Niall, I did. I killed *Signore* Rinoletti, because I drew him."

"Not possible, Sabine," he said.

"'Tis!" she cried. She dug her right hand frantically in her bag, twisted fingers fumbled for the scraps of paper, pulled out a fistful, and dumped them in her lap. She immediately lifted out two between the wreckage of her fingers, one paper large, the other quite small. She held the large one before Niall's face.

"Do you not see this? I completed it from memory while locked in my bedchamber, waiting the fate my father would hand me for daring to practice my art, for daring to fall in love. 'Tis *mon maître* as I remember him, as he allowed me to draw him. Can you not see what my father saw? This sketch is of an unclothed man, a man who willingly gave his body to my eyes and nothing more. I would have wished for more, even stole a kiss from him, but he would not sate a young girl's yearnings. He was a gentleman. My father could not see anything but an abomination in him and in my sketch!"

She dropped the drawing to the heather and took the smaller paper between thumb and forefinger. "This is what remains of the 'abomination' my father saw."

She showed Niall the face of *Signore* Rinoletti, sketched in charcoal, sketched from life, sketched from her heart. "'Tis all that remains of my portfolio. I found some of the scraps on the floor, beneath the chandelier, decorated with drops of *mon maître*'s blood. The rest of the scraps were stuffed in his mouth."

Niall took the paper from her and, without a second glance, slid it into her bag. He grasped her right hand, gently flexed her fingers outward, and rubbed the pad of his thumb over her flesh, sending shivers up her arm.

"Was this your fate?" he asked.

Sabine glanced at her hand before looking into Niall's eyes. *"Oui."*

"Your father's doing?"

"Oui."

Silence fell between them. Sabine searched her mind for the right way to tell Niall the unspeakable. There was no right way other than the truth.

"We grew apples at the *château*. Beautiful small *pommes,* of many colors, red, orange, green, yellow. Autumn was, at one time, my favorite season, when the apples were ripe, full of juice."

Niall gave her twisted hand a gentle squeeze. There was no pain in her hand, only in her words.

The words tumbled out over her lips. She could not help it. She had told no one, had never wanted to, until now.

"There was a pressing room under the château, for the apples. My father had an idea to turn them into wine. Grapes, grown so far away in Provence, were not good enough for him. He took me there . . . into the pressing room."

"Sabine," Niall said, "ye dinnae have to tell me more."

"I wish to," she whispered. "If I share this, perchance it will go away."

He drew her nearer, against his firm chest. Sabine placed her right hand into the folds of his linen tunic. She took a deep breath and continued. "My father could not do the deed himself. He ordered two of the servants to screw down the press while he held my hand in the sticky remains of the apples between the boards. The pain came slowly at first. It drowned out my screaming, thundered in my ears, but it could not drown out my father's threats. He was so certain he would steal my art. What he did was give me strength and a choice: the convent or royal servitude."

"Fortunately for me, ye chose royal service." Niall would not let her dwell in the pain of her past, this she knew. He held her so tight against the rough linen of his tunic, the warmth of his body beneath.

"I did not let my father win. Now he's gone, but my art lives. It lives in these Highlands. It lives when I look at you. But if you take that paper to Her Majesty and she sees the sketch on the reverse, you will die. She will think 'tis vulgar, and have you in the gaol before you can show her what is on the other side."

"Then I will read quickly to her those words. She will find them far more vulgar."

"I wish I never had that paper," she said. "You would not wish to take yourself into the lion's den if you did not have it. They will take you, Niall, and Her Majesty will have you executed because you are a MacGregor."

"And if I dinnae take this paper to the queen, she will die."

Sabine drew in a long sigh. "Then I will take it to my queen."

Niall pulled her away and looked harshly into her eyes. He had to know as well as she that their goal was one, but only she could carry it out.

"No, ye willnae," Niall said. "I for—"

"You forbid it?" she asked. Only her father, Lord Campbell, and her queen had forbidden her from anything.

Sabine rushed to stand, but Niall held her down, practically crushing her against his body.

"Let me go!" she cried.

"I will do what I'm bound for my clan. 'Tis my will," he said firmly.

"You cannot go to Her Majesty," she managed to say. "You must stay here, safely in your valley."

"And wait for Campbell to send all of the queen's men down upon us?" Niall asked.

"You said they could not find you."

"I am one person. And, aye, I can hide, but that willnae protect my clan . . . or ye, Sabine."

Niall leaned down and kissed her, dousing her fear for the moment. And for the moment, Sabine guessed, he most likely thought he had won their argument.

She swallowed. She had not told him all her secrets that day. One plagued her since early morning. Was it truth or her artist's eyes tugging too hard upon her good sense? When Rory had burst into the cottage, standing there in silhouette, his hulking body a monolith barring the doorway, her gaze and her heart had frozen. She could not bring herself to tell Niall that the man she had seen with Campbell, the intended recipient of that order to murder the queen, was his friend Rory. She prayed her eyes had betrayed her and it was not him.

● ● ●

W**omen are not allowed at the gathering,"** Niall told her that evening.

"Stay with Mum," he said, both hands on her shoulders, gently emphasizing his words. He looked deep into her eyes. "Aye? Will ye do that?"

She nodded slowly, her thoughts in another place. Perchance she was wrong. How could Rory have been the man in Campbell's chamber? He was Niall's old friend. Loyalty was as much a part of these Highlanders as the crisp air they breathed. She must have been mistaken. All she had caught of that mysterious stranger was a shadowy glimpse of profile. It could have been anyone.

Sabine placed herself back into Niall's blue stare. Was this denial wishful thinking? If she told him what she suspected, what would he think of her? He had known Rory all his life. He had known her for a mere blink of time. But what a blink!

"I have to go now," he said, fingers gripping her shoulders hard. The crease between his brows deepened. Was there something he had to tell her?

Sabine inched closer. Gave him the opportunity. Surely he wanted to take her with him to this wholly male gathering. She waited for an invitation.

"Bide with Mum. I'll be back soon," he said. Slowly he released her, paused, and leaned down, placing a small, but searing kiss upon her lips. He gave her a wink and left the cottage without another word.

Perchance he had nothing at all to tell her, just wanted a kiss.

She turned from the door, right into mistress MacGregor's stare.

"Well, lass?" she asked, raising one grayed brow. "Dinnae stand there like a statue. There's supper to be made."

Sabine's gaze shifted to the cauldron over the musty hearth fire. It was always there, with something inside, simmering. It seemed to her that supper was always ready in this cottage. Nevertheless, she was glad for the distraction. Niall would be with his clansmen, well and good, acting their leader—very well and good.

"And protected by those who serve him," she breathed.

"To it, lass!" Niall's mother shouted and tossed an onion at her. Sabine caught it securely in her left hand. Mistress Mac-Gregor eyed her right hand before turning back to her perpetual place at the hearth.

Sabine drifted to the pockmarked worktable, the onion in her fist. She dropped it on the table and glanced over her shoulder to see if mistress MacGregor had noticed. She remained hunched over the cauldron stirring, always stirring.

Sabine took up a knife beside several bundles of herbs. She had eaten this Highland cooking for four days now, and each time hoped the meals would not be so woefully absent of the flavor herbs could provide.

She took one of the bundles and raised it to her nose. Thyme. *Très bon.* She did not have to sniff the other to know it was dried violet. She laid the thyme on the table with the onion. As she quartered the onion, her gnarled fingers holding the knife surprised her with their steadiness and lack of pain. Niall would like her addition to the evening's repast. He had sampled the food in Her Majesty's court, whether invited to or not, he knew the French manner of cooking with plenty of herbs. She chopped the onion into tiny pieces, then began mincing the thyme into them. She hoped Niall would think it was nice—

"What are ye doing to my herbs, *outeral*?" The harsh whisper stabbed her in the ear.

Startled, Sabine almost chopped her thumb off. She dropped the knife onto the bits of onion and thyme, still clutching the remains of the herb bundle with her left hand.

She turned and looked into Agnes's lightning stare. All of the fury of a hundred storms lay in those pale eyes. Her blonde hair was a wild, knotted mass framing her angry face. With the quickness and agility of a wildcat, she snatched what was left of the thyme bundle from Sabine's grasp and wielded it before her eyes.

"This is to cleanse, and *this* . . ." Agnes grabbed the bundle of violets and thrust them under Sabine's nose. The spicy fragrance teased her nostrils. ". . . These violets are for a poultice."

She shoved Agnes's hand away from her face and tipped her chin high.

"That doesnae work with me, *outeral*," Agnes growled. "I

ken ye. I ken what ye want. Ye came here and made a good man break a vow to his dead father. Now . . ." She shook the herbs in Sabine's face and gave her a sly smile. ". . . I have to make amends."

Before Sabine could respond to the wild ranting, Agnes disappeared from the cottage. All that remained before her stunned eyes was a thick pall of musty peat smoke.

Ye came here and made a good man break a vow to his dead father.

What had Agnes meant by that?

Sabine turned toward mistress MacGregor. The old Scot stood upright from the hearth. Her bones creaked and snapped at the effort. She placed a spotted hand at the small of her back and tried to continue her journey to standing. Without a second's hesitation, Sabine stepped to the hearth and laid her hands on top of mistress MacGregor's and helped her to stand.

"Thank ye, lass . . ." she paused. ". . . Would ye be at wanting a bit of cake and broth?" Her question was tinged with more kindness toward Sabine than she had yet to hear.

Mistress MacGregor paused and eyed the pulverized onion. "Such wee bits are no' much good in my soup."

"Will add more flavor," Sabine said. Perchance she would ask a bit later. "If it's in 'wee bits.' Or so I've been told."

"In France?" Mistress MacGregor reached down and took up some small pieces of onion between her fingers. "Ye can cook?"

"My mother, she loved to cook, despite having the servants to do it for her. Sometimes I watched her."

Niall's mother rubbed the onion between her fingertips, gave them a sniff. "What is this herb ye've minced?"

"Thyme."

"It has a bonny scent. 'Tis used for healing herbs, no' for cooking." Mistress MacGregor sprinkled the onion and herb back to the pile on the table.

"So Agnes told me. She said it was for cleaning . . . wounds I guess, she did not say exactly."

"What did she say exactly?" Niall's mother asked, neatly laying out the opportunity for Sabine to ask a very important question without fear of incurring the Scot's wrath.

"Because of me, Niall has broken a vow to his late father."

Mistress MacGregor stared at her for several of the quietest moments Sabine had ever known before she said, "Let us sit by the fire, lass."

She pointed a gnarled finger at one of two chairs by the hearth. Sabine waited for her to sit first before she took her seat. Her *sac* dangled down from her hip. Sabine reached down and placed it on her lap.

"All Niall's father wanted for him was a lifetime of happiness. He knew the lad wouldnae be chief, with all of its worries and problems. That destiny was reserved for my eldest lad, Colin."

"Niall once spoke fondly of him to me."

"Aye, they were almost as close as Niall is to Rory . . . inseparable they were, with Rory oft in the middle, their champion. All was put asunder when my dear husband and my firstborn were murdered in Edinburgh, because of an order ratified by the father of *your* queen."

"But she is your queen as well, mistress. She did not levy the order. She has the power to—"

"To what, lass? Take back what has already been done? Bring my husband and firstborn back from their graves? Even your queen with all manner of good intentions couldnae do that."

"Your bitterness, mistress, is justified. But if Her Majesty can be convinced to take back this law against your people, then the lives of your clan will be spared, is that not true? And, your second born, your Niall, is the man to sway the queen to do that very thing. Yet, he would be in too much danger if he tried."

Mistress MacGregor offered her a small smile, a grin so like that of her son. "Ye will be by his side when he attempts this folly, lass? Is that what ye've a mind?"

Sabine could not answer to the bluntness of the Scot's question right away. She swallowed and gripped her *sac,* for the ball inside. Instead she grabbed a fistful of the papers through the soft leather. They crinkled.

"What have ye there?" Mistress MacGregor asked.

"Niall is very close to restoring the name MacGregor."

Sabine removed the proof of Campbell's treason from the *sac* and showed it to her.

"'Tis a great problem, mistress MacGregor. One, I fear, may take Niall to his death . . . and I foolishly brought it to him."

"A problem?"

"The undeniable evidence that Lord Campbell wishes the queen murdered."

Sabine offered the paper for her to see, but mistress Mac-Gregor waved it away. "'Twould do no good, lass. For I cannae read."

"Shall I tell you what it says? It is your native tongue, but I can recount what Niall told—"

"'Tis proof of Campbell's treason against our new queen, ye say. And my son has seen this?"

"*Oui,* he has."

"And what plans does he have regarding it?"

"To show it to the queen . . . at the proper time . . . soon, I fear."

"Yer feelings mirror my own." Mistress MacGregor leaned forward, bones creaking a little. She took both Sabine's hands in her own, pressing the paper between them. "Have ye another plan . . . one my son doesnae know about?"

"*Oui,*" Sabine said, tipping her chin up a little. "I will go to my queen without him."

"Will Campbell let ye near her? I hear he is her council on Highland matters."

"That is where I need Niall's help. I wish him to safely escort me back to Holyrood."

"Does he know this?"

Sabine shook her head. "He does not. That is why, I guess, he is at this gathering of men, his warriors, plotting a siege upon Campbell to get him out from between Clan Gregor and the queen. Battle cannot be the way. 'Twill need subtlety."

"No' a trait many men possess," mistress MacGregor quipped. "Especially my son."

She released her hold of Sabine's hands, the paper between her fingers. Sabine caught a glimpse of the drawing on the other side. Mistress MacGregor caught far more than a glimpse as she unfolded the paper before her eyes. "This sketch, I dinnae have to ken how to read to understand it."

Sabine bowed her head. "I . . . I did not mean for—"

"Dinnae apologize, lass. 'Tis a good likeness of my son, a *very* good likeness. Did he pose for ye?"

She could only reply with unflinching honesty. "*Oui,* mistress, he did."

"Well," Niall's mother said with a sharp breath over her lips, "I shall return this to your care. Keep it well hidden, lass, for my son needs it."

"I will, mistress."

The old Scot glanced off into the hearth, certain to take up her spoon and stir the soup. But she remained firmly in her chair.

"Mistress, is there something else you wish to tell me?"

"Niall's father wished him happiness. Wanted him to have the best wife, one of fortunate birth, one who could strengthen the clan by bringing more people to it. Our numbers are far fewer than most clans."

"Quality does not lie in numbers," Sabine said.

"But strength does, lass. Before his father set off for Edinburgh, Niall made him a promise . . . one I must tell ye now . . . one I am compelled to tell ye for no other reason than to spare ye from giving yer heart away."

"My heart is already Niall's willing servant," Sabine said quickly.

Mistress MacGregor took her right hand, rubbing her spotted, knobby fingers over it. "Take back yer heart, lass. This ye must do."

Heat built behind Sabine's eyes. "Why, mistress?"

"Because Niall is betrothed to another."

"No, mistress," Sabine breathed.

The world suddenly slipped out from under her into a void as deep and forbidding as the pits of hell.

"No one kens this, not even his future bride's brother . . . Lord Campbell. 'Twas the only way my husband saw to bring peace between our clans, by marriage."

Sabine grabbed hold of herself enough to ask a question. "Lord Campbell does not have a sister. I have not seen her in his castle."

"Lord Campbell does have a sister, one he is estranged from, one he would wish was dead. But her blood runs strong to his clan, and her marriage to Niall will bring support from some, if not all, of Campbell's people to us. They will have our land, we will have theirs. 'Tis an arrangement my husband thought best for Clan Gregor, best for Niall, our second son—"

"Who is she, mistress!" Sabine demanded, the tears swelling in her eyes.

"Agnes."

And the world turned to darkness as Sabine rushed from the cottage into the night to find Niall and, she prayed, find proof that his mother had told her one horrible enormous lie.

chapter 17

Two Betrayals

Niall gave his warriors, several dozen strong, a hearty, assuring wave as he turned from them. He felt their stares on his back as he departed the small clearing in the woods a quarter league from the cottages. He had left them with a promise that after first light, on the morrow, victory would be Clan Gregor's. Campbell would fall, and the queen would be saved. He did not bother to tell them that all these things hinged on the desire of one beautiful, spirited Frenchwoman to give him the proof against his enemy.

He decided long ago that she would not accompany him when he took the proof to the queen and brought Campbell down. Of course he had yet to tell her this. The prospect loomed more frightening than facing down Campbell. He did not wish to lose Sabine. She would be safe and well inside his glen. This he had to convince her.

"Not an easy task," he murmured.

Nothing that would happen from this time until dawn would be easy. It was a comforting and familiar feeling. He quickened his pace back to the cottages, then he broke into a run along the narrow path. The trees were more of a hindrance than the darkness of night. He knew this path well, the direction of it. He wacked branches out of his way and continued onward to the cottages. Rory had departed the gathering shortly before, to attend to business of a highly personal nature. Niall would join him soon, and they would ride through the night to Glen Fuil and await the clansmen.

Sabine had to give him the proof bearing Campbell's seal on such a harsh threat to Her Majesty. They had no knowledge of the identity of the man she saw in Campbell's chamber, the paper would have to suffice.

A sudden figure emerged from the darker-than-dark cover of the trees.

Niall did not miss a breath as he cleanly unsheathed the claymore that rode on his back and brought it forward with one smooth sweep over his shoulder.

"Who are ye?" he demanded.

The figure raised one hand.

"'Tis Agnes."

Niall stopped and lowered his sword.

"What are ye doing here?" he asked. *"Spying?"*

She huffed. "Ye would think so," she said. "Ye, who still sees me sided with a brother, *my* brother, who banished me from my own home."

"I cannae deny your name is Campbell," he said. "While I'm chief of Clan Gregor he willnae get away with the things he did when my father was head of this clan."

Agnes smiled. "Of course, he willnae. But ye've been a stupid lad nonetheless."

Niall narrowed his eyes. "Ye best stand aside. I've still my claymore in hand."

Agnes stepped forward, facing him. "Ye bring that Frenchwoman into this glen and think all will be well. She is betrothed to my brother, and yet ye've coupled with her. Is that how ye do better than yer da?"

"Ye know nothing," Niall snarled.

"I know from the look in her eyes, the same look I had the day yer father and mine agreed that we should wed . . . the very same day I gave my maidenhead to yer brother, Colin."

Niall stared at her, not knowing whether to feel relief that she would not pursue marriage to him, or whether to feel betrayal that Colin took his brother's betrothed to his bed.

"Colin is dead," Agnes said. "I want ye to avenge his death as well as ye do. Bring my brother down for casting me out after Father died."

"I will," Niall replied. "For that reason and many more."

Agnes smiled, then began to laugh. Niall winced. She cackled like a hag. Little wonder Campbell tossed her out. Who would want a witch in his midst?

Then suddenly, as if she could read his thoughts, or, more likely, the look of disdain that he could not conceal, Agnes shoved Niall hard. He stumbled backward, his claymore landing on the ground before he did. He hit the ground to the side of the path and felt as if he had fallen into a nest of angry hornets.

Worse. He had fallen into nettles.

I*s this how ye show your gratitude?" he asked, feeling the* sting of tiny thorns and the cool night air against the bared skin of his buttocks. "Shove me into nettles?"

"Ye gave me the same look my brother did before he banished me. I'm no' a witch. Or did ye look at me with the knowing that I have never loved you," Agnes said from behind and above him. "I always loved Colin. Is that what made ye look at me so?"

"It's a bloody relief that ye loved Colin," Niall said through gritted teeth. "I couldnae be more happy."

He rested the side of his face on a carpet of damp moss. His body was spread out under Agnes, his kilt was flapped up his back, giving leave for the chilly night air to cultivate row upon row of gooseflesh upon his bare arse. The moss felt soft under his body. It was the only comforting thing about this night, in addition to the fact his clansmen had listened to him and agreed to lay siege upon Castle Campbell. He would join them, aye, but not with an arse full of nettles. He could not ride in such a state.

"My bloody triumph awaits me," he said. "If I can ever get there."

"Hold still," Agnes scolded.

"Ye have me where ye want me," he said. "Dinnae take advantage."

"Of what? Yer wee arse? Such treasure is best given to fine French lassies. 'Tis the only way ye'll win her heart," she teased, giving him a playful whack on the backside. A fiery sting bloomed from where she struck him.

"Ow! To it! I've things to do . . . important things."

"Are ye gonnae ask the French *outeral* to be yer wife, now that we have gracefully stepped from yer promise to yer father and mine to unite our clans?"

"That's not been on my mind. Besides, she's betrothed to your brother, remember."

"A farce, ye ken that as well as I. My brother's tastes din-nae go for the lassies, never have. If I ken him, and I do even though I havenae seen him in the year since our father died, he has used the lass for his own means."

"He did, used her, blamed her for trying to murder Her Majesty, when it was his archer who all along shot the arrow intended for the queen."

"What archer?" Agnes placed a cool poultice on his back-side.

Niall flinched a little. "I wish I knew."

The undergrowth a few feet from where he lay rustled. Niall did not reach for his claymore. He knew who was push-ing aside enough bracken and shrubbery for three men. Thank God his friend had chosen to do his personal business well off the path. Rory stepped out of the forest almost on top of Niall.

"Oy! Watch yer step, ye gad!" he shouted.

"Don't move!" Agnes scolded.

"What're ye doing on the bloody ground?" Rory asked.

"Getting a good shagging," Niall snapped. "What does it bloody look like!"

"Betrayal," came the reply, with a French accent.

"Oh, shite," was all Niall could say.

*S*abine clenched her right hand into a tight ball.
It was not difficult for her to ignore the pain that radi-ated up her arm and struck her heart. She was too occupied searching for her strength. She needed it now more than she ever had. Her heart was breaking. It would take strong hands to mend it.

"Bâtard Écossais," she hissed.

"Now, wait, Sabine," Niall protested, trying to rise up from the ground. Agnes straddled him, her hands on his bare buttocks, massaging him there.

"You 'now wait,'" Sabine said. "I know about you and this *sorcière.* Your mother, she told me everything!"

"Apparently she didnae." Niall struggled to get out from under Agnes. "Get off me, woman!"

"Do not bother to rise," Sabine said, the fury surging within her, beginning at her toes. It grew like a snowstorm, inch by rapid inch. "I wish my last memory of you to be like this. I was a fool to think you worthy, thinking you honorable."

"Agnes was just—" Niall shouted.

"I know what 'she was just'!" Sabine shouted.

She had given him her heart. She had been such a stupid fool. How could a Highland *sauvage* give himself to one woman? He lived like an animal, and rutted like an animal . . . now, while he lay upon the ground, bared to the night, he had never looked so much like a beast. And she had fallen in love with him. Falling out of love was a most dismal prospect indeed, but an easy one with this sight before her.

Niall finally managed to get out from under his intended.

Sabine took several steps backward. She stared at Agnes, who rose boldly beside Niall.

"You have won, *sorcière,*" she said. "I give you your wish. I am leaving."

"NO!" Niall shouted. "Ye will *not!*"

Sabine turned away from him. Rory barricaded her way.

"I am leaving," she said flatly.

The mammoth just shook his head and stared down at her.

She stepped to the left of him, off the path. He mirrored her. She stepped to the right. He followed her move.

"No games!" she cried.

"No games," Niall said behind her.

She whirled around, the heat building in her eyes, blinding her.

"Hear me out," he said.

"You cannot tell me what I already know."

"Sabine—"

"Do not say my name. You could run me through with that large Highland sword of yours and do me no more pain than I have witnessed and heard this night. I wish now that the darkness would cover your face, so I may not ever look upon it."

"Ye must not . . ." Niall said, taking her left wrist. He pulled her against his body, that heated, firm body where she had once sought protection and love. How foolish of her.

The storm built within her, reached her heart. She did not care about Niall, his body, or any other thing about him. She had lost the trust, had lost the trust her queen had in her, had lost the life she had known in recent years, had grudgingly begun to accept, all because of this Highland man who had played with her heart and done as he pleased, without a by-your-leave!

"Listen to me!" he shouted.

Demands, always demands from men. Were they not good for anything else?

"I am leaving," she said under her breath. "And there's nothing you or anyone can do to stop me."

She looked through her hair and into his eyes. His blue gaze had lost its magic upon her. Betrayal had dulled the colors, made the hue normal, like everyone else.

"I have proof of Campbell's treachery against my queen. I will take it to her . . . and save her," she said. "I, alone."

"*We* will save her," Niall countered.

"There is no *we,* only me! All you have to take to the queen is your damned name and your worthless honor!"

Niall tightened his grip on her wrist. Was that red she saw in his eyes?

The snowstorm froze her heart, and its fury forced her gnarled fingers to ball into a tight fist.

"Release me," she growled.

"Not until ye—"

All she saw was the blinding rage of the storm within her. Then she felt Niall's face as it gave way to her right fist. For the blink of an eye, she hated herself. Then she hated Niall for making her feel that way, for making her do the unthinkable, for making her sink to Campbell's level, and that of her father.

Hell, where they dwelled, would be a welcome reward from this torment upon her now.

Sabine barely knew the woman who suddenly left destruction in her wake and escaped into the night, while inwardly cradling the remains of her shattered heart.

"Bloody woman!" Niall shouted into the star-filled night. But stars did not dance on the ground, did they?

He could only keep one eye open. The other eye, swollen shut, held the stars against a burning darkness. His head seemed to have been cut in two by an expanding fissure of pain and dizziness. No man had ever struck him as hard.

"Damn woman!" he cursed again. He managed to rise to his hands and knees.

"I'll get the lassie," Rory said from somewhere far away.

"Aye," Niall rasped. "Get her, drag her here if ye have to. I'll be along . . . soon . . . bloody hell . . . owwwww. " A fresh bundle of pain stabbed his eye right into the center of his head. He tore a fistful of damp moss from the ground and placed it over his eye.

He rose on shaky legs. Agnes tried to help him up, but he shrugged her away. "I'm fine," he lied.

"Och, aye, I can see that," she scoffed. "The French lass has a mighty swing in her fist, has she no'?"

"Tell me what I dinnae know," he growled.

He willed his legs forward. Why was the ground moving beneath him? Niall swallowed and tried to ignore the pain, all the worse because Sabine had delivered it to him.

If she had only heard him out, not been so stubborn. But he had seen the enormous hurt in her eyes, knew at that moment he should have told her about Agnes.

"What was there to tell her?" he grumbled to himself, while stumbling down the narrow path toward the cottages. "I had promised my father I'd marry Agnes as a weak effort to bring peace to these lands. It was a promise ill-conceived, not important. Telling her would have only burdened her with more strife."

He spoke these things aloud, practiced what he would tell

Sabine when he saw her. If it took Rory holding her down so he could tell her, then so be it.

As he made his way through the forested path, and through the pain, he pondered the question Agnes had so deftly posed to him.

Are ye gonnae ask the French outeral *to be yer wife?*

Such a powerful question. Niall had told her the notion had never entered his mind, when in truth it had, on several occasions. Sabine was betrothed to Campbell, but only in word, not in the banns. However, the queen had given her consent to the marriage, and the queen's consent was her command. Nothing could break it, nothing but the proof that Campbell was a traitor. He had to reach that step in his life before he could take another. So, he placed Agnes's question in the back of his mind and continued onward, this time breaking into a run, despite the burning on his arse and the fire on his face.

His claymore banged against his back as his feet pounded the ground. The faint glow from the tiny cottage windows guided him out of the forest and into the open glen, where the wash of a full moon illuminated the landscape.

He skidded to a full stop before the byre, freshly turned mud splattering his feet. He slid his gaze down to the softened earth. Deep and very fresh hoofprints met his eyes. He followed the prints, impacted into the ground from a beast that had been forced to make great haste, to the east, to the queen, to Castle Campbell Dubh.

"That foolish lass," he breathed. "Too bloody willful, but that's what I love about her."

He dashed into the byre, certain to find Rory there, holding his hand to his eye, another victim of Sabine's wrath. He expected to take another mount, for Sabine surely would have taken his, and he would catch her. By God he was certain of that . . . until he stepped into the dimly lit byre.

Rory was not within, neither was his mount, and neither was Sabine. Niall stood just inside the door. The emptiness of the stable gnawed at his soul. He stepped forward toward his horse. Something crinkled and gave way under his foot. It was not straw or manure. He stepped back and reached down to the gut strings that protruded from under a pile of soiled straw. He pulled gently and revealed Sabine's *sac*.

Immediately he looked inside. The proof of Campbell's treachery was tucked safely there with the gold coins.

"Why?" he whispered, tucking the purse into his plaid.

He glanced about the byre. "Why would she leave it?"

A horrid and confusing answer lay just a few paces from where he stood.

"No. . . ." he breathed, leaping forward to snatch it from the straw.

Niall stared down at his hand. Too many thoughts fought for purchase in his turbulent mind. Only one screamed in his ears. Harm had come to Sabine, and Rory seemed to be at the heart of it. Did his friend and champion betray him?

Rory never took the usual path for anything. He had to have his reasons. Niall could not grasp anything that made sense beyond what he saw before him.

He clenched his fist around the cruel, taunting evidence—a torn scrap of brocade from Sabine's gown, covered with blood.

"What have I done?" he said, ripping across the byre to his mount. "I sent Rory after her. By God, what have I done?"

*S*abine lay trussed like a sheep to be sheared across the back of Rory's mount. She could still smell the coppery scent of his blood caught under her fingernails. He had tried to tear her clothes off to get at the evidence against Campbell she had stupidly told Niall she would take to the queen. Her anger toward Niall had blinded her to her suspicions about Rory, had made her mouth divulge what she had in front of this Highland ruffian. Now she knew it was Rory inside Campbell's chamber. And she knew the evidence against Campbell was not on her. She closed her eyes and tried to find strength, tried to breathe.

Sweet Saint Giles let Niall find my sac. This I pray to your mercy, amen.

She jostled on back of the mount, her belly riding hard against horseflesh and muscle. Once in a while, over the thump-thumping of hooves on the Highland path, she heard the plaintive cry of an owl from the suffocatingly dense forest shadows. Only the moon guided Rory on this narrow path, or was it greed and disloyalty to Niall that guided him?

She knew where they were headed. To Rory's true master. Lord Campbell. That thought sickened her more than the constant bumping of her belly against the horse.

The beast slowed and eventually stopped to the sound of Rory's soft clicking. How could a man who spoke so softly to his beast be so cruel to his best friend?

"Tell me where this evidence against Campbell is, lass," he said. The first words he had spoken to her since he had taken her away from Niall's valley.

She looked up, the blood rushing through her head when she did so, making her dizzy. She blinked several times and saw they had halted on a precipice. The moonlight reflected across a shallow valley cut by a forest in the center. Up the other side of the valley lay a horribly familiar shadow—Castle Campbell Dubh.

"I will tell you nothing," she said.

Her heart froze at the thought of her destiny falling back into that dreadful place. She doubted the queen would still be within, having long taken her affairs back to the comforts of Holyrood.

Rory turned and looked down at her. His face was raked on either side with eight long scratches, the blood dried.

"'Tis a pity, ken," he said. "Ye leave me with no choice." He gestured with his chin toward the castle.

Sabine stared up at him. What did she care? Niall was hers no more. All she had was her strength and the will to save her queen. Getting as far as Castle Campbell was one step, not a good one, but a step nonetheless. She wondered if Niall would dare follow, and she knew the answer before Rory urged his mount forward.

Of course Niall would. And she was oddly cheered by the thought. Maybe she would give him a chance to explain himself to her, when they both sat in the gaol of Castle Campbell.

chapter 18

❦

Falcon's Flight

This chamber was far better than any gaol. For that Sabine should have been a little grateful. But how could she be grateful to the Devil?

"A fine confinement for a fine lady," Campbell said. He stood before the hearth, hands clasped behind his oiled leather doublet. The sword he wore at his hip, a slender blade with a golden, pierced hilt that glinted in the firelight, distracted Sabine from his words. She had never seen him carry a sword before. Circumstances were different now. The queen was a day gone from the castle. Her royal presence and her guards were no longer within the high, stark stone ramparts.

"You wear your smile and sword to shield your fright," Sabine said. She tipped her chin up.

Campbell took a broad stride away from the hearth. His hand moved to the hilt of his sword. One more bold step and he would be close enough to inflict more damage to her face. Sabine shuffled backward. She would gladly engage in this *pas à deux* with her captor to keep him from striking her again. Her ears still rang from his last blow. Yet, he could pound her to darkness on the plank floor and she would still refuse to tell him the location of the proof against him.

"I give you one more chance to give this 'proof' to me."

"You could give me a thousand chances," she said. "But I still have nothing."

Sabine gripped the bedpost, digging her fingernails into the wood.

Campbell stalked closer, until his hot breath pressed against her face. He raised his hand. She turned her face away, leaned into the bedpost, waited for another blow, another taste of blood to course over her tongue.

"No," he grimaced, "not that way . . . I have another method to get what I want. . . . Remove your garments."

A shudder chased through her. "I will not."

"Precisely what I expected you to say."

Before she could escape the vicinity of his nasty breath and his penetrating stare, he unsheathed his slender sword and slashed open the front of her gown. His cruelly expert swordsmanship cut the brocade from her throat to her navel. The gown separated and fell from her shoulders, revealing her shift. She tried to close the gown, but her heart screamed in her chest when Campbell reached forward and ripped the gown the rest of the way off her body.

"Evil!" she screamed. "Devil!"

"Yessss," he hissed and placed the tip of his sword under her chin.

Sabine lifted it high because he forced her, for those horrid moments he took her strength with his weapon and his demand.

Slowly he drew the blade down between her breasts. The linen tore and the tip drew a thin crimson line in her flesh. Sabine remained rigid, lest he dig his blade in deeper. His gaze melted her resolve more than the blade did on her bared skin.

"I have nothing for you," she managed to say, tone firm. "And what you want from me now, you will have to take."

He paused, the tip of the sword at her belly. Her breasts strained against the torn tunic. She breathed shallow and quick. There was nowhere for her to go from Campbell's blade.

He lowered it and placed it neatly in its sheath.

"No, *mademoiselle,* I cannot take what I know the Mac-Gregor possesses."

"Comment?" What could he possibly see and know? He could not have known that she had given Niall her maidenhood. The memory of that beautiful night uncloaked itself at the worst possible time. She would never forget it, no matter that she had lost Niall, and no matter that she would surely die under Campbell's acid touch.

He took a step closer, pressing his body against hers, hands at his sides.

"If there is evidence to the contrary of my undying loyalty to the queen, you would not have it—the MacGregor would. And what he has is rubbish!"

Campbell would find his only comfort with that lie, she thought.

He slowly turned, leaving a trail of French perfume behind him.

Sabine clasped her tunic closed as Campbell walked to the door, his gait nauseatingly civilized.

He took the door latch in his fist, turned, and regarded her.

"The MacGregor is certain to come and challenge me with this 'proof' if it exists." He paused and looked her up and down. "And I'll wager my lands and castle that he comes in search of you. I will be waiting for him."

And in a blink he was gone. The slamming of the heavy door boomed in her ears.

"Niall will not come after me," she said, clenching the tunic together in her fists. "I gave him what he needs for the queen. 'Twould be folly for him, 'twould mean his life. That he knows as well as I."

She stepped over the remains of her gown and walked to the table by the bed. A thick green glass carafe with wine and a goblet rested on the dark wood. She shakily poured herself a glass. Niall would not come after her. He should not. The last words she had screamed at him and the blow to his face that still made her right hand throb should have convinced him to take his proof and go to the queen . . . for the sake of his clan.

A lone tear escaped down her cheek as she gulped down the wine. She prayed to Saint Giles that Niall would not come to find her. He would do well to forget her, and she would do equally as well to forget him. They had been so foolish to mask the differences between them.

She poured herself another goblet of the wine. The rest of her life, however long that was, would be behind these gray walls. She would be Campbell's prisoner or his wife—little did it matter?

She crawled up on the bed. The wine made it very easy for her to forget where she was, but not to forget Niall. That would take her a lifetime.

With one hand Niall held his cloak closed under his chin. He kept his head bowed and his claymore hidden under the swath of dark wool. Under the canopy of gray midday clouds he observed his warriors, also disguised as farmers, dispersing among the crowd within the bailey of Castle Campbell Dubh. A few more steps and he would be underneath the portcullis to join them.

He hiked the fardel higher on his back and sighed in frustration at the sluggish procession. Some of the farmers glanced at him. Niall glared them into keeping their eyes to themselves.

He stole glances at the two guards as he shuffled under the portcullis, imitating the stooped gait of Campbell's tenants. The guards stood with hands on pikes, faces sagged by boredom. They could not have welcomed Niall any better. He stepped into the bailey, closer to Sabine, closer to finding a traitor whose name was not Campbell, but Rory. The thought lanced Niall's mind with anger and pain. He had asked himself over and again why would Rory betray him by siding with Campbell?

Now he had to place the question out of his mind and focus on the task at hand. The answer would come much later, after he saw that Sabine was well and removed from this nasty place—whether she wanted to be or not.

He quickly stepped from the procession into a dark recess near the gate. One of his clansmen, a young, eager lad, stood in the recess on the opposite side of the gate. He eyed Niall just before a cart loaded full with hay rumbled past. Stifling a sneeze, Niail looked through the dusty air at the lad, nodded, and sliced his hand downward. With a flourish he threw down the fardel and withdrew his claymore from beneath his cloak. The lad proudly did the same. Simultaneously they sliced the ropes that held the double portcullis up. The barred gates slammed down, sending up an enormous cloud of dust and a thunderous noise.

It should have been Rory helping him, and not this way with Niall hunting him down like the dog he was. He shoved the thought aside and turned away from his handiwork, catching the eye of another clansman. An old warrior who had seen many a battle with Niall's father held Campbell's factor hostage with his dirk to the man's throat.

"To it, lad!" the old warrior shouted. "Tell these good folk what they wish to hear."

Niall nodded and raced up the stair on the side of the bailey. Below him the warriors roared to life and took over the proceedings, subduing the surprised and stunned guards. The farmers stood around in confusion, their tithe to Campbell in purses dangling from their fists or bleating from the ends of short tethers.

"Oy! Oy!" he shouted to the farmers, raising his claymore high. "I am Niall, chief of Clan Gregor. I offer ye protection, not servitude! Join us now and ye may farm and live on my lands as equals, not as tenants!"

A shout rose from the farmers assembled there, a shout of "Aye!"

Niall nodded. "Done then! To it! Join us in bringing yer landlord to rights!"

He turned and raced up the stair and entered deep into the castle. He made his way along the darkened corridor. The interior of the castle was unusually silent. Had good fortune winked at him by driving Campbell to certain peril in the bailey? That was his fervent hope. But men like Campbell had ways to escape any situation, any trap.

He suddenly dropped back into a doorway. At the end of the corridor a pair of guards stood on either side of a large door.

"She's there," he breathed. "The most precious of Campbell's possessions would be so well guarded."

Niall slipped his claymore down the back of his tunic. He wrapped the cloak about his body and drew the hood up.

He walked piously down the corridor, head bowed slightly, and stopped before the guards.

"Who be you?" one of the men asked, placing another hand around the shaft of his pike. The other guard followed suit.

Niall eyed them but did not raise his head. *"Non omnis moriar."*

"What did say you, Father?" the guard. asked. They relaxed their grips upon their pikes. Just what Niall knew they would do. He raised his hands and face to Heaven.

"Non nobis, Domine."

One of the guards wrinkled his brow. "Father?"

Niall dropped his hands behind his head, pushing the hood down with them. He grabbed the handle of his claymore with both fists and swung it out. With two rapid blows he smashed the end of the handle on top of the men's heads. The guards quickly crumpled to the floor.

"Sleep well my sons," Niall said, making the sign of the cross over them.

Without another second to waste, he jabbed the tip of his blade into the keyhole. The door swung open into a dimly lit chamber. The faint glow of a fire dying in the hearth was the only light. He swept his gaze to the bed, the curtains open, a pale figure curled in sleep on top of the covers.

"Sabine," he whispered.

He rushed to the bed and stabbed his claymore into the floor beside it.

He sat on the edge of the bed, watching her sleep, before he noticed the distinct scent of wine. Carefully he placed both hands on her shoulders and gently rolled her to her back.

"Sabine," he whispered. "Wake up, lass."

The firelight reflected dried blood in the corner of her mouth and a purple welt below her left eye. His gaze traveled down to the slashed tunic, the thin line of dried blood from her throat down between her perfect breasts to the small swell of belly, stopping just above her navel. Any other time, just looking at her sleeping, her body partially revealed to him in the shadows and orange light, would make his heart scream with want and joy.

But this time all he saw was unencumbered anger.

"Campbell's handiwork, no doubt," he breathed. "He'll get a lot worse when I'm through with his hide."

He leaned down and drew Sabine's tunic closed against the chill of the chamber.

"My poor lass," he whispered. "I will avenge this done to ye." He licked his thumb and rubbed away the dried blood from her mouth. "A man who would do this to ye doesnae deserve to live protected within these walls. He will be punished, by God he will."

She sat up, eyes wide. The goblet that she had held in her hand crashed to the floor.

Niall straightened on the bed. He smiled to show her all was well, that he was here to rescue her from this place.

"Well, Sabine, no proper welcome for yer rescuer?"

She stared at him for a moment, then placed her right hand to her forehead. "I do not feel so well."

"That's the wine talking," Niall said. "But ye've got to get up now and come with me."

Her eyes suddenly opened wide. *"Non!"*

"No?" he asked. "Ye dinnae wish to escape from here?"

"Leave," a familiar voice said from behind him. "If ye wish to live."

"Rory!" Niall grabbed his claymore. He turned to face a man he once, not long ago, had called friend. Now all he could call him was "Ye bastard!"

"Ye've gone and spoilt everything for our clan just to save this lassie here?" he snarled. "Ye must leave, now."

"What're ye on about, doss bastard?" Niall demanded.

"Ye've got the *mademoiselle,* now," Rory said. *"Now, go."*

Niall blinked in disbelief. "Ye betrayed me because ye're jealous of Sabine?" he asked.

"Dinnae be a daft bastard!" Rory growled.

"Ye're a kidnapper and ye're a traitor to your clan," Niall snarled. "Ye're less worthy than the shite left in the heather by the sheep."

Driven by anger deeper than the black water of Loch Lomond, Niall smashed the flat side of his sword against Rory's face.

Rory wavered for a moment, blinking, as if he completely

expected the blow. As his knees weakened, he looked into Niall's eyes and said, "I have, I can help Clan Gregor more than ye know."

Niall raised his claymore high above his head, yet he had no conviction to dispatch Rory to that place where he could not return. The big man's words echoed over and again in his mind. *Help Clan Gregor.*

"How?" Niall asked. "How have ye helped my clan?"

His question was met with the solid thud of Rory hitting the floor.

Niall stared down at Rory and took in a deep breath. He turned to Sabine, who had stood beside him the entire time. She had not said a word.

"We must leave," he said. Of course, she would come with him. He did not wait for her to reply.

He raced to the bed and tore the curtains down. With every new breath his head cleared. The reality of Rory playing Campbell's pawn gnawed at him. Help Clan Gregor? How could anything that involved Campbell help his clan? He tore the curtain into strips. Aye, well, so damn Rory! He did not need him.

Niall knelt down and bound Rory's ankles and wrists together like a sheep before shearing with the strips of curtain. With as much strength as he could muster he shoved him across the floor and under the bed.

"Here," Sabine said. Her torn tunic flapped open, revealing her lovely body.

Niall removed his cloak and placed it on her shoulders. "Let me take ye from this gilded prison."

"To Holyrood," she said firmly, gaze set on him.

"Aye," Niall replied. "To Holyrood." He grabbed her hand and they raced for the door.

It swung violently inward at them.

"Mon Dieu!" Sabine screamed.

Campbell and his guards filled the doorway. The lord of the castle confidently, casually rested a hand against the door frame.

"Well, what good fortune for *me*," Campbell said. "Two conspirators, two *lovers,* too bad you both will die. Mac-

Gregor, do me the honor of dropping your weapon to the floor." Campbell aimed his sword inches from Niall's heart.

"Do as he says," Sabine told him. She placed her right hand on the door.

Niall placed all his trust in Sabine and obliged her.

He tossed his claymore to the side. It clanked to the floor, well within the chamber, well away from the swing of the door. He read Sabine's mind. This royal falcon and Highland fox were not going to stay trapped for long.

"I'm glad you see things my way, MacGregor," Campbell said, a smug smile upon his thin lips. "Now, come with me and tell your warriors who have taken over the bailey that you admit defeat, that you *will join me.*"

Niall stood firm, raising his chin a bit, just like Sabine.

"That will happen the day I see ye sent to the Danes, ye bastard."

"Look at him, *mademoiselle,*" Campbell sneered. "See how he desperately clings to a wee bit of false pride. So like you, how you pretend that your malady is not noticed by the queen and her court. All you've gotten from them is pity, never trust."

"Eeeeyyyyyaaaahhhhh!" Sabine screamed.

She swung the door hard, smashing the wood into Campbell's fingers. His howl of pain was immediately deafening. Niall slammed his body into the door, mashing Campbell's fingers harder, making him howl louder.

Niall looked at Sabine. "Ye are the best, my love." Dear God, I mean that, he thought.

He released pressure on the door, enough for Campbell to jerk his crippled hand back, then slammed the door hard.

"See how you like it!" Sabine shouted to the door.

"Rory's claymore," Niall said, still braced against the door, "get it."

She hefted the weapon from the floor.

"Now, put the blade into the keyhole as far as ye're able," he said. "Campbell did us a favor by not placing ye in that chamber with the odd door lock."

"*Oui,*" she said, taking aim with the blade, both fists gripping the long handle. "I see what you wish me to do."

Niall kept the latch firmly in hand, kept his back against

the door. On the other side the guards pounded on the door against the background of Campbell's curses and screams.

Sabine drove the blade into the keyhole.

"Back, Sabine," Niall said.

She released the claymore. It remained stuck in the keyhole. Niall smashed the heel of his foot several times into the flat of the blade. The claymore clattered to the floor. The tip remained embedded in the keyhole. He stepped back from the door. The pounding and screaming continued.

"That'll bargain us some time, but not much."

He reached out a hand to Sabine. She took it with her right and gave his fingers a powerful squeeze.

"'Tis time for us to leave this nasty pile of gray stone," he said.

Sabine stared at the door, then back at him. "How?"

Niall nodded to the window.

She shook her head.

"Oh, Niall, *non . . . non.*"

He took her by the hand and pulled her closer to the window. "If I dinnae miss my guess, there's a cart loaded to bear with straw right below this window."

"There could be the down from five-thousand geese on that cart, and I'm still not going to jump from this garret."

Niall threw open the window glass. He glanced down— not too far, the length of two men, maybe more. He pulled Sabine against him. "Dinnae look down."

With one hand he tossed the claymore to the bailey, where it landed in the straw and mud to one side of the cart. Sabine leaned forward over the window ledge.

"No," he said, shielding her eyes with a hand.

"Niall," she protested, "do not be so absurd."

"'Tis better this way. Pretend ye're a falcon, a royal falcon."

"A royal falcon who'll fly back to the palace," she whispered.

"Ye'll not fly there alone."

He pulled her to the sill. Gripping her hand tightly, he placed one arm tightly around her waist, then swung his legs out the window.

"Niall. . . ." Sabine said. She clawed at his hand over her eyes. "Foxes cannot fly."

"Relax. Close yer eyes. . . ." He looked down, now the length of three men at least. Niall swallowed.

The pounding on the door grew. Campbell had been joined by more guards, those who were not taking part in the melee in the bailey. Niall held Sabine tighter to his body.

"Let's fly, my love," he said. "To the palace."

"I've changed my mind," she said, struggling in his hold. "We cannot fly."

"That's because we have yet to try."

He pushed away from the ledge, spiriting Sabine with him. Her screams rang in his ears well after they had made a safe landing and quick escape through the narrow postern gate guarded by his clan. Faster than the west wind they rode away from Castle Campbell Dubh toward Holyrood.

The sun was setting, but Niall did not slow his mount. They would not rest. Sabine could sleep in the saddle if she wished, but he would not stop. He had to put as much distance between themselves and Campbell as possible, should he manage to escape his castle and the grip Clan Gregor held on it. Niall shivered a wee bit. Campbell would escape. The bastard knew the castle better than Niall's men.

"I should have taken the bastard out when I had the chance," he whispered. "Not cripple his hand."

"I crippled his hand," Sabine said suddenly.

These were the first words she spoke since she had stopped screaming after they had jumped from the window.

"Aye, ye did," Niall agreed.

"Stop," she said. "I wish to dismount."

He shook his head. "Sorry, cannae do that."

"You can," she said. "And you will."

The tone of her voice hammered the back of his neck. Niall took a deep breath.

"What's on your mind?" he asked.

"I will see the queen on my own," she said. "After you return my *sac*. I know you have it."

"We will see the queen," he said firmly.

"You are betrothed," she said flatly. "I cannot trust you with my *sac,* the proof against Campbell, if you would keep such a thing from me. We made love. It meant so much to me then, but now, it means very little."

"Lying doesnae wear well on ye, Sabine," he said. "Ye still care. Otherwise ye wouldnae have left your purse in the byre and ye wouldnae have come with me."

"You will marry Agnes," she said.

"I willnae," he said with a small laugh.

He felt her stiffen against his back.

"I saw you and her. She had her hands on your . . . on your backside."

"She was pulling nettles from my arse with a moss poultice. Agnes and I have never loved each other. We have never shared the same feelings that I feel for ye."

He paused, held his breath. What had he just stepped into? Sabine breathed short, warm puffs on the back of his neck. "What're you saying, Niall?"

He sighed. Best he go forward. Always . . . forward.

"I love your strength, the way ye stand up to adversity. I love your art, the way ye create life on paper." He swallowed. "Ye could say . . . *I* could say, um, Sabine . . . I love ye, with all my heart."

He felt her arms squeeze him tighter. He felt the pounding of her heart as she leaned against his back. He grinned for a long time afterward.

She did not speak, just held on to him, breathing gently.

This silence was wonderful. He wondered if it would last all the way to Holyrood and if Sabine would return the sentiment.

From the way she held him she did not need words. For now that was fine with Niall. She was safe and with him. He vowed never to let her from his sight whether she wished it or not.

She held to him tighter.

She did not wish it.

That was the one certain thing before him. The only one. He dug his heels into the horse's ribs and urged the beast forward on the darkening path.

chapter 19

❧

In the Duck's Nest

"Do not worry so, Niall," Sabine said. "We will get into the palace."

"Aye," he replied with yet another glance over his shoulder. "'Tis the method that vexes me though."

Sabine smiled and looked through the dingy panes of the shop window. The sun of early day could barely chase the gray mist away from between the teetering buildings of Edinburgh's High Street. She had seen Le Canard's carriage leaving the gates of Holyrood. It was her suggestion that they follow him. She hoped that her giant friend had not subscribed to the harsh rumors about her certain to have made rounds within the palace.

Monsieur Le Canard argued the price over some orange silk with the merchant. She could hear him quite clearly through the dingy glass.

"But this is not the best price for this silk. It is, I must say, an inferior quality," he said, waving the roll of fabric before the indifferent merchant's eyes. "Her Majesty enjoys this particular color though, so I will purchase it . . . *robber.*"

He dropped the fabric into the already-laden arms of a meager page boy. The lad's knees buckled. Le Canard reached for his bulbous purse, hidden away under the doublet covering his shelflike belly.

Sabine pulled back from the window. "He will be out in a moment," she told Niall.

He leaned against the stone wall, his plaid pulled up to hide his face. It did little to cover his displeasure. "Right," he said through gnashed teeth.

"Monsieur Le Canard has not the desire for you, Niall MacGregor. He is my friend and, dare I hope, my only ally in Her Majesty's court."

Sabine stared into his eyes. Despite the morning mist swirling all about them, they still shone spectacularly blue, captivating her. How could she ever be angry at him? He had professed his love. Captured in the moment, thrilled that there was nothing between him and Agnes, she had tried to say the same before Rory's intrusion. Yet, on their journey to Holyrood there had been few words between them, although the opportunity had been ample. With each mile closer to the palace, Sabine felt the burden of differences between them grow heavier. Social differences that had seemed so petty in the remote Highlands, in the sanctuary of his arms, were now a sturdy wedge that she could not dislodge.

Did Niall's frustration with her plan mirror her feelings? Did he consider, as well as she, that if Campbell's treachery was believed by Her Majesty that she must go back to royal service, and he must return to his beautiful wilderness? That was the truth of Sabine's future, should the queen believe the proof against Campbell. And the truth stung like a hornet.

"Look up my love," Niall said from the shadow of his plaid. "Yer ally is shifting his bulk from the shop."

"Alors, ma petite . . . ," Le Canard said to the lad. He took a glance down the center of Edinburgh at the rows of shops and taverns on the road leading to Holyrood. ". . . We shall return to the palace with our purchases. Where is that carriage?" He looked down the street. Sabine stepped into his sight, waiting for his glance to settle down upon her.

The giant took only a second to recognize her, and another second to break into tears. He quickly swallowed Sabine in his arms, pressing her against the great wall of his perfumed body, jasmine this day.

"Oh, *Mon Dieu, Mon Dieu! Ma Sabine!*" he wailed. "I have missed you so!" He released her, and once again she could breathe.

Niall stepped forward and leaned in toward Sabine. "As much as I enjoy a good reunion, having one in the middle of bloody Edinburgh isnae the best idea."

"Oh! *Mon Dieu!* 'Tis the bold and, dare I say, most handsome Highland fox!" Le Canard exclaimed just as one of the royal carriages rumbled up to them.

Niall leapt back into the narrow way between the shops, grabbing Sabine's arm, dragging her with him.

Le Canard peered into the shadows, his caterpillar brows knitted together in confusion. "What's wrong?"

"Do you not know?" Sabine asked him, stepping away from Niall. She shrugged from his hold on her.

"Sabine, dinnae——" he protested.

Le Canard nodded ruefully. "*Oui,* this about you I know, my sweet Sabine. But I did not believe a word. I know you love *Marie Reine* more than any of her court. You are not capable of wanting to kill her."

"Of course she isnae a murderer," Niall said, "but we have proof of who——"

Sabine jabbed him in the ribs with her elbow. All Niall could say was a startled "Oof!"

She turned her attention back to Monsieur Le Canard. "I need to see Her Majesty on a matter that is most urgent." She nodded toward the carriage.

Le Canard's eyes glinted. "Oh, *chérie,* you have but made me so happy. Of course, I will see that you get to the palace. And . . ." he paused to look her up and down. ". . . I will make you a beautiful new gown. I am sorry to say that in that cloak you look less the courtly lady and more the urchin of the hills."

She carried that as a compliment.

Sabine nodded. "We will go, now, *n'est-ce pas?*"

Le Canard's eyes widened. "We?"

Niall stepped forward. "Aye, big man, *we.*"

"Niall MacGregor has to deliver the message to Her Majesty. He must translate and put it into the proper context," Sabine said, inside her heart was telling her to grab Niall's hand and flee to the safety of the Highlands, but she could never live the rest of her life as an outlaw. Her queen needed her, even if she did not know it.

"You must put context in this thing you must tell the queen?" Le Canard asked, dismissing the servant boy to the carriage with a curt wave of his hand.

"I will tell you on the way," Sabine said, stepping quickly past him and up into the carriage. She took her seat and peered around the velvet curtain at Niall. "It has to do with the life and death of Her Majesty."

"Mon Dieu!" Le Canard exclaimed. "Then we must haste!"

"Aye, exactly," Niall said.

Sabine observed him allow Le Canard to enter before him. The giant climbed up. The vehicle groaned upon his entrance. He settled onto the bench beside Sabine, placing an arm about her shoulders. Then, after taking a few more glances up and down the street, Niall climbed inside. He hunched inside, staring at the space beside the heaps of fine silks, velvets, and linens.

She thought he had never looked more out of place or uncomfortable. For an instant she thought Niall would lunge from the carriage and race for the Highlands. It lurched forward and Niall tumbled onto Le Canard's lap.

"What a rare treat this is!" the Frenchman exclaimed teasingly.

Sabine suppressed a surprised giggle.

As if he were stung by a wasp, Niall leapt up, striking his head on the roof of the carriage. "Bloody hell!" He plopped down beside the servant, who stared at him warily.

Niall regarded the lad. "I willnae bite." He turned aside his plaid enough to display his sword against his back. "But my blade might if ye betray my presence to anyone."

Le Canard chuckled.

"Something witty in what I said, ye big pansy?" Niall asked.

Le Canard regarded Sabine. "Is this why you went into the Scottish hills?"

She smiled. "This Highlander kidnapped me. And once I was there, in his land, I found my heart." She felt a bit lighter for saying it out loud.

Niall nodded at her. A knowing grin played upon his lips. "Let's hope ye can keep it."

That, Sabine knew, was for Her Majesty to decide.

Monsieur *Le Canard's generosity flowed well beyond what* Sabine had expected. He had given her and Niall refuge and repast in his lavish bedchamber while he left to quickly fashion a costume for each of them for the queen's masque that evening. He had taken Sabine's and Niall's measurements with him. Hope filled her because good fortune of circumstance had smiled upon them. A masque! Her Majesty did enjoy her parties, thank goodness!

Sabine wrapped her naked body in one of Le Canard's silk robes and stepped from behind a gilded screen. Niall greeted her from the vast bed, velvet curtains cinched to the post with thick crimson and gold cords, revealing him in all of his Mac-Gregor glory. He lounged on the exposed sheets, one arm on the mound of pillows, propping his head up, one brow cocked at her.

"Loosen the robe, *mademoiselle*," he said.

Sabine drew the robe cord tighter about her waist. "And what good will that do me?" she teased.

"Come hither and find out."

"Hither?"

Niall grinned. "I'm not one for tender words. 'Tis the best I could do. Ye're a wee bit distracting."

"Only a 'wee' bit?"

She padded across the floor past the blazing logs in the hearth. The warmth from the fire was no match for the flames burning up and down her body. She slowly, teasingly shed the robe. His eyes and his grin widened. He offered her his hand. She joined him on the bed, entwining the fingers of her right hand in his. If this was to be their last time, let the memory burn deep.

He took her, gently so, down on his body. His hands explored her, stroking her, making her breathe deeper, then faster. With the deepest sigh as he filled her, Sabine nestled on top of him, their bodies a perfect fit. He reached up and cupped her breasts, kneading each engorged nipple beneath his palms as she began to command him with each fluid movement of her hips.

With growing confidence, Sabine bore down on him, taking charge. The look in Niall's eyes told her he did not mind, his actions emphasized that sentiment. He grasped her hips, pressed her down hard and mimicked her dance with his hips. She closed her eyes and imagined that they were not in the palace, doing the unspeakable in the royal house. She tried to imagine they were far from everyone. Their lives were laid out far and wide before them like the infinite Highland landscape. What a beautiful dream. The thought of ending their time together was worse than the possibility of the royal gaol. She might as well ask the queen to send her to the Danes than live her life without Niall.

She threw her head back. The ends of her hair brushed his strong legs as her body was racked with wave upon wave of sensation. Her breathing stopped, her heart stopped, as Niall took her with him to a place only they could go.

Their moans mingled with the crackling and snapping of the fire as they continued to make love. Their world was about to end but that was the farthest thing from their minds as they fell rapt into each other's arms.

"This is the end of our time together," Sabine whispered. She stared at the flames, knowing that night would arrive with the prospect of righting her name to her queen.

"Does it have to be?" Niall asked her, combing her hair with his strong fingers.

Sabine rested her head tighter against his chest. With one finger she toyed with the dark auburn curls against his pale skin. "What I wish and what the queen commands are two different things, *mon amour.*"

"Does she expect ye to honor yer betrothal to Campbell after what we tell her?"

"She will expect me to remain in royal service."

"Will she?"

Sabine looked up into his face. "Do you think she will allow me to away with a Highland . . ."

"Say it, Sabine. A Highland savage is what ye meant. Ye wonder if Her Majesty would condone one of her court to

leave service to hide in the bens and glens. I can tell ye the answer. 'Tis no." His tone was abrupt, sarcastic even.

He took a fig from the silver trencher beside the bed,
peeled off the thin outer skin, and took a bite. The juices exploded about his lips. He chewed, deliberately, before offering the fruit to Sabine. She declined it.

"What have I done to deserve such a tone in your voice?"

He swallowed. " 'Tis not ye, Sabine, 'tis the bloody way of
things." He dropped the remains of the fig on the trencher and
gathered her in his arms. "I have my own reasons for leaving
ye here as well."

Sabine closed her eyes. The warmth gathering behind her
lids threatened to ruin this beautiful time they had alone together, as if Niall speaking the bitter truth had not done
enough.

"My clan has invaded Castle Campbell Dubh. I have new
people under my protection, and I should haste back as soon
as we set things to rights here . . . with or without Her
Majesty's consent. I will find a way to them."

"What do you mean?" Sabine asked.

"I have a better chance of making it to the gaol than ye, my
love. My clan has a tainted reputation to say the least. Our
clan has long raided cattle from anyone, even royal holdings.
My father would sell the cattle at market and take the tidy
profit to his clan. That is not the way I wish to run our affairs.
I want our reputation, although partly deserved, to change. I
want to trade wool with the rest of Europe. We can make it
work from the shores of Loch Katrine. I know it can happen."

" 'Tis your dream?" she asked.

"Aye," he said, a faraway look in his eyes, " 'tis." He
breathed deep. "And my wish is that ye could be there with
me."

Sabine felt a tear trickle down her cheek. She opened her
mouth to tell him that her wish was the same just as the door
slammed open.

She quickly buried herself under the sheets. Niall left the
bed, his feet landing on the floor with a heavy thump.

Sabine slowly stuck the top half of her face from the
covers. Monsieur Le Canard stood just inside the door dangling Rory by his plaid. The Buchanan looked, at best, quite

ill used. Sabine doubted Le Canard had anything to do with that.

"Pardon," he said, throwing Rory to the floor at Niall's bare feet. "But I found this Highlander creeping around in Her Majesty's gardens. One cannot go out to gather blossoms for the most stunning costume ever created without being bothered by the denizens of this savage land."

Le Canard stared at Sabine, who sat, with shoulders bared, on the bed with the covers cinched about her body. He then regarded Niall. *"Mon Dieu!* 'Tis a formidable weapon you have."

Niall immediately grabbed his plaid from the end of the bed and wrapped it about his waist.

"What's this rubbish ye've brought me?" he asked.

"The savage says he must speak with you. Go gentle on him though," Le Canard said.

"Why should I?" Niall asked.

The Frenchman looked down upon Rory and with the toe of his shoe toyed the hem of his kilt up to his waist. Rory snapped upright from his place on the floor.

"Delicious," Le Canard said. "Leave a bit of the fight in him for me, would you?" He winked at Niall, who, in turn, winked back.

Sabine held fast to a laugh. Rory looked up at Le Canard, then at Niall. "Ye're no' gonnae give me to this big pans—"

Niall kicked Rory in the ribs. "Careful what ye say, bloody bastard, this big Frenchman is my friend."

"Bon, bon," Le Canard said. "I will be waiting for my reward then, MacGregor."

"Aye, after I find out what this piece of shite wants." He took Rory up from the floor by the tattered collar of his linen tunic.

Monsieur Le Canard took his leave.

"Ye're no' gonnae give me over to that buggerer, are ye?" Rory pleaded.

Niall patted the Highlander with one hand for weapons while holding him firmly by the throat with the other. His lips were drawn together in a tight grim line as he ground his teeth.

"I've no arms," Rory spit, pulling from Niall. "That

Frenchman took them from me, put them in his handful of posies."

"Resourceful," Niall mocked. "Why are ye here?"

Rory glanced at Sabine, then at the trencher of food. "I'm a wee bit empty in the belly, might I have a fig or pear first?"

"I'll fill yer belly with every inch of my claymore, ye bastard, if ye dinnae tell me why ye've come."

"Campbell tried to kill me," Rory whimpered.

"Bloody tragic for ye."

"He beat me and tossed me out the window for dead. A goodly amount of straw kept me from breaking my bloody neck."

Niall huffed and folded his arms across his chest. His silence and stare told Rory he had wished the other fate had befallen him. Sabine wished it had, given all the pain Rory had caused Niall.

She cleared her throat. "Why are you here?"

"I will tell ye," the Buchanan said, strolling importantly past Niall to the bed. "Because I bloody care about what happens to us all." He took a seat on the edge of the bed and took a pear from the trencher. "Without Clan Gregor I dinnae exist."

Niall stared at him.

Rory shrugged and took a bite of pear. "I have nothing except the will to survive in this shiteheap of a world."

"'Tis that way, because ye've made it so," Niall snarled, lunging forward, knocking the pear from Rory's hand. "Stop with the riddles and tell me why ye dared show yer face to me."

"You owe Niall that much," Sabine added.

"Aye, so I do," Rory said. "I want ye to forgive me."

"That willnae happen," he growled.

"What I did, I did for Clan Gregor."

"If I had more like ye," Niall spat, "I wouldnae need the enemies I've got."

"Campbell has money, coin, lots of it," Rory said. "He tried to lure yer da and Colin into his riches by negotiating a truce at the Canon Gait."

"They died at the Canon Gait," Niall said.

Sabine slipped from the bed, bringing the covers with her

like a toga, and stood beside him. She pressed a hand to his shoulder. He covered it with his hand.

"Aye, they did, but after refusing to join with Campbell."

"My father didnae tell me he was going there to bargain with Campbell."

"Because he knew ye'd want to come," Rory said. "He told me no' to tell ye. He wanted ye away from the Canon Gait, in case he and Colin—"

"Met with death," Niall breathed. "He knew Campbell well."

Sabine wrapped her arms about him. His body trembled.

"Ye were his legacy, Niall," Rory continued.

"Of course, I am his bloody legacy!" he roared. "Why did ye not protect them!"

"Yer father, in his dying, told me to away and find ye, protect ye. 'Tis what I have done."

"What ye've done?" Niall shouted. "Ye've got a bloody fine way of doing it!"

"I have taken money from Campbell for deeds undone." Rory reached into his plaid.

Niall grabbed Sabine and pushed her behind him. In an instant he grabbed his claymore from the foot of the bed. "Careful, ye bastard," he warned, the blade a whisper from Rory's throat.

"I wish to give ye this." Rory dropped a bag at Niall's feet. It jingled heavily.

"What is it?" Niall asked without giving the bag a glance.

"Coin, a muckle coin. For ye, for the clan."

"Campbell's coin?"

"Aye."

"The coin he paid ye to murder the queen?"

Rory fell silent. "'Tis coin, 'tis all ye need ken, that and Campbell is on his way here."

Niall snorted. "Ye bloody bastard, why did ye not tell us in the first place?"

A shudder coursed through Sabine.

"We have to see Her Majesty," she said. "Without a moment to spare."

The bedcover slipped from her body as she rushed for the door to tell monsieur Le Canard to haste with the costumes.

She caught Rory's blatant stare in her periphery. Sabine took up the robe from the floor and wrapped it around her body.

"Show the mademoiselle respect, ye bastard," Niall spat. "Or I'll kill ye where ye stand." Niall placed the tip of his sword on Rory's neck.

"I can bring to Her Majesty proof of the *mademoiselle*'s innocence," the Buchanan said hastily.

"She was never guilty, bloody bastard! Ye cannae prove her innocence because she was never bloody guilty!"

"Niall! Stop! Let him speak!" Sabine cried.

She lunged across the room and pushed the blade from Rory's neck.

"I know," the Highlander rasped at her, "that ye didnae try to kill Her Majesty."

"How d'ye know?" Niall demanded.

"Because I was hired to kill the queen. 'Twas my arrow, painted to look like Sabine's, that took ye in the shoulder, Niall. That arrow was indeed intended to pierce the queen's heart, but it didnae."

Sabine gasped. "I should beat you myself for trying to murder my queen, *your* queen."

"Campbell paid ye to do this thing?" Niall asked.

"For yon coin," Rory said. "But I never intended to kill the queen. I wanted the coin for our clan, for yer plan of building barges and sending wool to Leith from Loch Katrine. We're friends, Niall."

"What a misguided bastard, ye are," he snarled.

"I want yer protection," Rory said. "I have nowhere else to go."

"Nowhere but Her Majesty's gaol."

Sabine turned to the door. "Campbell is on his way," she said. "We've not time to tarry. Rory must go before Her Majesty."

"And place my head in the noose?" Rory asked.

"Or die by my sword," Niall threatened.

"Men!" Sabine exclaimed, rolling her eyes toward the ceiling. She opened the door.

"Where are ye going?" Niall asked.

Sabine swept a lock of hair from in front of her eyes. "I am going to find *monsieur* Le Canard and get our costumes.

Campbell will not wait, I fear, for an invitation to Her Majesty's masque. We must be there before him. We must be in the best position to strike forth with our truth to Her Majesty." She glanced at Rory, then at Niall. "We have proof, remember? Your friend need not place his 'head in the noose.'"

Niall's anger turned to a grin. "Did I ever tell ye that ye're full of the Highland spirit?"

Sabine offered him her own smile as she wrapped her right hand effortlessly around the door latch. "That, *mon amour,* I'll carry as a compliment. I'll return forthwith. You decide what to do with Rory, but do it quickly. We have an appointment with the queen."

"Such a bold lass," Niall quipped.

"Aye," Sabine said with a wink and stepped out the door. But the ebullient gesture masked the fear raging within her at the thought of seeing her queen without invitation, as a fugitive with a Highland outlaw.

chapter 20

The Wonder of Good Lives

You look splendid," Sabine cooed.

Niall scowled. "I wish ye wouldnae look at me like that." He glanced up at the carved ceiling of Le Canard's outer chamber. "And I wish I had my bloody claymore."

He shifted his gaze down to the mighty sword leaning haphazardly against a trestle table laden with silks and other fine fabrics. It did not belong there and neither did he belong here in Holyrood Palace, in this ridiculous garment.

"Aye," Rory commented around a mouthful of beef. "Ye look right a dandy in blue silk doublet and slit pantaloons. Nice stockings too, by the way."

"I've no' started forgiving ye, Buchanan. Best haud yer wheesht, as my fingers are playing me toward my claymore. Or would ye have me call in Le Canard and let him make his choice of pleasures known to ye?"

Looking warily at the door where the big Frenchman had recently left to fetch the masks he had created, Rory said, "I ken ye're in jest, but all the same I'll keep my backside to the wall."

Niall sniffed and took another painful glance at himself in Le Canard's grand glass. Rory, the bastard, was right. He did look a dandy. He did not recognize himself in the outlandish garb, the shimmering blue brocade doublet, the startling white linen underblouse with the ruff collar that threatened to strangle the Highlands from his soul, and the pantaloons. The bloody split pantaloons of the same blue as the doublet mocked him with the slices of bright orange silk peering out from between the blue. He reached down and scratched at the stockings that ran up the length of his leg all the way to his bits and pieces. He scratched there, too.

"Perchance you would like me to ease your itch, *mon amour*?" Scandalously Sabine reached down and gave a quick, satisfying scratch between his legs.

He seized her in his arms, not caring that Rory was watching, not caring that soon they would place their heads on the block before Her Majesty as they stole an audience.

Sabine kissed him, long and so very deep. Slowly she broke the kiss and stepped away from him as if the reason they were dressed so oddly had struck her. Niall held her out at arm's length. She could make any manner of garment look more radiant when she wore it. Le Canard had created for her a gown of crimson and gold, a garment worthy of displaying to the queen. And Sabine had made it into a rare treasure for the eyes. Her raven hair cascaded lavishly about her shoulders, the locks decorated by gilded stars and moons. Le Canard had interpreted Sabine's essence into a dazzling garment even a wool-and-towed-linen rube like Niall could appreciate. She wore a vivid interpretation of what Heaven must look like.

Niall could barely breathe when faced with such beauty.

Sabine glanced down, her long dark lashes sheltering her eyes from him. "We will have to meet our queen and tell her the most distasteful of things."

Absently he reached down to his sporran with Sabine's purse and Campbell's incriminating letter. Against Le Canard's wishes Niall had insisted on adding the sporran as part of his costume.

Sabine stepped forward and gave him a small kiss.

"*Monsieur* Le Highlander and *chérie* Sabine, please, please we do not have the time for this!" Le Canard declared. "Her Majesty is beginning to receive her guests. I give you both these masques. Then I show you the way to the great hall."

Sabine took her mask, a golden half mask, with moons and stars bursting from the top in a spray. She slipped it on. Was that the glisten of tears Niall saw in her dark eyes?

He had no time to consider anything when Le Canard strapped a mask over his face. He had to adjust it to see out the holes. Then he caught sight of himself in the glass.

"Och, bloody hell. . . ." he sighed.

Behind him Rory laughed. And Sabine, the minx, stifled a giggle.

Le Canard had done his magic and seen that no one, not even Niall's own mother, could recognize him.

"I'm a bloody . . . flower?" he asked.

"*Oui, monsieur* Le Highlander. I have made you into a noble sprig of, how do you say, *the heather*."

"And what a lovely wee flower ye do make," Rory teased.

"You are most handsome," Sabine added. Niall could not tell if she was serious.

He wore, like her, a half mask but the color was blue satin. Clusters of blue glass beads, representing heather, sprang forth from it.

"That bloody does it," he hissed. "I'm gonnae carry my claymore."

"But you cannot, not in Her Majesty's court," Le Canard said, shaking his head, the wattle under his neck scraping over the lace ruff collar.

Niall glared up at the giant Frenchman. "Ye're the maker of magic with yer beads and silks. I will carry a large stalk of heather on my back, a stalk that will serve my purpose if such a purpose arises."

"To what purpose?" Le Canard asked.

Niall did not offer a reply to him, instead he turned to Sabine. "Campbell will no doubt make his presence known to the masque. I intend to be ready with paper"—Niall patted his sporran—"and sword." He took up the claymore in its sheath and handed it to Le Canard. "Work quickly yer magic with the beads and silk, then Sabine and I will take our leave."

Canard glared down at him. "*Monsieur* Le Highlander,

you can leave the hills, but the beast remains in your soul, *n' est-ce pas?*"

Niall gave him a nod. "Aye." The bead clusters on his mask swayed back and forth. He slapped them still.

Sabine took him by the arm and pulled him away from Le Canard.

"Save your anger for when 'tis really needed," she said.

"Such time is near," Niall said as he stared deep into her eyes. "I can feel it as well as I feel my heart quicken when ye're near." If he could stop the sun, he gladly would spend more moments like they had had before. He swallowed hard. He could not predict what the outcome of stealing an audience with the queen would bring, he could only hope for the best. Yet, with a heavy heart he could clearly see the end of these days with Sabine.

He gave her a lingering kiss on her lips, despite and damn who was observing. Stolen moments were all he had with Sabine. Why could bliss not linger? He slowly broke the kiss. Bliss was never the Highland way . . . or the way of the MacGregor. He doubted the queen could change that, but he would certainly try to sway her.

He looked into the eyes of Heaven before him. His strength lived within her, and hers within him. It would take him to their queen.

Niall offered Sabine his hand.

"'Tis time to go," he said.

As much as Sabine had wanted to take Niall's hand, she could not. Her heart lurched as they parted once inside the great hall. T'was best this way, though, that they act as strangers, and mingle without notice into the crowd. She watched as Niall made his way around the fine-costumed lords and ladies as easily as he made his way through the Highland forests. He was a predator among the docile sheep, those who thought everything was right in their lavish world with their new monarch.

"*Signorina* Sabine, is that you, my dear?"

Startled, Sabine reached up to make certain her mask was

still on her face. It was and she dared look at the one who had recognized her, Davide Rizzio.

"'Tis you, *signorina*! Oh, it brings me great delight to see you!"

"Please, please, *monsieur* Rizzio, silence. For my presence here is but unknown to Her Majesty."

"*Si*, for I have heard of the lies against you. I did not believe them." He nodded his head and took a sip of brandy. His stocky, compressed frame was dressed in emerald and golden silks, his mask was that of a parrot.

"May I please have a sip?" Sabine asked.

"Of course, if you would favor me by divulging the identity of that striking person who escorted you to this masque?"

She almost dropped the glass. Rizzio reached under her hand and cupped the bottom of the glass. "He is the Highlander who you ran off with, is he not, *signorina*?"

"Is that the lie you believe?" she asked, taking the glass from him and gulping down a long fiery swallow. Tears came quickly to her eyes.

"I believe no lies, *signorina*. I listen and divulge what I know where appropriate."

"Well," she said, taking another, smaller sip, "I did not run off with the Highlander. But I did return with him for good reason." She looked about the masque. "Where is our queen?"

"I fear *our* queen has taken notice of your escort."

"*Comment?*" Sabine dropped the glass. It shattered on the floor. The crash was cloaked by the music and the many animated conversations.

Niall stood before the throne, the queen's hand in his, and his lips upon her great ruby and diamond ring.

"I must go to him, the fool," she whispered.

But Rizzio held her by the arm. She turned on him with the sudden viciousness of a cat cornered. "Let me go!"

"*Signorina*," he purred. "I would not allow you to muddle what your Highlander seems to be carrying out quite aptly."

She stopped struggling and stared at Niall with the queen. The Italian spoke the truth, much to her relief, much to her surprise . . . or was it? Niall had charmed her, and at one time Sabine had thought that a most impossible prospect.

"I wish to move nearer," she told Rizzio.

"And I shall escort you, *signorina.*"

Grateful to have the Italian, a trusted confidant of Her Majesty, with her, Sabine placed her hand in the crook of his arm. She walked slowly, but determinedly, toward the throne, practically dragging Rizzio with her.

"Let's pause here, *signorina,* beside the groaning board, behind the wild boar. We can observe unnoticed."

Sabine glanced at the cooked whole pig. The largest apple she had ever seen was stuffed between its honey-glazed jaws. "Are you certain the boar is not watching us, and I mean the pig, not Lord Darnley, sitting to the right of Her Majesty?" she asked with a smile.

Rizzio leaned against her a little, his small body quaking with silent laughter.

Sabine wished she could continue to share his mirth. She had no idea why she made such a biting observation about the roasted boar and the perpetually reticent object of the queen's affection. Despite the criticisms Sabine had heard the court level against Lord Darnley, Her Majesty seemed not vexed by them in the least. It was natural that she would be so attentive to Niall. He spoke to her in the clearest Scots he could manage. Le Canard had tailored one of his old doublets and pantaloons to Niall's firm body. Her Majesty clearly was charmed by his natural and confident manner, and the immortal blue in his eyes that echoed the supreme bravery and strength of his spirit. Sabine never had been so proud or enamored of him as she was now.

"You do honor me, good sir, with your compliments," Mary said. "For I have been in this country of my father, and still feel the stranger to it."

"How could Yer . . . ahem . . . *Your* Majesty be a stranger to Scotland," Niall said, giving her a slight bow. "When your royal presence brings a great light of hope to every corner of your realm?"

"The great flatterer, is he not, Lord Darnley?" Mary asked.

"Yes, Your Royal Highness," Darnley droned from behind his glass of brandy.

"Such charm is rare in all corners of Scotland, good sir," Her Majesty said. "Tell me, from which corner of my realm do you come?"

Sabine gasped and held her breath, she leaned forward on the table, craned over the boar, her ears pricked to every word. The groaning board shifted a bit.

"*Mademoiselle* Sabine," came a harsh whisper in her ear.

"Do not bother me," she said.

Niall continued to capture the queen in his sapphire stare. He would boldly tell her the truth, Sabine knew. Highland honor gave him no capacity to speak a lie. Sabine prayed he would hold his words a moment longer, enough for her to join him.

"*Signorina*, 'tis not I who wishes to speak to you," Rizzio said.

"*Mademoiselle.*" A great shadow dropped over her. She could not help but look up at *Monsieur* Le Canard. "I have to tell you of an urgent matter."

"What could be more urgent than what is taking place before Her Majesty?"

"The other Highlander, the cretin, he has escaped my notice."

"Rory? He's gone . . . well, good riddance. He has done nothing but bring Niall ill tidings," Sabine quipped. Why was everyone bothering her now of all times?

Monsieur Le Canard leaned on the groaning board. The planks beneath the white linen cloth sang with displeasure at the added weight. "The Campbell had arrived. He has caused more than a slight ruckus with the guards. I fear they had no choice but to let him pass."

"Sweet Saint Giles!" Sabine gasped.

Le Canard leaned forward more. The planks suddenly shifted, throwing him off balance.

The boar, along with a cornucopia of vegetables, breads, and fruit sailed through the air accompanied by the cracking of the table's planks as Le Canard crashed down. Sabine had no time to gasp before she tumbled forward. Her mask caught on the French giant's sleeve. The disguise tore from her face. She rolled unceremoniously down the shattered planks, over the ruined victuals to a stop at Her Majesty's feet.

"Well, *Monsieur* Le Canard," Mary said. "'Tis a grand *comédie* you have performed. You are to be commended."

The giant forced himself to his feet and bowed his bulk

back into the stunned crowd, leaving Sabine with a sympathetic stare.

Niall helped Sabine to her feet. She immediately caught her sovereign's harsh stare.

"Well, this *comédie* gets livelier, more intriguing. A return performance, no doubt. And, look, our Sabine is the principle player. 'Tis a shame her tenure will end abruptly with the gaol," the queen said.

"I beg yer difference, Yer Majesty," Niall said giving her a sweeping bow. "But 'tis another who deserves the royal gaol."

"Who are you?" Mary asked.

"Non," Sabine warned Niall. Some truth must be kept intact.

He gazed deep into her eyes, showing her the blue and hope. "I must, my love. The honor and the respect I bear for my sovereign compels me to continue."

He swept off his mask. His auburn hair spilled down to his shoulders, no longer hindered by the silken tie. Sabine felt her knees weaken. This was a mistake, them coming here. From the look in her queen's eyes, Sabine was certain Niall would surely die. She moved closer to him.

"The *comédie* grows," Mary said. "I shall refuse the encore by summoning the guards."

"Non," Sabine breathed.

"I must request yer audience, Most Gracious Majesty . . ." Niall stood upright. "I willnae beg ye for it."

"Beg, Niall," Sabine whispered to herself. "To save your life."

"A proud Highlander, are you?" Mary said. "Will such pride remain when you dangle from the noose?"

"For what crime, Your Majesty?" Sabine asked suddenly. The fear of defying her queen faded with her concern, her love, for Niall. "He has done nothing."

"You misspeak yourself," Mary snapped. Her pale eyes flashed as brilliantly as the hundreds of jewels bedecking her gown.

"Your Majesty, I tell the truth."

Sabine curtsied and glanced at Niall.

"Tell her," he said, "before the walls crumble about ye."

Tilting her chin up, a defiant gesture in the presence of her queen, Sabine knew that either she take the plunge into the fire now or remain silent and allow the truth of her innocence to keep her company behind the iron bars of the royal gaol.

"I would rather see my own grave, Your Gracious Majesty, before I would deem to see you in yours."

"Well spoken," Niall said, boldly taking her right hand and giving it a squeeze. Sabine squeezed it back, imagining she took some of Niall's strength with it.

"Yes, I daresay, t'was well spoken," Her Majesty said, "for a lie."

"'Tis not a lie!" Sabine shouted. "I love you, Your Majesty! Has my loyal service for five years not proven that to you?"

"No more than you have proved your contempt by spurning our desire to have you marry Lord Campbell, and instead, seeking this *Highlander*!"

Sabine pulled from Niall and dropped to the queen's feet. She clasped her hands together and looked up, forcing herself not to cry. Instead, she drew upon the strength she had taken to her heart from Niall's kingdom of the Highlands.

"Niall MacGregor has as much honor and fealty toward Your Most Gracious Person than the entire court present. His honor and courage to face the truth come from the most magical part of your kingdom, the Highlands. Those who dwell there have honor and truth in their everyday spirit. They use the beauty all around them and the kinship with each other to cloak the threats ever present in their lives. There is wonder in the good lives of those that crave the freedom to live in peace, and yet have been denied it."

"Denied it, by whom?" Mary asked. Sabine said a small prayer thankful that Her Majesty had deemed to hear her out and inquire more.

Sabine looked back at Niall. It was time for him to speak for his clan.

He stepped forward, bowing. "If ye'll permit me an indulgence, Yer Majesty . . ." He reached down to his sporran.

"No!" Lord Darnley rose from his stupor, tossed aside the glass with a crash and brought forth a small dagger.

Niall regarded him but continued to reach into his sporran. "Would it that I would dare lay a weapon at my sovereign's throat before a grand protector like yourself?" Sarcasm chewed at his words. "I would surely put my own head in the noose," he said to the wilting noble. "No, m'lord, I have a letter for Her Majesty." He removed the paper and snapped it open. The red wax seal glistened in the light of the hundreds of candles illuminating the great hall. "May I read it ye, Yer Majesty, or would ye rather? 'Tis in the Gaelic."

"A Highlander who can read," she said with a small sniff, "astounding."

"Aye, we are capable of a great many things, including saving Yer Majesty's life." He grinned.

Did Sabine's eyes suddenly deceive her? Was that the hint of a smile playing on Mary's lips? But of course it was. Niall's charm had touched her as well.

"I shall read that paper on my own," she said. "I do know some of this Gaelic."

Niall bowed and offered the letter to Her Majesty.

"Atrocity! Lies!" A voice shouted from the rear of the great hall.

"Campbell!" Sabine hissed. *"Mon Dieu!"*

"What is this disturbance in one's presence?" the queen demanded, taking the letter from Niall just as he turned away from her to face his enemy.

Campbell stormed through the crowd, sword bared, fire in his eyes.

He stopped before the throne, and gave the queen a quick bow, before turning his wrath on Niall. He was not allowed to pounce further before Her Majesty's guards grappled him, forcing the sword to the floor.

"How dare you intrude upon one's celebration like this!" the queen shouted.

"I've come to save Your Most Gracious Majesty from the lies of these traitors!"

"Traitor?" Sabine said, voice tight. "I love my queen! 'Tis you who are the traitor!"

Niall took her by the arms and pulled her back around his body, shielding her from Campbell.

She shook against his back, anger rocking her.

"Our Sabine has forgotten where she is," Mary said. "We

do not allow emotions to flow as freely as the pride of these Highlanders. We see that our Sabine has taken on their lively Highland spirit from your journey there."

Sabine nodded. "I take that as the highest compliment, Your Majesty."

"Order your guards to release me," Campbell snarled between gritted teeth.

The queen nodded to her guards. "Stay close though."

Campbell adjusted his doublet with a snap and gave her a quick bow. "I am sorry to see Your Majesty forced into such disagreeable company."

"Aye," Niall said. "Things were much more agreeable before ye came."

Sabine could not help but smile.

Campbell narrowed his gaze, then stole a quick glance at his sword on the floor.

"We will read this letter that has caused so much consternation," Mary said. "All concerned should remain before us in silence."

She raised the paper up before her eyes and began reading.

Sabine's sketch of Niall was suddenly displayed for all to see except the queen. A gasp shuddered through the court. Sabine looked at Niall, horrified. He, in turn, grinned and stood a little taller. Highland spirit, be damned, Sabine thought, that sketch could place both of them squarely in the gaol if the queen turned the paper over.

Sabine glanced at Campbell, who stood bathed in fury. He, obviously, had seen the sketch.

Niall took her right hand. She squeezed it tight and held her breath.

With a sigh the queen folded the letter. Sabine sagged in relief. Mary looked at Campbell, then shifted her gaze to Niall. "Highlander, you bring me a most interesting dilemma."

"And more," Niall said with a grin.

Sabine kicked his foot.

"He brings you nothing, Your Majesty!" Campbell bellowed.

"And how would you know this, Sir John, unless you have knowledge of this letter?"

"I have knowledge of no letter, Your Majesty," he said, craning his neck to see what she held.

"Liar," Sabine breathed. She stepped out from behind Niall and faced Campbell. "You are the traitor. I have proof—the queen has it—it is your letter bearing your seal and the order to have the queen murdered."

"Bloody bitch!" Campbell roared at her. In lightning progression, he leapt down, seized his sword, and stood, swinging it in an arc, keeping the royal guards at bay. In an instant he snatched Sabine against his body, crushing her. The nightmare had returned with stale perfume.

"Let her go!" Niall ordered. He reached back at the large sprig of false heather and unsheathed his claymore. Blue glass beads rained down on everyone, capturing the candlelight, sparkling as they bounced to the floor.

"I'll cut her throat and save Her Majesty the trouble of hanging her," Campbell threatened.

Sabine clawed at his arm, tightly ratcheted about her neck, cutting off her breath. Nialh lunged forward, claymore thrust in front of him. Campbell cowardly used Sabine to shield his own body.

"Cease this at once!" Mary demanded.

"I have to save Your Majesty from the savages that beg for mercy at your feet with their lies against me," Campbell protested.

"Her Majesty should be saved from ye," Niall said, stepping forward. "Release Sabine, now!"

The guards stepped up to either side of Niall. Sabine tried to shout out a warning to him, but Campbell had stolen her voice with his stranglehold.

"Take the Highlander," Mary commanded.

Campbell smiled in triumph.

Mary nodded again at her guards. "And take Lord Campbell, until we can decide what must be done with them."

"No!" Campbell cried. "I, a Scottish noble, will not rot in the gaol with a Highland outlaw. What of the proclamation against the MacGregors declared by Your Majesty's father? Have you no recollection of it?"

"We'll have no more of this insolence!" Mary said, rising from the throne. "Guards, obey my command!"

Both of them seized Niall.

"Wait!" a voice bolted from the crowd.

Sabine knew it well, so did Niall.

"Rory!" he shouted, turning around. "Ye bloody fool!"

Dressed in an outlandish costume, obviously of his own making, of different parts inexpertly pieced together, Rory bounded through the gaping crowd, a knife held fast in his fist. Without effort he tore the costume from his body, revealing his Highland plaid. Gasps quickly ran through the crowd. Rory stopped before the queen and made an exaggerated bow, more of a genuflection, to her.

"Niall speaks the truth, Yer Majesty, 'tis Campbell who is a traitor."

"Haud yer wheesht, ye daft bastard," Niall hissed, fighting the guards who held him fast against their armor-clad bodies.

"What proof have you, Highlander, other than because of the outrage I see before me now?"

Rory dropped to one knee, relinquishing his knife at her feet. "I was the one who shot the arrow toward ye. 'Twas no' *mademoiselle* Sabine."

The silence that followed Rory's confession was thicker than the Scottish mist that had greeted Sabine on her first day in this land.

The thunder that quickly roiled in deafened Sabine.

"You bloody bastard!" Campbell roared. "Your skill with the arrow was without measure. I paid dearly for that skill and received nothing in return!"

Sabine beamed at Niall. He, too, knew what Campbell had just done.

His grin sliced through the mist and the distance between them. "*Touché,* Campbell," he said.

Campbell paled and shrank back, loosening his hold on Sabine. She stole the advantage and ran to Niall.

"Release him," she demanded to the guards. "Campbell has fashioned a noose from his own tongue, can you not see that?"

The guards remained bound to their duty.

She looked into Niall's eyes, seeing the victory playing within. "We've won," she whispered.

"Aye," he replied.

A sudden shadow cast over his blue eyes. "Niall?"

She grasped his doublet, wishing it were his plaid. "What is it?"

"Bastard," he hissed.

Sabine turned around in time to see Campbell plunging across the floor toward them. He would surely cleave his sword through her to get to Niall.

"Die, MacGregor! And take this crippled bitch to hell with you!" Campbell screamed. Sweat ran down his pale face in rivulets.

"Non!" she cried, turning to face him.

Campbell rushed at her, the queen's guards in pursuit of him.

With a mighty shrug, Niall jerked from the guards and swept his sword up from the floor. He shoved Sabine roughly out of his way, right into the queen. For one moment Sabine thought the once-thinkable of him: *sauvage!* And then it was gone, forever. No savage could wear the doublet so magnificently and love his queen as much, and save her life for the price of his own.

"Onaraich mi Gregarach aqus Sabine!" Niall cried, bringing his claymore above his head.

"Damn you, MacGregor!" Campbell shouted, sword raised.

The two enemies struck their swords in a lightning clash. A hail of sparks soared through the air. Then laughter. Niall's.

Campbell stood holding the pathetic stump of his weapon. The rest of his slender blade lay at Sabine's feet. A humbling tribute from him, as it was clearly no match for Niall and his claymore.

Niall stared at Campbell as he lowered his claymore. "I honor my clan and Sabine." He looked at the guards. "Take this filth to the gaol."

"That, Highlander, is for me to decide," Mary said. She looked at Campbell's letter as her guards surrounded him. She regarded the words. "We have many missives from Lord

Campbell asking us for this and that. . . ." She turned the paper over. Sabine took a step away from her queen.

"Our Sabine, where are you going? We are in need of your practiced eye."

Sabine curtsied and returned to the queen's side.

"You have a keen eye for detail," her sovereign said.

"*Comment?* Your Majesty, I do not—"

"Ply me not with 'do not,' our Sabine. I have knowledge of your art." Mary regarded Niall. "And from what I can compare to the subject you have chosen here before me, your eye for detail is most accurate. Have you perchance given thought to creating our royal portrait?"

Sabine shook her head. "*Non,* Your Majesty . . . I . . . I would never presume to. . . ."

"Not like this of course, although . . ." She handed the paper to Lord Darnley. His eyes widened and he gave Her Majesty a small smile. She looked at Sabine. ". . . I wonder if Lord Darnley would ask you for a similar commission for us."

Sabine could not help but smile. *Marie Reine* certainly was a woman who knew her own mind, just like herself. "*Oui,* Your Majesty. Upon your royal command." Sabine curtsied again.

"Was it upon our royal command that you brought such melee to our court?"

Niall stepped up beside Sabine. "'Twas my doing, Yer Majesty. I insisted we come and tell ye the truth of this vermin before ye." He gave a swift nod at Campbell.

"So it seems," she said.

Sabine looked at Lord Darnley and then at her queen. "What manner of celebration is this, Your Majesty, if I may be so bold?"

"Yes," she said, "you may. Being that you were in the Highlands with this MacGregor you would not know that I have been recently engaged to Lord Darnley."

"A dreadful mistake," Campbell hissed.

"I will engage upon King Christian of Denmark for a favor. He is anxious that we meet his son. I will indulge that kindness in return for a small favor. Lord Campbell, you will be his special guest. You will be sent to the Danes."

Campbell paled anew. The sweat that ran off him could fill the North Sea. "No! I beg you!"

"That time is long past," Mary said. She stared straight into Campbell's eyes but spoke to her guards. "Send him to the Danes."

Behind her back, Sabine heard Campbell's screams and shouts as he was dragged away. Niall remained at her side despite the guards that surrounded him.

After the great hall had settled a bit, Her Majesty regarded Niall. "We regret that we must carry out our duty, MacGregor. You did disrupt this court with words and sword, and without invitation. You have kidnapped one of our court—"

"He did not kidnap me!" Sabine cried, kneeling before the queen.

Mary paused, then continued speaking to Niall. "By royal law you shall be placed in the gaol until such time that these disagreeable events can be sorted out."

"Then I will go with him!" Sabine shouted, rising to her feet and taking her place next to Niall. The guards pushed her away and took their places on either side of him.

"Remember your place," Her Majesty ordered her.

"My place is with Niall." She barely recognized her voice.

Sabine grabbed his doublet, burying her face into the ruff about his neck. This was far from right. She wanted his plaid, to feel the scratchy wool against her cheek, to invigorate herself in his scent long trapped in that cloth.

"Sabine, this ye cannae do," he said softly. "Abide yer queen. I will be well and good, for our sovereign will understand me."

"How can that be?" Sabine asked, leaning her forehead into the side of his strong neck.

"Open her eyes, Sabine. Ye've begun yer task by telling her of what ye ken of the Highlands, of the wonder of good lives."

She kissed him hard. The guards pulled Niall away from her. "I cannot bear to think of you in the gaol."

"I can bear the gaol," Niall said tossing her a grin, "because I will think of ye, my love."

Other guards surrounded her, keeping her from Niall as he was taken from her.

His last words rang to her across the great hall.

"Open Her Majesty's eyes. . . ."

Sabine turned to the queen and curtsied, head bowed low. She clenched her right hand. No pain, only strength. For Niall, for her heart, she would draw her sovereign a picture.

chapter 21

❦

A Beautiful View

Colors Sabine had discovered in her art released Niall from the gaol five fortnights past, color and the undeniable fact that he was innocent.

Mary had marveled at the paintings of the MacGregor's Highlands. They had taken Sabine three sleepless nights to complete. Afterward she had slept for days. No one disturbed her, although she wished they had. She had awakened with joy to discover Lord Campbell was on his journey to a Danish prison, but her happiness was short-lived when the page told her Niall had been released back to the Highlands.

She was delighted that he was free, thrilled beyond words that her paintings had helped garner his release, but she had dearly, secretly wanted to go with him.

Color had helped release Niall from the royal gaol, but it did not release him from her aching heart. It only made her longing worse. Mary did not release her from royal servitude, a proclamation Sabine had expected to follow her declaration for Niall's release.

Now, thirty and seven days after Niall had gained his freedom and left her without so much as a good-bye, Sabine sat in one of the swaying carriages of the queen's cortege. For each league of the journey she had tried to convince herself this was for the best. Niall was in his world and she was in hers. Saying good-bye would have made the inevitable so much worse.

Sabine sighed. More lies. They would have to suffice as bandages for her wounded heart.

She thumbed through the paintings on vellum she had made for Her Majesty. Scene after scene of the Highlands, of Niall's home, of his clan, of the bold chief himself passed before her eyes in the most vivid hues. While she studied her work, she straightened the fingers of her right hand and kept them that way, without pain, without caring.

"Do not look so forlorn," Lady Fleming said. "Her Majesty's generosity extends far to allow you to return to the Highlands."

Sabine slid the paintings back into the leather envelope, and closed it by twining a gut string around a bone button. "Her Majesty is bringing me along because I am and always will be a part of her court. 'Tis Her Royal Highness who wishes to see the Highlands. I am here to attend to her wardrobe, that is all."

"Bitter girl," the old Scot said. "Your aching heart blinds you from duty." She paused. "Your hand has healed. 'Tis a miracle or 'tis it love?"

Sabine glared at Lady Fleming. "Presume not to know my mind, m'lady."

"Hmm, that is something I would not want to do. Perchance you should've gone to the convent instead of royal service."

" 'Twould be little difference from my current situation."

She was as alone as she had ever been.

Sabine lifted a corner of the velvet curtain and peaked out at the landscape, at the green and granite mountains pushing at the sky. She had traveled this route before on the way to Castle Campbell Dubh. In the distance it sat on the crest of a small hill on the shore of a crystal lake, a *loch* Niall would say if he were here. His voice rang true in her mind in his odd inflection, with the occasional musical Gaelic words. Sabine closed the curtain and leaned back on the bench.

What Highland lord would the queen prevail upon this

time? There was rumored to be a Lord Bothwell who had caught her eye, a Border rogue, as much a part of his vacant wilderness in the Scottish Lowlands as Niall was of his Highlands. Mary was intended to Lord Darnley, but what did that matter? She was queen!

"She is queen," Sabine whispered. "With two suitors, and I cannot have one."

Niall. He was certain to be in his valley, his glen, in the shadow of the mountain he called *Tulaichean*, Little Hill. Nothing was little in these Highlands, everything, life included, existed grandly, no less.

The carriage came to an abrupt halt. Sabine canted forward almost onto Lady Fleming.

"Why have we stopped?" she asked. "The day is not half over."

"I do not question Her Majesty," Lady Fleming said, opening the door and stepping from the carriage.

"Sweet Saint Giles," she sighed and followed the lady to the outside.

Castle Campbell Dubh loomed all around her.

"Why are we stopping here?" she asked. Lady Fleming did not answer her, having hurried to the queen's carriage.

There was something different about this place. It was not gloomy and full of whispers and furtive glances by those who inhabited it. The bailey was filled with the glorious bustle of people, wares, and livestock. Some of the people wore the Highland plaid, some of them were dressed as peasant farmers, all of them wearing bright faces full of shining hope.

"*Mademoiselle* Sabine!"

She turned. Rory ambled up to her and gave her a tight embrace.

"Why are you here?" she forced herself to ask. "Is this not Campbell's castle and land?"

"My chief saved me from the gallows," Rory said. "But ye should ask why ye're here. I'm off to guide Her Majesty on a tour of the Highlands. She has asked me to lead her through the whole of her kingdom."

He sauntered off, cocksure and no threat to anyone, just a lost soul who had found that he had worth to queen and clan. And he carried with him the mystery of why he was in suddenly good favor with the queen. Sabine could not have been more confused.

A sudden, great clamor rose from one of the arched doors to the bailey. "Bloody beastie! I'll not let ye escape from being our dinner this night!" an achingly familiar Scottish voice shouted.

A black-and-white blur raced across the cobbles and scatterings of straw and manure. Sabine, eyes wide in horror, watched it come right toward her. Her entire body and mind focused on that demonic thing rushing at her. She cringed just as the thing was scooped up by strong hands, the same hands that had embraced every inch of her body, sending her into a feverish ecstasy. Sabine froze in terror and delight.

The world ceased spinning, her heart stopped beating, and her breath abandoned her.

Niall stood, a squirming, clucking chicken in the crook of his arm. He gave her a small bow. "Ye're a sight I'd never thought I'd see in *my* castle."

"Y—your castle?" she managed to ask.

"Aye," he said proudly, "'tis mine."

"'Tis *mine*," another Scottish voice said from behind her, one decidedly female.

Sabine did not take Niall from her sight. Agnes, the Highland witch, stepped into her periphery for only a moment.

"The castle 'tis mine," she repeated. "My brother hasnae use for it."

She swished away as quickly as she had come, attracting impolite stares from the men in Highland dress, all except Niall. He kept his gaze firmly on Sabine.

"The castle now belongs to my clan," he said.

Sabine stood still with Niall and so many questions before her. She asked the first one that came to her mind.

"You and Agnes . . . are you married to her? To join your clans?"

Niall dropped the chicken, and it angrily zigzagged away.

He seized Sabine and held her so tight she could barely breathe and did not mind. He kissed her there in the bailey before anyone who dared to watch. Before he broke the kiss, she had her answer.

"I will miss you forever," she whispered. "I leave my heart here with you."

"Warm comfort, my love," he said. "A treasure greater than all of Scotland."

"Greater than all of Scotland, you say?" a royal voice said.

Niall and Sabine straightened at the sound of Her Majesty's voice.

Sabine immediately curtsied and Niall bowed.

"Yer Majesty," he said with a nod.

"Is this castle that we have given you and your clan agreeable to you?" she asked.

Niall's blue eyes flashed. "With all due respect, Yer Majesty, ye have given me and my clan nothing. This has been earned by many generations of MacGregors who have been forced to hide and deny their name and right to peace. Yer wisdom is a great blessing to all of us, Yer Majesty."

Mary glanced at Lord Darnley, who stood quietly by, staring up at the surrounding walls. "Your blessing goes against that of a great many others. We hope to rule Scotland with fairness and justice for all of its subjects . . . including the Highlands."

Niall bowed. "I must ask though, Yer Majesty, as I have been amply rewarded for my service to ye, 'twas Sabine who brought the matter of Campbell's plot to my attention. What reward does she get?"

"The one which I have already given her."

Sabine stepped forward. "What is that, Your Majesty?"

Mary waved a hand, each finger adorned with a jewel-encrusted ring, at a valise sitting alone in the midst of the bailey. Sabine's. She had not seen anyone bring it from the carriage, had not seen much else since she saw Niall.

"*Comment?* I do not understand," she said.

Mary reached out and grasped Sabine's right hand.

With her free hand Mary reached into a gilded, velvet bag at her hip. She removed the miniature portrait of Lord Darnley that Sabine had painted just a fortnight ago. He had sat silent in his chamber, eyes distant, as if he was not sure he was up to the task of marrying Scotland's sovereign. Worried about this new challenge, Bothwell, perchance. Sabine looked at the portrait, painted in thousands of tiny brush strokes.

"I believe you have something similar on your person?" Mary asked, speaking to her not with her royal tone of voice, but with one of a woman speaking to another woman.

Sabine withdrew a miniature of Niall from the top of her gown, one she had painted from memory. She must have left it on the table in her chamber to dry. Anyone could have seen it, including her queen.

"Such vivid memory should not be allowed to fade," Mary said. "You will not have much use for that portrait in the future."

Mary paused and smiled. "I promised your father that you would marry a good man." She regarded Niall, gave him a lingering up and down stare. "Our Sabine, we leave it to you to make that decision. We are granting you release from our royal service. You, Sabine de Sainte Montagne, have earned that as much as the MacGregor has earned this castle and the surrounding land. We give you leave here. Whether you choose to stay or not is up to you. Holyrood will always welcome you. You make our masques most . . . interesting."

With that Mary turned and walked away with Lord Darnley a few paces behind her.

Sabine curtsied. *"Merci beaucoup, Marie Reine,"* she whispered, stunned.

Niall stepped forward. *"Deagh fortan, Màiri Rioghachadh."*

Mary stopped and turned. She nodded to him. *"Tapadh leibh, MacGrector."*

He sang with laughter. "Scotland is gonnae be sound and good. With a sovereign like that, there's hope for all of us."

The carriages rumbled away. Lady Fleming gave Sabine a curt wave and sharp nod of her head. She waved back. Rory, from his mount beside the cortege, gave a hearty wave to them.

Niall offered Sabine his hand. "Ye wish to take a walk?"

She nodded numbly.

They walked up the stone steps, out of the bailey. Below them the clanspeople and farmers carried out the contented routine of their daily lives. Peace had settled upon them. Sabine wished the same would do for her soul. Her Majesty had left her here to choose her own path.

She squeezed Niall's hand so tight.

"Ow!" he teased.

They walked beneath the arched doorway along the same corridor Sabine had traveled when her life was more condemned than hopeful. But what hope lay before her? Perchance she should reach out and take what she wanted and not allow fortune to decide for her.

"Or a little bit of both," she whispered.

"Sorry?" Niall asked. He led her up another flight of stone steps.

"Rory says you saved him from the gaol?" she thought to ask.

"He'll wish he was back in the gaol when he takes the queen to the glen to visit my mum. She'll have his head."

"Who? The queen?"

"Me mum. She'll think the cottage isnae properly clean, isnae the place for a queen."

"'Tis wonderful, Mary will see that. But tell me, how did you get Rory released? By employing the same trick you used to take me from the queen on the field of hunt so long ago?"

"This time I had to use my head instead of my heart, or my bloody shoulder," he replied. "I simply told Her Majesty that Rory is reputed to be the best archer in the Highlands, and that if he wanted to murder her, he would. Instead, he chose to aim that arrow for my shoulder and let me play the hero for the queen."

Sabine paused on the winding stair. "Really?"

Niall turned and looked at her from over a plaid-covered shoulder. "Bloody hell no! Rory had no idea I would be so daft as to spring into the arrow's path. D'ye think I willingly wanted that arrow in my shoulder? But the queen believed I did. But I kept the money Rory got from Campbell to do the deed."

"The one he did not do?"

"Aye . . . no . . . aye, now I'm bloody confused. Let's just press on, aye?"

"Where are we going?"

"Not much farther," he said cryptically around a grin.

"You are quite the mysterious one," she said. "Taking me up to where the angels dwell."

"Not until we get there," he said.

Up and up they traveled.

"What are you going to call your stone palace?" she asked. "Now that you have *earned* it."

"Castle Gregor," he replied. "What else would I name it?"

"That was the name I would have chosen."

His laughter rang down the narrow passage from the top of the stair. They had to walk single file only a few paces before they entered a small round chamber. A startled falcon flew from the window ledge, its cry a harsh wake.

Sabine walked to the window, and her breath caught in her throat. The whole of Niall's kingdom lay before her. The emerald valley and forests glistened full of life in the rays of sun that pierced the blue-gray clouds. The hills, the Highland bens, rose in the western sky, offering her a silent beckoning to return into the grandeur. She drew in a deep, cleansing breath. She was there as long as Niall was with her.

"Nice view, aye?" he asked, slipping up behind her, wrapping his arms about her waist.

"'Tis the most beautiful view I have ever seen."

"More so than your French mountains?"

"The beauty is different, the way I see things now is different."

"You have color now. I saw the paintings. Very bonny. Ye know the Highlands."

Sabine turned in his arms and faced him. "When did you see my paintings?"

"In the gaol, before they released me. The queen sent a page to bring them to me. Ye were sleeping. I gave them my approval, thinking that was what the queen wanted."

He took her right hand in his and kissed it tenderly. "What say ye about this chamber?"

"'Tis sparse, humble, and quite small," she replied.

"Is that all ye see about ye?"

She turned to look out the window. "And despite all that I have just said, this chamber also has all of the life of your Highland home, because I can see it all before me through the window."

"Aye. . . . ," he whispered. "I see the very same."

He turned her gently back around. "I have strength here in

this humble place with all the riches of the Highlands before me. It has given me the strength to tell ye one very important thing."

Sabine leaned into him, nuzzling against his firm neck. She closed her eyes, letting his words, spoken in his unmistakable Scots, wash over her.

"I love ye, Sabine."

"Say it again," she whispered.

A warm breeze played in through the window, teasing strands of her hair from the taut braid she had worn in royal service. Niall untied the silken strips that bound her hair. He buried his face in her breeze-tossed tresses, inhaling deeply.

"I love ye so very much, Sabine."

She pulled away from him, just enough so that she could look into his eyes.

He captured her in his eternal blue eyes as his words flowed from his lips. "I know this chamber is humble, but two people who love a good view can make it part of this castle, can make it their home."

"Their home?" Sabine asked.

"Aye," he said with a grin, "the queen abandoned ye here. I thought it best to ask ye to marry me."

His grin filled his face, making his lips disappear.

"Is that a proposal?" she asked, twining a lock of his hair about her finger.

"Ye heard me, or shall I ask ye in French?"

He did not wait for a reply. He gave her a kiss that shamed all kisses that had ever been in the history of everything.

Then he took her right hand. He opened her fingers effortlessly, painlessly for her, and he placed something heavy in her palm. Her *sac.* She squeezed it, feeling the woolen ball, the coins and her papers inside.

"'Tis yours," he said.

She shook her head. "'Tis ours."

Sunlight suddenly filled the small chamber, or was it the sunlight bursting forth in Sabine's heart?

Niall stared deep into her eyes. The blue!

"And yer answer is . . . ?" he asked.

Sabine did not have to glance over her shoulder to confirm what her heart was shouting at her. Niall had brought her to

Heaven. All she had to do was look in his eyes and listen to her heart to know that. And once she was in Heaven there was no need or want to go anywhere else.

"I love you, Niall MacGregor," she said, her heart filling so full that she thought it would burst.

He seized her up off the floor. In this Highland Heaven their spirits soared higher than the falcon.

Sabine laughed. "I will marry you!"

Niall laughed with her.

They kissed and slowly settled to the bare floor.

"Lack of a proper bed hasnae deterred us before," Niall commented, nuzzling her neck.

"I want nothing," she said, "except you."

Niall toyed with the laces on her gown, then brought his hand slowly to her belly. "I can think of one thing I want," he said, not breaking his gaze, "or two, or three, or four, or—"

She pressed a finger to his lips and smiled. She felt she would do so forever.

HIGHLAND FLING

Have a Fling...with Jove's new
Highland Fling *romances!*

The Border Bride   Elizabeth English   0-515-13154-7
No one can remember a time when the Darnleys and Kirallens were
at peace—the neighboring clans have been at each other's throats
for generations. At last, however, it seems like peace is at
hand—Darnley's daughter Maude is to marry Jemmy, Laird
Kirallen's son, bringing the bitter fighting to a wary truce.
But things aren't always as they seem...

Laird of the Mist   Elizabeth English   0-515-13190-3
Banished from his clan, Allistair Kirallen is a sword for hire and a
man with a dream: to avenge his brother's death. Until a very
different dream fires his imagination. She is his heart's desire, his
one true destiny—but she is only a fleeting vision...

Once Forbidden   Terri Brisbin   0-515-13179-2
Anice MacNab has just wed her bethrothed, the heir to the clan
MacKendimen—a family powerful in both name and arms. In the
years she has waited for this day, Anice has dreamed of becoming
the lady of the clan and its castle, and of finding love with her
handsome bethrothed. But her dreams of love are brutally shattered
on her wedding night...

AVAILABLE WHEREVER BOOKS ARE SOLD
OR
TO ORDER CALL:
1-800-788-6262

(Ad # B105)